D0456876

ALSO BY CHAIM POTOK

The Chosen

The Promise

My Name Is Asher Lev

In the Beginning

Wanderings

The Book of Lights

Chaim Potok

THE BOOK
OF LIGHTS

 Alfred A. Knopf

New York 1981

THIS IS A BORZOI BOOK
PUBLISHED BY ALFRED A. KNOPF, INC.

Copyright © 1981 by Chaim Potok individually and Adena Potok as Trustee for Rena N. Potok, Naana S. Potok and Akiva N. Potok

All rights reserved under International and Pan-American Copyright Conventions. Published in the United States by Alfred A. Knopf, Inc., New York, and simultaneously in Canada by Random House of Canada Limited, Toronto. Distributed by Random House, Inc., New York.

Grateful acknowledgment is made to the Jewish Theological Seminary of America for permission to reprint from *Jewish Gnosticism, Merkabah Mysticism, and Talmudic Tradition* by Gershom G. Scholem (1965 edition).

LIBRARY OF CONGRESS CATALOGING IN PUBLICATION DATA
Potok, Chaim.   The book of lights.

I. Title.
PS3566.069B6   1981   813'.54   81-47505
ISBN 0-394-52031-9   AACR2

Manufactured in the United States of America
First Edition

TO
DAVID FLEISHER
my teacher and friend

See how many hidden causes there are . . . hidden from the comprehension of human beings. . . . There are lights upon lights, one more clear than another, each one dark by comparison with the one above it from which it receives its light. As for the Supreme Cause, all lights are dark in its presence.

—THE ZOHAR

Out yonder there was this huge world, which exists independently of us human beings and which stands before us like a great, eternal riddle. . . . The contemplation of this world beckoned like a liberation.

—ALBERT EINSTEIN

Part One

1

He arrived in Korea in a snowstorm on a huge big-bellied aircraft named the *Thin Man*. A little over a week earlier he had written his farewell to the man whose reluctant disciple he had been for a long and strange year, and, in parting, embraced his aunt and uncle and the girl he thought he might marry.

He was raised by this aunt and uncle, who was his father's brother. He had been staying with them when his parents died, and he simply stayed on. He slept in a narrow bed in a small and dingy room. They lived in a sunless ground-floor apartment in an old five-story red-brick building where his uncle collected the rents for the owner no one ever saw. The house was the talk of their Brooklyn neighborhood. There was something wrong with it, something had gone awry from the very beginning. The furnace was whimsical and tended to die when it was most needed; valves stuck, pipes leaked, faucets gushed unevenly when turned on, or gave off explosions of air; electrical wiring shorted mysteriously; pieces of brick worked loose and tumbled to the sidewalk; the tar paper covering of the roof, no matter how recently replaced, became warped, then buckled and cracked. But the rents were low, the apartments were always filled, and his uncle, who earned an erratic livelihood from the badly organized and decrepit Hebrew bookstore he operated in the neighborhood, was kept very busy. Often his uncle himself fired up the furnace, on those early winter mornings when the janitor was in a drunken stupor from which he could not be roused. Janitors came and went. His uncle's job was not an easy one.

He was eight years old when his parents died. His sharpest memory of his father was of the day they climbed together to the head of the Statue of Liberty. "You want to go up in the elevator or climb the stairs? Choose," his father said happily. He chose the stairs. He was seven years old, and his father carried him the last dozen flights up. He clung to his father and smelled the odor of his strength. It was a brilliant blue day, and they looked out across the water at the distant curve of Brooklyn shoreline. "That's where we live, Gershon," his father said. "Yes, it's a beautiful world. But you must learn to make smart choices or it will hurt you." Later that evening they did a picture puzzle together. It was a gift his mother had just given him for his seventh birthday, a puzzle map of the world. He and his father spread the pieces on the living-room carpet and worked on it together until it was done. His mother laughed and held him, and he remembered her kiss and the warmth of her face and the sweet smell of her perfume.

That was almost all he really remembered of his parents. There were pictures of them in the apartment on the mahogany end table near the sofa, but he felt no connection to them. They had gone off to what was then Palestine to look at some seaside property near Tel Aviv that his father had purchased. This was in 1937. They went out one night to a café after having been warned that the streets were dangerous, and were caught in a crossfire between Arabs and Jews. That was a bad time in Palestine—riots, demonstrations, ambushes. They made a poor choice and were killed.

His aunt and uncle decided to have them buried on the Mount of Olives outside the Old City of Jerusalem, the most sacred of Jewish cemeteries. Another poor choice. The cemetery was captured by Jordan in the Israeli War of Independence.

He grew up with a cousin six years older than he. Tall, blond-haired, his cousin seemed to move through life with a special grace. He loved his cousin, followed him, emulated him, hung on his every word. His cousin was killed during the Second World War.

That was a bad time. He was about fifteen when his cousin died, and he dreamed about him a lot, heard his voice, had sudden sharp visions of him in odd places—trolley cars, crowded streets, classrooms, ballfields. In those visions his cousin would be somewhere outside him, clearly visible but not always easily located—he seemed to move about—and they would talk. Slowly, very slowly, the dreams and visions became sporadic, faded, ceased. There were pictures of his cousin in the apartment. He could never look at them for any length of time without feeling pain and bewilderment. His cousin had gone off to war with a jaunty smile and a promise to return. He was a fighter pilot, and they never even found his body.

His aunt never recovered from the death of her only child. She would often talk to herself as she went about the apartment in her apron—she was rarely without an apron. She asked herself questions, answered them, questioned the answers. "Are you listening? Listen to an old woman. Why against the Japanese? Ah? Why? Tell me. They are an enemy? There aren't enough goyim in America to fight the yellow people? If he had to die, it should have been against the Germans. Where is the sense? A wagon-driver runs his business better than you run the world. How could you waste such a life?" She was in a dark dialogue with the demons—or the God—of catastrophe.

His uncle, on the other hand, developed a hoarse dry nervous cough and lapsed into almost total wordlessness. His eyes turned to pools behind the rimless glasses; the white and dark of the sockets blurred, became indistinguishable. Their sole light seemed to come from the occasional sudden flarings in the sun or in the fires of the furnace. He continued to run the apartment house, but talking seemed to weary him. He would address tenants with an opaque brevity that bordered on conventional notation. "Can't." "Don't know." "Maybe tomorrow." "Too cold?" "Fix soon." "Even God doesn't." "Janitor drunk." "Plumber Thursday." "Insane world."

From the age of fifteen until the age of twenty-one he lived in the apartment world of his aunt's whispery talking and his uncle's coughs and brooding silence, and he did not know which was more frightening. For a while after his cousin's death he thought his family had somehow been singled out for a special curse. But he talked to friends and found that throughout the neighborhood ran a twisting river of random events: parents died in slow or sudden ways, children were killed, relatives slipped young from life. The world seemed a strangely terrifying place when you really thought about it. He tried not to think about it too often.

Sometimes to get away from thinking about it he fled to the roof of the apartment house. There, on the cracked and reeking tar paper, he would sit with his back to the brick wall of the stairwell and gaze up across the adjoining rooftops to the sky. Usually it was a smoky stench-filled sky, but on occasion it was clear. One night he saw the vast heaven of stars clear as he had never seen it before, stretching from one end of the city to the other. It was a cool summer night, and as he sat there he heard a soft whining sound and a stirring in the darkness. He was about sixteen at the time, a boy of the streets, and not given easily to fear. In a corner of the roof, near a cluster of pipes, vents, and bubblelike protrusions, he found a bitch whelping her pups. She was a black mongrel with a white spot over one eye, and she growled softly as he approached. He watched the pups come, listened to her soft whimpers, saw her tear and lick off the sacks, clean the pups, push them aside, lie back, and wait for the next. He had never seen life born before. He knew the street talk about pricks and cunts, had read the porno books passed around in school yards, seen the photographs of the various positions. But the birth of these pups stirred him in a strange way. He saw them emerge from the organ that he and his friends would talk about with leers on the street. But here on this roof the bitch and her body seemed filled with a singular radiance. Life was being created before his eyes. He trembled, soared, wanted to shout and weep, and remained very still. He reached out to touch one of the newborn pups, and the bitch raised her head and bared her teeth. Overhead the star-filled sky seemed to drop down upon him. He felt all caught up in the life of heaven and earth, in the mystery of creation, in the pain and inexhaustible glory of this single moment. He wanted to hold the bitch to himself, caress her, caress something. Instead he reached up and brushed his hand across the sky and felt, actually felt, the achingly exquisitely cool dry velvet touch of starry heaven upon his fingers. He cried a little and shivered in the chill night air. Finally he thought it time to go back down, his aunt would become concerned about his absence.

He returned there the next morning. No bitch, no pups, no sign that life had been created on that sodden smelly roof. He wondered if he had dreamed it. He asked around the house. No one knew anything about a dog on the roof. He wandered through the neighborhood, casually questioning friends. No one was peddling puppies. A mystery.

But that rooftop feeling of awe and that caress of sky and stars were unforgettable. What an encounter that had been! He never forgot that moment. He hoped it would return one day. He felt he would be changed in some extraordinary way if it ever returned. He began to wait for it.

His aunt and uncle were pious Jews. They sent him to parochial schools. He obeyed them docilely. His first school was a neighborhood yeshiva where he studied in poorly lighted rooms that badly needed painting. Most of the students in his class were Hasidic boys in sidecurls. His uncle was not a member of any pietist sect but wanted him to have a true Torah education. Also, this yeshiva was tuition-free to those in need. He was a good but passive student. He seemed afraid to raise his hand in class. He spoke very little, had few acquaintances and even fewer friends. He preferred the window to the blackboard. Nothing seemed able to excite him.

He was then sent to a very orthodox high school in the Lower East Side section of New York and to an orthodox college in upper Manhattan. There was a rabbinical seminary in that college, and he received ordination. None of his Talmud teachers was enthusiastic about him, but none could find reason not to ordain him after he passed the required examinations. "Cannot hurt, ordination," his uncle had said in his shorthand manner. "Want to do something, fail, take a pulpit."

He did not know what he wanted to do. He had majored in mathematics but could not see himself going on to graduate school. He could not see himself teaching or doing anything. He spent sleepless nights on his narrow bed in his airless room listening to his uncle cough and wondering what to do.

Then one of his classmates, a close friend, told him that he was planning to apply for admission to the Riverside Hebrew Institute, a non-orthodox seminary in Manhattan a few blocks from Columbia University; it stood on Riverside Drive near the east bank of the Hudson River between the Gothic-style cathedral that was Riverside

Church and the Roman-style mausoleum that was Grant's Tomb. More out of curiosity than any sort of ideological conviction, he applied too. His uncle's coughs worsened, the silences grew deeper; the nephew he had raised like a son was abandoning the hothouse truths of orthodoxy for the cold heretical teachings of a non-orthodox rabbinical school. His aunt was bewildered and had another subject for her frequent conversations with herself. But there was nothing they could do. He was twenty-one years old.

Two weeks after the spring entrance examinations to the seminary, he learned that his classmate had decided to go on for a master's degree in biochemistry after all at Columbia and in that way possibly make it into medical school. For nights afterward he lay awake in his room choking back feelings of abandonment. But there was nothing he could do. When the letter of admission came from the seminary, he wrote back accepting, though he knew his classmate would decline. Three days later the Korean War broke out. That was in June 1950.

There were twenty-three seminarians in his class, and they all felt themselves very far from the war, as did most Americans. News of the war came to them in the newspapers they read with their meals, over their car radios as they drove to the various teaching jobs with which they supported themselves, or from radios in their dormitory rooms as they woke, shaved, dressed, or lay in the darkness trying to fall asleep. Uijongbu, Han, Seoul, Kimpo, Taejon, Pusan, Inchon, Yalu. Strange Asian names, bloodied villages, battered marines, wandering refugees, charging yellow hordes, brutal hills, murdered civilians. It was there, distant from them. They had more immediate matters than that war to consider: ancient texts, new ideas, the need for fresh concepts to replace their crumbling fundamentalism. The school was heady with thought and talk.

He went about his studies without enthusiasm. He felt no special interest in any one subject and read casually in all subjects. He was a plodding student and stood out nowhere. His classmates and professors considered him rather dull. He lay awake often at night wondering what he would do after ordination. The rabbinate filled him with dread. The joys and agonies of people, the politics of communal life, the tumult of involvement. But what would he do once he was out of this school?

Then at the start of his second year a new man came onto the faculty. He bore with him the aura of legend. He was of German origin, an erstwhile mathematical genius and theoretical physicist, a confirmed secular Zionist, a linguist, friend to Martin Buber, Franz Rosenzweig, Walter Benjamin, and a host of other near-mythical twentieth-century European intellectuals. He had been recently widowed and was now on indefinite leave from the Hebrew University in Jerusalem. His name was Jakob Keter, and he taught Kabbalah, Jewish mysticism. His classes were crowded; mysticism was popular, romantic. He taught Merkavah texts, the mystical writings of the talmudic rabbis. These texts described arduous ascents through celestial palaces and visions of the Throne-Chariot, the Merkavah, of the Supreme Being, as well as the Supreme Being Himself. Later in the year he began to teach the Zohar, the fifteenth-century compendium of Jewish mystical writings. But he taught only the history of mysticism and the readings of texts, textual analysis, a dry and technical method of study. Also it turned out that he was a dry teacher with a mirthless razor intelligence. He heaped on reading assignments as if his were the only class in the school. To come unprepared to his class was to court a low-voiced, German-accented public flaying. All in his class labored.

He assigned a major paper for the end of the year. The students worked on that paper in a long agony of travail. Two days after the end of the term Professor Jakob Keter flew back to Jerusalem, taking the papers with him. For a week he sat in the garden of his Jerusalem home and read the papers. His mood oscillated between dismay and boredom. Then one afternoon as he sat reading one of the papers he lost his sense of time. He finished reading, then read it through again. He was suspicious of most students and now considered the possibility of plagiarism. And so he sat in his garden amid mint-leaf plants, white and yellow jasmine, purple bougainvillaea, tall full-stemmed red and white roses, and in his mind went through decades of published scholarship. He could find nothing. He had only a vague recollection of this Gershon Loran, the student who had written the paper. Shy voice, downcast eyes, fairly good reading of texts, good knowledge of Hebrew and Aramaic, and generally undistinguished class performance.

The next day Professor Jakob Keter mailed the class grades to the seminary and a week later flew off to a conference in Switzerland. The only student who received an A was the vaguely remembered Gershon Loran.

Classes resumed in October after the High Holidays and festivals, but Gershon Loran was not there. After a few days, Jakob Keter inquired about him from the dean of students, a short heavy-set rabbi in his early thirties, and was informed that Gershon's uncle was ill and he was staying home to care for his aunt, who was also not well. To Jakob Keter's obvious next inquiry the dean of students replied that Gershon's parents were long dead.

Gershon returned to the seminary in the first week of November. He came into Professor Jakob Keter's class and sat silent and withdrawn in the last row of the crowded room. Keter, who had had no clear memory of what he looked like, now remembered him. He saw a thin-shouldered pale-faced young man with wide dark eyes and thick dark hair. An aura of melancholy radiated from his pale and delicate features like some dark nebula. Keter himself was a trim long-faced man a little more than six feet tall, almost completely bald save for a fringe of graying hair over his ears and around the back of his head. He had a sharp straight nose and bright clear gray eyes and thin lips. His face was clean-shaven, pinkish, and curiously unlined. He seemed of no definite age, certainly not the fifty-five he was known to be. He listened absently to the student who was reading aloud the passage, "Rav Hiya said: 'The world was in a state of poverty and misery from the time Adam transgressed the command of the Almighty until Noah came and offered up a sacrifice, when its prosperity returned.'"

"Thank you, that is fine," Jakob Keter said. There was a dry, uninflected quality to his voice. "Mr. Loran, please continue to read."

Gershon had been gazing out the window at some pigeons perched on the stone ledge of the building across the quadrangle. The late morning sun slanted through the quadrangle and shone full upon the pigeons, giving them a brilliant iridescent look. He had been gazing at them curiously and without feeling when Jakob Keter had called out his name. He found the passage in the text and continued the reading. "Rav Yosi said: 'The world was not properly settled, nor was the earth purged from the defilement of the serpent, until Israel stood before Mount Sinai, where they laid fast hold of the Tree of Life, and so established the world firmly.'" He read on, stopping from time to time to respond to questions from Keter about the precise meaning of this or that phrase, the grammar of this or that term. As he read, he found himself slowly warming to the words and the web of images they were spinning before his eyes. "Rav Hiya said: 'Why did not Noah, being a righteous man, cause death to vanish from the world?'" He read about the "scum of the serpent" and about the "lower leaves of the tree." It seemed to him that he read a long time, though toward the end he was no longer aware of the passage of time, he began to like the play of words and images; this was the same kind of feeling he had experienced while writing last year's paper. When Jakob Keter stopped him he looked away from the text and out the window. The sun had angled away from the ledge and the pigeons were gone.

Gershon was on his way out of the room together with the others after class when he heard Jakob Keter call his name. He wound his way carefully and with a thickly beating heart through the tangle of desks to the front of the room.

Keter's large desk was on a platform. Standing behind the desk and gazing down at Gershon Loran, Keter looked an awesome presence in his dark suit, white shirt, and red bow tie.

"How are you, Mr. Loran?" Jakob Keter asked. He regarded the young man closely and experienced a brief sensation of distaste. Gershon's jacket and trousers were unkempt, ill fitting; he badly needed a haircut; there was dirt under his fingernails.

"All right," Gershon Loran began to answer, but the words caught in his throat and he had to cough. "All right."

"How is your uncle?"

"Much better. He's back home now from the hospital."

"Where did you learn your Aramaic, Mr. Loran?"

"An old man taught me. My uncle thought it was important to learn." He kept his eyes down as he talked.

"This old man is a scholar?"

"I don't know. He prays in our little synagogue. He learned Aramaic from someone in Odessa."

"Mr. Loran, is it your intention to enter the rabbinate?"

He wanted to say "I don't know" but again the words caught and he had to clear his throat. "I don't know."

Jakob Keter adjusted the small dark skullcap that lay on his bald head; he was a secularist, and that skullcap was his sole visible concession to the traditionalism of the school. "I hope your uncle remains well and you do not miss any more classes," he said to Gershon Loran, and gave him a nod of dismissal.

He stood behind the desk watching Gershon thread his way through the desks and out of the classroom. The door closed with a soft click. He gazed at the space in front of his desk, the space occupied a moment before by Gershon Loran, and it seemed to him that space now contained a dark and palpable sadness.

Later that week he assigned a research paper to the class, with mid-February as the completion date, and again Gershon Loran was the only student to whom he gave an A. On the last page of the paper he wrote in a European-style script, "Very well researched and written. Regarding Persian influences upon development of Kabbalah, see footnote 2b to my article cited in your footnote 7."

In the first week of March, three days after the celebration of Purim, his uncle fell ill again. The illness was not menacing enough to send him to the hospital but was serious enough to confine him to his bed. Gershon Loran moved out of his seminary dormitory room, which he shared with a young man from New England, and into his old small room in the apartment house.

His uncle coughed a great deal and had difficulty breathing. The doctor called the condition emphysema and said there was no cure. The coal dust had probably brought it on, though this particular attack apparently was the result of the rather spirited way his uncle had celebrated Purim. He was a devout man, fully at home in Jewish law and learning, though not a scholar, and he took seriously the moments of splendid joy commanded by the tradition. Purim, which celebrates the failure of a despotic Asian minister to do away with an ancient Persian Jewish community, is an occasion for heavy drinking. He drank, grew overheated, was called up to the roof to repair a sudden break in a pipe, and was in bed three days later with a mild bronchitis. The bronchitis threatened to aggravate seriously the emphysema. The doctor said if the emphysema worsened he would have to go back to the hospital. His uncle was a short gaunt man in his early sixties, white-haired, weary, his goateë gone all white and scraggly, his narrow face deeply lined. He lay frightened and silent in his bed, breathing tortuously.

Gershon slept on the narrow bed in the small room. His aunt cooked, cleaned, sat stiffly in the living room staring at the photograph that showed her long dead son in the uniform of a fighter pilot, or wandered about the small apartment talking raspingly to the ceiling and walls and windows. She was a thin-boned woman in her late fifties with almost milk-white skin on her face and hands, and deep-brown eyes that were large and somewhat bulging and surrounded by dark shadows. Often the way she wandered about talking made the skin rise on the back of his neck. Sometimes she put on her coat and hat and scarf and went out shopping. Mostly she remained in the apartment tending to her husband, and it was Gershon who would go out for the groceries, bring the Yiddish newspaper from the nearby candy store, medication from the pharmacy, shoes from the repair shop, shirts from the laundry. It was also Gershon who would rise with night darkness still on the window of his room, dress quickly in the chill air, go out of the apartment into the narrow fetid ground-floor hallway and down the worn and cracked cement stairs to the basement where rats scurried about in the darkness and pipes sweated and valves dripped and the furnace was still and nearly dead. With an iron hook he opened the furnace door; with a shovel he heaped coal onto the darkly glowing bed, feeling the heat on his arms and face. Coal dust rose from the bin, stirred by the stabbing shovel, and he felt it dry and gritty in his throat and as slippery powder on his hands. He shoveled and sweated. The fire rose in the furnace. Through the open furnace door he saw the writhing bed of flames. He shoveled more coal and felt the fierce beating of his heart and the ache in his shoulders and arms. When the fire was high and roaring he shut the furnace door and went back up to the apartment, shivering as his heated skin encountered the early morning air in the hallway. He stripped to the waist and washed off the coal dust with laundry soap. He could not get the coal dust out from beneath his fingernails. He prayed the morning service, had a cup of coffee and a buttered roll, and returned to his small room where he read until he heard his aunt or uncle wake. Then he would leave his room and tend to their needs.

He asked his uncle one afternoon why they did not move to another apartment. "The neighborhood is bad. The building is terrible."

His uncle coughed and said, "Move? Where?"

"Anywhere."

"Remain here. Move to the grave and the next world."

"Pooh," his aunt said. "Watch what you say."

"Not afraid. Can't hurt me anymore."

"You really ought to move out, Uncle Aaron."

"No. Memories. Bricks and walls and ceilings. Memories. Will not leave them. A new apartment? Emptiness."

"And who has money?" his aunt said. "Here we live rent-free. And will Saul come to a new apartment? No." Saul was the son they had lost in the war.

Gershon felt cold listening to them talk, and he did not speak to them again about moving.

He read and studied late into the night so as to keep up with his seminary classes. He began to find a strange solace in the mystical text he was studying with Professor Jakob Keter. He felt attracted to the frequent images of fire. "When God decided to create the world, He first produced a flame of a scintillating lamp. He blew spark against spark, causing darkness and fire, and produced from the recesses of the abyss a certain drop which He joined with the flame, and from the two he created the world. . . ." It was all clearly such fanciful poetry, but he began to enjoy it—he did not know why he felt himself moved by it—and he found it more pleasant to apply to this material the apparatus of scientific text criticism than to the texts of the Bible or Talmud, which held little mystery for him.

One evening he was informed by a fifth-floor tenant that the roof pipe recently repaired by his uncle was leaking once again. He had learned some rudimentary plumbing from his uncle, and he climbed the stairs with some tools to have a look at the pipe. The leak was from a bad spigot. He shut the valve, removed the spigot, and capped the pipe. He would get another spigot tomorrow and replace it. The outside segment of pipe had not been drained and shut down. His uncle must have been in a rush to get off the cold roof. Probably water had frozen and burst the spigot. The winter wind blew a March gale across the roof. He stood there in the wind a long moment thinking he could hear a familiar sound, a soft whimpering in the darkness. But there was nothing there save patches of ice and snow on the cracked and buckling tar paper. He picked up the tools and went back downstairs. A week later he took the subway to the seminary and moved back into his dormitory room.

His roommate, Arthur Leiden, a suave and handsome Harvard graduate from a suburb of Boston, said to him that night, "You ought to get them a nurse, Gershon."

"We can't afford a nurse."

"I mean a home nurse. Doesn't this barbarous city have an agency for home nurses or whatever you wish to call them?"

"They don't want strangers in the apartment."

His roommate regarded him with a look of pity.

"They're old people with strange habits," Gershon Loran said. "What do you want me to do?"

"You keep piling up absences, you'll never make it to your senior year. Don't you want to graduate this esteemed institution?"

"I'll make it. Tell me again how Keter explained that passage. Where was that parallel text?"

They worked together awhile on the text. Later they walked down Riverside Drive toward Columbia and went into a delicatessen for something to eat. It was a cold night. The plate glass window of the delicatessen was steamy with condensation. They had corned beef sandwiches and cream sodas.

"Malkuson killed me last week in class," his roommate said jovially. Nathan Malkuson was professor of Talmud. "I didn't have a chance to prepare, and he caught me. It was a blood bath. I am scarred."

"You're never prepared."

"Not never, not never."

"When are you prepared?"

"Well, true, hardly ever. To change the subject. How's your love life? How's Karen?"

"Fine."

"Do you see her?"

"Of course I see her."

"She intimidates me, you know. She's too damn smart. I'm intimidated by female philosophers."

"You had no female philosophers at Radcliffe?"

"Certainly we had. Certainly. But they concealed it adroitly. Yes indeed. Quite adroitly. But our Karen is obviously good for you. She brings a smile to your sober countenance."

"We ought to start back, Arthur."

"Ah, our Gershon is embarrassed. Easily saddened, easily embarrassed. Our poor Gershon."

"Come on."

"Certainly. Absolutely. Let's go back so I can prepare for tomorrow's class with Malkuson."

"You aren't prepared yet?"

"It's early. It's only ten-thirty. I am a night person."

They walked back along the cold streets to the seminary. In the room, Gershon Loran put an old book on his night table. His roommate looked at the title.

"This one is most assuredly not on the class reading list," he said.

"It's on my private list," Gershon said.

"What is it?"

Gershon told him.

"You don't say!"

"It describes a simple way of inducing trances. A medieval kabbalist used to do it. You put your head between your knees."

"Really? You don't say! You mean of all the people here whom I might have dormed with, I had to find myself a practitioner of magic, a crazy kabbalist."

"This is scholarship, Arthur. Only scholarship."

"Do you transform yourself in the night? Do you become a Rabbi Hyde? Tell me. I have a delicate nervous system."

"You have the nervous system of a Bengal tiger."

"You need it to survive Malkuson. No transformations in the night, please. That's all I ask, my sole plea."

"Good night, Arthur."

Gershon lay in his bed and listened to the radio for a while. His roommate sat in their study. The radio spoke softly of Congressional investigations, of the distant war, of battles for hills and valleys, villages and rice paddies. It spoke in murmurous whispers of blood and madness in Asia and of Arab infiltrators killing Israelis in the Middle East. He turned off the radio and read. He grew tired after a few minutes, closed the book, and switched off the bed lamp. It had begun to snow, and in the darkness he heard the wind blow the snow against the windows. He had a brief vision of his long dead cousin. Blond hair, jaunty smile. He had not thought of him in a very long time. In the vision Gershon was about seven years old, his cousin was about thirteen. They were working on a puzzle together on a carpeted floor. How swiftly they completed the puzzle! It was a map of the world. They hugged each other and laughed. Someone kissed him, a warm kiss, a woman's kiss. The snow beat on the windows. He fell asleep.

The next afternoon Gershon emerged from the dining room, made a rush for the closing door of the elevator in the dormitory building, and was startled to find himself alone inside with Professor Nathan Malkuson. The door closed. This was a notoriously slow elevator. It began to rise.

"Good afternoon, professor," Gershon said diffidently and cleared his throat.

Professor Malkuson formed the small and faintly disdainful smile that was a near permanent fixture on his plump and clean-shaven face. "Well, Loran," he said. "How is your family?"

"As well as can be expected, thank you, professor."

The elevator moved at its normal slow pace, its machinery humming softly.

"You read the Gemara well this morning, Loran," Professor Malkuson said. He was a man of medium height, in his fifties, with silvery hair and cold blue eyes. He wore a gray suit and a dark tie, and his head was covered with a small black skullcap. He held a key in his right hand. Gershon's arms were laden with books.

As the elevator continued its languid climb, they talked of the difficult passage of Talmud with which the class had struggled earlier that day. Gershon spoke timidly, his eyes gazing downward.

The elevator stopped at the third floor. The door opened. No one entered. They broke off their conversation and stood there in awkward silence. Apparently someone had grown weary of waiting and had taken the stairs. The door closed. The elevator resumed its crawling journey.

Professor Malkuson noticed the titles on some of the books in Gershon's arms.

"Ah, Loran," he murmured with his disdainful smile, pointing to the books with his key. "Much better you should study Talmud. This is such foolishness. You wish to become a scholar of foolishness?" It was not unusual in this seminary to hear members of the faculty openly attack and deride each other's ideas. This was the training ground for the souls of coming generations; these seminarians went out into the world to teach and conquer or to be defeated. A scholar's disciples constituted one measure of his immortality. Gershon Loran, cringing inside himself, felt the cold blue eyes of this greatest of living talmudists, Nathan Malkuson, move across his face. The elevator rose with tortuous indolence. Nathan Malkuson went on in his half-mocking tone. "I detect in you, Loran, a good head for Talmud. But you have no enthusiasm. You are without *éntheos*. You know what that means in Greek? No? You are without the feeling of possession by the divine. There is no fire burning in you. Do you have *éntheos* for that, Loran?" He pointed again at the books with his key. "Well, perhaps it will wear off in the service. Here we are. Aren't you getting out? It is the top floor. Good afternoon, Loran."

Gershon came out of the elevator together with Professor Malkuson. He turned away his burning face, too embarrassed to admit that he had been so flustered by the professor's presence in the elevator that he had forgotten to press the button to his own floor. He started toward one of the administrative offices, saw Professor Malkuson put the key to a door and enter, then doubled back quickly and took the staircase down two flights to his dormitory room.

Inside the two-room study—even the room with the sofa and easy chairs was lined with books—Professor Malkuson settled himself briskly behind his large glass-topped desk and removed from a locked drawer the manuscript of his current work on the Talmud. He unscrewed the cap of his Waterman's pen, thought of the sad face of Gershon Loran, and regretted having mentioned the service. That had been an inadvertent slip, an utterance voiced in a brief moment of annoyance over the power of Keter, whose subject seemed to be claiming yet another adherent. It was all demented nonsense. They studied the history of the texts of a foolishness and called that a science. What did Kabbalah have to do with life? Surely they knew that Talmud was the only consistently honorable subject worthy of study in Judaism; it alone affected one's life, one's daily behavior. A Jew molded his life according to talmudic law. To uncover the original smoothness and clarity of an ancient passage of Talmud; to rebuild it and return it to the sharp, keen wording it must originally have had when it was first uttered two thousand years ago, before becoming garbled in transmission; to give it new meaning, explain an early text correctly in a manner perhaps not even perceived by later talmudic sages themselves—there could be no greater achievement than that. It was an art form; it was like painting a Raphael. Smooth, clear, coherent, with a depth that was three-dimensional and lovely. Not the murkiness of Kabbalah with its bizarre flights of fancy, its God of divine nothingness, its emanations and angels and numerology and dark magic that bordered on oriental paganism. Still he should not have mentioned the service to that young man Loran; that was confidential information given only yesterday to a special committee of the faculty. But the young man seemed to have taken no notice of it. He was a dreamer, sad, burdened, not quite present in mind where he was in body. He seemed always to be listening for something, always to be looking around, as if he were waiting for something or someone, waiting. Professor Malkuson opened his manuscript, read for a few minutes, then smoothly resumed writing. He forgot about Gershon Loran. On the stone ledge outside his windows pigeons strutted back and forth, softly cooing.

Two floors below and three rooms down the hall, Gershon sat at his desk studying a kabbalistic text. The book was old, its rag pages darkened, its binding frayed and redolent of dust. He was trying to reconstruct a garbled text and restore it to its original coherence. It was a lengthy and intriguing text, similar to others he had read before in such works. It told how God had withdrawn the pure radiant sacred light of His presence from the world in order to make possible the creation of impure material reality, thereby bringing into existence evil and suffering. He worked intently for a while, then broke off to rest his eyes. Gazing out the window at a shaft of pale sunlight on the gray-brown grass of the quadrangle, he wondered idly what Professor Malkuson had meant by service. He felt always too shy to ask for explanations from Professor Malkuson; he feared the full glare of that disdainful smile. As he gazed out the window, a pigeon fluttered by and was quickly gone. He returned to his texts and was soon lost inside the words and images.

Voices in the hallway outside his room disturbed him. He looked up and saw Nathan Malkuson standing just inside the closed door near the bookcase. He was smiling thinly and regarding him with disdain. Gershon experienced a feeling of cold shock at this abrupt and startling vision. It seemed not to help at all that he knew it to be merely a vision, a clinging memory of his encounter in ·the elevator. There he stood—gray suit, dark tie, pale smile, silvery hair. You have *éntheos* for that, Loran? he distinctly heard the vision of Nathan Malkuson say. Perhaps it will wear off in the service. The vision faded. Gershon was left with his numbing sensation of surprise. His heart beat inside his throat.

He could not return to the text. Anyway, there was something he needed to do in the library. He came out of the room, took the elevator to the sixth floor, crossed through the connecting corridor to the library building, and took another elevator to the second floor. This elevator was crowded with students and secretaries. Inside the vast and marbled reading room he sat at a long table and copied a long passage from a reference book into his notebook. It was early evening. Some students sat gazing through the tall leaded windows as the last light of the winter day faded. The street lamps came on. Desk lamps sent splashes of yellow light all through the reading room. Gershon sat at the table working. He went out after a while to the catalogue room to check a bibliographical reference, and there, thumbing through a long thin drawer of cards, was the tall presence of Jakob Keter.

"Ah, good evening, Mr. Loran," he said.

It was not unusual to encounter Jakob Keter in the library. Gershon saw him there often, most frequently emerging from the rare-manuscript room that adjoined the reading room. That rare-manuscript room was one of the reasons Jakob Keter had come to the United States; it contained an extraordinary collection of medieval kabbalistic manuscripts, some whole, others in tatters, isolated chapters and fragments in vellum and parchment, remnants of past labors that had barely survived the centuries. Jakob Keter was working to sort them, identify them, match them with known manuscripts, give them some semblance of order.

Gershon experienced his customary sense of awkwardness. He never seemed to know with certainty what to say to his teachers; he was incapable of making small talk and felt himself inadequate for lengthy discussions of scholarship.

Jakob Keter regarded him dispassionately. So timid a young man, so clearly sad. A childhood friend of his in Berlin had been like that: somber, walking about in his circle of uncertainty; he had stayed on in Berlin when Keter had left for Palestine and had been murdered by the Nazis in Theresienstadt.

"I see on your face a faint hint of excitement, Mr. Loran. You have discovered something?"

"I think so, professor."

"Yes? What is it?"

Timidly, hesitantly, Gershon explained that he believed he had found in another kabbalistic text the final section of a Zohar passage that, in its present form, was clearly broken off in the middle. There were two other students in the catalogue room, and they looked at him curiously as he spoke. Jakob Keter listened, his long bald head tilted slightly to one side. When he was done there was a brief silence. The two students looked away.

Keter asked a number of terse questions having to do with style and syntax, and Gershon responded.

"Indeed," Jakob Keter said, regarding him intently. "That is a possibility. Yes indeed. I will go home and think about it. Good evening, Mr. Loran."

Gershon returned to the reading room in a pall of shame. What a fool he had been to think he might have discovered something new in a realm of bewildering mysteries! Sitting behind the long table in a wash of yellow light, he had a brief vision of Jakob Keter's long face broken by a mocking smile. He felt moist with humiliation.

In class the next morning Jakob Keter announced that Gershon Loran had discovered the closing segment of a Zohar passage. The statement came abruptly right at the start of the session. "Last evening I was informed by Mr. Loran that he had discovered . . ." There were envious glances. Gershon Loran sat in stunned surprise, his heart pounding. Someone slipped him a note. He read: "The crazy kabbalist has struck again! Spare me, Rabbi Hyde!" He looked around and saw Arthur Leiden staring at the ceiling, wearing a countenance of sweet innocence. Then he turned his attention back to Keter, who was saying something about Kabbalah as an academic discipline.

"You will permit me to make this statement, gentlemen. Yes? It is seldom that I make a polemic in a class or in writing. But now it becomes time to make a statement. There was once a time when no one believed it necessary or possible to make of Kabbalah a scientific discipline. The talmudists disapproved. The kabbalists disapproved. To this day they disapprove. Yes. To the former, Kabbalah is nonsense; to the latter, it is an untouchable sanctity. But to me it is neither nonsense nor untouchable. Yes. It is the heart of Judaism, the soul, the core. Talmud tells us how the Jew acts; Kabbalah tells us how Judaism feels, how it sees the world. We are Western secular beings today, rational, logical, yes, and so we are embarrassed by Kabbalah, which is so irrational, illogical. But the tradition was not embarrassed; for nearly two thousand years it was not embarrassed. Great talmudists were also great kabbalists. Yes. If, as some of my colleagues in this institution claim, Kabbalah was never regarded seriously, will someone explain to me why the Jews of Europe produced dozens upon dozens of commentaries to kabbalistic works all through the centuries? Explain it to me, if it is truly nonsense."

He spoke softly, without passion. The class was quiet. This was the first time since he had come to the school that he was talking *about* Kabbalah, defending it. Morning sunlight shone through the windows of the long room and spangled the floor and walls. It shone upon the desks and the texts, upon the hands and faces of some of the students, and upon one side of the platform where Jakob Keter stood. He stood there in his dark suit and red bow tie, talking.

"People say that certain of us have nothing better to do with our lives than make trouble for Jews. They say I make trouble for Jews by teaching an embarrassing and archaic form of thinking. But why is it embarrassing? Why is it archaic? Yes? Will someone tell me? I do not tell you to believe it, I ask only that we understand it, that it not be lost to scientific inquiry. What right does any talmudist have to consign to—how do you say it?—to oblivion two thousand years of a Jewish way of thinking? Will someone be so kind as to tell me what right?"

The class was very quiet. Overhead, distantly, an airplane droned by, softly rattling the windows.

There was a long silence. Jakob Keter stood still, gazing out at the crowded room. Minute particles of dust danced and whirled in the beams of sunlight.

Then Jakob Keter said, "Well, we have wasted enough good time this morning with our polemic. Certain voices had been raised against me, and so it had to be said. Now, enough. We return to our text. Mr. Leiden, you are awake? Yes? Good. Please read."

At the end of the class, with everyone filing out of the room, he called Gershon over to him. When they were alone he said, "If you do not enter the rabbinate, Mr. Loran, consider the possibility of an academic career. Yes."

Gershon, bewildered, could do nothing but stare at him.

"Consider taking a degree, Mr. Loran."

Still Gershon stared, speechless.

Then Jakob Keter said something Gershon did not understand. "You will perhaps have plenty of time later to make your decision, Mr. Loran. You will perhaps have plenty of time in which to read and prepare."

Walking alone toward the elevator a moment later, Gershon felt bewildered by the events of the morning. He had in fact stumbled upon that second text quite inadvertently in the course of a haphazard reading of the book he had taken to his room the day before. There had been no calculated search, no scientific plan of inquiry. Certain phrases and ideas had seemed familiar in the second text, and he had gone quickly back through the Zohar and found the text he thought it matched. He had offered his idea with much trepidation during the chance meeting with Jakob Keter. It was strange how cumulative events had moved him into the good graces of this giant of twentieth-century scholars—answers hesitantly offered in class; research papers submitted with dread; the long-forgotten meaning of an Aramaic term wrenched from memory and timidly presented when his classmates had exhausted all other effort at explanation. He did not think he wanted to make a career out of Kabbalah. He really did not know what he wanted to do. He could not feel a deep—what was the word?—*éntheos,* yes, *éntheos* for Kabbalah. He could not feel *éntheos* for anything. But he was pleased to have earned the public favor of Jakob Keter.

So was his roommate. "A triumph!" Arthur Leiden exclaimed when he came into their room that evening after teaching a late class in the Manhattan synagogue where Karen Levin's father was the rabbi. He stood in the doorway beaming at the shy and hesitantly smiling Gershon Loran. "I burst with pride. Come, my kabbalist, I will treat you to corned beef and cream soda. You are the subject of the day. You have replaced Senator McCarthy and the hills of Korea. Come, my Rabbi Hyde. On to the deli."

It was a cold clear night. "Salubrious weather," Arthur called it. "Harvard weather. I will eat a potato knish to warm and fortify my insides."

"Tomorrow I'll discover a whole new kabbalistic work," Gershon said with sudden uncharacteristic exultation as they turned onto Broadway.

"Then I will treat you to a whole steer, a veritable stockyard of steers."

They ate heartily amid warm talk and then walked back along Riverside Drive to the seminary. The dormitory elevator was out of order. It broke down about once a month, was repaired, and broke down again; no one seemed to know what was really wrong with it. They walked up the stairs to their room and went to bed.

Gershon could not sleep. The room was dark and still. Dark and still too were the dormitory and library and school buildings. The huge wrought-iron front gate was closed. A deep quiet enveloped the corridors and the quadrangle. Gershon fell into a dreamlike vision. He could feel the quiet as he moved in his vision through the dimly lighted corridors. Soon Professor Malkuson would emerge from his study. At precisely two o'clock in the morning he would cease his writing. He would walk through the silent corridors, his shoes tapping and echoing on the marble floors. What would he do tonight with the elevator out of order? Walk down the dormitory staircase? Cross over to the library building and take that elevator down? The guard would open the gate for him. Good night, professor. Every weekday night he left the school to walk home to his Riverside Drive apartment, a solitary figure in the pools of light cast by the street lamps. He walked briskly, wearing a coat and a hat. Gershon watched him walk. A wind blew across the river from the cliffs along the opposite shore. Gershon shivered. He watched as a tall thin man emerged from the shadows of an apartment house. He wore a dark coat and a red wool muffler. His nearly bald head glinted dully in the light of a street lamp. He approached Nathan Malkuson.

May I walk with you, Malkuson?

Why, certainly. Certainly. It is good to see you.

They walked together beneath the haloes of the street lamps.

This student of mine, this Mr. Loran, the tall thin man said. Very quiet, very shy, very bright. Difficult to discover his brightness. He rarely speaks.

I have discovered it, Nathan Malkuson said.

In Berlin I had a friend like that, the tall thin man said. Shy, bright, fearful.

Indeed? Indeed? said Nathan Malkuson. And did you convert your friend to Kabbalah?

The tall man said, I am a threat to you, my friend, am I not. You would like our world to be smooth and rational, would you not. You do not care to know of the rabbis, the great ones who were filled with poetry and contradictions. There is deep, deep within us the irrational as well. It is our motor energy, our creative demon. You think we know the world only on the basis of what we observe or can deduce logically? No, my good friend. As you grew up, did you meet no one who spoke of his experiences through the use of images rather than logic, who spoke of things that did not correspond to any reality we can observe? The irrational completes us.

You exaggerate, Keter, came the murmured reply. You have taken a tiny tributary and made of it a mighty river.

Ah, this is no tributary, my good friend. This is the soul of the matter, the soul, the life's breath. You know it in your bones and will not admit it.

You exaggerate, you exaggerate. You deceive the unwary with your exaggerations.

Deceive? Deceive? I deceive no one. I do not deceive this young man, this Loran. He comes to it naturally. He is—how do you say it? predisposed?—Yes. He is predisposed to it. I feel he is attracted to it from the root of his soul. I am convinced of it.

I will wager you will yet lose him.

Yes? You think so?

I will wager. He is too intelligent for Kabbalah.

How this wind blows! This is a clean cold wind.

And you, Nathan Malkuson said, you too seek to reconcile contradictions, restore fragments. We are both of the rational world.

But our substance is different. Yes?

Indeed it is. Indeed it is.

Shall we stop off somewhere for a coffee? I know of a small clean place on Broadway. Up this street. Yes. How cold this wind is! How clean!

2

᭞᭞᭞ The weather turned languid. He watched the quadrangle grass come slowly to life. Birds returned to the river. He spent the Passover festival with his aunt and uncle. Together they celebrated the exodus that led to the choosing. They sat around the Seder table: the fragile and brooding scraggly-goateed man, the white-faced and dark-eyed woman, the shy seminarian, singing and chanting haltingly, rarely together, almost always out of tune; three solitary individuals bonded by strange memories and inarticulate love.

The winter was gone; his uncle no longer rose in the dark mornings to fire the furnace. Tenants reported rats, and his uncle brought in an exterminator. A large crack developed in the section of the roof adjacent to the stairwell shaft, and men came to repair it. Gershon stood on the roof near a welter of pipes and valves and watched the men lay down the tar paper. He gazed around the roof and saw in the grimy muck of a nearby corner two beer bottles and a condom. The sky was moist and gray. Why were things always breaking down? The world ought not be that way! The odor of molten tar was strong in the narrow hallways and in the stairwell. He smelled it that evening in the apartment as he sat reading.

"Reading what?" his uncle asked him, and seemed startled by the response. "Sacred, sacred," he murmured, shaking his head and staring at his nephew.

His aunt said in her hoarse whispery voice, "I remember, yes, I remember my mother's father studied Kabbalah. In old age he lost his mind a little. No, it was my mother's grandfather. They kept him locked in the house. My mother told me of her visions of him singing strange songs. He sang Gypsy love songs to the Torah. Pooh! Yes, it was my mother's grandfather."

Two blocks away was the small synagogue where they prayed: an old brick building, a narrow vestibule, a room with a single aisle, wooden chairs, a podium, a lectern, an Ark with the Torah scrolls. Naked light bulbs hung from black wires in the ceiling. The greenish walls needed painting. In this synagogue he had recited the prayer said by mourners—the Kaddish. His uncle too had said that prayer. Gershon sat and listened to the old people praying; he was the youngest person there, and he was twenty-four years old.

After the service on the last day of Passover the old man from Odessa who had taught him Aramaic came over to him and said in Yiddish, "If I had known, I would never have taught you."

And Gershon stared at this old man, at his worn brown suit and battered old hat, at his white hair and long uncombed white beard and slightly protruding eyes, and remembered the two years of evenings he had spent with him in his musty book-crowded apartment.

"Torah you know?" the old man said. His mouth was stained yellow from the cigarettes he smoked. "Gemora you know? My uncle, may he rest in peace, studied Kabbalah. He was a healer, in Jerusalem. You hear? In Jerusalem. Always he went to the ritual bath before he studied. You go? If I had known . . ."

And he moved away, muttering to himself, and left Gershon staring at him in stupefaction.

After the festival he returned to the seminary. He saw the sun on the spires of Riverside Church one block up the Drive. There were buds on the trees. Gulls wheeled over a barge on the river. He came up the wide stone front steps and through the gate and crossed the open stone courtyard into the quadrangle. There were flowers now in the beds: tulips, daffodils, hyacinths. Along the western rim of the quadrangle was a bank of forsythia, yellow in the sunlight. On the stone ledge of the red-brick dormitory building, the north side of the quadrangle, pigeons strutted about, cooing. The air was warm and blue. He greeted passing seminarians and one classmate. The air was cool in the shade of the outdoor flagstone walk that ran beside the library building. He took the dormitory elevator and found his roommate unpacking in the bedroom.

"Hello," Arthur Leiden said cheerfully, waving at him a pair of Jockey shorts. "Welcome, welcome. I am returned from Arcady to this semi-barbarous center of Western civilization. How was your holiday? Mine was a surfeit of chicken fat and matza. My bowels murmur but will not move."

"Hello, Arthur."

"Did you have a good holiday?" Arthur asked.

"It was pretty good."

"Can I give you a hand with those bags? My God, what have you got in here?"

"Books."

"More esoterics for Keter? More hermeneutics for Malkuson?"

"A little of both."

"How are you, Gershon? Really."

"I'm all right. I'm glad to see you, Arthur."

"Why is it, my friend, that you never look glad when you say you are glad? Are you devoid of the smile muscles around your mouth? My mother is like that, you know. I never told you? Oh, yes. A single expression for all the vast multiplicity of emotions. She is, mind you, a marvelous woman, my mother. Her family dates back to pre–Revolutionary War days. Oh, yes. But she cooks like an Eastern European immigrant and possesses one and only one expression, a curve of lips that is a shade or two below the *Mona Lisa* level of outburst. Do you have any shaving cream? It appears I forgot to bring my own, and I would like to shower and shave. Thank you. Have you heard the latest rumor? We may be drafted into the service."

"Where did you hear that?"

"There and here, here and there."

"That can't be true, Arthur. Theology students are exempt from the service."

"Only as warriors, dear friend. Only as wielders of weapons and killers of men. Not as—guess, guess."

"As what?"

"As chaplains."

"The chaplaincy is voluntary, Arthur."

"That is what I said to myself when I heard this rumor. 'The chaplaincy is voluntary, Arthur.' Yet the rumor persists. We are all going to be volunteered for the chaplaincy."

"It's another silly rumor, Arthur. This place is full of rumors."

"Rumor and untruth are not necessarily synonymous, dear Gershon."

"Is there anything else you need? I have a styptic pencil."

"I have my own, thank you. I will dry my own blood."

"Your own pre–Revolutionary War blood."

"We need an incantation, Gershon. Against the ill winds of rumor. Give us an incantation. Whisper for us a kabbalistic word. One moment! One moment!"

"What?"

"I believe I am about to move my bowels. I cannot tell you how absolutely refreshing a prospect that is. Hold on with the incantation."

He picked up a magazine from his night table and disappeared with it into the bathroom. Gershon opened a window and stood there feeling the warm air on his face and listening to the pigeons on the ledge.

That Sunday afternoon he walked with Karen Levin to the Fire Department monument that stood at the end of 100th Street on the narrow upper road along Riverside Drive. The air was warm, and the Drive was crowded with strollers and traffic. Sunlight shone on the grass and the spring trees. It was about a twenty-minute walk from her family's Riverside Drive apartment to the monument. They walked along the upper road past tall elegant apartment houses of brown brick and gray stone. Wedged among the apartment houses was an occasional three- or four-story white stone house. These narrow houses, dwarfed by the immense buildings around them and yet possessed of a fragile grace, with their polished stone stoops and Ionic entrance pillars and wrought-iron grillwork and window boxes—these houses seemed to Gershon silent reminders of golden things past. Tiny balconies looked out from their second or third floors across the trees and the slopes of the Drive to the broad river that lay beyond the densely traveled city highway. Shrubbery lined the side of the road across from the houses. The leaves were still young, and through the breaks in the hedges he could see now and then glints of sunlight on the dark river. The river seemed to him filled with strange power, a resonance of menace, yet he was drawn to it. Always he returned to it, walking alone or with Karen or a classmate. On occasion he thought he had come to this seminary because it lay near this river.

They walked through the sunlight and shadows of the May afternoon.

"This is the first really warm day," Karen said. "Isn't it lovely?"

"We'll get some ice cream," he said. "There's usually a vendor near the monument."

"I can't. I had meat for lunch."

"Soda, then. All right? Or maybe some Italian ices."

She nodded happily. Slight, diminutive, wearing a plain white blouse and a bright-green skirt, she held his hand and gazed at a flock of birds wheeling above a grove of elms down near the riverbank. She was not a pretty girl—eyes, nose, and lips, separately well proportioned, had somehow been so arranged upon her face as to seem ever so slightly out of place and shape. She had short straight brown hair, brown eyes, a somewhat longish nose, and Cupid's-bow lips. Her father had served eighteen years as a rabbi in a large Boston-area congregation before moving to Manhattan three years ago, and she spoke with the expected regional accent, the flattened a's and the suddenly appearing r's. They had met at a party, had spent a summer discovering one another in a children's camp, found themselves at ease together, and saw each other often. For as far back as she could recall she had been without illusions regarding her looks and had given herself over to a relentless and grimly focused concentration upon her studies. This had finally yielded precious fruit: she had passed her doctoral preliminary examinations some weeks back and this past Thursday had been informed by her Columbia philosophy faculty chairman that her dissertation topic had been approved. She had an instructorship at Barnard. She looked forward happily now to the coming two or three years of teaching, research, and writing.

"How crowded the Drive is," Gershon said. "It's like a tribal picnic."

"It's wonderful. It's beautiful."

He looked at her. She wore no makeup. The sun shone on her face. "You sound very happy," he said.

She squeezed his hand. "You've noticed. How perceptive! Of

course I'm happy. You have no idea how long that tunnel was, Gershon."

"I have some idea."

"There were times I thought I'd never get out."

"I'm glad for you, Karen. Where are we? Three more blocks."

They walked on in silence. The Drive hummed with the sounds of people and traffic. Children played and ran along the grassy slopes beneath the shading sycamores and elms. They came to the monument. The pink marble of the fountain glowed in the sunlight. The water was off. The monument had been erected in 1912 and was a memorial to the men who had died in the service of the New York City Fire Department. A warm wind blew from the river with the moist fresh scent of water. They descended from the street on the pink marble staircase to the parquet brick parapet lined with benches and facing the wide lower Drive. The river was clearly visible through the trees.

"Let's sit down for a few minutes," Gershon said. "I'm a little tired. Arthur got back at three in the morning, woke me up, and spent an hour telling me about his date."

They sat on a bench in front of the monument. For a brief moment he sensed something behind his back and glanced around. He saw nothing but the white stone monument with the statues on its sides, one of a woman holding the body of a man, the other of a woman holding the body of a child. A few people sat nearby on the other benches. Set into the parquet floor in front of the fountain was the bronze tablet memorial to the horses that had died in the service of the Fire Department.

"Arthur can be a nuisance at times," she said, looking away from him at the trees and the river.

Her face, bubbling with joy moments before, had gone suddenly cold. He sensed the change in her.

"You don't like him very much," he said.

She turned her brown eyes upon him. He detected in them sadness and anger. "I only like him for bringing you over to me at the party. I knew him about five years in Boston. Remember my telling you? His family came to Boston right after the war. For as long as I've known him I haven't liked him. He's wild and flighty and irresponsible."

"I like him."

"I'm glad. It would be terrible if you didn't. He's your roommate. Gershon, I don't want to talk about him. This is too nice a day for us to talk about Arthur. Look at those kites. Aren't they lovely?"

They sat for a while in silence and watched the kites and the people and the river and the birds against the clear blue sky. A boat crowded with sightseers passed slowly before them heading down-river toward the ocean. He watched it go by: it would sail on and out and vanish in the endless sea.

"The river looks beautiful," he heard her say. "Doesn't it look beautiful, Gershon? Do you know how often I used to sit near my window at home, wanting to look and look at this river, and went back to my books instead? I used to sit and look at the Charles River on Sunday afternoons in Boston. That's a beautiful river. They use it a lot for sailing. Much more than they use the Hudson. Gershon? Hello. Are you there?"

"I'm listening," he said, distantly.

"You drift off sometimes. Your eyes go somewhere else."

"You were sitting on the Charles River in Boston on Sunday after-noons. I was listening, Karen."

He had in fact been listening and at the same time experiencing again the sharp memory of the huge boat that he had once boarded with his parents and his aunt and uncle. It was docked at a cobble-stone quay on this river. His parents had been very happy. The quay throbbed with passengers and porters. They would be back by the end of August. "You want to stay with your aunt and uncle or go to summer camp? Choose," his father had said. He had chosen his aunt and uncle. "You be good, Gershon," his father said now. Ger-shon was sad to see them go but happy at the thought of nearly eight weeks with his cousin. Perhaps they would be away longer than eight weeks. Perhaps he could be with his cousin a really long time. It was a hot July day. The wind from the cliffs felt scalding. They went into the suddenly cool interior of the ship and took an elevator down to his parents' stateroom. His father and mother were well dressed, elegant, young. They all sat around, laughing and talking. He kissed his parents. His aunt and uncle kissed his parents. Gershon will be a good boy, his father said. Of course he will, his mother said, holding him to her. Don't break any more windows with your baseball, his father said. The boy will be fine, his aunt said. Have a good trip, his uncle said, and added, Maybe you can buy a piece of land for me and make us all rich. Come, Gershon, we must leave now, his aunt said. He went back up the elevator with his aunt and uncle. They stood on the quay, waving at his parents. The ship slid slowly away and on down the river. He watched with the sunlight in his eyes until their faces were tiny and indistinguishable. He never saw his parents again.

"They use it a lot for sailing," he said. "Much more than they use the Hudson. Right?"

"You were with your parents again," she said.

"Yes," he said, and closed his eyes.

The noises of the warm afternoon came to him then in a sudden amplified rush: voices, cars, birds, barking dogs, the throb of a distant airplane. He felt the sunlight on his eyes. The wind was hot. Don't break any more windows with your baseball, a distant voice said. The ball had sailed away from his bat, and he had watched it in an ecstasy of joy and disbelief as he started around the bases of the backyard ballfield, watched it together with his teammates as it raced and soared and curved and crashed in a shower of glass through the window of a distant apartment. His father paid for the window. That was two days before they sailed.

He opened his eyes and saw Karen looking at him with concern. "Strong memories," he said, glancing away from her. "Visions and things. You know."

"Listen, I'm having a vision of someone down on the Drive selling Italian ices. Are you still interested in Italian ices?"

"A favorite pastime of mine is Italian ices."

"And visions."

"Yes. And visions. Come on."

They walked down the grassy slope and crossed the crowded Drive. The vendor had his cart on the sidewalk in the shade beneath a canopy of elms. There was a crowd around the cart. The vendor was an old thin man with white hair and a brown lined face. His hands shook as he scooped up the crushed ice, poured on the flavoring, and made change. He seemed a cheerful old man, and he kept saying, "I thanka you, I thanka you, if it no sweet enough, you tella me, I make it sweeter. Thanka you."

Gershon moved away beneath the trees, the ices in the paper cone chilling his hand. He sensed more than saw Karen beside him. Here and there thin shafts of sunlight came through the trees. He felt the alternating sun and shade on his eyes. They sat on a bench near the gray stone wall that faced the river.

She sensed his loneliness and fear and listened quietly as he looked out at the river and spoke. His voice was shy, hesitant, as if carrying with it an apology for burdening her with his memories. "When I was a kid I used to be afraid our apartment house would burn down. For some reason I had the notion that my uncle might one morning shovel too much coal into the furnace and set the whole place on fire. In school, whenever I heard fire engines, I always thought that it was our house burning and that I would go back and turn the corner and see the place a smoking ruin. I've never told you this, have I? I just remembered it now. I think it was the Fire Department monument. I never really looked at it closely before. Sometimes at night fire engines would wake me and I would think the house was burning. Memories."

She felt the heat of the sunlight on her face and the cold of the cone in her hand. The melting ice was running down the cone onto her fingers. She licked at the cone and watched him lick at his. His tongue was red from the cherry flavoring. He squinted his eyes against the sunlight and looked out at the river. Behind him he heard the vendor saying, "I thanka you, I thanka you."

He turned to her. "I don't know if I should tell you this or not. I don't know whom to tell. I don't know if it's even important enough to talk about. I think Arthur was a little drunk when he came back last night. I've lived with him nearly two years. I've never seen him that way before."

She gazed at him silently a moment. Dappled sunlight lay upon her straight brown hair. He had been in a torment of indecision about telling her and now was surprised at her calm. Was that a faint smile at the corners of her small lips? Was she thinking how naive and pure-minded he was? He fidgeted on the bench and licked at his ices.

"How do you know?" she asked quietly.

"He smelled it and sounded it. Look, Karen, I don't want to sound like one of your New England Puritans. I grew up on the streets of Brooklyn."

"Was he mean?"

"No."

"You're lucky, Gershon. I've seen him drunk a few times at parties in Boston. He gets talky and mean."

"They may expel him, Karen. They probably will, if they ever catch him."

"He told me he was through with that," she said. "No more wildness. When he told me he was applying to the seminary he said he wasn't doing it to avoid induction but because he really wanted to become a rabbi."

"I think it has something to do with the chaplaincy."

"What do you mean?"

"That's all he's been talking about the past few days. He seems scared. We're not even sure it's true. So far it's only a lot of rumors. Arthur talks as if we'll all be in uniform tomorrow."

"His brother was killed in the war."

"He was? Where?"

"In Europe."

"I didn't know that."

"Be careful, Gershon. Your ices are dripping on your pants."

"What does Arthur's father do?" Gershon suddenly asked.

"He teaches physics at M.I.T."

"Is the family traditional? Do they go to a synagogue?"

"No. They're thorough secularists. Except Arthur, of course."

"Isn't it strange? I've been living with him for two years and I don't know anything about him except that he likes corned beef on rye and girls who aren't too smart."

"And sometimes he drinks too much."

"Yes. That now too." Almost as an afterthought, he asked, "What does his mother do?"

"She's an art historian. She teaches at Radcliffe. Gershon, the ices are melting all over your hand."

He tossed the cone into a nearby wastebasket. His hand was wet and sticky.

"Thanka you, thanka you," the vendor intoned behind him. "You tella me, I make it sweeter. Thanka you."

"He chose you for a roommate because you're shy and don't talk a lot. That's what he told me, Gershon. He doesn't like inquisitive talkers."

"He does enough talking for the three of us."

"We went to school together in Boston. His talking used to drive the teachers crazy."

"He doesn't talk in Keter's class. Or in Malkuson's."

"Then he probably hides. If he can't talk, he hides. I remember that."

"He hides, yes. He hides." And Gershon had a sudden vision of Arthur Leiden sitting low at his desk behind the student in front of him, his shoulders squeezed together, his pale-blue eyes narrow and fearful, strands of his straight blond hair on his forehead. He had always thought of this as part of his roommate's frequent play-acting.

Karen threw her cone into the wastebasket. She regarded him with a tenderness that she knew bordered on love, but she feared a future of empty nights if he entered the rabbinate, and she doubted that he had the determination to do a doctorate with Keter. Anyway, all that was a long way off. She would make no commitment until she was done with her dissertation. And Gershon's life was now being planned for him by others. She would tell him what she knew. Her father, a rabbinic power broker, always knew things months before most others did. And so she said, "They are going to force you into the chaplaincy, Gershon. Daddy told me yesterday that the faculty has known about it for weeks."

He felt a sudden premonitory coldness. He heard the hot wind gusting through the trees and shaking the leaves. "How can they force us into the chaplaincy, Karen?"

She was grieved by the fear in his voice. "By making it a condition for ordination."

"How can they do that?"

"They'll ask you to sign a pledge."

"What if someone refuses to sign?"

"Daddy says they'll ask him to leave the school."

He stared at her. "Leave the school? Can they do that?"

"Daddy says they certainly can. He says there are sufficient Protestant and Catholic clergy volunteers, but not enough rabbis are volunteering."

"We're going to be drafted into the voluntary chaplaincy corps?"

"The yeshivas will be doing it too," she said.

Why was he suddenly so cold?

"Do you want a soda or something, Karen?"

"No."

"We'd better start back if we're going to a movie later."

They got up from the bench and passed from the shade into the hot sunlight. They crossed the Drive and walked up the slope to the parapet and the monument. He passed by the statue of the dead fireman. The stone was white. He felt deeply moved by the white stone face of the dead man, and he found himself wondering, inconsequentially, why the water was off in the fountain.

"One good thing at least," he said. "I won't have to decide between the rabbinate and Keter until I get out of the chaplaincy. Two years after ordination."

"Why is that a good thing, Gershon?"

He did not respond.

"I won't marry a pulpit rabbi," she said as they turned into the upper Drive. "I've had enough nights without my father. I don't want it from my husband. I've paid my dues. Don't you want to do the doctorate?"

He was silent as they walked along the narrow street past the tall apartment buildings and the small narrow homes. And then, abruptly, he spoke to her in an uncontrollable rush of words, as he did often when they were together.

"I wish I knew what I wanted, Karen. I wish I had your tenacity. Sometimes I think I'm afraid to make choices because whatever choices I make something will come along and blow them away. I know it sounds silly and infantile, but that's how I feel. I'm taking you home now, aren't I? Sometimes I forget where I am. Are we having supper with your family? Look at the way these small homes have stuck it out among all these apartment houses. Talk about tenacity. I wonder why they didn't take them down when they built these big places. I think you could put the house where I live inside the entrance hall of one of these buildings. God, the chaplaincy. What do any of us know about the chaplaincy? How am I going to tell my aunt and uncle? Maybe I'll decide about the doctorate before I go in. I'll talk to Keter. Why can't I get excited about a doctorate in

Kabbalah? Why can't I get really excited about anything—except you? Look at this pink house. Isn't it pretty? How small it is!"

They walked in the late afternoon sunlight. She held his moist and sticky hand and listened to him talk.

The next day Gershon sat in the classroom gazing through the morning sunlight at Arthur Leiden and listening to the angry voice of Jakob Keter. The sunlight was bright and full on Arthur Leiden's face; yet he sat wide-eyed and unblinking as the words directed at him from Jakob Keter filled the room. "You prepared nothing, Mr. Leiden? Nothing?" Jakob Keter stood like a tall, bald-headed predatory bird on the platform behind the desk. "You can tell us nothing? You can make no contribution to our discussion? I did not require of you such a vast amount of reading for this morning. A few passages of Talmud, a look at two bibliographic references. Can you tell us what is said of the figure of Metatron in the tractate *Hagigah*? No? Perhaps you looked at *Sanhedrin* or *Avodah Zarah*? Nothing? Nothing at all?"

He stood there, tall, dark, relentless, his eyes blazing.

"In Berlin I read five times the amount I ask you to read each week. Five times. Are all Americans so lazy or is it merely the Americans in this school? I am after all not asking you to read the literature of pagans or Christians. If I required that you read Kant or Hume, you would no doubt do your reading. This is the literature of your own people. You have so much contempt for it, Mr. Leiden? Yes? So much contempt?"

The class was hushed. A bus roared by on the Drive. Gershon saw Arthur Leiden sitting very still, staring into the sunlight. There was a sheen on his eyes.

"You know nothing about this strange angel Metatron?" Jakob Keter went on. "Where do we learn that he was once thought of as a second God? Yes. A second God. Not an insignificant figure, you must admit. You do not know? Where is Metatron identified with Enoch? Ah, you disappoint me, my Harvard graduate. Perhaps you can tell us something of the etymological difficulties connected with the name? No? Nothing? All right. Who can help us? Yes. Mr. Loran. Please."

Gershon talked and at the same time saw Arthur Leiden turn his face to the window. Arthur had risen that morning in gloomy silence; Gershon had the impression he had slept little during the night. It was strange how he stared straight into the sunlight without squinting or blinking. The sunlight turned his face milk-white. Gershon looked away from him and went on talking about Metatron. The name Metatron appeared here and there in kabbalistic literature, now as an exalted angel, now as a heavenly scribe, now as Enoch, "who walked with God," according to Genesis, now as an advocate who defended Israel in the heavenly tribunal, now as a servant before the holy throne of God, or as a lesser or second God—a notion bordering on heresy, for it came dangerously close to dualism. Kabbalistic literature was full of dangerous imagery and ideas, for it was involved often in an effort to make sense of the world's evil, and it ventured into rivers and tributaries considered treacherous by rigid non-speculative legalists. No one knew the origin of the name Metatron or what to make of the various roles assigned to this being. It was the sort of puzzle that delighted scholars and bored almost everyone else. Gershon went quickly through some of the etymological theories that attempted to explain the origin of the name. He sensed the boredom that weighed upon the men and, simultaneously, the tension that constricted the air. Few were listening to him. All, including himself, were waiting for the class to come to an end.

The back door to the room opened quietly. The dean of students slipped into a seat. He was a short roundish man in his middle thirties, an ordained graduate of the school. His name was Robert Taronson. He wore owlish glasses. He wiped his face with a wrinkled handkerchief and sat there staring down at the floor.

Gershon continued talking. He knew no one was listening. Still he went on. Jakob Keter raised a hand. Gershon fell silent.

"We will continue this discussion the next time we meet," Jakob Keter said. "By that time you will all have read the assigned material. Thank you, Mr. Loran. Your remarks were correct. Good day, gentlemen."

He picked up his text and notes from the desk and went from the room through the front door near the platform.

The dean of students got out of his seat, walked slowly through the room, and sat down behind the desk vacated by Jakob Keter. He looked solemn.

"Good morning," he said. "I don't have anything to tell you that's going to come as a big surprise. I'm a messenger from the higher powers. Just remember that. I answer to them, you answer to me."

"An ominous beginning," someone said.

"I think I should have gone into my father's ladies' underwear business," someone else said. "Saving souls is about to be dangerous."

"All right," said the dean of students, wiping his forehead. "All right. There's no point to making this more unpleasant than it already is."

"Maybe the Messiah will come and we'll be spared," someone said.

"Not until Keter gives the okay," someone else said.

"You want to hear this?" asked the dean of students.

There was silence. Gershon glanced at Arthur Leiden, who still sat staring into the sunlight that came through the window. How pale he seemed, and frightened.

"It's simple," said the dean of students. "You will be accepted into your senior year on condition that you agree to make yourselves available to the chaplaincy corps. The branch of service—army, navy, air force—is up to the individual. If you fail the physical exam, you are no longer under any further obligation to the school and you may enter the pulpit rabbinate. You will be asked to sign an agreement to that effect before this term is over. That's all. The Jewish kids in the armed forces need chaplains, and not enough men are volunteering. All the rabbinical seminaries have agreed to do it this way. That's it. That's the end of my message."

A brief tense silence followed. The dean of students stirred uncomfortably in his chair and wiped his face. He felt stripped and pierced by the looks of the men. But none of this was of his making. Their lives had suddenly veered off the smooth road from seminary to pulpit and onto a dark uncertain landscape. Well, there was a war on. Besides, he was only a messenger. He hoped the questions would be civil. He was in no mood to serve as butt for their frustrations. He would become nasty if he had to. It was expected of him by the higher powers.

"Are there going to be any exceptions made?" someone asked.

"Not many," said the dean of students.

"What if you're the sole support of your parents?"

"We'll have to talk about that privately."

"Are married men exempt?"

"Only if they have four or more children."

"What happens to your family if you're sent overseas?"

"The same that happens to any other chaplain's family."

"Why don't you start with the freshman class, or the new entering class? How can you make this a condition for our ordination? It wasn't a condition when we entered."

"The services need chaplains now," said the dean of students.

"What happens to someone who refuses to sign the agreement?"

"He'll be asked to leave the school."

Gershon sat listening to the questions and answers. He saw Arthur Leiden slumped down in his seat staring at his desk top. The sun was gone from his face. He sat with his head in his hands. Abruptly, in a pause that followed an answer, he raised his head and asked, "Is there any provision for exemption in the event that you lost a brother in the last war?"

Everyone turned to look at him. Gershon felt a sudden thick beating inside his chest.

The dean of students stared through his glasses at Arthur Leiden. "I haven't been told of any such provision, Arthur," he said. "Did you lose a brother? I'm sorry. I'll inquire. But I doubt it. Are there any more questions?"

There were more questions. It all seemed to Gershon to go on and on and, at times, to become quite heated. Most of the men recognized and accepted their obligation; they sat quietly, trying to reshape their visions of the coming years. Some were annoyed and angered by this sudden break in their lives. At one point Gershon heard the dean of students say loudly to one of the men, "It might turn out to be a good experience for you. You might find out what the real world is like. It's not the dream world of the seminary, I'll tell you that much. You might even be grateful to us for making you go. Look at it this way, a lot of good guys end up in branches of the service that are a lot worse than the chaplaincy. Don't complain."

The questions became repetitious. Arthur Leiden sat staring at the top of his desk. The dean of students stood. "That's it," he said. "If you have any more questions, please call my office for an appointment. From now on all matters pertaining to the chaplaincy will be handled through the mail. I've another class to talk to." And he went out through the front door of the room.

A babble of voices broke the tense silence. Chairs scraped noisily. Gershon was momentarily distracted: he bent to retrieve his Zohar, which had been knocked to the floor by the waving arms of an angry classmate. When he looked up, Arthur Leiden was not in his seat. He glanced around the room. Arthur Leiden was gone.

Gershon spent the afternoon and evening in the library. He returned to his room shortly after ten o'clock that night. Arthur was in the study bent over a pile of books on his desk. He looked up as Gershon entered. The desk light shone in his eyes.

"Good evening, chaplain," he said softly. "How goes it with the troops? Their souls are in order? Their morale is good? And the VD rate. What of the rate, chaplain? Is our rate of non-specific urethritis going to wrong us?"

"How are you, Arthur?"

"Embattled with Metatron."

"A tough adversary, Metatron."

"He really creamed me today. Keter, I mean. It was—unpleasant."

"Do you need help?"

"I'm not sure I understand the real reason for the difference between the six-letter and seven-letter Hebrew spelling of Metatron. Why are the six letters associated with Enoch?"

"Let me put my books down."

"You look sad, Gershon."

"I've spent most of the day trying to figure out how I'm going to tell my aunt and uncle."

"You mean because of your cousin?"

"Yes. And other things. I'm sorry you lost your brother."

"I should not have said that. It came out almost by itself. I tend to talk a lot when I'm agitated. A bad habit. Very un–New England. Yes. My older brother was killed. On Omaha Beach. Bad show, Omaha Beach. Very bad. His commanding officer showed up at our house one day and said that to my parents, among other things."

"Do you have any other brothers and sisters?"

"No brothers and one sister. I'll make a bargain with you, Gershon. I won't talk to you about my family and you won't talk to me about yours. Family talk is either boring or self-pitying. Or it's Gothic, like a Faulkner novel. Who needs to talk about it? It's enough to live it. Okay? Very good, dear friend, very good. Now tell me about Metatron. Why in God's name did I take this course with Keter? He's driving me crazy. Malkuson is a saint compared to Keter."

"That's not what you said the last time Malkuson caught you unprepared, Arthur."

"No? You see what a blessing the mind is, Gershon? You see how grateful we should be for the ability to forget? Please explain this text to me. I can't work out the Aramaic."

They labored into the night. Preparing for bed, Gershon turned on the radio, and they listened to news of the distant war in Korea and the domestic war in Washington.

"My mother despises that man," Arthur said.

"Senator McCarthy?"

"She calls him a demented clod."

"Does your mother smile when she calls him that?"

"My mother never smiles, dear Gershon. Is this Monday? Yes. This is the night of the week that I brush my teeth. You or me first into the bathroom?"

They read for a while in bed. The window was open, and the lowered shade scraped softly against the sill in a spring breeze. Arthur turned off his reading light and lay with his arm over his eyes.

"What do you know about amulets?" he asked.

Gershon put down his book. "What?"

"An amulet may be called for. What do you know about them?"

"Nothing."

"Nothing?"

"What are you talking about, Arthur?"

"Desperate people resort to desperate measures."

"Good night, Arthur."

"Are you a little afraid, Gershon?"

"Yes."

"An incantation. An amulet. What can it hurt?"

"I am a student of mysticism, I am not a mystic."

"Ah, the words of Jakob Keter. You cite in your defense the precise words of our esteemed master."

"Arthur?"

"Yes."

"Are you all right?"

"Not really." He took his arm from his eyes, propped himself up on one elbow, and looked at Gershon across the narrow space between their beds. "I have this strange premonition, you see. I'm going to end up there no matter how hard I try to avoid it. Everything is pushing me there."

"What are you talking about, Arthur?" Gershon felt strangely chilled.

"We'll see. Probably I'm dead wrong, and it's all ridiculous. Good night, dear friend. I won't bother you anymore tonight. Unless, of course, my demented bowel decides to utter a nocturnal statement. Good night, good night."

He lay back on the bed and turned his face to the wall and was still.

A dream woke Gershon in the night. He opened his eyes and found himself drenched in sweat. He could not remember the dream, though its quality of raw horror remained with him for long terrifying moments until it was finally dissipated by his need to go to the bathroom. On the way back he saw that Arthur's bed was empty.

The study was dark. He returned to his bed and lay awake until his eyes closed of themselves. He woke and saw a dim figure moving through the room outlined against the vague beginning of dawn.

"Sorry," he heard Arthur Leiden murmur. "Couldn't sleep. Went for a long walk. Really sorry, dear Gershon."

This time there was no odor of drink in the air. Gershon slept and said nothing of the matter when they woke in the morning.

He sat in the silent rare-book room of the seminary library surrounded by floor-to-ceiling dark-wood bookcases filled with precious books and manuscripts. It was early evening. Outside the air was soft with fading light. The room was windowless. Its light came from desk lamps and overhead fluorescents. The temperature in the room was kept constant all year long to stem the deterioration of paper, ink, and parchment. Visiting dignitaries were often brought to this room and shown its treasures. He liked this room, with its small marble-topped desks and dark-wood chairs and high ceiling and long shelves and manuscripts behind glass doors. He worked here often in book-enclosed silence. At times his mind would wander from an eye-wearying text. He would rest with his eyes closed. Then, slowly, he would become aware of a presence on the other side of the twin metal doors to the room. This presence, it sometimes seemed to him, was what he had been waiting for all the years since the night on the roof when he had witnessed life being born. But at other times the presence was dark and fetid and seemed to him to be the angel of death. He sat in the room with the few others who had been given special faculty and library permission to use these manuscripts—he sat in this room reconstructing texts, while outside death waited, barred from entry. He did not know what death looked like, though he thought it was dark; nor could he understand why he thought it to be outside precisely these doors. But he could sense it outside, chagrined, waiting.

Now, ten days after the class meeting with the dean of students, Gershon sat at a table in this room and experienced a strange vision. He heard the knobs on the metal doors turn violently. The doors flew open, and death entered the room in the form of an impenetrable icy blackness. He watched in horror as the cold blackness spread swiftly over the tables and manuscripts and lamps and went on up the walls to the ceiling. It felt wet and it encompassed him and he was left entirely without sight and it was icy and smelled of cold raw earth. The vivid quality of this vision frightened him. He came awake from the half-sleep into which he had slid while working over a text. He was completing his term research paper for Jakob Keter, rebuilding some garbled passages in a printed Polish kabbalistic work on the basis of two earlier manuscripts, and he had fallen into some sort of stupor while trying to make out the meaning of a passage about the sitra achra, the other side, the demonic realm of evil. It was a strangely convoluted passage, densely inhabited with specters and demons, and he had wearied of it. Also, Arthur had not slept in the room the night before, and he had lain awake in dread for hours wondering what to do. Arthur had returned, bleary-eyed and un-shaven, in time for classes. The stony glance from his eyes as Gershon turned to him had deterred any questions about the night. Now Gershon sat at the table clearing that vision of darkness from his eyes. He returned to the text.

He came into their dormitory room later that evening and found Arthur asleep at his desk. The lamp glowed on his blond hair. His face was buried in the bend of an arm. The fingers lay curled near the small gilt-framed photograph of his parents that stood in a far corner of the desk. The bulb of the lamp was close to his head. As Gershon bent to wake him, he smelled the musky odor of singed hair. He put his hand on Arthur's shoulder and shook him gently.

"It's fire," Arthur said in a muffled voice. "Everywhere." He buried his head deeper into his arm. "Why did you do it?"

"Arthur," Gershon said, shaking him.

"Why?" Arthur said. Then he stiffened and woke and sat up.

"Are you all right?" Gershon asked.

"Did I say anything?" He blinked and rubbed his eyes.

"I couldn't make it out."

"It was a bad dream. What time is it? I can't get started on this paper for Keter. My God, I slept more than two hours at this desk! Keter will be my death."

"Do you want help, Arthur?"

"Desperately, dear friend."

"We could study together on Shabbat. I'll stay over this Shabbat if you want."

"I'm off to Boston for the weekend, Gershon. A family conference or some such thing."

"Well, we could work tonight and tomorrow night, Arthur."

"Many thanks, much gratitude. Need all the help I can get. God, what a terrible dream that was!"

They worked together a long time and went to sleep late. Gershon woke in the night thinking he had heard Arthur cry out in his sleep; but he could not be certain. In the morning he woke with sunlight on his face. Arthur was in the bathroom. The bedroom windows were open, the filmy curtains parted. He could hear pigeons on the ledge above. An airplane droned by, rattling the panes.

Arthur flew to Boston that Friday afternoon, and Gershon took the subway to Brooklyn. He climbed up the stone stairway of the subterranean station and walked along dirty broken streets. The air was warm, and he could smell the refuse in the alleyways. The asphalt streets had sunk in spots and lay rippled and pitted. Traffic jounced heavily through these streets. It was late afternoon, and the sidewalks were crowded with children and street toughs. Three blocks from his house some of the buildings had been emptied by the city and boarded up. They stared blankly at the decaying neighborhood with reddish-brown walleyed faces.

He remembered the antique sunny loveliness of the neighborhood. He remembered accompanying his cousin through the streets, skipping to keep pace with his long stride. He remembered many things about the past. He knew why he was remembering all that now. He came from the street into the small entrance hall and went along the dim, faded yellow hallway that led to their ground-floor apartment.

He told them that night when they were done with the Shabbat dinner and the Grace After Meals. How he dreaded hurting them! He looked at their bewildered faces: lined, weary—dark mirrors of splintered dreams. He thought he could sense himself slipping through their eyes into the landscape of their pain. He recoiled as if from fire and turned away from their incredulous stares. It would only be for two years, he said. There was nothing about it that was dangerous, he said. Please don't worry, he said.

The candles on the table burned evenly in the warm still air. Their light fell upon the white cloth and the braided bread and the beaker of wine and the empty cups of tea. Through the open windows came distant voices and the occasional sound of a passing car. A dog barked.

His uncle asked, "What does it mean, Gershon? Forced? How?" And his aunt said hoarsely, "This head hasn't borne enough? What are you saying?"

He explained it to them again.

"All are going?" his uncle asked, and coughed.

He wondered how many in his class were living through this now. Was Arthur? Some had seen themselves as lambs being sacrificed to help allay a collective embarrassment. A few had threatened to leave the school. He could not leave. Where would he go? What would he do?

"I think all will go," he said. "Certainly most will go."

"Surely you will not go," said his uncle. "You will find a way not to go. We have not done enough for the country?" He tugged at the hairs of his goatee and coughed. Gershon heard his wheezing breaths —as if his abrupt return to the use of full sentences was draining his strength. "In middle age," his uncle said, and left the sentence unfinished. Then he said, "And now in old age too? How much do they want?"

"God will not permit this," his aunt said. "Never! How can He permit it?" She gazed across the room at the photographs of her dead son in the uniform of another war. And she asked hoarsely, "How much am I to bear? How much? And who will continue your father's name if something, God forbid, happens? Who?"

Gershon sat in silence and did not know what to say.

Later he slept in the narrow bed in the small room and was awakened in the night by the sound of fire engines. Two streets away was a major city thoroughfare. Fire engines went up and down often. He could not sleep. He stood at his window and gazed out at the dark concrete backyard. He stood there a long time in the chill silence. Pale fire crept onto the top-floor windows of adjoining houses: a dim reddish smear of distant light. He watched the dawn move ever so slowly across the shadows of the night. Nothing had changed. No miracles. A sunrise and now a return to his broken world. His head was heavy with lack of sleep, and his eyes burned. He went back to bed and fell asleep.

The old bearded man who had taught him Aramaic came over to him in the little synagogue after the Shabbat service. "What do I hear?" he asked. "You are going to be a soldier?"

"It's only the chaplaincy," Gershon said. "It's not exactly a soldier."

"I know about such things. I was in the Russian army in the First World War. Bombs and shells do not know about rabbis and priests. Listen. Take with you an amulet. A Jew needs protection everywhere, especially in an army filled with goyim. What can it hurt? I know a man who writes amulets. I will tell you, I will have an amulet written and pay for it myself."

"You don't have to—"

"No, no, please. My gift to my former student, even if he misuses what I have taught him and studies Kabbalah. You know that amulets are not only for kabbalists. My father, may he rest in peace, gave me an amulet when I entered the Russian army, and he was an enlightened man. He said to me, 'Words have power,' and he put the amulet around my neck. I returned unharmed. Tell me, you are still studying Kabbalah, Gershon? Yes? Be wary. Take my advice. I know a little about such matters. But I will get you the amulet."

And Gershon had not the heart to refuse.

His uncle came over to them.

"I promised your nephew an amulet," said the old man.

His uncle coughed. "He will not go. Save your amulet."

The old man looked at him. "What can it hurt? I will have it made, and if he needs it—"

"He will not need it. It has nothing to do with us. Nothing. The yellow people have nothing to do with us. You hear?"

"I hear," the old man said. "I hear. Let others hear too. What does it matter that I hear?"

He shuffled off, murmuring to himself.

Gershon returned to the seminary late the next morning. Arthur was not yet back from Boston. In the late afternoon he walked to Karen's apartment. Her mother opened the door and let him in. The Riverside Drive apartment faced the river and the afternoon sun. Shafts of sunlight came through the windows into the large and richly furnished rooms. The sunlight was reflected back by the ornate wall mirrors of the living room. The polished mahogany end tables and brocaded sofa and wing chairs, the leather-topped coffee table, the floor lamps and antique brass sconces, the Steinway piano and the oriental rugs—all seemed to shimmer in the glowing opalescent haze of mirrored sunlight.

Karen's parents were on their way out. Her father, a tall erect man in his late forties who exuded an aura of immense dignity and businesslike efficiency, greeted Gershon and inquired about Arthur Leiden. "My principal informed me he did not show up to teach his class this morning." He had a deep voice and knew how to modulate it for maximum effect.

"He went to Boston for the weekend," Gershon said hesitantly.

Karen's father said, his voice resonating, "And abandoned his class?"

"There must certainly have been a misunderstanding, dear," Karen's mother said. Tall and regal, meticulously garbed and groomed, she seemed the perfect feminine counterpart to her husband.

Karen, wearing a simple summer cotton print dress and no makeup, appeared rough-cut and out of place in that apartment. She gave Gershon a troubled glance.

"Untrustworthy," her father said. "I think at times I made a mistake encouraging his wish to enter the seminary. He was a fine physics student at Harvard. But he is not sufficiently organized. He will not succeed in the rabbinate. Perhaps I should not have taken him into the school. I thought he had changed."

"Isaac—" Karen's mother began.

"I shall have a talk with him," said her father.

Gershon said, "He's been a little strange ever since we were told about the chaplaincy."

"Indeed?" her father said. "A strange family. I could not make them out. Brilliant people, you understand. But strange."

"The mother is most certainly strange," Karen's mother said.

"Indeed," said her father. "A most unsociable person. Well, we must go. The chaplaincy will be a splendid experience for all of you, Gershon. Indeed. We must all serve our country in its time of need. I served during the last war. Proud of it. Come, we really must go."

"There's chicken in the refrigerator, dear," Karen's mother said at the door.

Gershon stood next to Karen at one of the tall living-room windows gazing out at the sunlight on the river.

"How goes the work?" he asked.

"Fine. Slow."

"Where is everyone?"

"Out with friends."

He felt her next to him and put an arm around her. "I told my aunt and uncle."

She was quiet.

"They are absolutely convinced I will not have to go."

Still she was quiet.

"Do you want to walk?" he asked.

She nodded.

They took the elevator downstairs and came through the spacious carpeted hall to the sunlit street. They walked slowly along the upper Drive to the Fire Department monument. The streets were crowded. They sat on a bench near the monument and looked out at the teeming lower Drive and the groves of elms and sycamores and the golden immensity of the river shimmering in the sunlight.

"Are you frightened?" she asked.

"A little."

"What service will you go into?"

"I haven't thought about it."

"The navy?"

"I don't think so. I heard that there's a lot of anti-Semitism in the navy."

"The air force, then. You'll look good in an air force uniform, Gershon."

"Will I? Somehow I can't see myself coming home to my aunt and uncle in an air force uniform."

She said nothing and looked away from him and out toward the river.

"I think that leaves the infantry," he said. "Yes. I'll stay on the ground. The infantry it is. Safe and sound. I'll read a lot to keep from dying of boredom."

Still she said nothing.

"Karen."

She looked at him.

"Don't you think we ought to get married?"

"Married," she said very quietly.

"I do love you, Karen."

"Dear Gershon. Will you want me to follow you to Texas or Oklahoma or God knows wherever you're stationed? And afterward, what? The rabbinate?"

He was silent.

"You see? If we both finish what we have to do these next years, we may have a good life together. You see?"

He remained silent. They gazed together at the crowded sunlit street. The afternoon sun stung his eyes. He sensed something behind him and turned his head. Dark sunspots floated before his eyes, marring his vision. He saw Sunday strollers, people on the benches, and the Fire Department monument with its statues and dry fountain—all blotched and faintly distorted by the slowly floating and gyrating sunspots.

"Look at the gulls over the river," he heard her say. "I love this river. You look so sad, Gershon. Please don't feel sad. I love you and don't want us to be hurt by each other. We can wait. Can't we wait?"

"Why not?" he said after a long moment. "I've been waiting a long time."

"What?"

"A little longer can't hurt. Can it hurt?"

"Gershon—"

"Let's go back," he said.

That evening they ate alone in the apartment, and later in her room he held her to him. He was still somewhat clumsy and awkward, but she was warmed by his hands.

"I love you, I love you," she murmured. "Am I wrong not to marry you now?"

"We'll wait," he said. "I'm getting good at waiting."

"You're getting good at other things too," she said, and laughed delightedly.

He returned to the seminary very late. Arthur was not back. He was gone all that night and was absent from classes the next day. In the late afternoon Gershon stepped into the elevator on the second floor of the library building, and there was Jakob Keter.

"Good afternoon, Mr. Loran."

Again he felt the abrupt disquietude, the uncertainty and diffidence. The elevator door slid shut. They started up together.

"How are you progressing with your paper, Mr. Loran?"

"It's almost finished, professor." He kept his eyes down.

"Yes? Very nice. Mr. Loran, you are entering the chaplaincy?"

"Yes."

"You heard perhaps that members of the faculty who were recently ordained will be exempted?"

"Yes."

"And Ph.D. students will be granted deferments of one or two years. Are you aware of that, Mr. Loran?"

"No." He raised his eyes for a moment.

"Probably you were not informed because no one in your class is a suitable candidate as yet for a Ph.D. Except, perhaps, yourself. Consider strongly the possibility of beginning your Ph.D. studies with me in the coming year, Mr. Loran. Unless, of course, you have already been invited by Professor Malkuson. No? I thought not. Consider it, Mr. Loran. It is not often that I invite a student to become my disciple. I am giving a seminar here next year which I would like you to attend. Yes? Ah, here is my floor. Good afternoon, Mr. Loran."

The door opened, and he stepped out. He seemed still to be present as Gershon rode the elevator to the top floor.

Arthur had not returned by evening. Gershon lay in bed after midnight listening to the radio. It was raining. He heard the rain on the window. He read and fell asleep with his bed lamp and radio on.

A voice woke him from a fitful sleep. He was unable to hold on to what he had been dreaming. The smoky vestiges of a trembling rage slipped quickly from him. He was frightened and drenched in sweat. He could not remember why the light was on. The voice in the room bewildered him. And someone was at the door. He sat up in the bed, feeling his pajamas sticking to his body. He identified the voice and shut off the radio. In the silence the knocking on the door was suddenly very loud. He went in his bare feet through the bedroom and study, unlocked the door, and pulled it open.

Arthur stood in the dimly lighted hallway. His clothes were wet. His face was streaming with sweat. He was unshaven. His suitcase sat on the floor.

Gershon stared at him and felt a queer and tingling coldness on his back. He thought the noise should have awakened everyone in the building. But the hallway was silent and warm. Yet he was cold, icy cold.

"Sorry, dear Gershon. Really sorry. I lost my keys somewhere and didn't realize it until I was at the door. My apologies. The Boston navigator has just landed."

"Not so loud, Arthur. Let me take your bag." The handle of the leather bag was warm against his cold hand.

Arthur came inside. Gershon closed the door. Arthur stopped in the middle of the study and looked around. He seemed dazed. "No," he said. "You're supposed to say, 'Are the natives friendly?'"

"What?" Gershon stared at his roommate and felt a shiver course through him.

"And then I'm supposed to say, 'Everyone landed safe and happy.' "

"What are you talking about, Arthur? You'd better get out of those clothes. Aren't you cold?"

"Very warm. Very rainy. Pouring. And the elevator was jammed. Had to walk up the stairs. My God, what a weekend! How good were you at navigating, dear Gershon? How was your weekend?"

"It was all right, Arthur. Were you in Boston all this time?"

"Oh, yes. Fierce discussion. Pros and cons. Does Arthur leave the seminary or stay? Much polite tense talk. You could detonate the sun with the power of that politeness. You don't know anything about it, do you? Look at me, I'm soaked. I need a towel. Thanks. Thanks. You're a friend. Must get out of these clothes. I'm exhausted. The politeness kills me. Fucking goddamn New England politeness. Excuse me, excuse me. Mustn't talk that way. Seminary and all that. Excuse me. You won't have to put up with me next year when we'll have our separate rooms. No more nocturnal nonsense from Arthur Leiden. Right? Need another towel. Look at me. Sopping wet. Am entering the navy. Yes, sir. Big family decision. Long navy tradition on father's side. Yes, sir. See the world. Did I miss much in class today? God, I'm tired. What time is it? I'm not prepared for Keter's class. Would you believe it? He'll kill me if he finds out. Sorry to wake you up, dear Gershon. Don't want to involve you in anything. Picked you for roommate after I saw you so quiet during the first year. No more involvement. I promise. The word of a New England gentleman. Do you think you could go over the Keter assignment with me now? He'll kill me, and I can't cut any more of his classes. My God, is it morning already? There's light in the windows. Please let's do the Keter assignment right now. Yes? But first I must go to the bathroom! I simply must! You look so sad, dear Gershon. Why do you look so sad? And cold. Are you cold?"

3

He left New York on a warm day in the last week of June and went to work in a children's camp in the northern hill country of Pennsylvania while Karen labored over her dissertation in the city. It was a Hebrew-speaking religious camp, and he had been hired in a last-minute effort by the administrative staff to overcome a counselor shortage; the year before he had worked in the library and canteen. It became quickly apparent that the administrators had made a bad choice: he was uncomfortable around children; he preferred solitude; he never looked at you directly when you spoke to him; and something seemed to be wrong with his eyes, a lack of focus, a strange glaze, a haunting softness. He played ball badly. He was a clumsy swimmer. He could not control his campers.

In early July there were warm heavy rains. Lightning played across the nearby hills. He lay awake and listened to the drumming of the rains on the roof of the steaming bungalow. White mold formed in damp dark corners. His campers grew restless and unrestrained. The bungalow seemed a war zone. Then the rains were suddenly gone. He let himself get burned by the sun and lay sleepless for two nights. He blistered and was in pain. His face peeled badly. He looked blotched, mottled.

On a hot July day a co-counselor informed him offhandedly that the armistice had been signed, and the Korean War was over. A few days later he received a letter from the dean of students: the chaplaincy commitment remained in effect.

Often he read deep into the night. He was rarely without a book. He was studying the historical development of the kabbalistic doc-

trine of *sefirot,* the ten stages of emanation that are the manifesta-
tions of the sapphirelike pure radiance of God and that make possible
creation, generation, and decay. Were these emanations identical with
God? Were they a radiation or an expansion of God's essence? Did
the process occur in ordinary time or in non-temporal time? He was
reading about the development of these concepts while he felt the
camp humming and vibrating all around him like some vaguely
bothersome noise. Many gave him queer looks as they watched him
wander about with his strange texts. On occasion he felt a burning
sensation in his eyes. He tried staying out of the sun. As much as
was possible in that mostly open and rolling terrain, he walked in
the shadows of trees.

Unexpectedly in late July he received a card from Arthur Leiden.
It had been mailed from Brussels and was dated 16 July. The handwriting was barely legible. Directly beneath the date was something
that looked like "Auuiv Dtk Lt." The card read, "Dear Gershon,
Here with Dad for physics confab. Meeting mother in Paris and off
to Rome and maybe Jerusalem for meetings with Hebrew University physicists. Dad not well so am tagging along. Keep the light of
your kabbalistic God pure. Babies born this day doing too well. Your
troublesome friend, Arthur." He read it through a few times and
could not fully understand it. Then he realized that the scrawl
beneath the date actually read, "Anniv Dth Lt." He puzzled over
the card for a while, then put it aside. Arthur's moods unnerved and
wearied him. The card had evoked in him a sharp recollection of
Arthur's handsome features and blond hair and nocturnal jaunts and
bathroom badinage. After a moment he returned to the text he was
reading and forgot about Arthur Leiden.

On a day in the second week of August he took an early bus into
New York and spent about an hour with his aunt and uncle in the
sweltering apartment amid the noise of traffic and children and the
foul odors of rotting alleyway garbage. "War finished," his uncle
said hoarsely. "Need chaplains? Why? Why?" His aunt served them
lunch. She kept staring at him and glancing at the photographs of
her lost son. Gershon wanted to ask them, "Why don't you get out
of this broken-down place?" He said nothing and ate his aunt's
borscht and noodle pudding.

Later he rode the subway to Manhattan and walked quickly through burning air and shimmering streets to the Riverside Drive apartment where Karen lived. They fled the heat by taking a river cruise around Manhattan. They sat on the deck and watched the city glide slowly by beyond the gray expanse of the river. Gulls wheeled languidly overhead. After a while they left the deck. Below, in a corner of the boat away from the summer crowd, they held each other tightly. She was genuinely happy to see him, knew she loved him, and felt fired by the tentative caress of his hand on her breast and the gentle brush of his lips on her cheeks and lips. No, she murmured. She would not marry him. They would wait. She saw only disorder and early sorrow in an immediate marriage. They came back out on the deck and ate ice cream and watched the late afternoon sun turn the river to burnished bronze. Her face, still flushed from their moments together below, seemed to gather in the sun and send forth its light in a blinding radiance. Her eyes shone. She clung to his arm as they came off the boat onto the quay. Later he returned to the camp by bus and much of the way back read a text that described in vaginal and phallic imagery the relationship between a number of the *sefirot*. On a residential street in a small upstate New York town, the bus nearly hit a dog.

He arrived at the camp close to midnight and discovered his bungalow a shambles as a result of a pillow fight. He cleared his bed of the carnage and found his mail, a postcard. He read it in the pale beam of his flickering flashlight. It was from Arthur Leiden. Beneath the date, 6 August, he made out "Anniv Hiroshima." The card had been mailed from Florence. It read, "Dear Gershon, Beauty is Florence and Florence is Beauty. In other words (Яf) Bf. Was there ever a school of Kabbalah in Florence? Dad resting after Brussels. Mother smiling. Yes! Mother smiles in Florence! Am weary. How are you? Soon off to Jerusalem. Almost wish back on mesa where travel forbidden. Your Boston navigator, Arthur."

His battery nearly dead, Gershon put the card away on a shelf and picked a path through the debris. He washed up and slipped into his narrow and uncomfortable camp bed. He lay awake wondering why Arthur had chosen to write to him now; he had never seemed eager for intimacy in the two years they had roomed together.

Through the screening near his head he could see the vast black canopy of the sky and the awesome cold-blue spread of burning stars. All the velvet sky was alive with jeweled light. He remembered the night on the roof when he had touched the sky, touched it. He sensed that nothing within himself had really changed since then. He would continue to wait.

He lay still, listening to the night. Somewhere a farm dog barked, the sound thin and forlorn in the darkness. One of the campers cried out in a dream. Gershon felt his skin crawl. The child fell silent. Gershon lay awake, listening. The night pulsed and murmured with the softly sonorous rhythmic stirrings of trees and insect life. Distant voices drifted toward him on currents of air through the darkness. He closed his eyes and thought of Karen and released himself slowly to the embrace of the other side. After a while he fell asleep.

He returned to the seminary in October after the autumn festivals. He was assigned to the room on the fifth floor that was directly below the study of Professor Nathan Malkuson. The room had the same configuration of study and bedroom as the one he had shared with Arthur Leiden. It faced the quadrangle and the morning sun. He looked forward eagerly to the solitude of private space. His first evening there, he quickly arranged with his customary neatness his books and desk and clothes and went in search of Arthur Leiden.

He found him in his fourth-floor room in a clutter of books and cartons. He was deeply tanned, his blond hair bleached flaxen. He was barefoot, wore old khaki trousers, and was naked from the waist up.

"Hello," he said cheerfully. "Come on in. I wondered where you were. I was going to look you up as soon as I got myself straightened out."

Gershon stood near the door and surveyed the chaos inside the room. Books and clothes and cartons lay in wild disarray on the sofa, the chairs, the desk, the bed, the windowsills, the floor.

"The apocalypse will come before you're straightened out," he said.

"How was your summer, Gershon?"

"It was all right. I read a lot."

"Kabbalah? Can you utter a right word and get this room straightened out?"

"No. But I can lend you a hand."

"What good is a kabbalist who can't change the world?"

"Probably no good at all. Do you want a hand?"

"I don't even know where to begin."

They worked together for an hour. The clutter diminished. Order settled slowly upon the room.

"Did you get to Jerusalem?" Gershon asked at one point, suddenly remembering the postcards.

Arthur was putting books on a shelf. He gave Gershon a surprised look. "How did you know I was going to Jerusalem?"

"You said so in the card."

"What card was that?"

"The postcard."

Arthur looked blank.

"You sent me two cards during the summer. Don't tell me you don't remember."

"The summer was very strange, dear Gershon." He looked at the books in his hands and put them on a shelf. "A little tense, the summer was. Very up and very down. Family problems and things." He gazed at the shelves and the open spaces that were appearing in the room. "You do have an eye for order," he said. "Remember the time I pushed in almost every other book in your bookcase?"

"I remember."

"It was a joke. I thought you would kill me."

"It wasn't very funny."

"You are a melancholy and humorless creature, dear Gershon. A perfect kabbalist."

"Are those physics texts?"

"Which?"

"Those."

"Yes."

"You didn't have them before."

"I brought them from home. I used them at Harvard."

"You really don't remember sending those cards?"

"It was, as I said, a strange summer. Listen, why don't we quit and go out and get something to eat? I'll put on a shirt and some shoes."

"All right."

They walked in the warm autumn night to the delicatessen near Columbia University on Broadway. Gershon ordered a corned beef on rye and a cream soda. Arthur ordered a corned beef on a roll, a potato knish, and a beer. He finished the beer quickly and ordered another. He was flushed and sweating. There were three other people eating at tables in the delicatessen. The fluorescents hummed softly and gave off white light. The air was warm and thick with the odors of hot spiced meat and mustard and sour pickles.

"It's good to be back here," Arthur said around a mouthful of corned beef. "No good delicatessens in Boston."

"Were you in Boston for the holidays?"

"Sure."

"You got that tan in Boston?"

"I went out west for Succot with my father. Desert country. Got burned in the Negev and tanned in the great American desert. Fine finish to the summer."

"You were in the Negev? Did you get to Jerusalem?"

"Yes."

"Did you see the Mount of Olives?"

"I saw it. I couldn't get to it. The Arabs have it."

"My parents are buried on the Mount of Olives."

He stopped chewing. "I didn't know that."

"You really do remember sending me those cards."

Arthur raised a hand to signal the waiter.

"Another beer," he said.

The waiter, a short elderly man with white hair and palsied hands, brought the beer. He looked at the small dark skullcap on Arthur's flaxen hair and at the two empty bottles on the table.

"Leave the bottles," Arthur said. "That way I can keep count."

"Certainly, young man," the waiter said. He turned to Gershon. "Will you have anything else?"

"No, thank you."

"You want something, I'm at the table in back."

"It's very bright in here," Arthur said when the waiter had gone. He was pouring beer slowly into his glass, watching the head bubble and foam. He put the half-empty bottle down and stared at the golden liquid and foaming crest in his glass. He drank and put the glass down. The foam left small white marks around his mouth.

"What were the dates on the cards?" he asked. "Do you remember?"

"No. I don't think so."

He took a bite out of the sandwich. "Probably July sixteenth and August sixth. Are they around?"

"The cards? I'm not sure where I put them. I may have thrown them out. You do remember sending them?"

"No. But if you got them I obviously sent them." He looked around. "They've done something to the lights. Isn't it brighter in here than it used to be?"

"It seems the same to me, Arthur."

"Do you want anything else to eat or drink?"

"No."

"Let me finish this beer and we'll head back." He emptied the bottle into the glass, watching the foam. He drank slowly, the foam against his mouth. He put down the empty glass.

"Summers are not good times for me," he said. "I get strange sometimes in the summers."

"How do you mean, strange?"

He looked down into his empty glass. His face clouded suddenly. "You're getting nosy, dear Gershon. You've asked more questions in two hours than you have in two years."

"I'm sorry, Arthur. Do you want to go back now? I asked about the cards. You sent them."

"Probably thought no one else to send them to. Send them to my sister? Too damn busy with her two kids. But really can't remember sending them. Must have been—how to put it delicately?—under the influence. That's right. Under the influence. Damn, these lights are blinding me. What did I write? Anything special? Coherent? Spectacular? What?"

Gershon recited the contents of the cards as best as he remembered. Arthur sat staring down into his glass.

"I've got to go to the bathroom," he said after a long silence.

Gershon watched him walk to the rear of the delicatessen and waited until he returned.

"Are you all right?" he asked.

"Let's go back," Arthur said. He looked tired.

They said quietly the Grace After Meals. Arthur murmured the words with special intensity, his eyes closed. He prayed always with the discomfiting zeal of one recently come to religion.

At the front of the delicatessen the man behind the counter wiped his hands on his apron, took their money, and punched down on the cash register keys.

"Are these different lights?" Arthur asked him.

"New fluorescents. Just had them put in."

"See?" Arthur said to Gershon. "Told you. Too damn bright." He turned to the man who was handing them their change. "Too much light. You ought to reduce the light."

The man looked at him. "Sure," he said. "Absolutely. Come again."

They walked along Broadway, then turned down toward the Drive. A strangely warm fall breeze blew dying leaves from the trees. Gershon felt the leaves underfoot as he walked. They entered the seminary building and took the elevator.

The door opened slowly to the fourth floor.

"Do you want me to come in and finish helping?" Gershon asked.

"No more work tonight, dear Gershon. Must go to sleep. Very tired." He held the elevator door open and looked up and down the hallway. "Listen. Appreciate it very much if you say nothing about cards. Have you told Karen? No? Good. Just a little awkward. Not a big thing. All right, dear Gershon? Good night. See you at the opening slaughter in tomorrow morning's Keter class."

He stepped out. The elevator door slid shut on his tanned and weary face.

Gershon rode up one floor to his new room and went to bed.

The weeks moved slowly. Summer warmth lingered into autumn. There was a drought. He walked along the riverbank with Karen in cascades of falling leaves. She was deep into her dissertation and talked of necessity and will and sentiment in Kant and Hume and others. Her face grew flushed, and the words tumbled from her, and he could barely follow her thinking and felt inadequate. At times she talked of her life in Boston, the loneliness of growing up not physically pretty, not mentally ordinary. She had loathed most of her classmates and almost all of her teachers. She had yearned for solitude and at the same time dreaded it when it had come in drowning doses. Now she was happy with her teaching and her writing. She clung to him beneath the falling leaves. They were falling early that autumn for the lack of rain.

He marveled at her focused will and envied her having chosen her way with such calculated passion. He himself felt vaguely fearful of choices. He was drifting slowly toward Kabbalah as a scholarly discipline only because the active rabbinate seemed to him unthinkable. He felt disinclined to hasten his decision. His drift toward the chaplaincy he knew to be determined and inevitable and not a matter of choice.

He told himself that he liked the solitude afforded him by his new room. There for hours on end he could forget that looming time when the choices would finally have to be made. He studied and read and listened to music and news and watched the sunlight on the walls as he woke and dressed and prayed. He saw less and less of Arthur Leiden outside the classroom. Arthur seemed the center of that cluster of the class at home in the beat and rhythm of the world, the smooth and witty ones, those marked for swift success, the ones with whom Gershon felt himself always ill at ease. Only at odd and rare moments did he see darkness obscure the light in Arthur's handsome face; moments when Arthur no doubt thought himself unobserved, in a classroom or the library or along the rim of the quadrangle, and when Gershon would turn a corner or raise his eyes and there was Arthur, sometimes staring directly into the sun, his face slack, his thick athletic shoulders sagging. Gershon sensed in himself the stirrings of concern during those moments but feared entering Arthur's sadness and turned away with the conviction that he was witnessing reflections of those fleeting moods to which all people are now and then subject.

Over his bedside radio one November night came news of an Israeli attack against the Jordanian village of Kibya in retaliation for the repeated Arab raids across the borders of Israel. In a sharp vision he saw hills and sand and sunlight and tombstones. A pale-gray sky over reddish earth and an echoing call of birds. Then a silent blue land, utterly deserted. The vision began to fade. He could not sleep. He repeated to himself the pages of Talmud he had memorized that day in preparation for his comprehensive examination with Professor Malkuson. He was memorizing more than three years of Talmud texts studied with Professor Malkuson along with commentaries and pertinent text-critical studies. He had to get through that Talmud test, together with comprehensives in all the subjects he had taken in that school, in order to qualify for ordination. Finally he fell into uneasy sleep, fatigued by the competing visions of pages of Talmud and hills of tombstones. He woke in the night in a sweat of terror but could not remember what he had dreamed.

He was in the rare-book room of the library the next afternoon when the door opened and a tall gaunt man entered, carrying an unlit pipe in one hand and a battered gray fedora in the other. The man looked to be in his middle fifties. His face, sharply angled and bony, with prominent nose and cheekbones, wore the remnant of a tan and was deeply lined along the forehead and near the corners of the eyes. He had thick uncombed brown hair that was going gray and pale-gray eyes set in circles of bluish darkness. He wore a dark-brown overcoat and stood near the door, looking around with an air of melancholy uncertainty. There were five students in the room. His eyes rested briefly on Gershon's pale features, narrowed with what appeared to be an effort at memory, then looked away. He turned and went out of the room. The door swung shut.

Gershon sat in his chair and stared at the door. He rose after a moment, went out of the rare-book room into the large main reading room, and saw the man standing near the elevator across the corridor from the reception desk beyond the open doors at the other end of the reading room. Next to the man stood a tall woman. The elevator door slid open. They stepped into the elevator. The door closed.

Gershon returned to his table and his text. He had recognized the man and woman from the photograph on Arthur Leiden's desk, and he wondered what Arthur's parents were doing in the seminary.

About an hour later he was immersed in a kabbalistic text on the Revelation at Sinai, and so he did not hear the door open. Five men and a woman stepped softly into the room. The click of the closing door startled him. He looked up from his text and saw Jakob Keter,

Nathan Malkuson, Arthur Leiden's parents, the chancellor of the seminary—a dark-suited, dark-bearded august presence—and a man of middle height, bare-headed, with straight sand-colored hair, ruddy features, and clear shell-framed glasses, whom he recognized instantly with numbing shock as Harry Truman. There were now only two other students in the room. All started to their feet, chairs scraping, eyes wide with astonished recognition. The chancellor raised a palm. "Please continue what you are doing, gentlemen." They sat down. Gershon bent over his text. He heard their murmured voices but could not make out their words. They moved slowly along the circumference of the room, sometimes the seminary chancellor, sometimes Jakob Keter or Nathan Malkuson explaining the significance of a book or manuscript. He had witnessed congressmen, governors, ambassadors, and foreign dignitaries being shown through this room. Now in a dreamlike state he heard the voice of the former President of the United States, and then a low-pitched male voice he took to be that of Arthur's father. The woman said nothing. They approached the wall of books near his table. He looked up and found himself gazing into the eyes of Professor Keter.

"—one of our finest students," he heard the chancellor say. "Mr. President, may I present Mr. Gershon Loran."

Somehow he managed the proper act and rose to his feet. He was shaking their hands, the warm fleshy hand of Harry Truman, the firm bony hand of Arthur's father, the cool smooth hand of Arthur's mother.

"I envy you, young man," Mr. Truman said in that easily recognizable voice. "I wish I could be back with books all day."

"Loran?" Arthur's father said. "Gershon Loran?"

"Yes, sir."

"Arthur's former roommate?" He had a low soft voice.

"Yes, sir."

"Do you know where Arthur is?"

"No, sir."

"We thought he might be somewhere in the building."

"He may be teaching today."

The woman regarded him coolly and said nothing. She wore a light-blue coat with a silver-gray fur collar. Her hair was long, her face smooth and oval-shaped, her eyes pale-blue. She was a beautiful woman. She glanced down at the book he had been reading. He saw her eyes move across the pages of Aramaic and Hebrew. She looked away with a vague air of uninterest.

"I understand you are a student of mysticism," Arthur's father said. The unlit pipe was between his lips.

"Yes, sir," Gershon said, and coughed and averted his eyes. He felt the blood pounding in his throat.

Jakob Keter regarded him without expression. Nathan Malkuson's face wore a faint look of disdain.

"We have a mutual interest in light then, don't we?" Arthur's father said.

Gershon looked at him, confused.

"Very different sorts of light." Arthur's mother abruptly spoke up.

"I thought you might have a look at the Rothschild manuscript before you leave," said the chancellor.

"Good luck to you, Mr. Loran," Arthur's father said.

They moved away. Gershon sat down. He saw the two students looking at him. His heart beat thickly, and his right hand felt strangely light, the skin tingling as if brushed by an electric current. They had stopped in front of the bookcase that contained shelves of kabbalistic manuscripts. He heard Jakob Keter's descriptions and explanations. They listened attentively, laughed at a witticism, asked questions. He heard Truman and Arthur's parents exchange the kinds of pleasantries that are the mark of long acquaintance.

"This stuff would be to Oppenheimer's liking, it seems to me," said Mr. Truman.

"I think you're right, Mr. President," Arthur's father said. "Eastern poetry and Western physics. Right up Oppie's alley."

"He's had enough," Arthur's mother said. Her face, pale and lovely, was startling in its blankness, its absence of affect. "Hasn't he had enough? Are they going to flay him alive? Lewis is such a clod."

"He's my appointment, Elizabeth," said Harry Truman.

"We all make mistakes, Mr. President," said Arthur's mother.

"You can bet we do," said Harry Truman. "How old did you say this manuscript is, professor?"

Jakob Keter responded with Germanic charm and propriety. Nathan Malkuson gazed at the ceiling. Harry Truman held the manuscript with obvious reverence, opened it, peered at its lines, returned it to Jakob Keter. The chancellor stood by, smiling, pleased.

"Where do you suppose Arthur is?" Gershon heard Mrs. Leiden say.

"We'll find him," her husband said.

"Permit us to show you that Rothschild manuscript before you go," said the chancellor.

They went out a small side door.

"Holy God!" one of the students said breathlessly.

"Don't wash that hand, Gershon," the other student said.

Gershon sat very still, waiting for his heartbeat to slow. Circles of light flared briefly before his eyes. He picked up his books and went into the main reading room, where he stopped to look up something in a reference volume. He came out of the reading room, took the stairs to the street floor, walked quickly through the tall front gate, stopped at the foot of the broad stone stairway, and looked around. A long black glistening Cadillac limousine was parked on the side street. A uniformed chauffeur sat behind the wheel. Gershon crossed the Drive and sat down on a bench. The air was warm and pale-blue. A river wind shook leaves from the trees. A few minutes later he saw the six of them come out of the building. They went up to the limousine. The chauffeur hopped out and opened the door. They were all shaking hands. Harry Truman climbed into the limousine. "Thank you," Gershon heard the chancellor say to Arthur's parents. "We are very grateful. Thank you." They got into the limousine and sat next to Mr. Truman. A small crowd had gathered, seeming to have materialized from the light and air. The limousine pulled away from the curb.

The three men—Jakob Keter, Nathan Malkuson, the chancellor —all in dark suits, stood on the sidewalk watching the limousine enter the traffic stream along Riverside Drive. The crowd began to disperse.

"Will he accept the award?" asked the chancellor.

"I am not sure," said Jakob Keter. "He is a strange person."

"Why did he stipulate him, I wonder?"

"What would you have done if he did not deserve it?" asked Nathan Malkuson.

"I would certainly have turned it down," said the chancellor. "Most certainly."

"Well, he has to pass his comprehensives first," said Nathan Malkuson. "Keter is right. He is very strange."

"I'm delighted that Leiden got Truman for us," said the chancellor. "This will be a feather in our caps. But I cannot understand why Leiden insists we start off this award with this young man."

They turned and went slowly into the building, talking earnestly and quietly.

Gershon Loran sat in the pale afternoon sunlight beneath the autumn trees. He could still hear all their voices, feel the touch of their hands. He closed his eyes. Immediately he saw a vast ball of white light flash across a desert night. An iron wall of wind and a tidal wave of fire. A black sky empty of stars. He opened his eyes to the pleasant and reasonable sunlit afternoon. After a while he went back into the building and took the elevator to his room.

He lay on his bed. Through the partly open window he could hear the pigeons cooing softly on the ledge above. A passage from the Zohar drifted through his mind. "And birds to fly above the earth. . . . Rabbi Simeon said: There is here a mystic allusion. 'Birds' refers to the angel Michael. . . . 'Above the earth': Rabbi Abba says, 'This is Raphael, who is charged to heal the earth, and through whom the earth is healed so as to furnish an abode for man, whom also he heals of his maladies.'" He lay on the bed a long time listening to the birds.

He saw Arthur in the dining room that evening.

"Anyone eating with you, Arthur?"

"No. Sit down, sit down."

"I met your parents."

"They called me. Be wary of the roast beef. It is manna for Cro-Magnon man."

"I didn't know your father worked on the atomic bomb. I read all about him in *Who's Who*."

"Not all, dear Gershon. Not all. What do we know about each other's parents? Families are private matters. I don't know anything about your father or mother."

"My parents are dead."

"I don't know what your parents did when they were alive. Are you going to eat the mashed potatoes? Didn't it move? I swear I just saw it move."

"My father was in real estate. He bought land, built houses. Things like that. He went over with my mother to look at a piece of land they had bought near Tel Aviv. They were killed."

"My father built atomic bombs. He's very much alive, as you no doubt noticed. You might think it ought to be the other way around. What does your kabbalistic soul tell you about that, dear Gershon? Is there any pepper on this table? My meat requires some revivifying force. Do you want to go out for a sandwich and a beer later on?"

"I need to study for my comp with Malkuson."

"Did you finally decide on the army?"

"I don't know."

"Everyone is betting you'll still be here next year working with Keter."

"I'm not sure I want to do that, Arthur."

"No one is ever sure of anything. People have to be nudged. But you'll be here."

"Is your father still building atomic bombs, Arthur?"

"Are you sure you don't want to go out for a sandwich later on? How can you eat this stuff?"

"It isn't bad, Arthur. Is your father—?"

"I heard you, Gershon. How's your teaching coming along?"

"It's all right. The kids are unruly. I don't enjoy it too much. It's a long subway ride out to Queens."

"You ought to have gotten a job where I teach."

"I didn't want to work for Karen's father."

"To answer your question. My father teaches physics at M.I.T. That's all I can tell you. And my mother teaches art history at Radcliffe. They are splendid people, but life would be simpler and probably better for me if I had been born to a carpenter and a laundress. I give up on this meat. I yield in abject surrender. Are you done? Shall we take the elevator to our monastic cells?"

They found themselves alone inside the slowly rising elevator.

"Are you going into the navy, Arthur?"

"Yes. Absolutely. Long family tradition."

"I'm a little afraid of going into the service."

"What could happen? The war in Korea is over. They might send you to Germany. Imagine being stationed in Germany as a conqueror. They should have dropped the bomb on the fucking Germans. Excuse me. I forgot myself. My apologies. Here's my floor. Good night. Good night. You're sure you won't want a sandwich and a beer at around ten or eleven? No? Good night, my sad-countenanced kabbalist." He stood in the hallway facing Gershon, his foot blocking the elevator door. He spoke rapidly in a soft tense voice. "Some of the Germans had the decency to take Hiroshima very hard. Otto Hahn actually considered killing himself when he heard about it. Did you know that? He was the one who discovered fission in uranium in 1938. But he had a few drinks and felt better. It was decent of him to think he might somehow have been responsible for all those incinerated bodies. Good night, Gershon."

The elevator door closed. Gershon stared at the door in bewilderment.

He rode the subway home that Friday afternoon and on the way to the apartment stopped at the neighborhood public library. He took down from a shelf two physics books: *University Physics* by Sears and Zemansky, and *Introduction to Modern Physics* by Richtmyer and Kennard. He walked the littered and broken streets, noting that two more buildings had been boarded up by the city.

That night and the next afternoon and night he sat in the bleak apartment, leafing slowly through the physics books. He slept uncomfortably and woke in darkness. Somewhere in the building voices were raised in argument. An infant cried. Sunday morning over breakfast he asked his uncle to return the books to the library.

"You look tired, Gershon," his aunt said in her whispery voice. "And sad. Pooh! Terrible to have the weight of the whole world on your skinny shoulders."

He did not know what to say and remained silent.

"Master of the Universe sad always," said his uncle. "Since destruction of second temple. Never laughs. Gemora tells us."

"Did you notice the staircase?" Gershon asked abruptly. "On the second floor?"

"Fix next week," said his uncle.

"Why don't you move? It's terrible here."

His uncle gazed at him and would not respond.

"Eat your eggs, Gershon," his aunt said. "You want another piece of toast? That one is burned."

He called Karen from the seminary that evening.

"Not tonight," she said. "Must finish a chapter. The writing is like splitting rock. How are you, darling?"

"Karen, did you know that Arthur's father was involved in the atomic bomb project?"

"Was he? I didn't know that. Will you call me tomorrow? I miss you."

He would call, he said. And heard her say, "Isn't it awful the way the weather has suddenly changed? I can see the park and the river. It's cold and raining leaves. Was Truman really in the seminary? With Arthur's parents? You'll have to tell me everything next time I see you. I must get back to my chapter."

November ended with a United Nations Security Council censure of Israel for the Kibya raid. The weather was gray and cold, and there came a brief flurry of snow. Class meetings were held concerning the chaplaincy. Two men chose the navy; four, the air force; the rest, the army. Gershon committed himself to the army.

In Israel Arabs crossed the borders. There were raids and killings.

The first serious snow fell. He woke to it early one December morning from a raging dream he could not remember. The snow tapped softly upon his bedroom window. He stood by the window and gazed out at the snow, at the sheathed quadrangle and the white street, at the tiny particles drifting downward and slowly, lazily, revolving through the opalescent light of the winter day. As he watched, the snow thickened and a wind blew the particles in white waves across the buildings and the quadrangle and the streets and trees beyond. His right hand, resting upon the cold sill of the window, tingled vaguely—the hand with which he had respectfully shaken the hands of the man who had helped to build and the man who had given the order to drop the first atomic bomb. He felt cold and weary with a strange and looming dread. What was it? He did not know precisely. It was perhaps his growing inability to bear his slowly heightening sense of the disconnectedness of things. Nothing seemed truly a part of anything. Even between himself and Karen the lines were tenuous and fragile. He felt the world as separate bits and pieces floating and whirling. All seemed to him discrete entities. Particles. Bits of cold dead light. His aunt and uncle, Keter and Malkuson, the old man in the synagogue, his classmates, the dean of students, Arthur—whom did he really know? And who really knew him? Choose. Choose what? Why choose? Events began and did not end. There seemed no firm structure to anything. He himself floated and drifted and blew about. He did not even know on what or whom to focus the rages he sometimes felt. Ahead was always some elusive enticing truth. Always ahead. But here and now all seemed random and terrifying, shot through with gaping holes and cluttered with severed lines. Why so sad, Gershon? Why so sad?

He stood there gazing at the snow and wondering what he would do with his life. He shivered in the cold air that radiated inward from the window. After a while he dressed and prayed and had breakfast and went to his class with Jakob Keter.

On a bitter cold and brilliantly sunny January day he was called to the office of the dean of students. The office was small and strewn with papers and books. The dean of students sat behind his cluttered desk, gazing somberly at Gershon through horn-rimmed glasses. He squinted and smiled at the stupefied look on Gershon's face.

"They didn't give me any explanations," he said. "I'm only a messenger and I'm telling you what they told me. You've been chosen because of your academic record. It's a new award. They're going to call it the Richard Leiden Memorial Award. I think it's in memory of the grandfather, who was an important physicist and a philosopher. Like Newton. That's all I know."

"But I'm not sure I want to do graduate work next year." His heart thudded.

"There are worse ways you could spend a year."

"I don't know what to do."

"Which branch of the service did you choose?"

"The army."

"No problem. We'll get you a year's deferment."

"But what good is one year of graduate work?"

The dean of students gazed at him through his glasses. From the outer room came the sounds of a typewriter: the clack of the keys, the tinkle of the bell, the slide of the carriage. The office had no windows. The walls were covered with books arranged in wildly untidy rows on sagging shelves. The dean of students spoke with ponderous urgency.

"This is an important award. No one can get you out of the chaplaincy. Forget it. Unless you fail the physical. You want to talk to the chancellor?"

Gershon squirmed in his chair. "Let me think about it."

"No problem. But don't take too long."

Two days later he was called to the office of the chancellor. He took the elevator to the sixth floor. It was late afternoon. The office of the chancellor was two doors down from Professor Malkuson's study. The chancellor sat in a tall-backed leather chair behind a long glass-topped mahogany desk. He wore a dark business suit, a white shirt, and a dark tie. He had a short dark beard and wore a small dark skullcap.

"My dear Mr. Loran," he said in his high excitable voice. "Please, please sit down. Yes. Fine."

Gershon had never before been in this office. The floor was carpeted. There were books in glass-enclosed cases along the walls. The windows, tall and clean, looked out upon the quadrangle. He sat stiffly in a plush chair and caught himself reflected in the polished glass front of a bookcase. A warp in the glass rippled and distorted his features. His hands were cold and his mouth was dry.

The chancellor regarded him silently for a moment, cleared his throat, and spoke. "Mr. Loran, I understand, I fully understand and appreciate your hesitation. A big step, an important decision. Of course."

Gershon sat in rigid silence and listened to the beating of his heart. The chancellor gazed at him and sensed clearly his indecisiveness. He saw the pale features and the clutching of the fingers upon the arms of the chair and quoted to himself a rabbinic text. "Do not regard the vessel but what is in it." Malkuson and Keter had discovered the mind within the shell of fear and shyness and alerted the chancellor and members of the faculty. The young man was fortunate; the pulpit rabbinate might have consumed him. Why was he unable to choose? He seemed in a torment of indecision. Why was he so hesitant?

"Mr. Loran, perhaps you are not clear as to the nature of this award. The opportunity it affords you is not insignificant. It will support you amply for an entire year and permit you to do graduate work. In an informal manner, Mr. Loran, the family urged that you be its first recipient. The reason for that is not clear to me. It is a highly irregular request. The family, probably through Arthur, was aware of your academic strengths. Do you know the family?"

"No, sir."

"In any event, we are all of us most fortunate that you are indeed deserving of the award, else we could not accept that stipulation. You understand me, Mr. Loran? Am I making myself perfectly clear?"

"Yes, sir."

"Fine."

The chancellor waited. Gershon sat silent. The polished desk and bookcases reflected harshly pinpoints of high light from the afternoon sky. The chancellor stroked his beard. When he spoke again his voice was uncomfortably high.

"Perhaps, Mr. Loran, perhaps you are not fully aware of the—the significance of this award. To yourself, of course, and to the school. We must not forget that we are part of a great academy of learning. We are not permitted to forget that. The award will be endowed. It is given us by a great American family. It will be for our institution a source of enormous prestige. It may well put us in touch with the scientific aristocracy of the country. Other awards will come in its wake; perhaps, Mr. Loran, perhaps even an endowed chair, a new department. Deeds follow deeds. You recall what the rabbis tell us. One brings another. The faculty urges you to consider this with great care. Which discipline would you pursue were you to accept the award?"

"I don't know."

"Which would you feel inclined to follow?"

"I don't know. Maybe—I don't know."

The chancellor was quiet. He gazed at the young man, at his pale and moist countenance and his hesitant and squirming demeanor. Why was he unable to make up his mind? Anyone else in that class would have leaped for this award.

"Consider it, Mr. Loran. Consider it."

"Yes, sir. Do I have to give you my answer now?"

"In a few days. The family wishes to know in a few days."

"Yes, sir."

"Good day, Mr. Loran." He shook Gershon's cold hand.

Over the phone Karen urged him to accept it. Her voice was exultant.

"But it just delays everything by a year. What good is it, Karen?"

"It's an honor. Take it, Gershon. We'll be together."

"You can tell me about Hume and free will."

He asked Arthur, "What's it all about?" They were in Arthur's room. On the desk was a new photograph: a large Tudor-style house set on a wide green lawn amid towering oaks and elms and vast beds of flowers.

"I have no idea," Arthur told him. "Ask my parents. They don't include me in their plans. They don't even tell me when they're coming to the seminary with a former President of the United States. They are very busy people, my parents. Busy, busy."

"Why do they want me to start off the award?"

"I haven't the faintest notion, dear Gershon. They know you were my roommate, and I told them you were a very good student. That is all. Take the award, Gershon. How can you possibly refuse it?"

Gershon spent the Shabbat with his aunt and uncle. "A blessing," his uncle said, coughing. "Answer to my prayers."

"It's only for one year, Uncle Aaron."

"Who knows what can happen? One year a long time. Be in grave in one year."

"Pooh!" his aunt said. "This is a happy moment and you talk like that?"

"Truth is truth," said his uncle, and coughed.

That Monday morning he informed the dean of students that he was proud to accept the award.

"Will I be able to dorm here?"

"I'll see what I can do," said the dean of students.

"I won't have to take my army physical?"

"Forget the physical. Congratulations."

"I don't understand what's happening. I haven't even taken my comps with Keter and Malkuson yet."

The dean of students regarded him with amusement. "No one's worried about your comps, Gershon. Just do what you've been doing the past three years. For God's sake, smile a little. You look like tomorrow is the apocalypse. Gog and Magog. Armageddon. Smile, for God's sake."

The winter was cold. There were heavy snows. He trudged in the snow to Karen's home and to the subways. He hated the cold. It hurt to breathe. His eyes watered in the freezing winds. By the end of February he was done with all his comprehensives save those with Jakob Keter and Nathan Malkuson.

He dreaded the comprehensive with Malkuson.

On a gray afternoon in early March he made a rush from the dining-room entrance to the elevator and found himself alone inside with Professor Malkuson. The door moved. He watched helplessly its slow closing slide. The elevator made a loud clicking sound and began its languorous ascent. It uttered strange humming and scraping noises as it rose slowly through the shaft.

"Good afternoon, Loran," said Professor Malkuson.

"Good afternoon, professor." He felt his heart begin to speed.

"You are coming to see me tonight?"

"Yes." The appointment for his comprehensive was for nine o'clock.

"Are you prepared?"

"I—hope so."

"Do you remember, by any chance, the discussion concerning thoughts and contracts?"

"Thoughts and contracts?"

"Yes."

He groped wildly through his memory. "In *Kiddushin*? Yes. Page forty-nine b. I think."

"Well, Loran, can an unspoken condition, a mere thought, break a contract?"

"No."

"A thought has no effect?"

The elevator rose slowly, ponderously.

"One can tithe produce to a priest through thought," he heard himself say in a dry-mouthed panic.

"And?"

He flailed about desperately, searching. "The Rashba says that one can say 'I am,' and think 'a Nazirite,' and he is a Nazirite. Thoughts can bring on sanctity. In certain cases."

He heard the talking but was uncertain the voice was emanating from inside himself. He felt disembodied, a sensation of floating.

The elevator hesitated, lurched, scraped against the shaft, continued upward. It seemed an interminable journey.

"In certain cases. Yes. Loran, do you remember perhaps the story of Eleazar ben Dordia?"

Gershon stared. It was a simple, well-known tale. One was not asked about tales in a Talmud test.

"*Avodah Zarah*. Yes. Page seventeen a."

"A terrible man, Eleazar ben Dordia. No? Immoral. When he repented he sat between two hills. What did he ask of the hills and the sun and the moon and the stars?"

"To plead for mercy for him."

"And they replied?"

"They couldn't pray for him. They needed mercy themselves."

"And what did he say?"

"He said, 'The matter depends on me alone.' "

"Yes. And what did he do?"

"He put his head between his knees and cried."

"And?"

"He died."

"And?"

"A heavenly voice proclaimed that he was destined for the life of the world to come."

"Yes. A strange story."

The elevator stopped. The door opened. They stepped out. The door closed.

"Is there anything curious about the story?"

They walked together along the hallway.

"Nothing in the story struck you as curious when you went over it?"

They stopped at the door to Professor Malkuson's study.

"I wondered what he heard or saw," Gershon said.

Professor Malkuson regarded him placidly.

"Inside himself, I mean. As he sat with his head between his knees. I mean—"

"Yes?"

"There were kabbalists who used that position to—" He stopped in confusion, his heart racing. "I remember reading—"

Professor Malkuson opened the door.

"It is, as I said, a curious story. You are right to wonder what he might have felt and what he might have thought. Abandoned by his hills and his sun and moon and stars. But I doubt it had to do with kabbalists. All right. Very good. You need not come to see me tonight, Loran."

Gershon's mouth dropped open.

"You have just taken your comprehensive. Good afternoon, Loran."

He stepped into the study and softly closed the door.

Gershon stood in the hallway staring at the door to Professor Malkuson's study. Two secretaries came out of an office and walked through the hallway chatting. He could not still the wild racing of his heart. He took the stairs to his room and lay down on his bed and looked at the afternoon light on the pale-green wall.

After dinner he went to Arthur's room. There was no response to his knock. He returned at nine and found Arthur sprawled on his sofa in despair.

"I'll never make it. He'll flunk me. I should have stayed with physics. Michelson and Morley, where are you?"

"Malkuson won't flunk you."

"Physics is safe, it's neat. Memorize this, calculate that, measure, experiment, mathematize the universe, and perform an occasional inductive leap. Simple. Talmud with Malkuson and Kabbalah with Keter are driving me out of my mind. Hey! What are you doing here? It's nine o'clock. You're missing your comp with Malkuson!"

"I took the comp, Arthur."

Gershon recounted the elevator ride.

"I don't believe it!"

"It's true, Arthur."

"In the elevator?"

"Yes."

"I'll be absolutely damned!"

"I don't understand it, Arthur."

"Why bother, dear Gershon? My God, why bother?"

"I have to go back to my room now. My comp with Keter is in two weeks."

"In the elevator! My God, I can't get over it!"

"I can't either."

"Why aren't you laughing? How about a little smile? A teeny smile? God, you and my mother ought to get together. The sober sisters. Get everyone in the right mood for a proper sense of doom. Step right up, ladies and gentlemen. See the faces of man and woman on doomsday. Step right up. You want to go out for a sandwich and a beer?"

"No, thanks, Arthur. I really want to read some more for Keter."

"You mean there are books on Kabbalah you haven't read yet? Come on, Gershon. I need a break. A quick sandwich and a beer."

"It's too cold outside. I don't like walking in the cold."

"Doomed to spend the whole night studying for Malkuson. Doomed."

"I wrote your parents yesterday to thank them for the award."

"Oh?"

"I won't have to take my physical until next year."

"I've already taken mine. Passed with flying colors. Look, if we're not going out for something to eat, then scram. You go to your books and I'll go to mine."

"Sure, Arthur."

"Congratulations on the comp with Malkuson. What a story! The operator in the elevator. Incredible!"

By ten the next morning the entire class knew of it; by afternoon the entire school. Gershon walked through the halls in the wake of awed stares. The librarians spoke to him in hushed tones. He sat in the rare-book room. Pages brought him books and acknowledged his thanks with murmurs of respect.

Two days later he was asked to report to the office of the dean of students. A man in a neat dark business suit sat in a chair next to the cluttered desk. He looked to be in his thirties. He had close-cropped light hair and gray eyes.

The dean of students stood up as Gershon entered.

"Mr. Roger Wolfson, Mr. Gershon Loran. Mr. Wolfson is with the Federal Bureau of Investigation."

The man did not offer his hand.

The dean of students came around from behind his desk.

"I'll leave you two alone," he said, and went out of the office.

Gershon watched him go, then looked at the man.

"Please sit down, Mr. Loran. We're engaged in a routine security check for the navy. An individual from your graduating class has applied for a commission. I'll need to ask you a few questions about him, if that's okay with you. We would appreciate your cooperation. His name is Arthur Leiden. You do know him?"

"Sure."

"Do you know him well?"

"Of course I know him well. Do all navy officers undergo security checks?"

"How long have you known him?"

"We dormed together here for two years."

"Did you know him before?"

"Only as a classmate during our first year."

"You didn't dorm together during your first year?"

"No."

"How are the dormitory arrangements made?"

"You choose someone. He chose me."

"Though you didn't really know one another."

"Yes."

"What sort of a relationship did you have with him?"

"Friendly."

"Was it close?"

"Not really."

"Did you ever talk about your families?"

"He didn't like to talk about his family. He said he chose me for his roommate because he thought I wouldn't pry into his private life."

"Do you know anything about his family?"

"I know his father is an atomic physicist and his mother teaches art history. He lost a brother in the Second World War. He has a married sister. I think he mentioned once that she has two children."

"What sort of reputation does he have?"

"Very good. He's very popular. Very good sense of humor."

"Do you know of anything bad that is said about him?"

"Bad? No."

"To your knowledge, is he a member of any organization that advocates the overthrow of the United States government?"

"No."

"In your opinion, is he the sort of individual who can see a job through to the end?"

"Yes."

"What sort of work habits does he have?"

"He works very hard."

"Organized?"

"A little—disorganized."

"To your knowledge, does he have any idiosyncrasies?"

Gershon hesitated. "No. He likes corned beef sandwiches and beer."

"Does he have any disconcerting habits?"

"He goes to sleep late. He writes funny postcards."

"What sort of reputation does he have among his fellow students?"

"As I said, he's very popular. We like him a lot."

"Thank you, Mr. Loran. That's all. We appreciate your help."

Gershon went out of the office and took the stairs to his room. He was covered with sweat. His heart beat thickly. He found Arthur in the dining room during dinner.

"Can I join you?"

"Sit."

"The F.B.I is doing a security check on you, Arthur. Someone was asking me questions."

"Did they ask my opinion about the food in this place?"

"I blurted out about the postcards, but he didn't ask me anything about them."

"They probably know about the cards. We found out they've been checking our mail. The penalty of greatness in bomb-making. Intelligence agents have been following my father for years."

"What's wrong, Arthur?"

"I signed some left-wing petitions in college. The navy likes its officers politically pure. All will be well. Eat. Don't sit there not eating. You'll hurt the feelings of our esteemed chef."

"I don't think I said anything that might hurt you, Arthur."

"All will be perfectly fine. Worry not."

"It was a funny feeling, being asked all those questions."

"Yes," Arthur said. "I'm sure it was. Listen, do you have time to come up to my room? I'm stuck on something I'm preparing for my Talmud comp."

"Sure, Arthur. Absolutely. I don't think I've ever met anyone like that F.B.I. man before. He was very—unemotional."

Arthur smiled vaguely. They ate for a while in silence.

"He asked if I knew your parents," Gershon said.

"Did he?"

"I told him I didn't know them. I wonder who else he's asking."

"Oh, many people. Many. Are you finished? Come on. Did they fix the elevator? It was on the blink when I came down."

"It's fixed," Gershon said.

They took the elevator to Arthur's floor. An early March snow-storm raged outside. Gershon stood by the window listening to Arthur struggle with a passage of Talmud and watching the snow fall through the winter darkness. He could see the flakes in the pale circles of light cast by the street lamps. He stood there listening to the strange dry heaviness in Arthur's voice.

On a chill sunlit afternoon in the last week of March, Gershon came slowly out of the seminary and stood for a moment on the top of the wide shallow flight of stone steps that led down to River-side Drive. He could see about a block away, on the hill overlooking the river, the granite-paved plaza that led to the columned dome of

Grant's Tomb. The gray granite of the mausoleum shone stark and bleached in the early spring sun. He walked down the stairs to the street. Hillocks of dirty snow lay along the curbs. He crossed the narrow side street and went on down along the Drive. Pigeons strutted on the sidewalk near the West Portal of Riverside Church. The 400-foot tower rose white into the pale-blue air. He felt through his overcoat the cold wet wind that blew across the river. He walked on awhile and turned into the wide carpeted entrance hall of an apartment house. Elegant floor lamps gave off subdued lights. The hall was furnished with soft chairs and low tables. Dark antique oils with rococo motifs and thick gilt-edged frames adorned the papered walls. A uniformed doorman called upstairs to announce his presence, and a uniformed elevator operator brought him swiftly and smoothly to the tenth floor.

He knocked on the apartment door. The lock turned. Jakob Keter stood framed in the open doorway.

"Hello, Mr. Loran. You are early. Come in." He had on a light-gray baggy wool sweater over a tieless shirt. His dark-gray trousers were rumpled. His long pointed face looked elfin. He peered at Gershon without expression. "Please come in and sit down. I am finishing something. Let me take your coat. Can I get you a coffee? No? You are sure? It is no trouble. All right. Make yourself comfortable. I will be only a few minutes."

He left Gershon in the living room and went down the corridor that led off the entrance hallway. A moment later Gershon heard the skilled and rapid clacking of a typewriter.

The windows of the living room looked out onto the river. He saw barges on the river and the steep dark rise of the cliffs along the Jersey shore. The autumn sun was high and laid down a wash of gold upon the water. He moved away from the windows and sat down on the sofa. The room was painted white and was richly furnished with plush chairs, highly polished end tables, tasseled lamps, a rich deep carpet. Impressionist paintings of Parisian street scenes hung from the spackled walls. In decorative ceramic pots on the windowsills, coffee table, and the ledge over the buffet stood a variety of indoor plants—philodendron, bleeding heart, purple passion, wandering jew, jade. Gershon wondered whose apartment this was; who had rented it to Jakob Keter for the years of his stay in New York. He heard the sounds of the typewriter and wished Keter would finish and come out and get the comprehensive over with; he was weary of books and study and nights of dreams darkly luminous with symbols and images that spilled from his texts into his sleep. He sat back in the sofa and closed his eyes. He was tired. He had not seen Karen in weeks. The typewriter noises were steady, rhythmic, monotonous: tapping of keys, ringing of bell, sliding of carriage, efficient and expert noises. How had he learned to type like that? He was a prolific scholar; he published nearly everywhere, in scholarly journals and popular magazines, and nearly everything he wrote was of significance. Gershon had methodically tracked his writings with an increasing sense of awe for Keter and despair over his own inadequacies. He felt small in the presence of this man and cold with apprehension as he sat waiting for the written words to end and the spoken words to begin.

The typing went on. Through his closed eyes, Gershon sensed the light of the sun on the white walls. Pages of text rose from memory and floated before the inner vision of his eyes, printed texts and written texts, rippled paper dark with age, stiff sheets of vellum that would last a millennium, wavy lines of print, firm lines by master hands, texts vivid with clearly described symbols and images, texts that seemed the obscure ravings of furnace imaginations. He was suffused with Kabbalah, glutted with it, filled to overflowing with its historical development and basic doctrines, its major authors and their ideas, its philological problems. Up from the street and through the closed windows drifted the distant wail of a fire-engine siren. The typewriter clacked and pinged and whirred. Tell me about apocalyptic literature and Merkavah mysticism, he said to himself. Tell me about Ezekiel and his vision of the Chariot and about the Book of Enoch and the vision of the elements of creation—the hills of darkness, the rivers of fire, the abode of the spirits, the sun, the stars, the Throne of God. And what sort of relationship is there between the *Book of Creation* and Gnosticism? Now, about the time of its composition. Eighth century? Third century? Earlier? Do you think the language system indicates Greek influence? The author tells us God created the world by means of ten numbers and twenty-two letters, elemental letters. What do you suppose he meant by the idea that letters constitute elements? In what way? Can you relate them in any way to our notion of the elements in chemistry and physics? Now let us talk about the Zohar, Mr. Loran. How was Graetz both right and wrong when he gave the Zohar a late date? Tell me a little about the twelfth-century school of kabbalists in Provence. What was its link to Greek and Arabic thought? Tell me about the *Book of Brightness*. How did it perceive the universe? What is of special interest about its understanding of the Divine Presence? Tell me about the school of Isaac the Blind. What do these two schools have to do with the beginnings of medieval Kabbalah? Tell me about chiromancy and demonology and meditation in Kabbalah. Tell me about the Metatron problem. Tell me about Moses Cordovero and Joseph Gikatilla. Let us talk about the problem of evil, Mr. Loran. Where do we read about evil as a separate manifestation, as a result of too abundant a growth of the quality of judgment separated from the quality of mercy? What school of kabbalists regarded the sitra achra, this realm of evil, as no longer a part of the World of Holiness and set up what seems to be a cosmic dualism? What do you make of the view in the Zohar that there is a spark of holiness even in the demonic realm of the other side and how do you reconcile this with the view of Gikatilla that denies the metaphysical existence of evil? And, Mr. Loran, what are we to make of the language in the strange passage we find in—

He opened his eyes. The typing noises had abruptly ceased. Jakob Keter came through the corridor into the living room holding a sheaf of papers in one hand and a large manila envelope in the other. He put the envelope on an end table and said to Gershon, "I am sorry to keep you waiting. A call from Jerusalem this morning required that I write a lengthy letter to the university and I was unable to complete my work. This must get out today. It would be most helpful to me if you could read this for typing errors while I complete the last page. May I get you a coffee? No? Well, I will get one for myself."

Gershon heard him in the kitchen, then saw him go back up the corridor with a cup of coffee. The typing resumed.

Gershon glanced at the papers given him by Jakob Keter. The title on the first sheet read "JACOB HA-KOHEN's BOOK OF LIGHT: *A Comparison of the Milan and Vatican Manuscript.*" He recognized immediately the author and the work. A thirteenth-century Spanish kabbalist who wrote about visions accorded him in heaven. Very personal theosophy, no relationship with the contemporary schools; his ideas originating from his visions. The verse "Let there be light" means the formation of the light of the intellect in the shape of Metatron. Many of his mystical teachings based on numerology. The power of the Emanator is invisibly spread through the sacred spheres until it reaches the sphere of Metatron. . . .

The paper was a dry linguistic analysis of the two manuscripts, clearly written, with a meticulous attention to details. He had said often in class: Pay attention to details; tiny details in a work can give a light to a large darkness, to our understanding of the meaning of that work and its location in place and time. *Der liebe Gott lebt im Detail.* The beloved God can be found in minute details. The English style of the paper was brisk, with only an occasional Germanic locution. How many other languages was he able to write?

Gershon finished reading. He had found two typing errors. The typewriter became silent. He sat still and waited. The afternoon sun shone through the sheer curtains onto the light-gray carpet, the green indoor plants, and the rich colors of the paintings. The oils were luminous with Impressionist light. Horse-drawn carriages on wide boulevards. Sunlight on Seine excursion boats. Lovely ladies in silks and bonnets and handsome mustached men in tall hats and waistcoats. A church shimmering in morning sunlight. A row of bluish trees alongside a wide sun-washed river that wound toward hazy violet hills and a sweeping green-blue sky. . . .

Some minutes later Jakob Keter came into the living room. He had put on a jacket and bow tie. He wanted to know if there had been any errors, and he made the corrections quickly with a black fountain pen. He stuffed the sheets of paper into the envelope.

"I must mail this. You will come with me. We will go for a little walk." They were putting on their coats. "I learned to type when my wife died. Now I am a very good typist. Come, Mr. Loran. We will take in the scenery of Riverside Drive. It is very different from what

I am accustomed to on Ramban Street in Jerusalem. But it has a quality all its own. Come."

They waited in the carpeted hallway for the elevator.

"An interesting man," Jakob Keter said, indicating the manila envelope in his hand. "An individualist. Very strange, very courageous. Nothing in common with the kabbalists all around him. Jacob ha-Kohen. Yes. Very strange."

The elevator arrived. They stepped inside.

"Good afternoon, professor," the uniformed operator said. He was an elderly man with white hair and watery eyes.

"Good afternoon, John. How is your wife?"

"Not too good, professor."

"Take care of your wife, John. Take good care of her."

"I'm trying, professor. I sure am trying."

Gershon felt in the calves of his legs the smooth swift descent of the elevator. In the entrance hall the uniformed doorman put two fingers to the peak of his cap as Jakob Keter went by. They came through the heavy glass doors into the sunlit street.

"It is cold," Jakob Keter said. "I like the cold. In Jerusalem the cold is often cruel. In Berlin the cold penetrated the soul. We will walk along the Drive. There is a mailbox on the next corner."

He was hatless. He felt no need to raise the collar of his coat. Gershon blinked in the sting of the river wind. They walked together along the upper Drive. The wide boulevard that was the lower Drive was lightly covered with pre–rush hour traffic. The naked trees seemed tremulous in the wind. Beyond the West Side Highway ran the river, dark and choppy and burnished with shifting pools of reflected sun. They stopped at a mailbox, and Gershon heard the soft slide and thump of the swallowed envelope. They passed the apartment house in which Karen lived. She was home, probably, working on her dissertation. That was all she did now: teaching and writing. She would have it done in a year, she said. A year. At the most, two. He wondered how long it would take him to do a dissertation with Keter. How many years before he could even begin the dissertation? How many kabbalistic texts to study? How many scholarly monographs to read? How much history and philology to master? How many languages—German, French, Arabic, Greek—

to learn? It seemed an interminable travail, and he felt no force impelling him to undertake it. Was that what most people did—drifted uncertainly into a patch of world to which they offered with doubting hearts much of the fire of their lives?

They crossed a wide street. In the tall apartment houses that faced the river, windows flashed and glowed like mirrors as they caught the high afternoon sun. The wind had stiffened and blew sharp gusts across the river and the Drive. People huddled in their heavy coats. The naked branches of the oaks and elms jerked about stiffly. The air was clear and blue and strangely luminous with the chill afternoon light.

"This is splendid weather," Jakob Keter said. "I walk every day. Do you exercise, Mr. Loran? You should exercise. In Switzerland during the First World War I learned to enjoy walking. Jerusalem is a city for walking. You have never been to Jerusalem? You must go one day. A beautiful city. I have three favorite cities. Jerusalem, Lucerne, and Florence. In that order. Be careful here of the broken curb. Why do they take so long to fix the streets in New York? You know, before the Israeli War of Independence I used to walk to Mount Scopus once a week. That is a long walk. I would go to the amphitheater and look out at the Dead Sea. It is an extraordinary view. Yes. You must see it one day. You will, you will. The Arabs will not have it forever. At times, you know, my imagination would take possession of me. I would see the people of the Dead Sea sect along the edge of the water below the caves in the hills. I imagined I could hear them teaching and studying their Book of Enoch and their other books. Possibly it begins with them, you know. Bultmann believes that to be the case. I am not convinced. You have read my books on this. Of course. But if they did not start it, they certainly helped transmit it to the rabbis of the Talmud. Apocalyptic ideas, magic, accounts of the angels, the vision of the Throne on its Chariot —the vision that was seen by Ezekiel—the enigmatic teaching on the measure of the body of the Creator, and all the other mystical and esoteric traditions found in the literature of the rabbinic period. It cannot be that all this came to us from Persia and Greece. This is an independent Jewish mystical tradition. You have read my papers. Yes? Good. I will now cease lecturing. How cold and clean this wind is! It was always windy on Mount Scopus. Always. I imagined I could hear their voices and see them walking about in their white robes. Yes. Once a week I walked to Mount Scopus. Often my wife walked with me. Be careful. There is a car coming. We do not want to be run over by a twentieth-century chariot."

They crossed another side street and walked on briskly. Gershon was finding it an effort to keep up with Jakob Keter. Ahead was the Fire Department monument, with its horses and white statues of the dead. They came down the steps to the stone parapet and stood gazing out at the wide lower Drive, the brown grass and naked trees, and the turbulent surface of the river. Gershon shivered.

"When do you enter the army, Mr. Loran?" he heard Jakob Keter ask.

"A year from June."

"I congratulate you upon the Leiden Award."

"Thank you."

"You deserve it. There was a certain point in my life when a year of study was crucial. Yes. There is no question that you deserve it."

"Thank you."

"We will read together certain texts next year. I am working now on a critical edition of a puzzling text from Provence. We will study it together. Yes? You will need to know some Arabic. You can begin this summer on your Arabic and Greek."

Gershon felt the wind on his face and listened to the dry expressionless voice of Jakob Keter.

"It is an interesting text. Numerology and angels and emanations and lights. It has much about lights. The *Book of Hidden and Revealed Lights*. No doubt a Gnostic text, filled with allusions about the notion of the hidden God. Certainly some rabbis considered it a heresy. The manuscripts are in the seminary library. Yes. In the rare-book room—not far from where you always sit, as a matter of fact. Lights. They were so obsessed with lights, our mystics. Jerusalem, Provence, Spain. Lights. Did it ever occur to you why they were so taken with light?"

"No."

"It is of course incorporeal substance; so they thought. Appropriate for God and emanations. Today we speak of waves and particles.

But quite possibly it had something to do with the Mediterranean sun. You have not seen our sun. There is a special quality to its light. In Poland there was no special sun, and the Jews became obsessed with the realm of the sitra achra. They were in a great war against the demonic world of the sitra achra. They saw evil and corruption and malignant spirits everywhere. Probably it was because of the pogroms. But it also may have had to do with the absence of sun. Yes. But that is psychology and has nothing to do with our work. What do you suppose American Jewry will produce as its mysticism? Every Jewry has had its mysticism. The ancient Palestinians spoke of angels and sacred names and saw visions of the Chariot and the Throne and the palaces of heaven; the southern and western Europeans left us their visions of the upper and nether worlds, of God and the feminine Presence, of the emanations and the Creation; the Safed mystics taught us what to do with the sparks and shells of this broken world; the eastern Europeans told us about the realm of evil. Do you think your American Jews will ever produce a mystical tradition? This land of movies and chewing gum and McCarthy and bingo and big urban pots of melting immigrants. What do you think, Mr. Loran? Yes? An interesting question. The mysticism of American Jewry. Intriguing. At any rate, we will read together next year. Yes? Now, I will ask you some questions and you will answer them. This is so I can report to the administration that I gave you your examination. Tell me, Mr. Loran, what do you think of Belkin's attempt to reduce the *Midrash ha-Ne'lam* of the Zohar to the status of a Hellenistic composition?"

Gershon heard himself respond briefly. "He doesn't succeed."

"Tell me why."

Gershon told him.

The wind was biting cold. Gershon squinted against the sun, and the river and the cliffs seemed to leap toward him. He could make out details on the water and the cliffs: the white curls of cresting wavelets, a pale snaking path along the dark face of the towering west bank. What was it that sailed so slowly over the surface of the river, turning, hovering? A bird?

"Yes," he heard Jakob Keter say. "Now tell me about some of the different scholarly views concerning Greek and Persian influence on early Palestinian mysticism. What do Widengren and Reitzenstein think about the influence of Persian religion on Jewish apocalyptic thought in the second temple period? What do Baer and Goodenough do to convince us of a link between the Greeks and the Palestinians?"

The benches near the monument were deserted. There were few people in the cold streets. The gasoline fumes of the cars and buses vaporized in the air and were blown about by the wind. The bird wheeled smoothly in the wind, a white wide-winged bird turning and wheeling in wide circles low over the water. Gershon heard himself talking, distantly, and watched the bird. It rose and flared brilliantly white in the sunlight. The river seemed so close to him now, as close as the lower Drive, closer. It churned darkly in the wind, but over it sailed the bird in smooth graceful dips and turns, its white feathers strangely unruffled somehow, as if bending the wind away from its fragile loveliness.

"I doubt that Goodenough is so convincing," Jakob Keter said. "Do you think that the accounts of the Chariot visions are intended to be allegorical?"

"No," Gershon said. "They're literal."

"The details of the upper world, the rivers of fire in front of the Chariot, the bridges across the rivers, the seven palaces in the firmament, the angels that throng the palaces, Ezekiel's account of the Chariot—all this is literal?"

"Yes," Gershon said. "Yes."

"You are right," Jakob Keter said. "I believe so too. Though I cannot fathom it. The appearance of the Glory of God in the form of supernal man—that too is literal?"

"Yes."

"What are we to make of it?"

"I don't know. A kind of monotheistic Gnosticism?"

"Perhaps, Mr. Loran. Perhaps. Tell me about some of the places in the Talmud where we find Chariot mysticism."

Jakob Keter listened to him cite the passages in the tractates *Hagigah, Shabbat, Sukkah, Berachot, Chullin, Megillah.* Gershon's voice was tremulous, barely audible. His eyes were fixed on the river. What was he seeing with such intensity of gaze?

"By the way, Mr. Loran. From where do we derive the term Merkavah, the word we translate as Chariot? The term does not appear in Ezekiel."

"From First Chronicles, chapter twenty-eight, verse eighteen. It's found for the first time with the meaning of Merkavah mysticism in Ecclesiasticus, chapter forty-nine, verse eight. 'Ezekiel saw a vision, and described the different parts of the chariot.'"

"Yes." Jakob Keter raised the collar of his coat. "Fine. Now, Mr. Loran, tell me this. If I use the term 'Gnostic topology' what do you think it might mean?"

Had the dark slate slabs of the churning river moved closer? Yes. The water lapped at the foot of the parapet. And there was the bird, so very white, sailing placidly over the water, wheeling, its pinkish legs tucked against its soft mound of bottom feathers. Gnosticism? The name given to various kinds of Jewish and non-Jewish sects and systems of belief that were non-normative. The period of the Talmud. A collective name meaning knowledge, often secret knowledge, possession of which saved you from the clutches of the evil and material world. First and second and third centuries. Fought by the early Christians. Christian Gnosticism was borrowed from Jews, not the other way around. Gnostic ideas probably remained embedded in the thought of Jewish and Christian sectarians all through the centuries. Most people frightened by these ideas. "'He who sees them is terrified by them.'" Hai Gaon, tenth-century leader of a great academy of learning in Babylonia, talking about mystical writings. Yes, terrified. With good reason. Dualism, the hidden God, the evil Creator God, the Presence as the feminine counterpart of God, knowledge of the inner nature of God, radical depreciation of the visible world, the power of the realm of the other side. Topology? The ideas that remain basically the same even when taken up by other systems of thought. Mysticism. The hidden motor energy of Judaism. Merkavah mysticism is Jewish Gnosticism, as is much of Jewish mysticism all through the centuries. The Jewish mythic consciousness creating its own reality. Fashioning the world in its own image. Dreaming light into existence. Charged, volatile, explosive, soaring in the imagination free and away from the yoke and discipline of the Law and the Covenant or using it as a path toward the deepest meanings of the

Torah and the Commandments. . . . Someone was talking to him. Had the wind turned warm? Strange how it blew warm now across the water. But Keter had his coat collar up. Strange.

"—briefly the problems involving the dating of the *Book of Creation*."

Early, early, not late as was once thought. Early, embedded in the heart of Judaism, present in the early centuries of rabbinic civilization; third to sixth centuries, no later. The word "Kabbalah"? Tradition. First precise use? Thirteenth century, Isaac the Blind, southern France. Earlier terms for mysticism and mystics? Secrets of the Torah, the Work of Creation, the Work of the Chariot, masters of the mystery, those who descend to the Chariot. What does that mean? Those who descend to the Chariot? He was not certain. Perhaps, he heard Jakob Keter say, perhaps it refers to those who reach deep into themselves in order to have a vision of the Chariot. Perhaps. You know the story in the tractate *Avodah Zarah* about the sinner Eleazar ben Dordia? Yes? Perhaps. Are you all right, Mr. Loran? You should button your coat. It is quite chilly now. Tell me this. What do you think is the basic assumption behind the use of letters and numbers in the *Book of Creation*? Can you explain that, Mr. Loran? That letters and numbers are like elements? They have ontological value? They create reality? They are operational agents that produce being? Yes. Yes. No, the wind is quite cold. Are you all right? The wind could not be cold, for it blew now with a kind and silken caress across his face, and the bird flew in it with a special grace, and he could see it soft and white and feathery in the sinking afternoon sun. It dipped down into the river and drank and wheeled upward, its beak red. It seemed to be calling, but he could not hear it. What do you suppose, Jakob Keter was saying, what do you suppose gave rise to the medieval picture of the Jew as magician and sorcerer? The bird rose and plunged and wheeled. He thought he could hear the beat of its wings on the wind. The river was slowly moving back. The sun was low. The chill was returning to the wind. A pale-gray wash had begun to spread across the sky. The bird hovered over the slowly receding waters. He opened his eyes fully. Yes, Jakob Keter said. Indeed. We have had our share of magicians who dispensed their services to all customers, not only Jews. Indeed.

Come. We will go back now. Mr. Loran? I am afraid I kept you too long. Come. But the river and the cliffs were now back in place, and he was watching the white bird hover low above the water, wings stiff and still. And, slowly, it dulled and faded and winked out and was gone. He felt a moment of deep aching sadness and the swift surging beat of his heart. His eyes hurt. He followed Jakob Keter up the stone stairs to the street. They walked together along the upper Drive. The sunlight began to fade. The wind turned cruel.

Inside the warm and elegant hallway of the apartment house, they waited near a wall of mirrors for the elevator. Tall green plants grew from moist earth in a low stone bed before the mirrors. The leaves were broad and pointed, their intricate webbing of arteries colored pink in the light of the fluorescents set in the ceiling above the mirrors. Gershon, looking at the plants, saw himself in the mirrors, and looked away. He heard Jakob Keter say, "I forgot to water the plants in the apartment. It is nearly a week. How irresponsible of me. Yes. I have undertaken to care for the plants. They belong to the people who own the apartment. He is an embassy official. They are away in Europe. I knew him when he was a student in Princeton. Now he is with your State Department. You will come up with me for a coffee? Yes? Good. I will tell you something about the article I mailed off today. A little gossip. To be told only in a whisper. Also I will show you something I am writing concerning an Aramaic inscription on an amulet found in Turkey. Dupont-Sommer saw in it early Jewish dualism. He was wrong. He made errors in reading and translation. A pity. When one misunderstands a text or dates it improperly, one does violence to the intellectual history of a people. Imagine someone two thousand years from now dating your Declaration of Independence and Bill of Rights and—what are they called? —your Federalist Papers, imagine all these dated to the time of Senator McCarthy. Well, it is good to see a smile on your face. Ah, here is the elevator. Come, Gershon. Come."

4

☙☙☙ Now he entered upon weeks of exhilarating freedom. He felt a lightness of mind and body. He was done with school; the hill had been climbed and he stood on its crest gazing into the sun. He woke in the mornings filled with energy, dressed and prayed and watched the sunlight upon his walls. How new the world looked, how young! He listened to music and came in those weeks to a special passion for Bach. Sonatas and Brandenburg Concerti spun upon his phonograph. Alone or with Karen he went to movies, concerts, plays. Often she was lost in thought, brooding over her dissertation, which was moving along tortuously. But he was free, free. With Arthur he indulged in late-night corned beef sandwiches and beer. Arthur was still waiting for his security clearance and seemed troubled. "Will be in limbo until cleared," he said. "Very tedious. You notice he hasn't done anything here about his lights?" In later years Gershon would come to realize that in those weeks he had already taken the first steps along the twisting path that eventually led him from his school and home to the tragic dusty valley in Korea. But he could not have known that then in those sun-filled weeks between his examination with Jakob Keter and his graduation.

Curious echoes of that examination remained inside him. In the past the texts he had memorized for his comprehensives would encase him in their distinctive rhythms and ideas. As new texts were absorbed, the old ones would be relinquished to the horizons of memory, not forgotten but no longer resonant. Now he had only to wait until June for graduation and ordination; and he thought it strange that the texts memorized for Jakob Keter lingered with odd persistence. No one, not even Karen, sensed a change in him; but he went about in the sunny and warming air of those weeks of spring accompanied with the silent ringing of ancient phrases. He listened to the rhythmic double verses of four plus four words or four plus three words or three plus three words—the hypnotic beat of the original Hebrew and Aramaic. Prose texts recounting danger-ous ecstatic ascents and poetic texts that were celestial hymns would drift through the darkness in his room after he turned off his radio and reading light; or they would in the day become intertwined with the contrapuntal climbs and descents of a Bach concerto. He would hear within himself the words of the great sage Rabbi Akiva: "In that hour when I ascended to the Chariot, a heavenly voice went forth from under the Throne of Glory. . . . 'Before God made heaven and earth, He established a vestibule to heaven. . . . He in-vited man to ascend on high, to descend below . . . to contemplate the splendor . . . to know the meaning of the living, and to see the vision of the dead, to walk in rivers of fire, and to know the light-ning. . . .'" And these words, also from Rabbi Akiva: "I beheld and saw the whole universe, and perceived it as it is; I ascended in a car-riage of fire. . . ." And the words of Rabbi Ishmael: "Come and be-hold the letters by which the heaven and the earth were created, the letters by which the seas and rivers were created. . . . And I walked by the side of Metatron and he took me by his hand and raised me upon his wings and showed me those letters, all of them, that are graven with a flaming style on the Throne of Glory. . . ." He would hear the words that described the "rivers of fire which pass before the Presence like streams of water mingled with fire . . ." and the words of this poem:

A quality of holiness, a quality of power,
A quality of fearfulness, a quality of sublimity,
A quality of trembling, a quality of shaking,
A quality of terror, a quality of consternation,
Is the quality of the Garment of Zoharariel yhwh, God of Israel,
Who comes crowned to the Throne of His Glory. . . .
And of no creature are the eyes able to behold it,
Not the eyes of flesh and blood, and not the eyes of His servants.

And as for him who does behold it, or sees or glimpses it,
Whirling gyrations grip the balls of his eyes,
And the balls of his eyes . . . send forth torches of fire,
And these enkindle him and these burn him. . . .

And the warm spring weeks wound on. He returned to the rare-book room and resumed his sober reading of the past. How long could he remain an idle worshiper of his own achievements, a self-indulgent mirror gazer? And, as the weeks went by, the resonating texts slowly dimmed and weakened; and one day they were gone, their inner music silent and lost.

On occasion he met with Jakob Keter. One sunny morning he ran into Professor Malkuson along the rim of the quadrangle. Was he studying Talmud? Malkuson wanted to know. There were many things a man could study, but Talmud one had to study. Yes, he was studying Talmud. . . .

In May he began to pack his books—he would be returning soon to the old apartment—and found, inside a book he had read the previous summer, the two postcards sent him by Arthur Leiden. He read the cards and put them on a pile of papers on his desk.

He saw Karen often now. She had given up hope of completing her dissertation by the summer; she had been ill for a time with a bout of flu and was still plagued by headaches, and she had slowed her research and writing. She would be spending the summer with her parents in the Berkshires, and he would remain in the city and take summer courses at Columbia to improve his French and German, the languages of many of the difficult monographs he would be reading all next year. He sat in her room one Sunday night with a section of her dissertation and was impressed by its smooth self-control, by the ease with which she had handled abstruse ideas. She was good, all right; it would be wrong to have her relinquish her academic career and follow him into the army. What could they do? Wait? For how long? And when he came out of the army, what then? Nothing had changed. Everything remained as he had thought it would. His acceptance of the Leiden Award had been less a decision than a delaying tactic of dubious worth.

They went to a movie and returned to her room. Some hours later he wandered along the silent river at first light, the water a mirror beneath a still, thin mist, and came up the stone steps and through the gate and past the sleepy stare of the security guard, who recognized him and touched his cap in greeting. The smell of her, the warmth of her—lingered. He slept deeply, without visions or dreams.

Two weeks later, on a warm sunlit afternoon, he was graduated and ordained. It was the second Sunday in June, a day tremulous with the high sense of endings and beginnings. He came out of the subway with his aunt and uncle and walked along the Drive to the school. He saw with some surprise the number of police on the street and the many black limousines along the curb. Wooden folding chairs were arranged in neat rows on the freshly cut green grass of the quadrangle. He smelled the scent of the grass and saw the sunlight brush a haze of gold over the audience. Particles of dust drifted through the haze. In a room off the quadrangle he and his classmates donned their academic robes and mortarboard caps. The black robe tugged at his shoulders; the black cap lay tight upon his head; the black tassel dangled and danced in the air. They put on their red and black hoods, chatting among themselves amiably, exchanging memories of the school years, all the while gazing at one another with barely concealed exultant looks of wondrous accomplishment. Remember the time Malkuson caught you unprepared? Remember that research paper Keter handed us? Hey, Gershon, you studying any texts on kabbalistic magic? How about getting me out of the army? He got himself out of the army, that's what he did, our canny kabbalist. Didn't you, Gershon? I swear to God that's Truman out there. No! Where? Isn't that Einstein? What's going on?

"What's it all about, Arthur?" Gershon asked quietly.

"How do I know, dear Gershon? I'm an innocent, caught in the whirl of blind forces."

"Truman is getting an honorary Doctor of Laws," someone said. "Look at the program. Didn't you get a program?"

"Any word on your security clearance, Arthur?"

"Am on forty-eight-hour notice."

"What does that mean?"

"Can be cleared and taken any time now. Can't make plans. I'll go home and wait around. Damn unpleasant business."

"I think they're calling us, Arthur."

They had lined up in alphabetical order. Gershon followed Arthur out of the room. The procession formed up on the cement rim of the quadrangle behind the waiting audience. The academic hoods splashed patches of vivid color onto the sober air of the wide, red-brick enclosure. A hush fell upon the quadrangle. Overhead an airliner flew by, vibrating the still air. The procession comprised the faculty, the top administrators, the chairman of the Board of Overseers, guests of honor, and the graduating seminarians. In front, flanking the chancellor, were Albert Einstein and Harry Truman, both impressive in their robes and caps. Truman wore no hood; Einstein's hood had the yellow color of a doctor of science. Malkuson and Keter followed: dark caps and gowns, golden tassels, white and blue hoods. Between Malkuson and Keter stood—Gershon was startled—Rabbi Isaac Levin, Karen's father, tall, silver-haired, in dark cap and gown, gold-colored tassel, and white and blue hood. Gershon saw him say something to Keter and Malkuson, watched them bend toward him to catch his words, and then saw them laugh. How strange to see the normally expressionless face of Jakob Keter break into a laugh!

Behind the faculty were guests of honor—faces familiar from newspaper and magazine accounts of the controversy among scientists that preceded and followed the explosion of the American hydrogen bomb two years before. He thought he recognized Enrico Fermi, Edward Teller, Leo Szilard. There was Arthur's father—gaunt and, yes, tanned—talking earnestly with Enrico Fermi. All five wore dark robes with the three velvet bars on the sleeves, dark caps with gold-colored tassels, and yellow hoods. Gershon had a swift momentary vision of the world aflame, rivers boiling, mountains melting.

The audience rose. A chorus of seminarians burst into a hymn. The procession left the walk and entered the quadrangle. Gershon felt the grass beneath his shoes and the sun in his eyes. He bumped heavily into Arthur, who had stopped for a moment. "Sorry," he murmured. Arthur said nothing. The line moved on. Somewhere in the audience were his aunt and uncle, Karen, and Arthur's family.

He felt eyes upon him and looked down. They were approaching the empty front chairs, stepping between the rows, finding their seats. The chairs on the stage were filling with gowned men— Einstein, Truman, Leiden, the chancellor, Karen's father, Keter, Malkuson.

The singing ceased. There was silence. A bird chirped in the silence, and there was the clearly audible cooing of the pigeons on the ledge below Malkuson's study. The chorus led the singing of the national anthem. Then all were seated.

Gershon glanced quickly through the program that had been placed on his chair. Karen's father was the presiding officer of the graduation ceremonies. None of the nuclear physicists appeared on the program.

Arthur leaned toward him, reading the question in his eyes. He whispered, "Some very ill, weren't sure they would make it. Also, security problems. Too much of our atomic future in one open place. You know what I mean?"

Gershon nodded, looking at him. He seemed so weary, his handsome face pale, his eyes dark. He remembered him entering their room in the early morning, drink on his breath. He heard his banter, his laments about Malkuson and Keter killing him, his gaiety. He had not been much of a friend to Arthur. But Arthur had not really wanted friendship. Instead, he had wanted—needed, it seemed—some measure of companionship, to be available on request; and that, Gershon felt, he had given him. He might have given more if he had felt himself being called upon—despite his dark memories of past abandonments, of the world withdrawing itself from him: parents, cousin, the high-school friend who had persuaded him to enter the seminary with him, and then had gone elsewhere. Now Arthur sat next to him looking tired and sad; and soon they would separate. Perhaps it was better this way, better. Too many abandonments. Too much remembered pain and the feeling of the breaking apart of things. . . .

He sat lost in thought, and only a part of him attended—dimly— to the pageant on the stage: the introductory remarks of the presiding officer, Karen's father—clear, loud, amplified voice—about the nature of this gathering on the soil of this free land, whose future

is in the hands of those who not only toil with their hands upon
visible reality but also bend to higher purpose the unseen worlds of
spiritual and physical reality. "Never was there a greater need than
now for a vision of our future," Gershon heard him say, his voice
somewhat oracular, his pronunciation tinged with New England
accents. "We have it in our hands to make of ourselves a burnt cinder
or a star of the spirit." He felt Arthur stir beside him. Karen's father
went on a moment longer; Gershon was no longer listening. The
sun glowed warmly upon the quadrangle, lighting some windows.
He heard applause. The chancellor rose and went to the podium.
Professor Malkuson approached him and asked to present the dis-
tinguished former President of the United States, Harry S. Truman,
for the degree of Doctor of Laws *honoris causa.* Truman rose. A
citation was read by the chancellor. Malkuson and Keter accompanied Truman to the podium and placed on his shoulders a hood with
purple velvet on the outside and blue on the inside. There was much
applause. The applause died away. Everyone sat silent. Truman stood
alone at the podium, smiling, looking around. The tassel accompanied with slight swaying dances the movement of his head; his
glasses glinted and flashed, as had the windows on the tall buildings
along Riverside Drive the day Gershon had taken his comprehensive with Keter. Why did that seem so long ago? It had only been
March. . . . What was he saying, in that same twangy slightly nasal
voice that had once announced the end of the European war, the destruction of Hiroshima by an atomic bomb, the end of the war with
Japan, the tactics in the dread Cold War with Russia, America's
recognition of the State of Israel, our entry into the Korean War,
the thermonuclear experiments on a Pacific atoll? He seemed so
much a man like other men. How influence and power had once
issued forth from him! He was talking about the Bible, about how
much he liked to read the twentieth chapter of Exodus and the fifth
chapter of Deuteronomy. "The fundamental basis of government
started with Moses on the Mount. He taught the God-given law, and
he influenced the whole world. Moses is dead about three thousand
years, and he still influences the world. That's moral power, and I
think it's more lasting than political power. That's what you young
men are going out into the world with—moral power." He talked

about the moral vision of Isaiah. "My mother had a great big gold-back Bible. . . ." Gershon watched a fly sail lazily through the sun-light. Insects hopped about in the small green world of grass near his feet. What had this man really felt after they had exploded the test bomb at Alamogordo? He had held the power of the sun in his hands. And after Hiroshima? Gershon had a piercing vision of where he had been when the news had come over the radio. In his small sunless room. In the decaying red-brick apartment house with the odorous halls and peeling walls and the drunks and whores and the man who chased his wife down the stairs with a butcher knife and the black-metal fire escape like a zigzag scar down the face of the building. Yes, he remembered. An August evening in 1945. He had climbed to the roof of the apartment house that night and gazed out at the stars and witnessed the whelping of the pups. Strange how they had all vanished from that roof. He had brushed a hand across the sky and felt, felt, the touch of the stars. But the bitch and her pups had disappeared. How easily broken was this brittle world. You did not need bombs to break it. It seemed able to break of itself. And this man had ended a savage war by incinerating two cities with two bombs. The soul doubled back on itself in a murderous clash of conflicting moralities. "I think the United States is the greatest gov-ernment in the history of the world. Our continued existence is absolutely essential to the welfare and benefit of all people who would be free." Who could have taken them from the roof? How cool the air had been, how blue and cool the stars. No fires. Death was a distant dream. "And I think the men who wrote the Constitu-tion wanted a document that would be a lasting instrument of gov-ernment. But they didn't have any more idea of what the future would bring forth than we have today. They didn't know how it would work out. Moses didn't know how the law of God would work out. So far they both have worked out, maybe because they both have benefited from respectful and constructive interpretation and revision." A distant automobile horn blared; someone in the audi-ence coughed. The air was warm, very still. What had someone called the flash of the exploding bomb at Alamogordo? He now remembered the stories. What? Yes. Death light. A university student blind fifteen years had seen it through her blindness. Yes. He remembered. Death light. "And I thank you for this great honor and this most memorable day." He felt himself rising, joining in the applause. He looked around but could see neither his aunt and uncle nor Karen. Perhaps his aunt and uncle were not standing; the long subway trip had been difficult for them. He glanced to his left. Arthur stood very still, his hands at his sides, his face rigid. He saw Gershon looking at him and looked away. In that brief joining of eyes, Gershon had seen in the eyes of his former roommate rage and pain and a frightening darkness. The applause subsided. All took their seats. Karen's father stood at the podium. An aircraft rumbled overhead.

"I have the honor to present the graduating class. . . ."

One by one, as their names were read off, each rose, went up to the podium, received his degree of ordination from the chancellor, shook his hand, and returned to his seat. Gershon glanced at the awards section of the program and saw his name followed by the words *"The Richard Leiden Memorial Post-Graduate Fellowship Award."* He was first on a list of ten awards. He heard Arthur's name called, saw him rise, make his way between the rows, and go up the stairs to the stage. Arthur shook the hand of the chancellor. He hesitated. His father half rose from his chair. Arthur came over to him. They shook hands. Gershon saw Truman bend sideways in his chair and offer Arthur his hand. Then Arthur shook the hands of Albert Einstein, Karen's father, Keter, Malkuson, and the chairman of the Board of Overseers. He was coming down off the stage and returning to his seat.

"Gershon Loran."

He felt himself rising and moving. He sensed clearly the hushed silence, the grass beneath his feet, the cooing of the pigeons, and eyes, eyes, upon him. He looked at the grass and at the movement of his legs as they thrust forward beneath the gown. The cap was tight, tight; the tassel swayed. Carefully, up the stairs. Carefully. The stage. He raised his eyes. An ocean of faces glowing in the sunlight: his classmates, the faculty and guests, the audience, the men on the stage. Truman, Einstein, Keter, Malkuson. . . . There was the face of Enrico Fermi. First atomic chain reaction. Chicago. There, Leo Szilard. Drafted the letter signed by Einstein and sent on to Roosevelt. *Sir: Some recent work by E. Fermi and L. Szilard . . . leads me to expect that the element uranium may be turned into a new and important source of energy in the immediate future. . . . This new phenomenon would also lead to the construction of bombs. . . . He* had read all that in a science book. Long letter. Did presidents read such long letters? All the faces and eyes in the sunlight. Waiting. Golden globes of light. Where was Karen? He was shaking the chancellor's hand. Out of the corner of an eye he saw Arthur's father motion to him. He felt himself moving again. His hand was gripped by Arthur's father, and he found himself staring into gray sad eyes set in circles of dark and bluish skin. The nose was straight, the mouth delicate, sensitive, curiously curved into a smile that seemed a mixture of poignant sorrow and weary determination. Next to Arthur's father sat Albert Einstein. "Congratulations," Einstein said to him, shaking his hand. He found himself shaking the hands of the others, Truman, Keter, Malkuson, Karen's father. . . . He was on the grass, moving. His heart raced wildly. He felt a tightness in his throat and chest and took some deep breaths. He was sliding into his seat, shaking Arthur's hand, other hands. "He's not well," he heard Arthur murmur. "Not well at all."

"Your father?"

"Einstein."

"Is your mother here?"

"Of course. She's the one not smiling. I saw Karen. She looks great."

"Why are all these scientists here, Arthur?"

"They're friends of the family. To be accurate, all were once friends. Today some are enemies. Joined together by our common humanity, so to speak. God, I wish they'd hurry this up."

The names of the graduates continued to be called. Arthur sat fidgeting on the wooden chair. Gershon, sweating, his heart still beating rapidly, sank into a dreamlike reverie of no feeling and no thought; a static sense of floating in a pool of opalescent air. He heard deep within himself the words of a Merkavah celestial hymn: "A quality of holiness, a quality of power. . . ." Who was that rising now? Karen's father? ". . . not on program for reasons we feel are best left unstated. My honor and privilege to introduce one of the immortals of our time. . . ."

As if suddenly jolted from the grassy earth, all the audience rose simultaneously. A heavy and respectful thunder of applause reverberated through the warm and sunny air of the quadrangle. Albert Einstein stood at the podium: dark cap and gown, golden tassel, yellow hood. The wide bristly mustache, the shock of thick white hair, the dark hooded eyes, the deep lines etched into the forehead and running from the outside corners of the eyes across the hills and hollows of the cheeks. All were applauding and gazing in awe upon this man. How old was he? About seventy-five? He stood bowed, weary.

The applause subsided. The audience was seated. A deep resonant hush fell upon the quadrangle.

Gershon saw Arthur staring straight ahead at the podium, his mouth partly open, his eyes wide, somewhat glazed. "A quality of holiness, a quality of power." Gershon felt the rise of the words within him. "A quality of fearfulness, a quality of sublimity. . . ."

Through the silence came the muted sounds of the Sunday afternoon traffic along the Drive. A warm breeze stirred the air of the quadrangle. Einstein stood at the podium. The yellow of the hood caught the sun, and Gershon felt a flash of light upon his eyes. Einstein spoke in a barely audible voice and with the heavy accents of his native Germany. This was a day of ironies and healings, he said. A day when many opposites have come together. A day when many things broken are being repaired—if not permanently then at least temporarily. "All my life I have hated war. It is the greatest curse of man's history. War. It comes from absolute ignorance, absolute greed, absolute cruelty. I fled from Nazi Germany because the Nazis were all these absolutes joined together. My brilliant and shining and civilized Germany turned and went in the opposite direction, toward darkness and barbarism. I will not return. Some paths a man takes cannot be retraced. Some acts cannot be undone."

The high thin voice, feeble, drifted with curious strength through the luminous silence of the quadrangle. Gershon felt a coldness on the back of his neck. All on the stage were listening intently.

"There are times, I must tell you, when I regret a certain act of mine. I made perhaps one great mistake in my life—when I signed the letter to President Roosevelt recommending that atom bombs be made. There was some justification to that act—the danger that the Germans would make them. They did not succeed. We succeeded and dropped them on Japan. It ended a terrible war. But also it stained us forever. All that cannot be undone. It is damage human beings have done to themselves that cannot be repaired. Do you wish to know what a dear friend of mine, a man I have known for decades, said to me before he returned to live in Germany after the war? He said to me, 'Einstein, the Americans have demonstrated in Dresden, Hiroshima, and Nagasaki that in sheer speed of extermination they surpass even the Nazis.' The comparison is, of course, wrong. But the stain of the act remains. Perhaps it was a choice between evils. Perhaps that is the nature of all serious acts of choosing. Nevertheless, I feel we are all stained."

The faces of the men on the stage were impassive. Truman sat unmoving, staring at the back of Einstein, the black robe, the black cap, the yellow hood. Gershon heard Arthur take a deep, trembling breath. Tiny winged insects whirred through the still air.

Einstein continued, his voice rising slightly. "You are perhaps aware that the Nazis referred to theoretical physics as 'Jewish physics.' We should perhaps be grateful that Hitler so hated the Jews that he stripped his Germany of its best physicists and was himself uninterested in the possibility of nuclear fission. Speaking for myself, I wanted only to understand better my universe, not to help make bombs. My colleagues and I—not all of them Jews—gave the gift of atomic power to a benevolent land, to America. How this gift will be used is in the hands of the makers of policy. I try to be of influence. But this is now the voice of an old man who loves his chair and his sweater and his books more than he does the tumult of the world."

He stopped and passed a hand before his eyes and was silent. He gazed down at the top of the podium and seemed for a moment to have slid in thought away from the quadrangle and the stage and the sunlight and the simple pious reality of a seminary ordination. Gershon sensed clearly the tension of the collective waiting. Einstein looked up and blinked his eyes. Yes. He had been away somewhere. Gershon felt again the coldness on the back of his neck.

Einstein continued. "If we have indeed erred by giving this gift to the world, we in part rectify this error by our act today. All of us here, Jew and gentile, join together in homage to a family's vision. Embedded in the tradition of the Jewish people there is a love of justice and reason. The Leiden family displays such a love. In doing so, it helps to balance our past poor choices, the evils we do and that are done to us; it helps relieve life of something of its earthbound heaviness. The Leiden and Einstein families have been friends for decades. This goes back to the days of the Kaiser Wilhelm Institute, where a young American once came to study physics. I will not burden you with the memories of an old man. This good family lost a dear son in the war against the Nazis. It has chosen after many years of sorrow to convert the ashes of its grief into a light of hope. To study, to teach—that is the hope. It is a way to help overcome ignorance, greed, and cruelty. The Leiden family has given the name of the fallen son to an endowed graduate fellowship which has been awarded for the first time to Mr.—to Rabbi Gershon Loran of this graduating class. Loran. That is, I believe, also the name of a navigational instrument, is it not? You see? I am not so much a lover of a life of quiet contemplation as to be unaware entirely of the outside world." There was a stir and a wave of soft laughter. Gershon sat with the blood surging in his ears. He saw Arthur smiling faintly. "By such an act the Leiden family shows that it remains faithful to the moral traditions which have enabled the Jewish people to survive for thousands of years despite the heavy storms that have broken over our heads. And it is a personal honor to be here and participate in this act of healing, this act of placing a garment of grace upon past stains."

He turned away from the podium and, in the applause that rose through the quadrangle, moved slowly back to his seat. Gershon felt classmates thumping his back. Arthur applauded but said nothing. All were standing and applauding. Truman was applauding. Einstein stood with his head bowed. An airliner flew by overhead. The sun had dipped behind the library building.

The names of the other award winners were announced. The chancellor spoke briefly. The choir burst again into song. Gershon found himself moving in a line with his classmates. He came from the grass to the concrete rim, then went through a door. All around was the din of disintegrating order, happy voices. He was in a room with his classmates. Arthur was nowhere to be seen. Congratulations, Gershon. Congratulations. Handshakes. Back thumps. Hey, Gershon, does Einstein know you're a kabbalist? How's that for a day of ironies? Einstein giving an award to a kabbalist. The whole world is nuts! No, I don't know where Arthur is.

Wearing his cap and gown, Gershon went down a corridor and into a men's room. He saw Arthur bent over a sink washing his face. Water dripped from his chin onto the gown.

"Are you all right, Arthur?"

"Where are the towels? What happened to the towels? Never mind. I'll use my handkerchief. Too much emotion out there. Too damn many memories. Interferes with my thinks, as Uncle Albert would put it."

"I didn't know the award was in memory of your brother. The dean said it was your grandfather."

"The dean was mistaken. Can I borrow your handkerchief? Never mind. I'll manage. What a day! Uncle Albert went on a bit long. I thought I would burst. What's the matter, Gershon?"

"How did the award get to me, Arthur?"

"What do you mean?"

"I mean I don't really think I deserve it. How did it get to me?"

"You deserve it."

"No, I don't, Arthur. Listen. I sat in classes here four years and wasn't sure from one minute to the next if I was right or wrong about most of the things I was listening to. I wrote papers, took exams, took notes, answered questions—and I was never sure. I'm not that good, Arthur. I don't like getting an award in your brother's name that I really don't deserve."

"Gershon, you really do—"

"How did it get to me, Arthur?"

The door was pushed open, and two of their classmates came in. Hello! Hello! How nice to meet you here, rabbis. Hello! Gershon followed Arthur out into the hallway. Loud laughter echoed from a distant corridor. The hallway was deserted.

"Why are you so upset, Gershon? What's the matter with you?"

"It's wrong. I don't deserve it. You won't get me to take his place."

"What are you talking about? My parents wanted to set up a scholarship in my brother's memory. They wanted it for Harvard. I told Karen about it, and she told her father. He went to work on my parents and got them to change their minds and give it to the seminary. I suggested to my parents to make it conditional upon your acceptance of it, provided you were deserving of it anyway. From there it went to the chancellor and to Keter and Malkuson and to you. That's all. You deserve it, you crazy kabbalist. All I did was push you into making up your mind."

"I couldn't have deserved it," Gershon said in a low small tremulous voice. "I don't feel—"

"Listen, I've got my family waiting for me out there."

A group of students rounded the corner into the corridor. Congratulations! Congratulations! Great speech by Einstein. Great! Good luck!

"Come on," Arthur said. "Don't you have an aunt and uncle out there somewhere? Don't you have a girl friend? Listen, if I don't see you again today—take care of yourself. Sorry for all the trouble I may have caused you. Late nights and things. Sorry. Take good care of yourself, Gershon."

They were outside in the joyous confusion on the quadrangle. He searched and found his aunt and uncle near the flower bed, looking distraught. They embraced him with murmurs of awe. Albert Einstein! This was the camp of the enemy, this non-fundamentalist citadel of renegade Judaism—and yet here their nephew, sole hope and remnant of the family, had been honored. They seemed bewildered and unable to focus a coherent reaction upon the day. "Proud, proud," his aunt said. "Blessings on your head." "Einstein," his uncle said. "Can't understand. What did he mean? What?" Gershon could barely hear them above the noise. People moved by in a stream, offering their good wishes. Someone thrust a cup of coffee into his hands. You will come up with me for a coffee? Yes? I will tell you something. . . . A little gossip. To be told only in a whisper. "We will go home now?" asked his aunt. "Your uncle is very tired. His lungs. . . ." There was Karen, so beautiful in a lacy summer dress. Her mother, younger sisters, brother. She embraced him, almost knocking the coffee from his hands. Proud, so proud.

Awed sibling stares; warm handshake and cheek kiss from her
mother. Karen's face wore a high flush of excitement. "Will I see you
later?" "I have to take my aunt and uncle home." "Call me, please."
"Sure." "You're marvelous," she said. "And I'm so proud." She took
the cup away. "Hello, Karen," Arthur said from somewhere behind
him, and before he turned he saw the flush deepen to crimson on her
face.

Arthur stood there in his cap and gown, tall, strands of blond hair
pasted to his moist forehead. There seemed a sadness to his eyes. He
was flanked by his parents, his mother elegantly dressed in a dark-
blue dress and long white gloves, his father still garbed in cap and
gown.

"Our congratulations," his father said to Gershon.

"Yes," his mother said.

"Thank you," Gershon said.

"How are you, Karen?" Arthur's mother asked.

"Thank you, fine," said Karen.

"Mrs. Levin?"

"Well, thank you."

"You must come and see us if you're ever in Boston, Rabbi Loran,"
she said, turning to Gershon. Her face was smooth and pale, and her
pale-blue eyes were sharply focused and cold. Arthur looked down
as she spoke. "We would be delighted to have you stay with us. Our
home is kosher. Arthur saw to that."

"Thank you," Gershon heard himself say.

"What will you be studying?" Arthur's father said.

"Kabbalah."

"Yes," he said after a moment. "That's right. With Jakob Keter.
That was mentioned to me. Why did I forget it?"

"I think we ought to start thinking of leaving, Charles," Arthur's
mother said. "There may be traffic on the way to the airport. Come,
Arthur. Goodbye, Karen. Mrs. Levin. Do think of visiting, Rabbi
Loran. I would like to get to know the individual who has received
the first fellowship in my son's name. Goodbye."

Arthur shook Gershon's hand. "She means it," he said in a low
voice. "Take care of yourself. Maybe you can utter an incantation
and make us a miracle and let the next years go by smoothly. A little

practical Kabbalah, a little white magic. What good is all that study if it can't be put to some use? Goodbye, dear Gershon. Take care of yourself."

He followed his parents into the crowd.

Gershon said to Karen a moment later, "I lived with him for two years, and I still don't understand him."

Karen started to reply and stopped.

"I'll call you later," he said.

"Gershon," his aunt said. "Your uncle is very tired."

"I have to get out of this cap and gown."

"I love you in that cap and gown," Karen whispered, leaning toward him.

"How well did you know Arthur?" he asked.

She said, after a moment, "Very well."

"I'll call you as soon as I get home," he said, and went off toward the dormitory building.

Near the door to the building stood Jakob Keter, Nathan Malkuson, and the chancellor, deep in conversation. Keter saw him. "Mr. Loran. Rabbi Loran. My congratulations."

He shook their hands.

"Loran forsakes the Torah for the Kabbalah," said Professor Malkuson. "You have won the wager, Keter."

The chancellor looked on, smiling, paternal.

"We will wait a little longer before declaring the winner," Keter said. "In the meantime I wish you a pleasant summer, Rabbi Loran. Study your languages. I leave tomorrow for Jerusalem and will return in October."

Gershon left his cap and gown in the room where he had earlier donned them, and put on his jacket. Was it all over already? So quickly?

In the corridor he met the dean of students, who was still in cap and gown, and perspiring.

"Congratulations."

"You didn't tell me the award was named after Arthur's brother."

"Who knew? I thought it was the grandfather. What difference does it make? Listen. I don't think I'm going to be able to get you a dorm room for next year. The bosses on high say rooms are for seminarians only. I'll keep trying. Congratulations, rabbi."

He came back out to the quadrangle. Long shadows lay upon the grass and the disheveled rows of chairs. The crowd was thinning. His aunt and uncle stood near the flowers. Karen was with them.

"They look a little forlorn," she said. "I didn't want to leave them alone."

"When are you going up to the Berkshires?"

"The end of next week. Here's my father."

"Quite a day. Marvelous day. A coup for the seminary. Proud of you, my boy. Keep working hard. The world will hear great things from you one day."

He shook Gershon's hand. He shook the hands of his aunt and uncle.

"Splendid day. Splendid. Goodbye, my boy. Good luck."

Some minutes later Gershon walked slowly with his aunt and uncle out of the gate and down the steps to the street. He walked with them along the Drive, past tall apartment houses. It was early evening. The sun hung low over the river and the hills, a dull, red burning disc into which he could gaze without difficulty. Make us a miracle, Gershon. A little practical Kabbalah, a little white magic. He walked slowly between his aunt and uncle, holding their arms. They took the subway home.

He lived at home all the next year, in his sunless room, with its narrow bed and bureau and small desk and shelves of books. There were many fires in the decaying neighborhood. Empty buildings burst into flames in the cold hours of the night. He woke often to the sounds of fire engines and lay in the darkness listening to the sirens move through the streets. One morning he walked by a house that had burned the night before: charred windows, blackened and gutted interior, debris on the roped-off sidewalk. The stench of the fire thickened the air. People sauntered by in silence, faces vacant. No one seemed to know who was burning the dead buildings of the neighborhood.

Karen had urged him to rent a room near Columbia. He would have been happy with a dormitory room in the seminary. But a rented room of his own away from his aunt and uncle seemed some- how an act of abandonment. He did not know why he felt that way;

but he knew that he did and so lived at home and woke to the fire
engines and walked past the skeletons of cremated buildings.

Three times a week he took the subway to Manhattan. He studied
languages at Columbia and Kabbalah with Jakob Keter in his Riverside Drive apartment. On the subway he read and dozed, resigned
to the dirt and the screams of tortured metal and the dim lights and
the lurching cars. The subway train was his throne-chariot, he once
said to Karen after a ride in which he had sat in the darkness of a
suddenly dead train for nearly half an hour. "Dirty metal in place
of sapphire; conductors in human form. See Ezekiel, chapter one,
verse twenty-six. Did I ever tell you that *sefirot* comes from the
word 'sapphire' and not from the word 'sphere'? I told you. I feel
like a *Zwischenmensch*. A word I'm coining. Remember it. A
between-person. I don't belong anywhere. Not Columbia, not the
seminary, not Brooklyn. Nowhere. I'm in-between. I think this year
was a mistake. What can I do? I'll go on traveling in my chariot.
No, I don't hear anything. Are your parents due back so soon? It's
only a quarter to one."

He experienced a curious turn in his reading. In addition to his
languages and Kabbalah texts he began to read works having to do
with the atom, atomic power, atomic bombs. He read newspaper
and magazine articles on Los Alamos. He read the Smyth Report on
the making of the first bomb. He read about Albert Einstein, Enrico
Fermi, Leo Szilard, Robert Oppenheimer, Edward Teller. The name
Charles Leiden appeared often in his reading; something about the
implosion principle and the concept of fusion.

One November afternoon Gershon ran into the dean of students
near the entrance to the subway outside the Columbia campus.
Arthur Leiden? Fine, as far as he knew. Teaching in a Hebrew high
school near Boston. No, his clearance hadn't come through yet. Any
day now. No, a part-time teaching job. "You look pale, Gershon.
How's your year? Don't work so hard. Don't take everything so
seriously. When are you due for your army physical? Good luck.
Good luck."

Karen completed her dissertation in December and submitted it to
her adviser. She spent three weeks working on the list of suggested
revisions and submitted it again. It was accepted. Her dissertation

defense was scheduled for the last week in February, a few days before Gershon's army physical. She went about in a torment of anticipation—her own kind of betweenness, she said to Gershon.

"Am I impossible to be with?" she asked him one night.

"Just about," he said.

"I'm frightened."

"You'll do fine."

"There will be at least one person on the committee who really doesn't like me."

"You will think him into the ground."

"It's a her."

"You will think her into the ground."

"Do you have an incantation that might help?"

"No," he said. "I don't even have one for myself."

"What good are you?"

"No good at all."

"I'll show you what good you are. Come here to me. We don't need incantations. We're twentieth-century people. Come here, you sad-eyed kabbalist."

In late February, with winter snow on the ground, she went to her dissertation defense, and passed with ease. They shook her hand, standing around the long conference table, smiling at her. Afterward she stood on the street and found herself crying. Later in her room she was still crying. Gershon came over after his evening seminar with Keter and held her and listened to her cry. She was trembling and crying. Her parents were happy. "Dr. Levin," her father kept saying. "Dr. Karen Levin. I like it."

At Gershon's army physical later that week, a doctor ordered a set of chest X-rays, and a cardiologist asked him if he had ever felt pains in his chest. "Very rapid heartbeat," the cardiologist said. "Tachycardia. No pains, ever?" The walls of the drafty room were white and lined with glass cabinets filled with instruments. The floor was of white tile. The cardiologist, a short man with thin graying hair and a graying mustache, waited. Gershon looked at him. The cardiologist stood there quietly, white-frocked, waiting, stethoscope dangling from his neck. "No," Gershon said. The cardiologist nodded and wrote something into a file. Afterward Gershon walked to the subway and found his hands were trembling. A gate had been swung open for him onto a safe and certain path, and he had turned away. Why? Because whatever it was that he was waiting for would never come to him in this twilight urban world of fragments? He did not know.

He passed the physical. His aunt and uncle stared at the letter advising him that he had been made a commissioned officer in the United States Army. The miracle they had expected had not come. The week he was informed that he had passed his physical, two houses in the neighborhood burned. His aunt, horrified, took that as a bad omen. "It is a sign, a sign," she whispered fearfully. "Dear God, help us." He turned away from her dread. "Again a soldier?" his uncle said. "Cannot endure it. Cannot. Flesh and blood. No more. Cannot endure." He was ill for a day, then returned to the bookstore. Gershon stopped by the store one morning on the way to the train and found him in a dusty clutter of books and ritual objects. "You could do nothing?" his uncle asked. "Nothing? A wasted year?" He could do nothing, Gershon said, and wondered if he spoke the truth.

In early April he submitted to Jakob Keter a research paper on which he had worked since the start of the year. Keter read the paper the same day he received it, remaining awake late into the night. He was reminded of the first paper he had read by Gershon Loran—in the garden of his Jerusalem home. He sat now in the living room of the rented apartment, amid the green of potted plants, and finished reading the paper. He put it aside and read it again a few days later.

They walked in the warm spring air along the Drive and talked about the paper. It was very technical talk concerning methods of dating the theurgical descriptions and magical names found in mystical texts generally ascribed to the early talmudic tradition. Were the abracadabra passages as early as the hymns and prayers and Throne-Chariot descriptions found in the text or were they later additions? Were they original to rabbinic Judaism or inauthentic accretions? They talked into the early evening, then walked over to the delicatessen on Broadway near Columbia for supper. Gershon ordered a corned beef sandwich and a beer. He ate slowly. The ceiling fluorescents hummed and flickered. The place was crowded and warm with the odors of sour pickles and hot spiced meats and sauerkraut—the scents remembered from the many times he had eaten here with Arthur Leiden.

"You have on your face more than your normal measure of sadness," Jakob Keter said. "What is wrong?"

"Memories," Gershon said. "And anticipations. Do you really think I ought to go up to Harvard to have a look at that manuscript?"

"Yes. If a microfilm is unobtainable. It will, I think, substantiate your inclination to date the magical material early. I would suggest Oxford, but that is untenable."

"I might drop in on Arthur."

"Leiden?"

"Yes."

"The dean tells me he is in the navy, or is very soon to enter. They are an interesting family. Do you know them?"

"No."

"The father is a great physicist, and the mother is a splendid art historian. She specializes in oriental art. I met them in Berlin soon after they were married. I knew many of the physicists. I thought once to become a mathematician or a physicist. They were a small international family. Everyone knew what was in everyone else's pot."

"Arthur and I roomed together for two years, and I never found out why he left physics and came to the seminary."

"Indeed? Your reticence conceals much. And his exuberance conceals much. I think, if you will excuse me, that reticence and exuberance are often splendid soil for talk that is in essence silence. Yes? You agree? Where is the waiter? The roast duck was passable. I think I shall have a black coffee and a strudel."

"Will you call the people in Harvard, if I have to go?"

"Certainly. You should see the Munich manuscript. It is in splendid condition. But Munich and Oxford will be for another time. Yes? I have been back to Germany twice since the end of the war. I saw Dresden. In my darkest imaginings I could not envision such destruction. An ocean of fire from American fire bombs. Yet I felt no compassion for the Germans. And that distressed me. To think that Germany had succeeded in destroying a man's capacity to feel compassion toward human suffering. That is perhaps her greatest sin. No, I made no mistake when I left for Jerusalem. Those who remained, they made the mistake. Ah, finally, our waiter."

The waiter was the same palsied, elderly man who had over the years served Gershon and Arthur.

"Where is your friend?" he asked now. "The handsome one with the blond hair and the fancy accent?"

"In the navy," Gershon said. "A chaplain."

"You don't say? He should come home in good health."

They ordered dessert. He cleared the table and went off. The noise inside the delicatessen was loud. Waiters shouted their orders to the aproned men behind the front counter. The flickering fluorescents had begun to trouble Gershon's eyes. The walls and tables dimmed and flared. They returned to technical talk over dessert.

"Malkuson may be able to resolve that for us," Keter said at one point. "It may appear in a parallel rabbinic text. I should have studied more Talmud in my young days. It was a mistake. Did someone tell me you received ordination from a yeshiva?"

"Yes," Gershon said, and named the school and his teachers.

"May one ask why you left Talmud?"

"I don't know. I ask myself often. I answer that I don't know. It doesn't hold me. It doesn't seem to grasp my feelings and imagination. But I really don't know."

"How interesting. Are you done? Come. I will walk with you to your subway station. It is a pity you must travel now all the way to Brooklyn. Come."

To the man behind the cash register Gershon said, "You ought to fix those fluorescents. They hurt the eyes."

"Sure thing," the man said, punching keys. "Got a guy coming in this week. You got two pennies?"

Outside the evening street was crowded with strollers. The air was cool and clear. They walked slowly together.

"I am able to recollect clearly why I left mathematics and physics," Jakob Keter said as they slowly crossed a side street. "I had a vision one day that science in our century would lead to death. There were many roads in my vision, all marked with the word for science. The roads twisted and turned and became a huge road marked with the word 'death.' It is certainly a vision that was unfair to science. But it showed me my feelings, and I went elsewhere. I did not wish to become what I had beheld. You understand? Yes. Be careful. Why is there such a piece of wood in the middle of a sidewalk? And so I decided instead to explore the demonic that leads to life, rather than the demonic that leads to death. It seemed to me that nothing was more demonically creative in all of Jewish history than Kabbalah. I was not mistaken. Shall we buy a newspaper? I hear Einstein is quite ill. Yes. You have not heard? We nearly lost Truman last summer. We lost Fermi in November. And, I am afraid, we are about to lose Einstein. How intriguing that all were at the graduation last June. This is your station. Yes? Good night, Gershon. I will see you on Tuesday, and I will tell you then about Harvard."

He rode home and walked through the littered streets of his neighborhood. Which house would burn tonight? In the morning he heard over the radio that Einstein was dead. He had a vision of him standing at the podium in the dark cap and gown and yellow hood. "A quality of fearfulness, a quality of sublimity. . . ."

Jakob Keter was profoundly upset when Gershon saw him the following day. That was the first time he saw Keter's face without its mask of expressionlessness. "I cannot come to terms with our mortality," he heard Keter say in the living room of the apartment. "I simply cannot. It is all one vast obscurity, one vast hopelessness. A veil. We know nothing, we can hope for nothing. Nothing." He paused, standing by the window and gazing out at the river and the late afternoon sun. His longish face was drawn. A blood vessel beat visibly on the side of his bald head. He put a finger to his bow tie. Gershon looked past him at the fading day. Then Keter said, still staring out the window, "It will not be necessary for you to go to Harvard. There is a microfilm, and they will send it. We will have a coffee and return to our work. It is a fine sunset. Yes. Very fine. Come, we go back to work." He turned away from the window. "I did not tell you. This will probably be my final year here. I will know definitely soon, but I think I will be returning to the Hebrew University after the summer. It is almost certain." He gazed at Gershon, his face once again impassive. "So. You go west, and I go east. Yes. Well. Shall we have a coffee and return to our text? Come, Gershon. Come."

In the weeks that followed, the weather turned warm and the trees grew lacy with young leaves. He walked often with Karen along the riverbank and near the monument. In May he bought his army uniforms, and in June she walked in cap and gown and white hood and received her Ph.D. She had earlier received an appointment to the philosophy faculty at Barnard. She walked about in a daze of joy and said to him the night after graduation, "It's like a dream. I can't believe it."

"It better not be a dream. Your mother is telling the whole world."

"How shall we celebrate?"

"Let's read a kabbalistic hymn."

"Gershon!"

"Let's not go anywhere. Let's just stay here."

"There's a little club on Seventy-second. I'm in the mood."

They took a cab and sat in the cool dimness of the club and had drinks and danced. The music was soft and sweet. He held her gently against him.

"Enjoying?" she murmured.

"Very much. You?"

"Yes," she said. "Yes, dear Gershon."

Later they returned to the apartment. She said at one point during the night, speaking softly into the darkness, "Gershon, did I make a mistake?"

"How do you mean?"

"Should we have gotten married?"

"You're asking a biased judge."

"We'll get married when you come back."

"I will be a desiccated monastic."

"Not very likely, my Gershon. Not even at eighty. I know about your secret kabbalistic powers."

"Sure. Abracadabra. You and Keter. He says I have a splendid way of expressing myself on paper. Splendid. Half the time I'm not even sure I'm coherent."

"My poor Gershon."

"I'm tired, Karen. The year is over. Gone. Nothing has changed. You should see the looks I get at home from my aunt and uncle. I'm really very tired."

"All the late trips on the city throne-chariot. Poor darling."

"They look like they're expecting doom. My aunt and uncle. Doom."

She said suddenly, "Gershon, hold me. Why am I so frightened? Have I made a mistake? You'll come home changed. I'll have stayed the same, and you'll be different. Will we want to make the effort to grow toward each other if we're not married? I'm really scared."

They were silent awhile. The window was open. A night wind stirred the curtains and brought into the room the chill scent of the river.

"Don't worry," he said finally. "I'll make magic against radical change. Don't like radical change. Prefer smooth drifting to and fro, to and fro, like so, to and fro."

"Gershon."

"I do love you," he said. "You doctor of philosophy."

"You kabbalist. Gershon. Oh."

Later, in the early morning, he came out of the subway and walked deserted filthy streets that were washed with bleak pre-dawn light. Cats played in the open garbage pails. The apartment house was silent. The floors creaked beneath his feet. He got into bed and saw sunlight on his windows and fell asleep. He woke at noon.

He put his insignia on his uniform that day and stood before the tall mirror in the living room. He was alone in the apartment. The uniformed officer in the mirror was a stranger to him. He felt his heart beating rapidly. He took the uniform off and put it back into the closet. He would not tell himself how frightened he was. He spent the day reading.

It rained much of that week. He saw Karen twice, traveling back and forth by subway. At the end of the following week, on a wet day, he sat on the edge of her bed, watching her pack. She was going with her family to the Berkshires for the summer. She would use the summer to prepare her lectures, she said. He told her he would be in chaplaincy school all summer, in Fort Slocum, outside New Rochelle. There was little chance they would see each other.

"Will you write me?" she asked.

"Yes."

"Where will they send you after the summer?"

"I don't know."

"I feel cold. It's so dreary outside. Please hold me, Gershon."

He returned home by subway and spent Shabbat with his aunt and uncle. The apartment was dense with their sighs and silences. He lay awake Saturday night listening to the noises of the neighborhood. The year was crumbling slowly away, and he held in his hands nothing.

He took the subway to New York that Sunday afternoon and went up to Jakob Keter's apartment. Two valises stood neatly packed in the hallway. The curtains were open. Through the windows Gershon saw the river covered by heavy mist. He could not see the cliffs. The indoor plants stood full and leafy. Who would water them now? Were the lessees of the apartment returning? In the study he watched Jakob Keter neatly packing papers and a few books into an attaché case.

"I am taking your paper with me," Keter said. "I will return it to you by mail."

"You can send it to my home. It will be forwarded."

"Is there a chance you will be sent overseas?"

"Yes."

"Well, if you are sent to Europe, perhaps you will visit me in Jerusalem." He closed the attaché case and stood there looking at Gershon. "Well," he said. "It is finished. I have been away too long." He paused. "When you get out of the army, what will you do?"

"I don't know."

"Yes. I understand. It can be a long and uncertain passage. Yes."

Gershon said nothing.

Jakob Keter gazed at him. "You will continue to read. Yes? Take with you what books you can. Come. Let us sit in the kitchen. I will make some coffee."

They came into the small, brightly lighted kitchen. Keter puttered about. He wore a dark suit, a white shirt, and a red bow tie. His bald head shone in the light. He put cups of coffee on the table and sat down across from Gershon.

"Do you know yet where you will be assigned?"

"No."

"I was in the German army briefly during the First World War. I detested it. But I was not a chaplain."

Gershon said nothing. An electric clock hummed softly on the wall.

Jakob Keter sipped slowly from his cup. "It is not pleasant to be alone. Keep yourself busy, Gershon. Read, write, move about. Do not permit yourself to brood. Can I give you another coffee?"

Later they came out of the elevator together into the wide and elegant entrance hall. The tall leafy plants shone before the wall mirrors in their bath of artificial light. The sky had cleared. Afternoon sunlight warmed the air. They walked together to the subway station on Broadway.

"You have my Jerusalem address?" Jakob Keter asked.

"Yes."

"Write to me from time to time, Gershon. Do not hesitate to call on me. I will make every effort to respond."

"Thank you," Gershon heard himself say.

"Goodbye, Gershon. It was a pleasure to be your teacher. Goodbye."

They shook hands. Gershon took the subway home.

That night he came out of the apartment and climbed the stairs to the roof. He stumbled on a rickety step during his ascent and bruised his knee. The building smelled of mold and moisture and decay. On the roof he walked to the low stone parapet and gazed down at the street. In the pools of light cast by the lamps lay the refuse of days. The street was silent save for an occasional car. Ruts and bumps caught the lights in a dance of shadows that gave the asphalt street a rippled liquid look. It was a clear hot night, its redolence borne to him by gentle currents of air. The roof, with its fissured tar and rusting pipes, was empty. No bitch whelping life on this rotting roof tonight. Only a vast emptiness of sky and earth. What had he really accomplished all these past months? The year lay behind him like a shallow trench, a murky indistinct betweenness. He wished Arthur had not forced the choice upon him with that curious gesture of helpfulness. He wondered where Arthur was, what base, what ship. Distant street lights winked in the darkness. The sky seemed cold, as if its galaxies and debris mirrored an ancient abandonment. No one could really climb the transcendent heaven now. The rabbinic mystics with their strange ascents—a different time, a different place. The secret face lay silent behind a thousand seals. He could touch

Einstein's heaven, Arthur's father's heaven, yes. But it would remain closed, and icy to his fingers. No chariot into the chambered heaven. No. Still he felt himself waiting. For what? He shivered in the hot night air and was nearly overcome by a sadness that had no face and no name. It was a deep and fearful sadness, a palpable realm, a *sefirah,* as real an emanation of the Divine Being as were royalty, wisdom, understanding, power, grace, and the others. He gazed into its melancholy darkness and saw again all the abandonments of his life, all the incompleteness. Warm breezes bore in upon him with vagrant scents: the musky odors of an ailanthus, the thick smells of frying meat, the stench of alley garbage. If he were to climb now, attempt the ascent, storm the palaces with all the things he knew, he would perhaps see the Throne. Yes. And upon it would be the Essence of all Being—encased in dark shrouds of melancholy. He needed no such ascent. His small trench of earth was a parallel sadness. Still—he stood on the roof and waited.

From the east came a distant hum and the twinkle of living lights. An aircraft came slowly into view, low overhead, its cabin lights visible, its wing lights flashing, exhaust flames pouring from its four engines. It shook the air as it passed, roaring. He followed its rise, watched its westward flight until its sound was gone, and only its lights winked in the darkness that was background to the cold stars. Then the lights were gone. He stood there, waiting. And after a while he knew that nothing would come that night. He went slowly from the roof and down the stairs and into the apartment. It was a long time before he was able to sleep.

The next week he put on his uniform and took a train, a bus, and a ferry to Fort Slocum, a tiny island close by New Rochelle and the Bronx. Gulls wheeled over the slate-gray water near the dock on the island. There he spent the summer, in sweltering heat, attending classes with other uniformed men. Weekends he spent in Brooklyn. He was unable to read, and gazed upon all around him as if in a dreamlike trance. He marched and saluted and listened in a strange stupor to lectures on counseling, map-reading, combat, administrative procedures. He felt himself entered upon a twisting passage, a fearful course of space and time, and he shielded himself from dread with a wall of melancholy indifference.

In later years he would remember almost nothing of this curious period. Pieces of paper began to pass him from command to command. In September a bus brought him to Fort Knox, Kentucky. There he lived in a small room with a narrow bed, a desk, a bureau. Heavy vehicles woke him in the mornings. The distant thunder of artillery rattled the windows. Young soldiers lunged in bayonet charges and broke their hands and crushed their fingers in the machinery of tanks. He lay in tents in the field in cold and rain and listened to barked commands drift through morning mist. Helicopters flew overhead, chopping the air. He conducted services and counseled frightened young men who told him of fears that mirrored his own. The division, with its men and armor, was due to go to Germany in the coming summer—and just as he began to look forward to that, began to grow accustomed to the specters of death in which he was enmeshed, he was told that a mistake had been made, he did not qualify to move with the division, he would be out of the army too soon, less than a year, after the move. He lay on his narrow bed and listened to the tanks and the artillery. He wrote to his aunt and uncle, to Karen, and to Jakob Keter. He received no reply from Keter. Then he received a new piece of official paper, new orders. He had little to pack and no one on the base to whom he really wished to say goodbye.

In late January he took a bus back to New York. That was a bad time. Karen wept and wondered if they had made a mistake. Her dissertation was being prepared for publication by a prestigious university press; she loved her teaching; she lived alone in an apartment near her parents—and she lay against him and cried. He said little, and afterward remembered nothing of his words to her. His aunt and uncle gazed at him with a special sort of horror in their eyes—but toward the end, when he was soon to leave, they seemed to change. They would help him through it, they said. They would send him packages, magazines, newspapers, food, whatever he needed. "You need Kabbalah books, Gershon," his uncle said, coughing, "write and I will send." "Yes," his aunt said, clinging to him. "We will help." The old man in the synagogue who had taught him Aramaic gave him the amulet. "What can it hurt?" he murmured through his tobacco-stained beard. "It means nothing. But what can it hurt?"

In the middle of February he boarded a commercial airliner—a double-decker Stratocruiser—that carried him to Seattle near Fort Lewis. He flew in pure terror, staring down at the distant, gliding, snow-covered earth. He signed into Fort Lewis and spent Shabbat in Seattle in the home of a seminary rabbi who had been ordained nine years back. The rabbi's wife had a master's in art history from the University of Chicago. The meals were noisy. There were three young children. The phone rang often. "Make sure to see Kyoto," the rabbi's wife said. "And Nikko." He went to the Friday evening service and, back in the house, read into the night. The rabbi had a splendid library. Many of the books looked unread. "You read the Cordovero?" the rabbi said the next day. "I haven't had a chance to look at it yet. Not much time for reading. The publishers sent it to me. I don't much like Kabbalah. Spooky stuff." "Make sure you get to Kyoto and Nikko," the rabbi's wife told him as he left on Saturday night. "Make sure." They stood in the doorway with their children and watched him get into the cab.

Two days later a Military Air Transport Service DC-6 brought him to Hawaii. He walked in sultry night air beneath luxuriant palm trees, felt beneath his feet the sand of a golden beach, listened to high, dark waves, and saw a vast stretching sky filled with cold stars. The next day he boarded a navy Constellation. Somewhere over the Pacific they lost a day, and he lost track of time. He slept a great deal and ate little. He would wake from dazed sleep in the canvas seat, his body stiff and aching, and ask himself what time it was, what day. They landed on Wake Island to refuel. His eyes felt singed by the sun on the white lava. They flew into the night, and he saw the wing lights flashing and blinking and the exhaust gases burning behind the engines. They landed in Japan, and he slept in a stupor of exhaustion on a cot in a bachelor officers barracks in Camp Drake near Tokyo. Thirty-six hours later a huge, big-bellied, double-deck-ered C-124 Globemaster named the *Thin Man* brought him to Kimpo Air Force Base in Korea. The journey had taken ten days.

Part Two

5

They landed in late afternoon on Friday in blowing snow. He saw granite hills and bare brown valleys. A frozen river flashed by just before he felt the heavy touch of the wheels on the tarmac.

He trudged with the others in a fierce wind toward a nearby cement building. In the tall windows the name *Thin Man* on the Globemaster showed in reverse. The outside walls bore the leprous tracings of war: stark pits and gouges of bullets and shells. He saw all and saw nothing. The wind whipped against his face and blew snow into his eyes. He felt himself still on the aircraft. The ground yawed and swayed and oscillated beneath his feet. As they walked, a huge aircraft went into its takeoff run. The windows in the building shook, blurring the reversed name *Thin Man*. Inside, a potbellied oil stove gave off heat. His eyes ached with the fatigue of travel and altered time. Soon they were herded into a bus. He gazed out a window and through a thin film of snow saw barbed wire fences and empty fields. All in the bus were officers, and all sat in silence. It was late afternoon, the air gray with the shadows of clouds. A strange landscape floated by: pale, globular lights, dense shadows, blurred figures, wet vehicles, misshapen dwellings, horse-drawn carts, women with vacant faces, children with running noses and facial sores. Objects drifted toward him out of the snow and flashed by and vanished. All this he saw, and yet he saw nothing.

The bus brought them to a replacement depot, and he walked again in the snow. A jeep pulled up, and the driver called out his name. He felt eyes staring at him through the snow. The jeep had a canvas top and plastic side and rear windows. The driver took him quickly along pitted roads and through the streets of a torn city to a chapel in a military compound. "Welcome, welcome," the Jewish chaplain greeted him. "How I have been waiting for you! Welcome!" The interior of the chapel was very hot. The chaplain was a major, round, cheerful, pink-cheeked. "Take off your coat. Relax. Stay awhile. Ha, ha! Can I get you a cup of coffee?"

He stayed there Shabbat and attended services. Saturday night and Sunday they celebrated Purim. The night service was well attended. Afterward he sat in the chapel office with the chaplain, who was methodically emptying the contents of a bottle of bourbon into himself. "Why don't you join in?" the chaplain kept asking. "Jewish law says to get tight on Purim. Must join in. Celebrate. Happy Purim. Have one. Have two. Go ahead." The office was hot. The lids of the oil stoves in the chapel glowed pink. The chaplain leaned across the desk and said to Gershon, "Listen. Watch out in this place, you hear? Watch yourself. Many temptations. Beware. Where there are no men, you be a man. Understand? Have another drink. Place full of pits and traps. I leave untouched. Two more months and goodbye. Hate this place, hate it. But I leave untouched. Not like so many others. No, don't touch the stoves. Like it to be warm. Like it toasty. Cold outside, hot inside. Like it that way. Finish your drink. Freshen it up a bit? Two more months. My God! This is not a place for Jews."

The next afternoon Gershon reported to the Eighth Army chief of chaplains. "Glad to have you with us, chaplain. Please sit down. Tired?" He was a short trim man with warm, gray eyes and a kindly face. "I'll bet you're tired. Well, we can put you with headquarters in Seoul, and you can take over the Jewish chapel when he leaves, or we can put you up north with a division." He gazed across the desk at Gershon and waited. The wind blew against the translucent plastic windows of the office. Gershon looked at the maps on the wall and the Bible on the desk and at the cross and silver birds on the chief of chaplains' uniform. "North," he said, and was not sure why he said it. The chief of chaplains looked at him a moment, nodded briefly, and shook his hand.

That afternoon a jeep returned him to the replacement depot. He slept on a cot in a wide room filled with officers. A bus brought him to the railroad station in Seoul the next morning. He rode north in an old rickety train with wooden seats and protective iron grates outside the windows. The train was cold and crowded with officers and enlisted men. Some were returning from leave in Japan and were raucous with happy memories. Others sat staring out the windows. It was snowing hard. The train moved slowly, stopping often. Gershon sat next to a heavy-set infantry major who was asleep. Thick blowing snow had obliterated the landscape. A blank whiteness pressed against the windows. He rode through the day and watched the snow slowly darken. On occasion the snow was parted by a sudden gust, and he saw thatched huts and narrow valleys and steep hills. Once a dog ran alongside the train for a moment, then vanished. The windows turned slate-gray. The train stopped with a jarring lurch and was engulfed in dense, driven, buffeting clouds of snow. He could feel the car quivering in the wind.

They started up again, slowly, and went on slowly a long time. It was dark when they came to their destination, and all inside were silent with exhaustion. He stood on the station in the snow, and someone called out instructions. He rode in the back of a two-and-a-half-ton truck over rutted snow-packed icy roads. In a replacement depot whose generator was inoperative he handed over his field 201 file and was processed by the eery lights of flickering candles. Long shadows danced on the floor and walls. A dark form materialized at his side. He felt a tap on his shoulder and saw, vaguely, a hand motioning to him. They went over to a dark corner away from the others. The young man introduced himself in a low voice. "Charlie Taron, rabbi. Headquarters. I never thought we'd get a Jewish chaplain this far up north. Boy. Welcome. Listen. You need any paperwork done real fast, rabbi, you pick up the phone and call me. I got friends all up and down. We'll walk the work through for you. Won't sit a minute on anyone's desk. Okay? Just pick up the phone. Great to see you, rabbi. Really great."

Later he walked through drifting snow to the mess hall. He ate the vegetables and ignored the fried chicken. He had coffee and accepted the cigarette offered him by a medical captain. He coughed as he inhaled the smoke and had a clear vision of his uncle—white goatee, lined, pallid features, weary eyes, coughing. What time was it now in the States? He did not know. His eyes were heavy, and he felt the quickening beat of his heart.

He slept in a cot in a crowded Quonset, and in the night the oil stove died, and he had in his life never believed such cold could exist. He woke into the cold. He lay on an icy pillow. His sheets were icy. He dared not move. He listened to the snow blowing against the Quonset. He opened his eyes and stared into utter un- relieved darkness. The Quonset was silent save for the deep breath- ing and snores of sleeping men. He shivered uncontrollably and felt all his body naked to the air. To take his mind off the cold, he reached into himself and summoned forth remembered Merkavah texts of ancient ascents through chill skies. He lay in the darkness and imagined letters and words playing clearly before him in the icy air. "Rabbi Akiva said: 'In that hour when I ascended on high, I made marks at the entrances of heaven . . . and when I came to the curtain, angels of destruction went forth to destroy me. God said to them: "Leave this elder alone, for he is worthy to contemplate My glory." ' " And Gershon saw too the words spoken by Metatron, the prince of God, the messenger, to Rabbi Ishmael: "Come and behold the letters by which the heaven and the earth were created, the letters by which the mountains and hills were created, the letters by which the seas and rivers were created . . . the letters by which the planets and zodiacal signs were created . . . the letters by which the Throne of Glory and the wheels of the Merkavah were created. . . . And I walked by his side and he took me by his hand and raised me upon his wings and showed me those letters, all of them, that are graven with a flaming style on the Throne of Glory. And sparks go forth from them. . . ." And he remembered these words of Rabbi Akiva: "I beheld and saw the whole universe and perceived it as it is; I ascended in a carriage of fire. . . ."

The texts were of no comfort. He fell into a fitful sleep.

In the morning a jeep took him between roadside hillocks of snow to the office of the division chaplain. Sunlight shone on the snow and hurt his eyes. The tents and Quonsets of the division lay buried in the snow. Men were digging paths behind the barbed wire fences. He rode to a Quonset at the foot of a low hill.

The division chaplain was a short, portly lieutenant colonel with a completely bald head, slightly bulging blue eyes, and moist lips. He had short fingers, a pudgy hand, and a protruding belly. "Hello, hello. They told us you were coming. The place takes getting used to, doesn't it. Well, let's see. What'll we do with you? Haven't had a Jewish chaplain on division level yet. No. Fort Knox? Really? Imagine. Big army. Right hand doesn't know left hand. Didn't think you guys ever went below corps. Okay. Anyway, anyway. Let's see. Schmidt is going, so is Rose. Thompson coming in. So. Okay. It looks like this. Got a spot for you. Nice spot. Put you in the medics. You'll take care of the battalion and all the Jewish personnel in the division. Wait until you see the chapel. Nicest one in the whole division. Needs some finishing. But beautiful. New. The present assistant is not Jewish. A Mormon boy, I believe. You can change him if you want. All set? Good luck. Give me a call if you need anything. That's my job. Keep you happy, keep me happy. Okay?"

That afternoon a jeep took him to his new unit, and a company clerk directed him to his quarters. He would live alone in one of the Jamesways in the officers' section of the compound. It was a small, hutlike canvas dwelling with a wooden floor, a cot, a makeshift desk and washstand. Two walls curved inward to form an arching roof. The windows were plastic. He lay awake that night and listened to the wind blow fresh snow against the hut. After a while he fell asleep. Sometime in the night the fuel line attached to the oil drum outside froze, and the fire died in the potbellied stove. He woke and lay very still in the narrow bed. The air grew so cold it seemed to burn. He lay awake and listened to the rapid beating of his heart. He had been gone now fifteen days.

He woke to a bitter cold morning brilliant with sunshine.

Similar days followed. An icy sun had settled upon the land. The winds seemed strangely cruel, and when he asked about them he was told that they blew down from the Siberian tundras in the north. He went about in boots, long underwear beneath his woolen uniform, a fur-lined parka and hood, and gloves, and was always cold. He seemed unable to adjust to the new cycle of time, caught himself dozing at odd hours of the day and lay wide awake long into the nights. He had little appetite during meals. His eyelids and head felt weighted. From time to time he gazed at his reflection in mirrors and did not know who he was.

On the morning of his first full day, he had reported to the battalion commanding officer, a short trim man with red hair, pale eyes, and a small mouth. "Anything I can do to help, chaplain. Anything. Let me know. Morale is very important in my outfit. Keep it high. Men get the blues, work falls to pieces. Learned that in the big war. I flew the big bombers. That's right. Bombed the hell out of Japan in the big war. When morale in a plane goes down, so does the plane. Did you see the chapel? It's a fine chapel. I'm very proud of our chapel. Did you see the hospital? We definitely need a new hospital. Well, good luck. Welcome aboard, chaplain."

Later that morning he met his assistant and was taken through the chapel. The assistant was a shy lad fresh out of high school, blond-haired, ruddy-cheeked, smiling, his deep blue eyes covered by shell-rimmed glasses that gave him a misty daydreamer's look. His name was Roger Tat. He wore neatly pressed olive-greens, polished boots, and the maroon scarf of the medical battalion, and he showed Gershon around the chapel. The office at the rear of the chapel was large and neat. There were two desks and filing cabinets and chairs and bookcases. There were windows, a typewriter, a field telephone. The room had its own oil stove. The air was warm, comfortable. But Gershon felt cold.

"And here I keep the Bibles, sir. And the prayer books for the different services. Here are reading material and the wine." He spoke in a soft voice.

"Where are you from, Roger?"

"Salt Lake City, sir."

"Is that music paper on your desk?"

"I write music, sir. But only in my spare time."

"Can you drive a jeep?"

"Oh yes, sir. And I'm very good with a weapon."

"You are?"

"Yes, sir. I am required to carry my weapon whenever we travel outside division by jeep."

"Where are the Jewish services held now?"

"At regiment, sir. The Jewish prayer books are there."

"I think I'll want the services moved here. I don't travel on my Sabbath."

"Yes, sir. Seventh-Day Adventists are here now Friday night and Saturday morning, sir."

"They are?"

"Yes, sir."

"We'll have to think what to do about that. Do we get our own jeep, Roger?"

"Yes, sir. I've already arranged for that, sir. I also called division air and told them you'll be flying about a lot."

"You did?"

"We have a regiment in the hills beyond the thirty-eighth parallel, sir."

"We do? No one told me that. How far beyond?"

"More than an hour away by jeep, sir. Over a range of hills."

"Show me the rest of the chapel, Roger."

It was a fine chapel: white walls, clean cement floor, metal chairs, large pulpit with lecterns, flags, candelabrum. A stove stood in the center of the floor between the rows of chairs, the flue climbing out through the curved ceiling. My first synagogue, Gershon said to himself. A pulpit rabbi. In Korea. But the chapel still wore a raw look; it had about it an air of incompleteness. He gazed at the altar and the lectern: lacquered light wood reflecting the diffused sunlight that came in through the closed translucent windows; brass candelabrum polished to a high shine. He felt for the first time since leaving New York the vague warmth of a comforting eagerness.

They spent some time together in the office, setting up the files and records and counseling hours. The field phone rang a few times, inquiries from various units about the truth of the rumor that a Jewish chaplain was now with the medical battalion. Gershon sat behind his large dark-wood desk and listened to Roger Tat's replies. The oil stove burned smoothly, warming the air. Still he felt cold. Later, on the way to the officers mess for lunch, he thought to circle the chapel to have a look at it from the outside. It was clean and white. Patches of snow clung to the roof. A narrow bed of crushed whitish rock, much of it covered with snow, gave it a neat border and a New England look. In the morning he had entered the chapel through the rear door that led to the office. Now he stood at the front of the chapel. Wood panels reached from its base and were smoothly molded to the curve of the roof. The door was also of wood, its brass knobs and hinges glistening in the sun. The wood had been stained a rich walnut, the grain showing in undulating

circles and loops and arabesques. Incised deeply into the panel next
to the door, and taking up nearly the entire height of the entrance,
was a cross. On the roof above the entrance rose a delicately angled
steeple topped by a short white wooden cross that glinted in the sunlight. Gershon had seen the crosses the day before; yet he had not
seen them. Now he stood there looking at the two crosses. After a
while he turned and walked the length of the compound to the
officers mess.

The compound lay in a flat valley alongside the main supply route
from Seoul. This was a wide unpaved road crowded with military
traffic. Beyond the road was the railroad. The division airstrip lay
parallel to the tracks. Single-engined L-19's and Beavers came and
went regularly. A line of snow-covered hills bordered the airstrip.

Gershon sat alone at a table in the officers mess and gazed out
the glass panes of a window at the hill behind the battalion. He ate
the scrambled eggs which he had asked the chef to substitute for the
ham menu, stipulating that the eggs be fried only in vegetable oil.
The chef, an elderly Korean with brown, leathery skin and shiny,
dark eyes, had nodded agreeably, uncomprehendingly. Beyond the
mess was the bar and club room, which was empty. Officers ate
quickly and left. There were brief introductions, handshakes. Some
of the officers were from New York. What's new, chappy? Anything
new? Anything? You hear about that cold wave in the east? Yeah,
in *Stars and Stripes*. Good to have you with us. Join you, chaplain?
How was the trip? Is that all you're eating?

He returned to the chapel after lunch. Two young soldiers were
waiting to see him. Counseling. Roger busied himself sorting book-
lets, polishing brass, preparing the jeep. Later Gershon came out of
the chapel office into the cruel and bitter cold of the early winter
night, went around to the entrance, gazed at the crosses, and trudged
across the frozen compound to his quarters.

He wrote a letter to his aunt and uncle, requesting certain books
and canned meats. He washed in a basin with potable water from
a five-gallon can, shaved with his electric razor, which he had attached with extension cords to the three-way plug in the ceiling
wire into which also was screwed an electric bulb. The interior of
the Jamesway, with its cot and makeshift desk and old wooden

chair and rickety bookcase and packing-crate dresser, looked jerry-built but neat and clean. A Korean boy, whom he shared with other officers, cleaned, did his laundry, polished his boots. The boy had appeared in the early morning—"I your houseboy, sah"—and, without a further word, had gone to work. Gershon stood near the basin, combed his hair, gazed at the face in the hand mirror that hung from a nail he had found protruding conveniently from one of the Jamesway ribs, and saw the pallid skin and the dark circles beneath the eyes. He saw the face and did not see it. He went out of the Jamesway into the cutting wind. It seemed to be watching for him, that wind, waiting to pounce and clutch. He walked quickly to the officers mess.

The battalion commander hailed him from a table. His small puckered lips formed a small smile around his cigarette. He tilted his head, closing one eye against the smoke. "How'd it go today, chaplain?"

"Fine, sir."

"What do you think of our chapel?"

"It's quite nice, sir."

"I built that chapel. It beats dropping bombs, I'll tell you that. Is your assistant working out okay?"

"He seems very good, sir."

"Glad to hear it, chaplain. Enjoy your dinner. Our steak is also very good."

Gershon joined two doctors at their table, waived the steak, and ate the vegetables. The doctors talked about two men brought in the night before. They had drunk anti-freeze in an attempt to keep warm. A guard had found them in a jeep near the quartermaster compound. One had died that morning; the other had survived but was blind. Mountain kids. The Ozarks. Keep warm and die. Don't even realize that booze makes you colder. Koreans know how to keep warm. Fire on one side of hooch, smoke under floor and out other side. Keeps you warm. Was the boy going to die? Gershon asked. "No," one of the doctors said. "Too bad, chaplain," the other doctor said. "He's better off dying," the first doctor said. "All concur there was brain damage." The two doctors got to their feet and sauntered into the club. Gershon returned to his Jamesway.

He lay in his bed reading a Kabbalah text that he had brought with him. Promptly at eleven o'clock the battalion generator shut down. The bulb went brown and died. He stared into the darkness. The oil stove burned with a low, even flame. He thought to use the piss tubes behind the hut, but he feared the cold. He closed his eyes. After a moment he had a blurred vision of his aunt and uncle. They stood before the chapel gazing at the entrance panels and the steeple. He saw them speaking but could not make out their words. He fell asleep.

In the night the fuel line froze, and the fire died. He woke and felt the cold like flaming air upon his skin. The next morning he learned over breakfast that one of the tents in a nearby infantry regiment had burned down during the night. The stove had been set too high in an effort to keep the line from freezing. No one was hurt.

He finished his breakfast, crossed the compound, and came into the hospital. The boy who had been blinded by the anti-freeze lay in a cot, asleep, breathing shallowly. He had blond hair and skin the color of chalk. There were tubes in his arms. An orderly stood near the cot.

"He's going out by chopper to the evac hospital," the orderly said in a low voice.

Gershon stared at the boy. "Did someone call the division chaplain's office?"

"I don't know anything about that, sir."

Gershon could not take his eyes off the boy. The blanket over his still form rose and fell slowly with his breathing. He turned abruptly and went back out through the hospital and crossed the short intervening ground to the chapel. The hospital comprised lines of parallel Quonsets connected by short corridors that leaked air and were cold. The Quonsets were dingy and dilapidated and poorly lighted. Beyond the hospital were the tents of the noncommissioned officers and enlisted personnel. The tents and Quonsets were a dreary olive-green in the morning sunlight.

Roger sat at his desk, reading. He looked up when Gershon entered.

"We ought to call division about that blind soldier," Gershon said.

"I've already done that, sir." He closed his book and placed it with stiff care on his desk.

"You have? Well, good. What are you reading, Roger?"

"The Book of Mormon, sir."

"Could they have been that cold? To drink anti-freeze?"

"They weren't the first to do that."

"Is there anything that needs to be done by me this morning?"

"We ought to set up a schedule of services, sir."

"Yes. All right. Thank you, Roger."

They sent memos to the division commander, attention office of the division chaplain, requesting that Jewish services be moved from regiment to medics, that the Seventh-Day Adventist service be moved from medics to regiment, that the Jewish prayer books, synagogue vestments, and religious articles be moved from regiment to medics, and that the new schedule of services be approved and published in the division bulletin. To the battalion commander went a memo requesting that the battalion carpenters construct a set of Jewish tablets for the chapel, estimated time required one hour.

"Best to include a drawing of the tablets, sir," said Roger.

"Thank you."

Later in the morning he counseled a sergeant whose wife back home was threatening to leave him and a corporal who had been caught the night before in the nearby village with a whore.

"She keeps me warm, chaplain, sir." He sat in the chair and spoke directly and unashamedly to Gershon. "I can't take the cold. I go to the village all the time. Damn MP's got nothing to do but raid."

Later Gershon was on his way out to lunch when he heard the helicopter. It landed quickly on the frozen earth, enveloping the valley in its buffeting noise. Men rushed from the hospital and strapped to the helicopter stretcher a still form. The helicopter raised itself from the earth, circled tentatively, and flew off toward the range of hills in the west. The small crowd that had gathered began to disperse.

Gershon crossed the compound to the officers mess. During lunch he sat quietly with some doctors and listened to them talk about non-specific urethritis. "Outpaced only by upper respiratory infections," said one doctor. "I don't have any statistics, but my soul tells me I'm right." "His soul," another doctor said. "That's your department, chaplain." "A figure of speech," the first doctor said. "I don't know about souls," a third doctor said. "All I know is that if this weather doesn't warm up soon, we may run out of penicillin because of all the guys going to the village to get out of the cold." "It doesn't change when the weather gets warm," the first doctor said. "All agree it doesn't change one bit."

On his way back to the chapel after lunch, Gershon stopped near the H and H Company Quonset and stared across the compound. He had a sudden brief vision of his aunt and uncle. He saw them go past the entrance guardpost that faced the main supply route. They moved slowly past the rows of ambulances, shuffling on the frozen snow. His uncle held his aunt's arm. They wore their old dark coats. His uncle had on his gray fedora, and his aunt wore a gray woolen scarf over her white hair. Their eyes were moist with cold. They stopped at the entrance to the chapel and looked up. He could not hear their words. He saw his uncle's goatee move agitatedly. Then they turned and walked slowly out of the compound and went on up the main supply route and, as Gershon watched, an old Korean came down the wide icy road bent nearly double beneath a load of brush he had brought down from the hills to keep his village hut warm.

Aside from a few kabbalistic works, he had also brought with him a small Hebrew Bible and a thin volume of Talmud. He spent part of the afternoon preparing his sermon for the Friday evening service, then wrote out a memo to the commanding general, Eighth Army, requesting two altar chairs and sixteen pews with kneelers for the chapel. He titled the memo "Beautification of Medical Battalion Chapel" and sent it to the attention of the Eighth Army chaplain through channels. He wrote: "There are no pews in our medical battalion chapel. Folding chairs are used for pews. These are inadequate because of lack of kneelers. It is estimated that sixteen pews can be constructed for approximately $350. This will do much to enhance the beauty of the chapel. Further, the pulpit at present has no chairs. The folding chairs that are now being used detract considerably from the beauty of the altar. Two pulpit chairs can be constructed for approximately $160. All construction can be accomplished with the use of Korean carpenters."

To Roger's look of surprise and admiration, he responded with, "I asked around during lunch. I got a little bored listening to all the talk about non-specific urethritis. Is it all right?"

"Oh yes, sir."

Roger quickly typed the memo on the old Underwood on his desk, and Gershon signed it. Outside the air grew dark. He went back to his Jamesway to prepare for dinner. The wind blew knives of ice across the compound. The mucus froze in his nostrils. He saw the guards slowly circling the perimeter fence and could not understand how they suffered the cold.

That night after dinner the battalion commander invited Gershon to join him for a drink. They sat at the bar. Gershon had a Scotch. The major was drinking bourbon. The night lay black upon the windows. Men sat at tables drinking and playing cards. Three doctors were rolling for drinks at the bar. There was a mirror over the bar behind the shelves of bottles, and it reflected the naked bulbs that hung from the ceiling wires. The walls were bare and unpainted. At the rear of the club near the door that led out back were stacked unopened cartons of beer.

The major looked to be in his early forties. He had a thin, high voice and a nervous look in his eyes. He was a short man, with thick red hair and small florid features. There was reddish down on the backs of his hands.

"Here's to you, chaplain. Good luck."

"Thank you, major."

"Yes, sir, I built that chapel. Took some of the material that should have gone into this club and put it into the chapel. Yes, sir."

"It's a very good chapel, major."

"Needs to be finished, you know. Need to finish this club too. A scandal, this club. We haven't had a chaplain here in about a month. The man who preceded you was a scandal. Enough said. Have another drink, chaplain. Keep you warm."

"Thank you."

One of the company commanders, a burly man with a barrel chest, called from a table, "We're getting a game going, Doug."

"Be there soon, Harry," the major called back. He sipped from his drink. "You're from New York? I flew over New York once in a B-29. I looked down and wondered what it would be like if the city were bombed. I never looked down at the cities we bombed. Except the night we really fire-bombed Tokyo. I looked down at that." He sipped again from his glass. "God, I loved flying those planes. I loved the way the seat would grab my backside during takeoff. I loved that."

"My cousin flew fighters during the war," Gershon said, and immediately wondered why he had offered up that memory.

"Did he?" The major's smallish face lit up. Gershon found himself bathed in an unexpected stream of admiration. "I couldn't qualify with fighters. Reflexes weren't sharp enough. What outfit was he with?"

"I don't remember. He was shot down. They never found him."

"Sorry to hear that." The major was silent a moment, puckered lips in somber thought. "My bombardier kept saying, 'We don't have to look down at the fires, do we? I'll drop them but I won't look down.' Damn good bombardier. He could put one down a smokestack. But he wouldn't look down afterward. Nice kid from Cedar Rapids. Nice kid."

"Hey, Doug," the company commander called. "We're aging rapidly."

"I had a quick look at your request for pews, chaplain. Good. Very good. Can't leave the chapel the way it is. Scandalous. Finish it. Back you all the way. Have another drink on me. Hey, Paul." He turned to the orderly behind the bar. "Give the chaplain another drink and put it on my tab. Take it easy, chaplain."

He slid off the bar stool and went somewhat unsteadily to the table, a short, thin man, holding his drink with care.

A few minutes later Gershon crossed the compound in a freezing wind. He shivered at the piss tubes near his Jamesway. The warm air of the Jamesway interior was of some comfort as he got out of his clothes. He felt a faint buzzing in his head from the alcohol and seemed unable to rid himself of the sensation of cold. He lay in the cot reading the Kabbalah text by the light of the naked bulb. The wind whistled mournfully against the canvas of the Jamesway. At eleven o'clock the light dimmed and died.

He slept fitfully and woke in the night and listened to the dying of the oil stove. It made loud banging cracking sounds as it con-

tracted into death, the same sounds that would come from the
radiators in the old apartment house when the furnace fire went
low and the janitor was too drunk to rise. For a moment he thought
to go outside and kick at the fuel line to dislodge the ice that was
blocking the flow of oil. But he dreaded the cold. He lay very still
as the canvas walls vanished, and outside and inside air mingled
and seeped through his blankets deep into his bed. He felt the crawl
of the cold air across his helpless form, felt the cold in his jaws and
teeth and hair follicles, felt entombed in black ice. He slept, finally,
in a paralysis of exhaustion.

He woke in terror. Along the fringes of a mist-filled dream he had
seen the vaguely outlined but unmistakable form of Arthur Leiden
beckoning to him. The sight of the figure had filled him with dread.
Now, awake, he had no memory of the reason for his fear. He got
out of the cot, shivering in the icy air of the Jamesway. You dressed
swiftly with numbed fingers inside the frozen membrane surround-
ing you; you went out to the piss tubes; you kicked at the fuel line.
You returned to the Jamesway and dropped a lighted match into
the stove. The oil caught. You poured water from the five-gallon
can into the basin, put the basin on the stove. The air in the Jamesway began to grow warm. You washed your hands and face and
brushed your teeth and shaved. You prayed the morning service.
You lingered over passages like "Sovereign of all the worlds: not
because of our righteousness do we bring before You our pleas,
but because of Your many mercies. What are we? What is our
life? . . ." And over passages like "Praise the Lord. . . . His word
moves swiftly on its course; He sends down snow white as wool; He
scatters hoar frost thick as ashes; He hurls pieces of ice like crumbs."
And you lingered at some length over the words "Praised be God for
the infinite wisdom with which He created the radiance of the
sun. . . . The stars all about the heavens proclaim His might. . . .
Be You praised, O Lord our God, for the excellence of Your handiwork, above all for the stars radiant with light, which You did
create. . . . May Your name be praised forever, O our King, who
fashioned unseen forces, ministering angels who stand in the heights
of the universe . . . and with soft and clear tones chant together a
sacred melody: 'Holy holy holy is the Lord of hosts, all the earth is

filled with His glory. . . .'" You lingered over these words because their meaning was suddenly no longer so clear as you had once thought. Then you finished praying and removed your tefillin and put on your parka and gloves and fur-lined cap and went out into the frozen compound where the wind lashed your face and brought tears to your eyes and stiffened the mucous membranes inside your nostrils. . . . No doubt the prayers had been written with only a Mediterranean climate in mind. What had the words meant all the centuries to those in the vast northern wastes of Russia and Poland? Dreams? Visions? And, as he walked over the frozen snow, glimpsing through wind-induced tears the traffic on the main supply route and soldiers huddled in their parkas, he saw with no sensation of surprise the tall, trim, hatless figure—dark coat, red scarf, longish face, bald head—of Jakob Keter outside the door to the officers mess, where it waited long enough for him to get within about twenty feet of it before it misted over and disappeared. He felt a strange sense of elation and sat at a table with some doctors and chatted and ate a large breakfast.

The elation vanished when he entered the chapel. He found waiting in his office the orderly whom he had met at the bedside of the blinded soldier. Roger was seated at his small corner desk; he sat stiffly, reading, his back very straight, his knees together.

"Can I talk to you, rabbi?" the orderly asked.

Gershon removed his cap and gloves and parka.

"It's very personal," the orderly said. He had curly dark hair and black eyes and a pale intense face the color of paper. On his uniform was the stenciled name Rosen. The stove burned and the air was warm. The orderly stood, waiting.

Roger put down his book. "I can tend to the jeep, sir."

"How did the major get that memo so quickly, Roger?"

"I walked it through to his desk, sir."

"Thank you."

Roger put on his parka and left.

"Sit down, Rosen. What's your first name?"

"Gabriel, rabbi."

"Where are you from?"

"New York. Brooklyn. Borough Park." He spoke softly in a tone cadenced with tribal familiarity.

Borough Park. A citadel of the very orthodox. Private homes with lawns, spacious apartment houses, clean tree-lined streets, large stores, bright with light. There, no houses burned suddenly in the night. There, Jews went about carrying with ease and certainty their freight of inherited responsibilities as guardians of the ancient covenant. Gabriel Rosen was a long way from home.

"What can I do for you, Gabriel?"

The boy's pale features suddenly put on an intimate look, a barely discernible recognition signal: a faint upturning of the lips, a slight narrowing of the eyes. Gershon felt himself being tested for tribal loyalties.

"The others chose me to represent them, rabbi. There are six of us in the hospital. Pharmacy, X-ray, things like that. Six of us."

Gershon sat behind his large dark-wood desk and waited. Old annoyances had begun to stir within him like awakening ghosts.

"They said to say welcome, rabbi. We're all real glad you're here. It'll make a difference, you know? Sometimes they give us a hard time." He paused, smiled thinly, waited. When he realized Gershon would not respond, he wet his lips and went on. "They asked me to ask you about the assistant. That's the biggest question. The assistant."

Gershon, not understanding, said, "What assistant?"

Gabriel Rosen said, "Your assistant. The goy."

Gershon said, "What about my assistant?" The annoyance had mounted swiftly, uncontrollably, at the deliberate epithet, the tribeword. Why was his long-forgotten yeshiva past suddenly returning to him in a chapel in Korea? Weariness? Lack of sleep? Change of time zones? Abrupt exposure to below-zero cold? Repressed realization of how close he had brought himself—without really understanding why—to this cliff-edge of death? Tanks, rifles, artillery, aircraft, soldiers on whose faces lay the stultifying boredom of waiting and the easy familiarity with war and death—how wistfully some returning noncoms talked of Korean battlefields and the major talked of his years as a bomber pilot! Had he, Gershon, been chafed to rawness by only three days in a front-line battalion? Who was this white-faced, skinny kid from Borough Park who had begun to raise the gorge in his throat, the silenced rage no one had ever heard or seen? Gershon hoped he could retain self-control, could keep the scraping annoyance and buried rage out of his voice. He said, again, "What about him?"

Gabriel Rosen said, with no indication of backing away and with the egalitarian tone of one Jew to another, "We think the assistant should be one of us. A Jew. Not a goy."

"He's my assistant, Gabriel. No one else's."

"It's against Jewish law. *Yayin nesech*. We can't drink wine he touches."

"You think he'll dedicate the wine to pagan gods, to Jesus, to Buddha? Don't worry about it. I'll pour the wine. You can pour your own wine. If I decide to keep him."

"The others all say it's wrong, rabbi."

"I'll decide. Not the others."

"You don't have to get angry, rabbi."

"Where did you go to school, Gabriel?"

He named a yeshiva in Brooklyn.

"You were drafted from a yeshiva?"

"My marks weren't good. The teacher had it in for me."

"What else can I do for you, Gabriel?"

"The assistant said services will be held here starting next week."

"That's right."

"The crosses, rabbi. What can we do about the crosses?"

"I'll think about it, Gabriel."

"A goy for an assistant and crosses on the shul. Who'll believe it when I write home? It's upside down here."

Gershon sat alone afterward, echoes of the conversation churning within him. Street words lurched through his head, the language of rage. The smug superiority of those certain of salvation. Long-dimmed visions of teachers in dingy classrooms teaching the road map of relationships with the Higher Power, the carefully delineated turns and bends, highways, byways, bridges, the surfeit of text and commentary, the richness to the point of glutinous choking, no new lights, no unexpected visions that chilled the spine, and a sharp voice if you turned to stare out the window at the way the pigeons strutted along the sidewalk in the sunlight. How could a lone soldier in this distant outpost of American power have awakened those dormant memories? He was tired, tired. He needed the coming Shabbat. He would rest.

Roger returned, his face flushed with cold. Icy air blew in through the momentarily opened door. They went through the mail, administrative newsletters of information from division, from army: preparations for Easter and Passover; a late spring retreat in Japan; items to include in the monthly chaplain reports; how to apply for welfare funds; how to keep a record of chapel collections. Words, dead words built of dead letters. "Rug sets for cantonment chapels are stocked at the Columbus Depot, United States Army, Columbus 15, Ohio. The color of the carpeting is Apple Green. . . ." "It is requested that an individual budget for each chapel in Korea be prepared and submitted on attached blanks following instructions furnished in paragraph 4 of Inclosure No. 1 hereto. . . ." "Completed budget forms in quadruplicate will be forwarded by supervisory chaplains. . . ." He found himself staring at his hands: white, bony, dry with cold. Why was he fixed on his hands? He felt he could not move them. He sat in his chair at the desk and had the strange sensation that he would never again be able to move. He would will himself to movement, but nothing would happen. Motionless. He felt within himself a cold and heavy weight. Before his test for ordination at the yeshiva he had felt this way: a freighted joylessness; everything known, the mapped road of reading marked and memorized, no lights, no lights, no bursts of surprise, no ascent from the choreographed landscape of text and commentaries. He took the test and had the distinct sensation he had remained motionless through all the hours of tense questioning in that small room with the long, glass-topped table and the wooden chairs and the cigarette smoke like stale fog through which hummed and shone the ceiling fluorescents. Why was he remembering all this now in this flat and broken valley in this torn and ruined land?

That afternoon it began to snow again. It was a soft powdery crystal fall of thick, dry flakes, and it came without a wind in a straight descent from a milk-white sky. The air was cold, five below zero, but the absence of wind effected a benevolent deceit upon one's face and eyes. There could be no thought now of attempting the long walk to regiment that night for the Friday evening service. Today's *Stars and Stripes* had headlined the death of forty-four Korean soldiers in a snowslide northeast of Seoul. This was ice-age snow, malevolent, deadly.

Gershon crossed the compound to his quarters. The Jamesway was swept clean, the bed made, the five-gallon can filled, underwear laundered and folded, washbasin clean and dry, stove burning. The houseboy—what was his name? Something Kim or Kim Something —had come and gone, invisibly. Gershon washed and shaved and prayed the service alone in the Jamesway. A long moment of calm descended upon him. "Awake, arise, for your light has dawned!" he chanted softly. "The Presence of the Lord has shone upon you!" And, a while later, he murmured, "And the heaven and the earth were completed and all their host. And on the seventh day God had completed His work. . . . And He rested on the seventh day from all His work. . . ." And, outside, the snow continued to fall, silently, through air strangely still and barely cold. He walked through the snow to the officers mess and chose to eat alone. The mess was noisy; the bar was crowded. He returned to the Jamesway. The snow had mounted quite some inches above the foot of the door and a hillock tumbled into the Jamesway with the opening of the door and proceeded immediately to melt and form puddles on the plywood floor. For a while he sat very still in the chair and stared into the dimness of the corner across from the washstand. The bulb burned at the end of its naked cord; the stove gave off its waves of warmth. The hut was quiet, the canvas walls unmoving. A deep, thickening silence was falling upon him, a dense white cloak of cottony snow. He felt drowsy in the warmth but knew he was awake.

And then he had a vision. He saw clearly Arthur Leiden and Jakob Keter strolling across a large green lawn, talking together inaudibly. In the distance beyond white birch trees lay a crystal lake. Tall leafy oaks graced the summer sky. Along the lawn came Arthur's mother, bearing a tray of afternoon tea things. She moved gracefully across the grass, lovely but unsmiling, and called to Arthur and to Jakob Keter. They turned their heads toward her. From the sun porch of the house—a large stately Tudor—came Arthur's father, together with Albert Einstein and Harry Truman. All converged upon a round glass-topped iron lawn table with white filigreed legs. Deep in conversation, they had their tea. Now, abruptly, Arthur was the only one speaking. They sat around the table on white iron chairs, listening intently to Arthur. Suddenly Arthur's mother put down her cup and walked off the lawn into the house. Arthur's father, with a gesture of weary resignation, excused himself and followed. A moment or two later Truman and Einstein went off together into the woods alongside the house. Arthur sat alone, gazing at the lake and the birches. He brushed a hand across his eyes. He sat there staring at the birches and the lake, and weeping. Albert Einstein and Harry Truman emerged from the woods and came over to Arthur. All three then sat at the table, talking softly. The vision—utterly soundless—faded.

He sat in the Jamesway, chilled and unnerved, and did not know what to do. The unheard anguish in Arthur filled the air of the hut like a dark snow upon the landscape of a soul. He trembled as he got up from the chair. When he went out to use the piss tubes he found himself nearly knee-deep in snow. The night was muffled, the mounded earth a pale ghostly white without form and contour. He lay in the cot and tried to read his Kabbalah text. Snow rumbled softly off the curved roof, burying the Jamesway to nearly half its height. Precisely at eleven, the generator was shut down and the light went out. He fell into an agitated sleep in which Karen appeared, and he held her, and she clung to him, and both yielded to the fever that possessed them. He woke to the sounds of the dying stove. The flame leaped and flickered; through the space along the rim of the lid he saw its gasping dance. It died, and the cold invaded the hut, and he fell finally into a helpless sleep. A moment before he slid into darkness he realized he would be unable to light the stove in the morning; fire was forbidden him on his Sabbath. That was a moment of deepest despair, that final flickering moment of consciousness.

He was awakened by distant scraping sounds. He opened his eyes. Faint light filtered through his windows. There was a loud thumping noise on the side of the Jamesway; it was repeated a number of times. Then someone knocked on his door. He rose into the cold and went to the door and stood aside as he pulled it open. He saw Roger and the Korean houseboy. They came quickly inside.

Gershon stared at them. They were red with cold and flecked with snow. They smiled. They had dug him out, Roger said. He had remembered about the Jewish faith and fire on the Sabbath, he said.

He and Sammy Kim had dug him out and broken the ice in the line. Did he have the chaplain's permission to light the stove? Sammy Kim would warm some water. Was the chaplain all right? Everything was buried in almost twenty inches of snow. The entire division, paralyzed. Sammy Kim smiled timidly, puttered about in silence.

Gershon looked at Roger Tat and Sammy Kim as they moved about the Jamesway. Roger's shell-rimmed glasses were wet. With his long thin fingers he adjusted the nozzle on the fuel line to control the flow of oil. The houseboy—short, thin, lithe, yellow-brown skin, high cheekbones, dark slanted eyes; about fourteen years of age—glanced shyly at Gershon. "Okay, chaplain, sah?" He put the heated basin of water on the stand.

"Thank you," Gershon said. He looked at them and saw them.

The fire leaped, danced, whirled, a long yellow curling tongue of flame. The air grew warm. They left. Gershon dressed and washed and prayed the Shabbat service. He gazed at the light in the stove.

In the weeks that followed he made a number of choices. This was during the period of time when in the outside world Eisenhower decided to run again for the presidency, Syrian anti-aircraft fire brought down an Israeli plane, a cold wave in Europe killed 919 people, four Swedish jets flew into a hill, and New York City was buried in a monstrous blizzard. He worried about his aunt and uncle in the old apartment house. These were the choices he made. He informed the division chaplain that he intended to keep Roger Tat as his assistant. He set up a schedule of services for the infantry regiment above the thirty-eighth parallel and traveled by jeep with chains on the tires and a weapon on the floor next to Roger. The roads were heavy with traffic, and alongside the roads, across the shallow river they forded to avoid the frozen mountain passes, were the mud and straw houses of prostitutes, smoke pouring from the chimneys and jeeps parked at the doors.

In the middle of April, about two weeks after Passover, the Seoul Jewish chaplain went home. "Untouched," he said exultantly to Gershon. "God was good to me. Now you can request to be moved to Seoul. They will do it. Let the man who replaces me be assigned to division."

But Gershon made no such request. He did not know why he decided to remain in the battalion. The warming sense of security and satisfaction he felt whenever he thought of Roger Tat and the friendly battalion commander? The few doctors he was getting to know and the work he was doing? But all that could not entirely explain why he chose to remain. Simply, he did not know.

His footlockers arrived with his books. He was given a wide new bed and a new bureau. His bookcase looked fine with the books neatly lined up on the shelves. No Arthur Leiden here in this broken land to poke in his books—Arthur Leiden, suave, swaggering, polished, a navy uniform, a posh officers club, high talk. Gershon's schedule of services in the battalion chapel was fixed. The snows ended. Roger functioned smoothly, often anticipating Gershon's wishes. Gershon admired his assistant's cheerful gentleness and the quiet tenacity of his faith; once he even tried reading The Book of Mormon but found it nearly incomprehensible. Gabriel Rosen attended services. He sat always in the same front pew, praying devotedly, in white-faced gloom. He drank the wine. From time to time he mentioned the two outside crosses on the chapel.

In late April Gershon went to the division PX, purchased a phonograph and a number of classical and popular records. He took to listening to music in the late evenings after dinner. The officers club, with its new wall paneling and card tables and floor lamps and bar stools, was always crowded at night and often noisy, and he did not stay around too long. Sometimes, alone in the hut with the music, he thought of Karen and Arthur. He had no more visions.

In the first week of May the altar chairs arrived, and three days later came the pews. He went alone through the chapel early the next morning. He saw its beauty, the clean and shining lights on the pews, altar, chairs, lectern, lights from the sun that streamed in through the open windows—and he liked what he saw. After a long moment he went to the office and wrote a memo to the battalion commander. He wondered why he had waited so long and did not know. Roger typed the memo and walked it through to battalion headquarters.

Three days later four men drove up to the chapel in a jeep. They removed the crosses, placed a weather vane on the steeple and a new panel of stained wood next to the entrance door. The weather vane was of dark metal that became quickly clogged with airborne grit and ceased to turn with the wind. The new panel was stained too dark and did not quite match the others.

The division chaplain rode up one day, looked at the chapel, and rode away. It was the third week of May. Dust clouds climbed into the pale sky from the traffic on the dry roads. The dust yellowed Gershon's face as he was driven about in the jeep; it powdered the tents and Jamesways and hospital Quonsets on the compound. Sammy Kim was suddenly gone a few days, then returned. Gershon learned that his mother had died and was buried on the shoulder of the hill behind the battalion.

He had watched her being buried without knowing what he was seeing. At lunch one day he had gazed out the window and spotted a procession moving along the shoulder of the hill that lay beyond the rear perimeter fence of the battalion. White-garbed elderly men in stovepipe hats; women; younger men; a long box on a plank carried by some of the men. He saw the procession stop and the box lowered into the ground and the grave filled. They went back down the hill, leaving behind a bare unmarked mound of new earth.

The next day, on the way up to the northern regiment in the jeep, he saw a similar procession on the road near the river. "A funeral," Roger said. They passed it quickly, sending up swirls of dust. Did the living worship the dead in this country? Gershon knew nothing about these people, had little desire to know. They entered the dry riverbed—sandy bottom and smooth pebbles and shallow streamlets and sunlight glinting on the clear, slow-moving water—and came out near the house of one of the prostitutes who lived along the riverbank. It was a low mud house with a thatched roof and a front yard marked with bamboo poles. She stood in the doorway, a pretty girl with dark hair and a red skirt and red lips and dark eyes. She waved as they went by. Her breasts, full and pendulous, were clearly visible. Gershon felt the heat rise in his belly. Roger looked away. They remained overnight at the regiment and drove back in the morning, and there she was again in the doorway of the house, waving at them, the tips of her bare breasts brown in the sunlight.

The next day they drove to Seoul, the day after to I Corps, and the day after that to the infantry division in the mountains near Panmunjom, where the armistice had been signed during his disastrous summer as a camp counselor. How long ago had that been? he thought, gazing across valleys and hills at the nearby enemy who no doubt stood gazing back at him. There were millions of them out there, millions, and he was not certain he knew why he was here looking at them. Everywhere in the brush he imagined he saw enemy eyes; behind boulders in the hills, everywhere. He and Roger rode back through the odorous shanty towns and blasted villages, half-naked children everywhere and stone-faced adults, all looking ravaged and hungry. He felt himself a vile intruder. He stared at much and saw little. They would drive in silence for lengthy stretches of time, Roger intent upon the road. The dust of the land blew into the jeep. Gershon wondered if village air bore diseases he might contract merely through travel. He had to travel. He was the only Jewish chaplain in Korea. There was some trouble about finding another man. No one told him what the trouble was; no one seemed to know.

Sometimes he traveled by plane. The L-19's were light, fast, two-seater aircraft. You sat behind the pilot strapped into a parachute, the seat a form of entombment, and the aircraft bounced and yawed and careened above the hills and valleys, and you had no faith it could be landed safely—too much gusting air, too many towering hills, too fragile a machine, that one propeller, that thin fabric of papery metal. Sometimes he saw from the air a rash of pinkish glows in the shrub-covered hills and the curling rise of gray smoke. There were frequent fires in the hills, set by the Koreans, and no one seemed to know the reason for them. "It's to kill the rats," a pilot said. "They're getting rid of the weeds that cause hemorrhagic fever," the battalion commander said. Others offered other reasons but no one really knew. The winds blew through the fires, and he wondered what would happen if he ever crashed into one of the burning hills. Light aircraft seemed always to be crashing. An L-20 Beaver went down near Seoul in March: one man was killed, three were injured. A division L-19 crashed into a rice paddy after takeoff one April day, and they brought the pilot into the battalion and stitched him up and sent him off to a rear hospital. Gershon came away from those rides drained, with a shivery weakness in his knees and always needing to use the piss tubes.

One afternoon Roger met him with the jeep at the division airstrip after a three-hour flight from Pusan. There were clouds blowing across the tops of the hills. The first drops of rain came as they turned into the battalion compound. By dinner the rain was heavy. He ate and watched the rain pelt the grave on the hill. Later in his Jamesway he sat reading and listening to a Brandenburg Concerto and heard the rain on the canvas roof. The air was warm and damp. It rained through the night, and in the morning it was a wall of water pouring endlessly from a slate-dark sky, and he realized the monsoon season had begun. And now he traveled on roads that were often slippery rivers of mud.

The battalion commander said to him one evening, "How's it going, chappy?"

"Fine, sir."

"You're losing weight. Are you feeling all right?"

"Yes, sir. I'm really fine."

"All that traveling around. They ought to get another man. Can't be all over the peninsula. It's a scandal. Must be careful."

"He's becoming more and more spiritual," one of the doctors at the table said. "Can't you see it?"

"No one becomes more spiritual in this place," said a second doctor. "Not even chaplains. Isn't that right, chaplain?"

"You ought to start eating meat," the battalion commander said. "It's bad for you to be losing all that weight. Bad."

"They'll send you home in a pine box, chaplain," the first doctor said. "This place has diseases we don't even have names for yet. The tuberculosis here alone could have killed off the dinosaurs."

"Why don't you make a blessing over this ham and call it chicken?" the second doctor said. "Can't you do that?"

"If I could make a blessing and call it chicken, I'd make a blessing and call it steak," Gershon said.

They laughed and let up on him, and he finished his food with neither interest nor appetite. He was rarely hungry. The canned kosher meats his uncle sent him by boat mail were inadequate and inedible. He ate eggs and bread and vegetables and cereals and was often tired but had yet to be ill. Sometimes he would find himself alone at a table, and he would eat quickly. Often during those times he would become aware that he was looking out the window across the perimeter fence at the solitary grave on the hill. Why was that distant mound so singular an attraction? It lay facing southward on the bare wide sloping shoulder of the hill, with ridges stretching along the east and west and with the long length of the valley at its feet.

"Was your mother old?" he asked his houseboy one rainy day.

"No, sah," Sammy Kim said, looking past him. "Not old."

"Was she sick?"

"Yes, sah. Sick. Taksan sick. She die." And he turned his head away and bent down over the boots he was polishing.

"You live with your father?"

"Yes, sah. Abuji. Yes, sah. In little village other side of hill. No can see from here. Very little. Very old village. Yes, sah."

"Do you pray to your mother?"

"Pray, sah?"

"Do you talk to her, ask her for things?"

"Yes, sah. Oh yes. Amuni watch all the time from hill. All the time. Yes."

Yes. The word echoed. *Yes.*

"Amuni do for us good things," the boy said. "Happy things. Amuni have nice place and see *cu-cak*. Amuni see all to south from bright place, from place full of light. Yes, sah."

"Where did you learn your English, Sammy? From soldiers?"

"Yes, sah. American soldiers, sah. Know good English, speak many words. I talk good, sah?"

"Yes," Gershon said, and looked at the small lithe form bent over his boots and polishing them to a high shine. Outside the rain fell steadily. White mold had formed in some of his books, and now twice a week the boy took the books from the shelves, riffled the pages, and replaced them neatly in their straight lines. The grave on the hill seemed unaffected by the rains, and Gershon wondered

about that until one morning when he saw a man on the hill rebuilding the mound after a punishing rain. The man was brown-
skinned and muscular, and when he was done he stepped back and
looked a long time at the grave and turned and went down the far
side of the hill.

There were days he did not travel. He worked in the chapel. He
counseled men, wrote sermons and character guidance lectures, answered his mail, sent off memos, made out reports. One morning a
request came up from the office of the Eighth Army chaplain for
photographs of the interior and exterior of the chapel. He sent a
letter of request to the division signal officer for the photographs,
explaining that the request was being sent by letter rather than by
a DA 11-161 form because the forms were unavailable within the
battalion. That was one of the many things that could not be ob-
tained in adequate amounts, or could not be had at all. There were
shortages of boots, ordnance, jeep and ambulance spare parts, tank
spare parts, fresh vegetables, greens for salads, fish. Beer and liquor
were plentiful. Sergeants who were on their second tour of duty told
him they longed for war, supplies flowed in war, what you really
needed you could swap for or steal with ease. This twilight armistice,
this no-war and no-peace, was a special hell of paperwork, boredom,
low morale, a pervasive sense of things having broken down irrep-
arably. In the midst of this he had somehow completed the chapel,
and wherever he traveled now they had heard of the chapel and
cheered him for it. There was a story on the chapel in *Stars and
Stripes*. He rode down to Seoul to tape a radio broadcast on the
meaning of the Festival of Shavuot, and was introduced as "the
chaplain of the well-known medical battalion chapel." As often as
he could he sat alone in a front pew, in silence, and gazed at the
altar and the lights. Its interior was clean and white, the wood
glistening, the cloths velvety. Once he thought he saw sitting there
the old man with the beard who had once taught him Aramaic and
given him the kabbalistic amulet he wore together with his dog
tags; but it was too brief and shimmering a vision and he could not
be certain he had in fact seen him.

He walked into the chapel one morning and found Roger sitting
there alone in the second row. Roger started to rise and Gershon
signaled to him to remain seated.

"I didn't mean to disturb you, Roger."

"I was thinking I had only two more months here, sir. I was thinking of my family." His voice was soft and his myopic eyes swam behind the lenses. "Two months. I was thinking how hard it is to believe that."

"I've got twelve months. It's hard to believe that too."

Roger smiled sadly. "You'll make it, sir."

"The doctors don't think so. They think I'll disappear before the end of the summer. I will be a vanished wraith."

"How were the tests, sir?"

"All negative."

"You should eat, sir. You don't eat."

"If the doctors here told you that you should drink tea and coffee, would you do it, Roger?"

"I think I would write home and ask what to do, sir."

"You wouldn't ask for a vision, a voice in the night?"

"Oh no, sir. We don't do that sort of thing. We're not primitive, sir."

"Right. Yes. Well. As soon as you can, Roger, come into the office. There are some memos we need to get out."

They drove into Seoul in the early afternoon for a routine meeting with the assistant who was responsible for the maintenance of the Jewish chapel. It was a searing, dusty day; there had been no rain for nearly forty-eight hours. Farmers worked the rice paddies. The human excrement spread on the fields for fertilizer thickened and fouled the air. They were going through Seoul on their way back to the battalion, and at an intersection a runaway horse attached to a riderless cart came plunging toward them. They were nearly through the intersection, and Gershon did not see it, and then it was upon them, filling all his vision, suddenly, a dark-brown wall of motion, and Roger pulled on the wheel and they swerved and the maddened horse hurtled past, and Gershon saw its blood-streaked eyes and the white foam on its mouth, and he felt its heat, felt the heat of the horse hotter than the heat of the day, a palpable heat against his face, and it was gone, the cart clattering crazily behind it. Only when they were out of the city did he become calm enough to realize clearly that a collision with that crazed horse might have killed them both. And he began to tremble.

"You're a damn good driver," he murmured.

"Thank you, sir." Roger's soft voice shook.

"No. Thank you."

"The heat must have made the horse go crazy. The heat and the dust. It's awful."

"How ridiculous. I mean the idea of being killed in Korea by a crazy horse. How absolutely ridiculous!"

The dust and heat blew against his face, but he could not stop trembling. He had once seen a horse in his neighborhood drop in its traces, tilting the ice wagon forward on the front wheels. The ice-man kicked it, then began to call to it endearingly. "Charlie," he called. "What're you doing? What? Get up. It's too hot here. Charlie. Get up. Extra bucket of oats if you get up. Come on, Charlie. Hey. Hey! Oh, my dear Charlie is gone!" Who collected the dead horses? Had the dead horses of the New York Fire Department ever run into moving automobiles? How ridiculous! Why had he thought of that monument now? And he thought too of Karen and Jakob Keter and the walks along Riverside Drive.

They rode the rest of the way to the battalion in silence.

It rained early Saturday morning, then cleared and turned hot and rained again briefly in the afternoon. Sunday they followed the valley north along the main supply route, crossed a low range of hills, and came down onto a broad plain. Terraced fields climbed into the hills. Children played at a game of oriental jump rope in the dusty earth before a peasant hut. Men were removing fertilizer from a horse-drawn cart. A scrawny dog lay asleep in the sun by the side of the road. Women in baggy pants were doing laundry near a rushing stream; they turned to stare briefly at the jeep as it went by.

It was a clear day, the air still cool with morning. The riverbed stretched dry in the sunlight, and they started across it, the pebbles crunching beneath the tires. In the heart of the riverbed was a trickle of water, and he heard the sounds of the water and the pebbles. There was the briefest of moments as he sat in the jeep with eyes closed, feeling the warm morning sunlight on his eyes and the cool morning air on his face and the gentle lurchings of the jeep in the riverbed—when all that Korean world vanished, and he imagined himself in some distant sunny land of gentle valleys and kind hills bathed in the softest and most caressing of lights. The noises of the jeep altered slightly, and he opened his eyes. They were hubcap deep in water. Ahead as far as he could see was a boiling torrent of water, and they were in it, and it was stretched out all behind them and alongside them. They bounced and lurched, and the water rose. Roger shifted expertly into four-wheel drive and put his foot down hard on the pedal, and the engine whined. There was water on the floorboard and water came pouring into the sides of the jeep. Gershon stared at the water and raised his feet and stared at Roger's feet buried now deep in the water on the floor of the jeep. He heard the rush and the roar of the cascading river and the whine of the struggling jeep and saw the wheel jerking in Roger's hands, saw Roger's face set, intent, his eyes narrowed to slits behind the glasses. The water ceased rising, and they were in it a long time. And then they were out of it, the water falling away, the jeep coming up the opposite bank, shedding water like some sea amphibian. Roger shifted back into drive and continued on. Dust rose behind them. The hills were green and violet and streaked with yellow flowers. The prostitute stood in the doorway of her hut, breasts bare to sun and sight. Roger looked away.

"It was yesterday's rain, sir," he said after a long time.

"Are you all right?" Gershon said. "Shouldn't you dry your feet?"

"I don't want to stop, sir. I may not be able to get it started again. I was frightened, sir. We'll take the mountain road back."

When they returned to battalion late that afternoon they learned that a jeep had attempted to ford the river some miles above them and had foundered and been swept away by the force of the water. The driver had made it to the shore. The captain was still missing. Two days later they found his body, miles away, near the steel bridge that crossed the river and led up to the mountain road.

All week after that river ride, Gershon slept badly for the dreams that filled his head. He retreated to his books and music. He lost himself in Bach and kabbalistic numerology. Safe, safe. And calm. The flow of music, the weave of numbers and words. He read and reread the letters from his aunt and uncle and from Karen. He had heard nothing from Jakob Keter. It seemed to him that random events now sought to control their lives. Strange things were happening everywhere, deadly things. Anti-personnel mines planted during the war and long dormant were moving beneath the ground in the drenched and shifting earth, and people who always walked with great care, placing their feet on tested patches of land, now trod on earth that blew them to pieces. Officers went hunting in the hills and stepped on the mines. Enlisted men were blown up near the huts of whores. One day a child was brought to the battalion, a girl, with an arm gone. Those were the early days of June. There was no war, but people kept crashing into shards of the world that broke their lives. He tried not to think about it too often. He spent as much time as he could in his Jamesway with his records and books and letters; and much time in the chapel with its sunlight and silence.

Then Sammy Kim was gone a few days, and Gershon found he missed the boy's timid presence. He asked around; no one knew where he was. The boy returned with bruises on his face and arms. Gershon asked one of the doctors to look at him.

"Some kids beat him up," the doctor said over lunch. "He wouldn't kick in protection money. They did a good job on him, the bastards."

"Korean kids beat him?"

"Why not? You think only Americans bang on each other? It's a great world out here. All join in the fun."

Gershon looked out the window at the hill. The man was up there again, repairing the grave.

"Damn slicky boys. Feed on us. Feed on kids. Why not? Talking about feeding. Listen, chaplain. You really ought to start eating meat."

"Tell him, doc," the battalion commander put in from the adjoining table. "He doesn't listen to me. Tell him."

The doctor, who was the division psychiatrist and had the rank of captain, said, "Your religion isn't one of those that says get sick and die, is it? It's not one of those kinds of religion."

"Are you telling me as a doctor that I really might get seriously sick?"

"Go ahead, doc. Tell him." The major looked at Gershon and smiled paternalistically.

"It's not a good idea to play around with your health in this place, chaplain. You can get beat up. Right now my dog back home eats better than you do. What's the point to getting beat up? All concur it makes no sense."

"You'll need to eat good these next weeks," the major said around the cigarette he was lighting. "Listen to the doc. Don't get beat up. Very bad idea."

"I'll think about it," Gershon said. "Seriously."

"You're a stubborn man, chappy," the battalion commander said. "You're good for the morale of my boys."

"Why do you suppose that's the only one on the hill?" Gershon said.

"What?" the battalion commander said.

"The grave on that hill."

"What grave?" He looked to where Gershon pointed. "I'll be damned," he said. "This is the first time I noticed it." He stared out the window and puckered his small lips. "I wonder whose headache that's going to be. Where are you off to today, chappy?"

"Artillery."

"Have a good trip. Stay out of riverbeds."

"Yes, sir."

"And eat meat," the captain said. "All concur?"

"Right," the battalion commander said.

In the second week of June, Gershon flew to Japan. He took a train to the town of Oiso, which lay on the Pacific coast about forty miles south of Tokyo. The weather was warm, the sky a clear sparkling blue. He felt exhilarated by the newness of the land, by the bursts of color from flowers and clothes, the lush green of the hills, the neat narrow lanes of villages swiftly glimpsed, and once, the train slowing for some reason, he saw a geisha framed in his window on the corner of a street, and her fragile balance of face and garb was of such transcendent beauty that he felt as if struck, and he heard the breath leave his lungs in a long sigh of pleasure.

For three days, at the invitation of the Japan-based Jewish chaplain, he participated in a Jewish religious retreat, lecturing to around eighty men from Japan and Korea. They lived in a seaside hotel that was an army retreat center. In the company of others, he walked along the sand beaches and through the tiny seaside town. They stood in a crowd one afternoon and saw costumed men carrying a large pagodalike edifice on poles and dancing with it, dancing and singing—and he thought of Simchat Torah and Jews dancing with Torah scrolls. It was a gay and festive afternoon, and there were many children, and women nursed infants, and the people and the streets were festooned with a shimmering array of colors. He spent the night in Tokyo, where he had a fish dinner in a lovely tatami-floored Japanese restaurant and then walked the crowded, brightly lighted streets. He wore the sport jacket, slacks, shirt, and tie he had purchased the first day of his arrival in Japan. He had a drink in a club and danced for a while with one of the Japanese girls. At first she did not understand what a chaplain was. He flew back to the battalion the next day.

It was ninety-one degrees in the officers mess the first morning he was back, and by noon it was one hundred and three. His head was filled with pictures of his time in Japan—visions played themselves out repeatedly before his eyes—and he gave little attention during the next few days to what was happening around him in the battalion. Repeatedly he saw the geisha on the street and felt against him the warm and soft body of the girl in the club. There had been a small band and dim smoky lights and the drinks and the girl against him, long straight dark hair and narrow dark eyes and high cheekbones and her flesh moist beneath his hands as they danced slowly on the crowded floor. He sat sweating in the chapel office and worked with Roger on his accumulated mail. He traveled by aircraft and jeep to Seoul, Pusan, Uijongbu, to I Corps and the distant division near Panmunjom, to the regiment in the north, and again to Seoul. He sweated and showered and ate and traveled and lay awake in the hot nights, staring into the darkness and wondering why he was no longer seeing visions of Arthur and his parents, of Einstein and Truman. He remembered a vague sensation he had experienced while watching the religious parade and festival in Oiso: heat and fire and smoke and burning flesh—a sudden quick, swiftly gone filter of darkness across the color-splashed joy of that afternoon. He saw and did not see what was changing in the battalion. He knew they were preparing to move to the hill, had known for some weeks, as had everyone else. They would build a new compound and a new hospital to be away from the dust of the main supply route, and the chapel would be moved and rebuilt and enlarged—on the highest point along the shoulder of that hill. It was one of the things he had known and not known, and he had paid it scant heed since his return from Japan.

Now in Korea, about a week after his return, it rained six days straight, and the battalion compound became a shallow lake. He could travel nowhere; aircraft were grounded in the pummeling rain, roads were washed away. He looked up one day from a meal of vegetables and saw the hill and realized that the grave was gone. He thought it had been flattened by the rains, but after two days of sun and furnace heat no one had come to repair the mound, and he knew it had been moved.

He said to his houseboy that afternoon, "Where is your mother now, Sammy?"

"Ah," the boy said, squeezing his thin shoulders together and not looking at Gershon. His small face was pinched, wooden.

"Where? Tell me."

"Not a good place, sah. Move. Not a sparrow place. Not see cu-cak. Soldiers tell to move, sah. We go to hill?"

"Yes."

"Bad for amuni, sah. Bad for abuji. Bad for village. Oh, bad."

"What do you mean?"

"Bad people come to village, sah. Bad women, bad men. To make money from Americans. Oh, bad, bad."

He said to Roger the next morning, "They had to move the grave to make way for the battalion. Did you know that?"

"What grave, sir?"

"The grave of Sammy Kim's mother."

"Is that right? I didn't know her grave was there."

"It was on the hill. Yes."

Roger was silent, gazing myopically off into space through his glasses.

"What a hell of a thing," Gershon said. "To have to move your mother's grave."

"You know, sir," Roger said, "I was thinking we might live in California after we're married. Central California. I could go to school and get my degree in musicology. My folks could come and visit. It's not so far from Utah. I hear nice things about California, sir."

Gershon stared at him.

"I'll be home in about four weeks, sir," Roger said. "Four weeks. I can't think of anything else. Shouldn't we be getting you a new assistant?"

"Yes," Gershon said. "Right."

During lunch he said to the battalion commander, "Are those our men on the hill?"

The major narrowed his eyes and looked through the window. "They better be," he said, "or I'm going to chew some ass."

"I don't see any machinery."

"We won't get any, chappy. The engineers need it for the roads and bridges."

"And the new officers clubs," one of the doctors said. "Don't forget the officers clubs."

"Are we going to cut the drainage channels in that hill by ourselves?" another of the doctors asked.

"That's the idea, doc."

"With our medics? You're kidding!"

"Those are my orders, doc, and that's what we're going to do."

"Not smart, major. All agree. Not smart."

"You want to come up with me, chappy, and have a look? Be good for the men to see you there. Going up at fourteen hundred hours. Boost the morale."

They rode together in the major's jeep. After passing the battalion guardpost, they made a right turn onto the main supply route and rode a few hundred feet and turned right again and went up a dirt road that was suddenly wide and steep and led out onto a broad slightly sloping ridge that was the shoulder of the hill behind the battalion. The wind blew hot, but there was no dust. They could see across the battalion and the valley to a distant range of southern hills. A yellowish haze hung over the valley. There were battalion trucks and jeeps on the hill and men with shovels digging the drainage ditches against the next rains. The view across the valley was sweeping. Gershon had not thought the shoulder to be so high; it had not seemed so high from the window of the officers mess. He wondered if the sky could be seen from here at night. Did the obscuring dust clouds rise? Were the stars visible?

He walked alongside the major, greeting and chatting with the men. They worked stripped to the waist in the relentless beating heat. The concrete platforms for the buildings were to be poured in early August. If the drainage work wasn't completed all would be swept away by rains. Gershon looked slowly around at the broad slope of the hill, feeling the sting of the sun through his dark pilot's glasses and wondering how they would ever do that without heavy ditch-digging equipment.

They had climbed to the rim of the future compound, its northern perimeter. From there the shoulder and the battalion and the division and the airstrip and all the faded green and dusty valley lay before him—a weary and mottled expanse of troubled earth. Behind him, at the foot of a steep, brush-covered hillside, he saw a tiny village of about a dozen mud and straw huts and neatly enclosed yards and terraced fields. Oxen grazed in the grass. Men worked in the fields. Children played in the shade of the huts. There was the distant barking of a dog.

"Here we put the chapel," said the major. "Right here. Facing the valley. Nice? Make up a little for all the bombs. Telling you this here and now, chaplain. Private. It was war, and it had to be done. But I didn't like it. Swore I'd get out of it. Couldn't look down. You know what I mean?"

They walked back down the slope past the lines of laboring men. An officer came over to them and saluted.

"How's it going, lieutenant?"

"Hot, sir. Worried about sunstroke."

"Salt tablets, lieutenant. Salt tablets. And water."

"Yes, sir."

They drove back along the dusty road to the battalion.

Two days later Gershon—a month overdue for his rest and recuperation leave—flew to Japan. He was in Japan ten days. With a Jewish lieutenant he had met at battalion services, he traveled to

Kyoto, Nara, Takarazuka, and Kamikeo. He was stunned into speechlessness by the temple beauty of Kyoto. They took a flat-bottomed boat along with other Japanese and an Australian widow in her early fifties and they traveled along the Hatzu River through mountain gorges and shot the rapids and, in the silences, listened to the singing of nightingales echo back and forth among the cedars and pines that lined the tall cliffs along the banks. They took the train back to Tokyo and rode along the ocean. Gershon looked and saw the awesome rise of Mount Fuji, vast and wide and filling all the train window and the far sky. He spent that night in the Imperial Hotel in Tokyo and the next night in Camp Drake. He flew back to Korea and arrived at the battalion in a rainstorm.

From the window of the officers mess he watched a river of rain wash across the shoulder of the hill. The drainage was inadequate. The channels dug by the men flooded and collapsed. Day after day of rain followed. The work on the hill ceased. The men began to grumble. There were fights in the tents and a sudden sharp rise in the battalion's venereal disease rate. Gershon walked the compound and saw the men tired, angry. Why weren't the engineers building the new compound? Why were medics digging ditches? Where was the engineer ditch-digging equipment? Wasn't there anything the battalion could trade for that equipment? Then the noncoms were angry, and as Gershon wandered the compound they talked to him. Ditch-digging equipment had been seen parked in the nearby engineer compound; other diggers were working over at regiment, at division headquarters, on the main supply route. Why everyone else and not us, chaplain?

The battalion commander grew somber.

"You won't get it done without engineers, Doug," one of the company commanders said over breakfast one morning.

"Can't get engineers."

"One ditch-digger, Doug. Just one of the machines."

"Out of the question. Can't budge the G-4."

"Why?"

"Don't know. He doesn't have to explain himself to me."

"It won't get done, Doug."

They stared out the window at the rain on the hill.

On a rainy morning Gershon and Roger stood in the chapel office.

"I want to thank you, sir," Roger said. "I appreciate all you did for me."

"Good luck to you, Roger."

"I appreciate your keeping me on, sir. I know it was—awkward."

"Take care of yourself. Write the world some good music."

"Yes, sir."

Roger saluted, Gershon returned the salute. They shook hands.

"Have a safe trip, Roger," Gabriel Rosen said. He was standing near Roger's desk.

"Thank you, Gabriel."

Roger went out the door into the rain. Gershon sat down at his desk and looked at the mail and did not see it. The air was steaming; it had the odor of fungus and drowned earth. He saw Gabriel Rosen sit in Roger's chair. Rain fell on the roof in a ceaseless drumming torrent.

"Is there anything we have to do, rabbi?" Gabriel asked after a while.

Gershon said nothing.

"Rabbi?"

"There's always something to do. Listen. Please don't call me rabbi. Call me either sir or chaplain. Okay?"

Gabriel's dark eyes flashed surprise against the papery whiteness of his face.

"This isn't Brooklyn, Gabriel. This isn't Borough Park."

"Yes, sir."

"Find something to do. There's plenty to do. I'm going out for a cup of coffee."

Later the rain ended, and the clouds broke. A fierce sun shone suddenly from a pale-blue sky, and the earth began to dry. When he entered the officers mess for lunch he noticed that the wall thermometer was registering eighty-two degrees. Over vegetables and coffee he saw that the work had resumed on the hill. In the afternoon the heat rose to one hundred fourteen degrees. One of the medics on the hill passed out and was brought to the hospital.

Gabriel said to Gershon the next morning, "There's a lot of complaining going on, sir."

"I hear."

"The men don't want to dig ditches. They ought to get machines to do the ditches. The one who passed out yesterday—he had sunstroke. It was bad."

At dinner that day the battalion commander said to Gershon, "You want to ride up to the hill with me tomorrow, chappy?"

"Tomorrow's my Sabbath, sir. I don't ride on my Sabbath."

"Oh. Yes. Right. Right. Sunday, then."

"Yes, sir."

"Afternoon. Go up and boost the morale. Becoming a problem. You hearing anything?"

"Yes, sir."

"Serious?"

"It seems to be, sir."

"Damn. One ditch-digger. One machine. Can't pry it loose from engineers. Don't know anyone, and they don't owe us anything. They keep their pants on. Pure, the engineers."

On Sunday afternoon Gershon rode up to the hill with the battalion commander. They left the jeep at the foot of the hill and walked to the crest. The sloping shoulder was entirely without shade. Gershon felt his heart racing and sweat on his face and neck. On the other side of the hill the tiny village seemed asleep. He had never known such heat; the air seemed aflame.

Standing next to the major, Gershon saw a man stumble into a ditch. He had a clear momentary view of the man's eyes as he fell, wide and all white, the pupils gone up beneath the lids. A cluster of men formed quickly around him. On the shoulder, not far from where the grave had once been, stood an ambulance. Two men were quickly loaded inside. Gershon had not seen the second man fall. The ambulance started downhill toward the road and the battalion.

A lieutenant came running toward them up the hill. He saluted. His uniform was stained with sweat.

"That's the third and fourth today, sir."

Gershon gazed down the hill. He could see the men leaning on their shovels. They were all looking up at him and the major, and waiting.

"What do you think, chappy?" the major said.

Gershon looked at the men waiting in the sun and heat. They all seemed enveloped in flames.

"I don't know how much more of this we can do, sir," said the lieutenant. "It's over a hundred degrees up here."

"Isn't there someone at division we can meet with and talk to about this?" Gershon asked. He did not know what else to say.

The major stared down the hill at the waiting men. Beyond the hill, all along the valley, Gershon saw the climbing dust clouds of vehicular traffic. An L-19 rose from the runway and flew on straight south, leaving behind no sound.

"Damn good idea," said the major. "Have a meeting with the G-4. Get the division surgeon in on it, and chief of staff. Clear it up. Good idea. You come along and make a morale report. Right?"

"Yes, sir."

"Get the men back to the battalion, lieutenant. Don't want anyone else hurt unnecessarily."

"Yes, sir."

"Damn good idea, chappy. I owe you a drink. Let's get into some shade. Brain beginning to boil."

The division psychiatrist said to Gershon that evening, "Clever idea, chaplain. All agree. Clear the air."

"Damn right," said the battalion commander. "Smart chaplain."

Gershon was finding it bewildering that so simple a suggestion was eliciting so enthusiastic a response. He saw the major talking excitedly with the adjutant, a short thin gloomy man who rarely spoke and never drank. "Couple of days, Doug," the adjutant said. "If they go for it." Some sort of machinery was being set into motion as a result of his offhand suggestion. He could not understand what he had done. "Tuesday, maybe Wednesday," the adjutant was saying. "At the latest Thursday. Frank will be there."

"Have another beer, chaplain," said the major. All were drinking beer that evening. The ice for their drinks had been used earlier to pack the sunstroke victims. The entire division had been scoured for ice.

Gabriel said to him the next morning, "Everyone's talking about it, chaplain, sir. You're a hero. They asked me to tell you."

"We've got to go to Seoul today."

"In this heat?"

Gershon looked at him.

"Yes, sir," Gabriel said. "I'll get the jeep. But this is a terrible heat, sir."

They rode to Seoul. Much of the way they were behind a convoy of two-and-a-half-ton trucks. The ride took nearly two hours. Gershon spent half an hour with the Eighth Army chaplain on preliminary plans for the High Holiday services in September. "Don't know what's going on," he said to Gershon. "They had a man, something went wrong. New man is coming around the end of August or early September. Don't have a name, no. You're sure you don't want to transfer to Seoul? All right. We'll put the new man into Seoul. Nice Jewish chapel here. I can't leave it too long without a chaplain. Not enough to have an assistant running it. You're sure you don't want a transfer?"

He arrived back in division in time for dinner. On the wall near the door of the officers club the thermometer registered eighty-six degrees. The odor of cooked ham assailed his throat. He saw the major wave to him. "Meeting all set, chappy. Tomorrow, fourteen hundred hours. I owe you a drink." The major shaped his small lips into a smile. "G-4, chief of staff, division surgeon, you, me, John here. Anyone else, John?"

"That's the lot, Doug," said the adjutant.

"Damn big meeting. We're counting on you, chappy."

He slipped into a chair and ate bread and vegetables and drank coffee. He smoked the cigarette offered him by one of the company commanders and joined the major at the bar.

Some time later he came out of the officers club into the hot night. The air lay heavy and without movement. An occasional jeep and truck passed along the main supply route, headlights flaring obliquely through the darkness. A red light blinked on and off atop a tall tower somewhere in the vicinity of the landing strip. Helmeted guards walked the perimeter, checking the fence for breaks by slicky boys, the South Korean thieves who moved skilfully, invisibly. He walked along the compound past the Quonset of the Headquarters and Headquarters Company, past the barber-shop run by the old Korean with the wispy white beard and the gnarled hands who hummed and sang as he snipped and cut, past the Hong Kong tailor shop and the Quonset that housed the offices of the major and his adjutant and their noncoms and clerks. Even in the starless darkness of the steamy night the hills stood clearly against the sky, blacker than the night, and the chapel carved its sharp silhouette out of its background of hospital buildings. And even in the darkness he saw the bleak, slovenly, scraped and battered walls of the battalion buildings, dusty, begrimed, and he smelled in the sultry air the stench of the fertilizer on the fields and the strong sour odor of the kimchi, the fermented cabbage that was the national food. Only the chapel stood clean and white on the compound. There was a stirring in the area of the tents beyond the hospital. Were they bringing in the prostitutes even on so hot a night? Gabriel had told him: the enlisted men lined up for the whores brought in by some of the noncoms from the village beyond the landing strip and the Korean market. What did they want from him, the major and the adjutant and the doctor? He was a Jewish chaplain; how had he become caught up in this? And yet he felt pride in his involvement; he was a part of them. He had managed in ways not clear to him to gain their trust. Noncoms came to him with their lives open; he counseled men from cities and suburbs, farms and towns, from Texas and Maine and the Dakotas, from the Ozarks, the Adirondacks, the Sierras—and somehow he was liked. He could not understand it, could not grasp it; he was liked by men whose lives he could not begin to conjure in visions. Gabriel reported what was said of him by the men in their tents—just as Roger had reported before. "You know how fast he pushed my morale leave through?" "Jesus, he really cares." "Yeah, he got out of bed at eleven o'clock and talked to the sarge in the chapel with a flashlight for an hour." "Yeah, he's all over the place." "Yeah, he was on the hill again today." "Yeah, it's the nicest chapel north of Seoul." He had thought little about the things he had done here; mostly he had tried to live with his books and records and letters. Yet now in this summer a clear and palpable resonance of regard echoed around him. Yes, he would be at that meeting and tell about the hill and the morale of the men. In ways mysterious to him others were seeing in him what he could not see in himself: a strength he knew he did not have, a certainty he knew he was far from possessing. This was his battalion. These were his men. He would talk up at that meeting. Yes.

He turned and started back across the compound to his Jamesway, stopping on the way at the piss tubes. He stood at the edge of the gravel bed and urinated into the angled metal tube set in the gravel-covered earth, and when he was done he turned to go to the Jamesway, and as he did, he saw, standing at his door, clearly outlined in the darkness, the tall, thin, trim figure of Jakob Keter. He stared and shivered and closed his eyes. When he opened his eyes, Keter was gone. But there remained in the space he had occupied the faintest of luminosities, a dim pulsing bluish light, like the light of a distant cluster of suns. It faded slowly before Gershon's astonished eyes.

He came into the Jamesway and prepared for bed, but it was a long time before he was able to sleep.

They met in a small room adjoining the office of the chief of staff. The air was damp and hot. Through the screening on the open window came bright sunlight and the occasional sounds of a vehicle. They sat at a rectangular dark-wood table. A single unlit naked bulb hung from the black wire attached to the ceiling.

From somewhere in the distance came the air-chops of a helicopter. Gershon, his back to the door, shifted nervously in his metal chair. An emergency in the battalion? He saw the swirl of dust, the orderlies rushing toward the helicopter, the doctors poised. The battalion commander sat opposite him, looking unconcerned. The adjutant was silent.

The chief of staff, a tall thin bird-colonel with close-cut graying hair and glasses, had the air of a kindly schoolmaster. The G-4, a lieutenant colonel, was short and stocky; his square face wore a dark look. The division surgeon, a portly lieutenant colonel, normally a jovial man, appeared troubled and chewed repeatedly at the fringes of his mustache with his teeth and lower lip.

Gershon knew none of these men; had, in fact, never seen them before.

The chief of staff cleared his throat and looked around. He said, in a mild voice, "Gentlemen, I've been told we have a serious problem over at the medics. What's the problem? Gil?"

The G-4 spoke. He would report on the hill construction project, he said. He didn't know anything about a serious problem. He had prepared a progress report. Date project had begun; dates of expected completion of drainage, platforms, buildings. The medics were doing the drainage. The engineers would construct the platforms and buildings. He knew of no serious problems, he said.

Gershon looked at the battalion commander and the adjutant. They sat very still, looking down at the table top.

"Doc?" said the chief of staff.

The division surgeon sat forward in his chair, belly pressing against the edge of the table. He was prepared to report on the status of the old and new hospitals, he said. The dust problem in the old hospital had been a major factor dictating the move. The transition had been carefully planned; the new equipment was either already in Korea or on its way; the hospital would successfully make the shift from temporary field operation to permanent camp facility. He knew of no serious problems, he said, and at present anticipated none. He sat back in his chair.

There was a brief silence. The helicopter circled the division area. Gershon saw the battalion commander and the adjutant looking down at the top of the table.

"Major, what did you want this meeting for?" the chief of staff asked. "I don't hear a problem."

The battalion commander looked up, caught Gershon's eye, and coughed softly. He was afraid, he said, that there was a problem. He hesitated, then continued. The use of his men to dig the drainage ditches had created something of a difficulty for the battalion, he said. The ditches were constantly being washed away by the rains; the sun and heat had begun to take a toll; there had been cases of sunstroke—

"We know about your sunstroke, major," said the chief of staff. "We had no ice for quite a while that evening. The Old Man was hopping mad."

"Those boys were very sick, sir," said the battalion commander.

"I'm sure they were if they had sunstroke," said the chief of staff. "Don't you know how to keep your men from getting sunstroke, major? Is sunstroke your problem? Talk to Doc. He'll straighten you out on sunstroke. Right? Did you call for this meeting to talk about sunstroke?"

"No, sir. There's something more, sir."

"Yes? What?"

"I'm afraid we have a serious morale problem, sir."

The chief of staff looked at the battalion commander and said nothing.

"The chaplain can report to you on that, sir."

The chief of staff turned to Gershon. They were all looking at him. He felt their eyes on his face, on his insignia, on the single bar of his rank.

"Go ahead, chaplain," the chief of staff said. "Let's hear about the morale problem."

"Thank you, sir," Gershon heard himself say. He forced himself to look directly at the chief of staff. Easier to look away, not feel a presence, a threat, a hurt. He looked at the smooth-skinned pinkish face of the chief of staff, this man who was second in command to the general. His heart beat loudly. He had been on the hill often, he said. He had gone up on the Fourth of July and on a number of Sundays to see the men at work. There had been the normal amount of griping at first, he said, and he had joked with the men about it —they were building a magic mountain, a hospital with a view, trading their tents for solid walls. But then the endless rains had come, and the exhaustion had begun to set in. Worse, a sense of futility had developed as the men watched rain after rain destroy their work. Battalion morale had been adversely affected by the work on the hill. The doctors were talking about the poor performance of the men at their normal hospital duties. There was growing concern over the possibility of a serious medical accident as a result of fatigue. Was it sensible to cut down on the time-off periods of the medics in order to make them ditch-diggers? he asked. He did not want to cause trouble, he said. He understood that there were valid reasons for the way certain things had to be done, and it was not his wish to interfere. His responsibility was to boost the morale of his unit. He understood that. But it was also his responsibility to report to his commanding officer whenever morale was being seriously undermined. He hoped everyone understood that he was acting in what he honestly believed were the best interests of his battalion.

He fell silent. His mouth was dust-dry, as if he had just returned from a jeep ride to Seoul, and his heart beat in a thick drumming rhythm.

He looked away from the gaze of the chief of staff. Outside, the helicopter noise was very loud; it was overhead. The helicopter was setting down somewhere nearby. Abruptly the noise ceased.

"Chaplain, with all due respect, how do you know?" the chief of staff asked.

"Sir?" Gershon said, raising his eyes.

"How do you know all this about the morale of the men? How are you measuring it?"

"They talk to me, sir."

"How do you distinguish it from normal laziness and loud griping?"

"I know what goes on in their tents, sir."

"How do you know that, chaplain?"

"My assistant keeps me informed. The noncoms tell me."

"I mean no disrespect, chaplain, but is your estimate of battalion morale based on the word of your assistant and some noncoms?"

"Not only, sir." He sensed that they regarded his words as negligible abstractions drawn from the kingdom of the intangible over which he was thought to rule. How to make it real to them? "There has been a sharp increase in the battalion's venereal disease rate," he said.

The G-4 broke in. "For Christ's sake, Luke—"

"All right, chaplain," said the chief of staff, ignoring the interruption. "Let's assume for the sake of argument that your battalion has a morale problem because it's been ordered to dig some drainage ditches. We can't have engineers digging drainage ditches for every compound. An American infantry division has only one battalion of engineers. You are aware of that, chaplain, aren't you? Fine.

What do you recommend be done to solve your problem?" He looked at the battalion commander and the adjutant. "Major?" He looked at Gershon. "Chaplain?"

The adjutant gave every appearance at that moment of wishing himself invisible. The major looked down at the table top. He said, without raising his eyes, "If engineers are entirely unavailable to us—"

"They are unavailable, major," said the chief of staff.

Gershon said, "Even one ditch-digging machine would help. If the men could see the one machine there, sir."

The chief of staff said, "Chaplain, this isn't a haggling session at some flea market in—" He stopped. There was a brief awkward silence. He said, "I don't think there's any point to—" He stopped again. His eyes widened.

Behind Gershon the door to the room had abruptly opened. The men around the table looked up and jumped to their feet with a sudden loud scraping of chairs. Gershon rose and turned and saw framed in the doorway the huge, bull-necked, baldheaded figure of the commanding general. He had seen him only once before, in a jeep, from a distance. Now, up close, he was an enormous man, well over six feet tall, long-faced, with small cold blue eyes and a protruding lower jaw. A pistol was strapped to his hip, and he carried his helmet in his hand. He was looking at the chief of staff.

"Luke."

"Yes, sir?"

"What the hell is going on out there?"

"Sir?"

"I just flew over the area and saw some of the men swimming in the streams. Those goddamn streams are polluted and off-limits. What the hell do we want here, typhoid and polio and bubonic plague?"

"No, sir."

"I want every major commanding officer called immediately by phone. I want those men out of those streams."

"Yes, sir."

The general's eyes flashed scalding through the room. He stood a moment in the doorway, his eyes running across the faces of the men around the table. He paused over Gershon's face. Gershon felt the cold and raging eyes, saw the eyes move to his insignia, the tablets and the Star of David. He saw the pistol and the helmet and the glistening twin stars of his power and the thick muscular frame that bulged against the meticulously neat uniform.

Then the general turned and walked off, leaving the door open.

The air in the room vibrated softly.

The chief of staff, rushing out, said, "I'll call you later, major."

The G-4 followed him from the room, brushing by Gershon without a word.

The division surgeon said to the battalion commander, "You'd better alert your guys, Doug. The shit will hit the fan if we've got men in those streams. What a dumb-ass way to beat the heat in this place."

"That's right," Gershon heard himself say. "And probably they weren't even digging ditches."

The division surgeon looked at him, nodded vaguely, and went from the room.

In the jeep on the way back to the battalion the major said, "You were great in there, chappy. Very eloquent. Wasn't he great, John?"

The adjutant, who had not spoken a word during the meeting, said yes, the chaplain was great.

Gershon felt tired. Something about the meeting was wrong. He had sensed an awkwardness, a barely concealed embarrassment, a tone of indignation. The heat and sunlight hurt his eyes.

Later that afternoon he rode with Gabriel to the artillery unit in the hills across the steel bridge. He conducted a service and a discussion session and slept over. The next morning he returned to the battalion. There was no one on the hill. He was eating a lunch of scrambled eggs and coffee when the major came into the officers mess.

"Chappy, o-eight-hundred tomorrow on the hill. The general is coming up to look around."

"Holy shit," someone said from one of the tables. The room had fallen silent.

"You'll ride up with me. We'll leave at o-seven-thirty hours."

"Yes, sir."

"Have you been in the hospital today?"

"No, sir. I just returned from artillery."

"We've got more than a dozen men in there with high fevers. They were all in the streams."

"I'll see them, sir."

"Yes. Be good for their morale."

Gershon went over to the hospital, then spent the remainder of the afternoon in his office with Gabriel Rosen, working on his correspondence and his July monthly reports: number of services held, number of discussion sessions, social events after services, how many attended, number of character guidance lectures given, religious retreats, orientation lectures to incoming battalion troops, hospital visits, evaluation of the month's activities, general comments. He wrote nothing about the battalion's morale problem or the meeting. He would wait to see how it all turned out.

He sat in his chair and gazed at the sunlight on the window. He heard Gabriel Rosen's laborious typing and closed his eyes. He felt tired. Why was he so tired? Probably his diet, his lack of fresh meat. He regretted having chosen Gabriel Rosen. He had yielded to his relentless importunings: he needed to be saved from the hellish job of hospital orderly; they mocked his Jewishness, were contemptuous of his personal habits and religious needs. The accusations had been vague, the pleading leechlike and without end. Try me, try me, please, rabbi. If you don't like me, send me back. Please. I'll have a nervous breakdown if I stay in that hospital. Well, he did not like him—he was a reluctant worker, a careless driver, a slow and inept typist—but how could he send him back to the hospital? And what certainty was there that another assistant would not be worse? He thought often of Roger Tat as he sat watching Gabriel Rosen.

That night after dinner the major drank too much. Gershon sat next to him at the bar in the battalion club. The heat was intense. There was a noisy card game in progress at one of the tables.

"It grabbed your ass and squeezed," the major said. "There was no feeling like it. You put on the juice and you could feel it grabbing. I loved it. You know what I mean? The plane would jerk up like a balloon every time we dumped the bombs. You knew they were out of the belly. I didn't like looking down. Listen. Never told this to anyone but can tell it to you, you're a man of integrity, deep faith. Lost my co-pilot in a dumb jeep accident on Okinawa and morale of crew went into tailspin. Very popular guy, the co-pilot. Took some flak the next time out and lost a gunner. Second time out lost an engine, barely made it. Fourth time out with new co-pilot, elevators went for mysterious reason, landed too fast, went off runway, blew up, lost two guys, was in hospital three months, quit flying. My morale all shot to hell. Know what I mean? Loss of will. Have another drink, chaplain. Proud of you. Man of strong will, strong convictions. Admire such men. Proud. Going now? Right. See you o-seven-thirty hours. Big day tomorrow. Big."

The night burned with dark moist heat. Gershon slept badly. He dreamed of his aunt and uncle and their decaying neighborhood. Houses burned in his dream; rain poured through the cracked tar paper of rooftops. He woke and went out to the piss tubes. The morning lay bathed in the rose glow of early sunlight. Except for the perimeter guards, he seemed the only one awake on the compound. A tranquil silence covered the land, beguiling, a moment of light and airy enchantment. He dressed and prayed slowly the morning service and had a breakfast of dry cereal and milk and coffee. He rode with the major to the hill.

They stood there waiting in the morning sun, all the officers of the battalion, tense, silent. Gershon waited beside the major.

At two minutes to eight a dust cloud appeared on the main supply route. It moved with stunning swiftness. There was the sound of sirens. The cloud turned off the road and Gershon saw the row of jeeps racing toward them along the shoulder, dust churning, sirens abruptly silent, the lead jeep with the white stars on the field of red. The jeeps halted suddenly, clouds of dust boiling upward. About a dozen officers and military police poured from them and followed the towering man moving toward the line of battalion officers, who suddenly snapped to attention. Gershon felt his heart racing, his mouth dry.

The general stood on the edge of the shoulder and surveyed the hill. He was flanked by the retinue of officers and a phalanx of military police.

The general said, "Bill."

A captain approached with an open notebook.

The general said, "I want this hill ready for buildings in two weeks." He spoke rapidly in a low voice. "I want it graded and the drainage ditches in. I want it done by engineers."

"Yes, sir." The captain wrote into his notebook and stepped back.

The general stood there a moment longer. He turned and glanced at the battalion commander. Then he looked again at Gershon. His face was expressionless.

"Major," the general said, nodding briefly. "Chaplain."

He turned and strode rapidly to his jeep. The retinue parted, dissolved, scrambled for the jeeps. Sirens cut the morning silence of the hill. The jeeps turned and roared away, followed by a rising boil of yellow dust.

"We did it," Gershon heard the major say softly in a tone of disbelief. "It was your idea, chaplain, and we won."

That afternoon two mechanical ditch-diggers were brought up to the hill. The next morning a flatbed truck moved slowly up the shoulder with a bulldozer. Gershon crossed the compound to his office and listened to the throb and roar of heavy engines.

Gabriel Rosen reported to him the feelings of the men. "They told me to tell you they think you're a great guy, sir."

"Are you ready for the trip to I Corps? Where's the jeep?"

"I Corps? Again? Didn't we just go to I Corps?"

Gershon's houseboy, Sammy Kim, said to him one morning later that week, "Hill soon finished, sah? We move?"

"Yes."

"You keep Sammy Kim, sah?"

"Sure, Sammy."

"Village not happy, sah. Bad people coming to village. Abuji say village become big, village become bad. Slicky boys come. Bad women come. Bad, sah."

Gershon said nothing.

"Not your fault, sah. You soldier. You make hill build fast. Not your fault." The boy did not look at Gershon as he spoke.

At the end of the second week of August two buildings appeared on the hill. Gershon drove up to the hill with Gabriel Rosen and walked among the toiling engineers. The buildings were freshly painted. He saw the G-4 conferring with a captain over blueprints.

"This is going to be a nice place," Gabriel Rosen said.

The G-4 glanced up, noticed Gershon, and looked back at the blueprints.

Gershon returned to the hill some days later. The area teemed with men and machines. Along the perimeter of the area, on the crest above the small village, two women squatted, waiting. They wore skirts and blouses, and their lips were painted bright red. He saw an engineer noncom walk over and chase them off. They went back down toward the little village, laughing.

The days were still hot, but the nights had begun to turn cool. Gershon would sit at his table in the officers mess and gaze out the window at the hill. He no longer thought of the grave or the village. Building after building had come up. Paths had been marked between the buildings. The new stone-lined drainage ditches constructed by the engineers had easily contained a recent heavy rain. Soon the hospital buildings would come up and then the chapel. New, all new. He looked at the hill and felt quietly exultant.

And that was the way he was feeling on the morning not long afterward when the new division chaplain walked into his office unannounced and asked if they could talk alone. Gershon sent Gabriel away.

The division chaplain had been in Korea less than two weeks. His lean, bespectacled face wore a sober look. Quietly he declined the chair offered him by Gershon and said in his soft voice that there was really no easy way for him to do this, he had not wanted to do it by phone, so he had come in person.

Gershon thought immediately of his aunt and uncle and felt the sudden surging thud of his heart.

The request had come from high up, the division chaplain said in a pained tone. Chaplain Loran was to be transferred out of the medical battalion.

Gershon stared at him. The beating of his heart became a rush of noise. He heard it in his ears.

"What did I do?"

"I don't know, chaplain."

"Who requested the transfer?"

"They didn't tell me. It came from someone in the office of the general and was relayed by one of the majors on the staff. It troubles me greatly."

"When do they want me transferred?"

"As soon as possible, I'm sorry to say."

Gershon looked around. Had the sun slipped behind a sudden cloud? When he turned back to the division chaplain he did not look at him directly; he looked past him at the bare wall.

"No one knows why?" he asked.

"They didn't tell me, chaplain. If I can help you in any way, let me know. I cannot begin to tell you how deeply this troubles me."

He went away, leaving behind him an air of apologetic and helpless regret.

Gershon crossed the compound to the office of the battalion commander.

"What are you talking about?" the major said in shocked surprise. "You're kidding. I haven't been informed of any transfer. Let me find out what's going on."

He made some phone calls. He told Gershon at lunch, "It's high, all right. Somewhere right around the Old Man. No one is saying anything else. Absolutely don't understand what's going on."

"Don't you, major?" The division psychiatrist leaned over from the next table. "The gods want blood. Can't agree to mortal demands without exacting blood. Chaplain our sacrificial lamb. Simple. All agree? Time-honored custom. Law of nature. Price of moral success is blood."

Gershon felt deep inside himself the fearful pain of old abandonments and the beginnings of rage.

He returned to his office and was greeted by a distressed Gabriel Rosen. "I heard it. Everyone knows. What are we going to do?"

"We're going to Seoul."

"Now? Right now?"

"Get the jeep, Gabriel."

"Yes, sir."

They drove to Seoul in the blistering afternoon heat. No, the Eighth Army chaplain said. Gershon could not be transferred to Seoul. They had already slotted the new man into Seoul. He was a career man, and it wouldn't be right to change things around at this late date. Also, there was a second man coming. He and Gershon would cover the two line divisions.

Gershon rode back to the battalion.

"It isn't fair," Gabriel Rosen said as they approached the division area.

Gershon said nothing.

"Will you take me with you?"

"I don't think so, Gabriel."

"But your replacement will probably be a goy."

"Work hard and convince him to keep you."

The orders to his new unit came through the following morning. Gabriel Rosen and Sammy Kim helped him pack. It was the last week in August. Gabriel Rosen, packing Gershon's books, said, "I didn't know you were interested in Kabbalah, rabbi."

"Watch how you handle those books, Gabriel."

"You made magic and got the engineers on the hill."

"Right. I'll make magic and get you to disappear if you don't stop wasting time."

"Yes, sir."

That afternoon Gabriel Rosen and Sammy Kim loaded his belongings into the jeep.

"Goodbye, Sammy. Take care."

"Yes, sah. Goodbye, sah. I miss you, sah. You good man, chaplain, sah."

The boy averted his eyes as he spoke.

Gershon had already said his farewells to the doctors he knew and to the somber-faced major. "Can't understand it," the major had said. "Bad for morale." Now, as Gabriel drove him out of the battalion, he saw the chapel white in the sunlight and the gleaming steeple and the weather vane. The varnished panels around the entrance door caught the high sun. They turned left into the main supply route and went on a few hundred yards. At the Korean market—a line of huddled shantylike stores along the road across from a teeming odorous village—they turned left again. They drove into the heart of the division area, past a tank company, a military police company, a reconnaissance company, an infantry regiment with a large building on which was painted the word LIBRARY. They turned left again and went past a guardpost into a compound whose buildings looked strikingly clean, neat, painted. Paths were clearly marked with whitewashed stones. Vehicles were parked in orderly rows. The compound—channeled, graded, terraced—sloped gradually toward the crest of a hill.

Gabriel Rosen brought the jeep to a stop before a long, white, angle-roofed building.

"This is it, sir."

"Goodbye, Gabriel."

"The guys told me to tell you they heard this is a tough outfit. Spit and polish and everything. Don't you think you'll want me? Won't it be hard to break in a new assistant?"

"I don't give a shit about what kind of outfit this is. Find out where to take my things."

Gabriel stared at him, open-mouthed.

They had stopped in front of the headquarters building. The sign near the door contained the name of the unit and a picture of a bulldozer painted in deep red and green colors. Gershon climbed out of the jeep and went slowly toward the building.

6

He followed a sergeant up the path to one of the terraced areas some yards below the crest of the hill. They were completing the new quarters for the officers, the sergeant said. He would have a private room in four or five weeks. In the meantime, did he mind sharing a Jamesway with one of the lieutenants? He did not mind.

He unpacked and set up his books and desk and clothes. He came out into the hot late afternoon air and walked down a narrow, winding, stone-lined path to the officers club. There were introductions and drinks. The officers were young, smartly dressed. The club had a new bar and new chairs and tables. The battalion commander, a well-built man with flat black hair and sharp gray eyes, stood drinking a martini and talking to a major. He nodded to Gershon and introduced him to the major, who shook Gershon's hand briskly. They went back to their conversation.

"What's the movie tonight, Stuart?" a second lieutenant everyone called Skippy asked the orderly behind the bar.

The orderly named a movie.

"How long is the first reel?"

"It's a two-beer reel, sir."

"Thank you, Stuart."

Gershon did not remain for the movie. He returned after dinner to his quarters and sat at his desk. Behind him were the desk and chair of his roommate. Their beds were on the other side of the Jamesway, each bed against a wall. It was not unlike the arrangement he had once had in the seminary with Arthur Leiden, save that here no wall separated desks from beds.

To the left of his desk was a narrow bookcase, its four rows of shelves almost filled with his books. The books were arranged in neat rows. He took down from the top shelf a kabbalistic work by Chaim Vital, a sixteenth-century kabbalist from Safed and Jerusalem. It was a while before he could lose himself in its pages. He was gone deep into the book when the door opened and his roommate entered.

"Awful movie. Awful. A sinful waste of time."

The text blurred, slipped away. Gershon looked up.

"I can't stand those dumb Westerns. The horses are smarter than the people. Where did I leave my writing paper? Here we are. Need any writing paper, chaplain? All set up? God, you really brought along some books, didn't you." He peered at the English titles, then looked over at Gershon with a grin. He was in his early twenties, an electrical engineer, with short, light-brown hair, a wide smile, and a warm and friendly air. His name was John Meron, and he was from a small town on Long Island not far from New York City. "Kabbalah?" he said. "Wow. Maybe you know some prayers that can speed the time up around here. Were you with the medics?"

"Yes."

He seemed about to remark something, thought better of it, and said instead, "I've got to write my nightly. If you need anything, give a yell. I like to keep on the right side of God."

"Which side is that?"

Meron laughed. He had a light high flowing laugh. "If you don't know, we're all in trouble."

"How long do you have left here?" Gershon asked.

"Until next June."

"That's how long I have."

"It's too long." His youngish features grew somber for a moment, then brightened. "We'll make it. You better believe we'll make it."

He sat at his desk, writing. The letter took him a long time. He filled many pages, read them slowly, folded them carefully, inserted them into an envelope, sealed the envelope, addressed it, and left it face-up on his desk. He went out for a few minutes, returned, and prepared for bed. As he took off his shirt, Gershon noticed around his neck what he thought to be a Catholic crucifix: the body of Jesus on the cross.

"Good night, chaplain. The generators go to sleep at midnight. You need anything?"

"No. Thank you."

Gershon sat at the desk awhile longer, reading. Then he too went to bed.

He could not sleep. He lay awake in the cool late August night and listened to the sounds all around him: an occasional vehicle; the quiet voices of officers passing by in the darkness outside; oriental music and then a news announcer from a radio in an adjoining Jamesway. He heard, barely audibly, something about British and French reactions to the recent Egyptian seizure of the Suez Canal; the election campaigns of Eisenhower and Stevenson; a plane crash somewhere in Europe. For a few moments he drifted in and out of sleep. Then he came sharply awake.

There was someone in the Jamesway. He sensed someone near his books. He opened his eyes and raised his head from the pillow. His eyes, accustomed now to the darkness, saw no one. Yet there was someone there. He lay back on the pillow. John Meron breathed softly in deep sleep. Distant laughter drifted through the darkness. He thought briefly of the medical battalion and the officers he knew and the major and the chapel on the hill. He felt nearly over-whelmed by a swamping sense of abandonment. Old wounds opened; buried visions stirred, awakened: a trans-Atlantic steamer sailed slowly away from a Hudson River quay; a handsome face smiled at him jauntily from the rectangular world of a photograph; twin graves stood on an inaccessible hill in a distant sun-drenched land. How he hated the night and its dark visions! Light, he needed light.

In the morning he rose and dressed and used the tubes tucked discreetly behind the Jamesway in a sheltering rise of earth. He washed and prayed the morning service. Meron, dressing quietly, glanced at him from time to time, taking in the phylacteries on his arm and head, the closed eyes, the intense concentration. He sensed the small sacred space Gershon carved out around him as he prayed. A boyhood friend, now a Jesuit priest, would pray like that: strange carriers of an otherworldly luminosity. The chaplain—pale skin, dark eyes, thick dark hair—looked gaunt, almost skeletal, a curious intensity on his boned features, a blended aura of anger and sadness hovering about him. He saw him touch the fingers of his right hand to his eyes and murmur some words. There was sanctity here, the holiness of altars and candle-lit chambers of meditation and quiet groves on green hillsides—places his Jesuit friend had once shown him when they met after a long separation and recounted their young lives. And what was John doing? Generators, power lines, power plants, transformers; John was supplying warmth and light to the world. All right? Each to his own light. His Jesuit friend had laughed and placed on John's shoulders an embracing arm. Meron watched the chaplain a moment longer, then went off to breakfast.

"Heal us, O Lord, and we will be healed," Gershon prayed, standing, eyes closed, seeing clearly the words. "Give us Your help . . . grant us a complete healing. . . ." Then he prayed, "Bless us, our Father, all of us together, with Your light. . . ." The words hovered before him, the letters shimmered. He could climb the letters, yes, and enter the sixth firmament and wander for the remainder of his time here through the Chamber of Healing and the Chamber of Building and on through to the million lights in the Chamber of Glory, where sat the most perfect of beings on the most exquisite of thrones. And what of those here? To hell with them! What was he to Korea and Korea to him? To hell with all of them!

He opened his eyes. The room—desks, chairs, beds, bookcase— leaped into view. He saw on Meron's desk the envelope with the letter he had written the night before, and he took it down with him to breakfast.

"Thank you, chaplain. Appreciate it. A lot on my mind this morning," said Meron. "Where are you going? Join us."

"I'll be back in a minute. I've got to teach the mess sergeant how to feed a card-carrying Jew."

He walked away, trailed by the curious and amused glances of the engineer officers around the table.

From the officers mess a path ran level for some feet, sloped downward, turned sharply, and continued on down until it vanished into the flat low area of the compound, a stretch of terrain on which stood Quonsets, buildings with angled roofs, the battalion motor pool, and a length of chewed-up earth crowded with neatly parked heavy construction equipment. There was no chapel.

Gershon had been assigned an office in the battalion headquarters Quonset. It was a large office, with two windows, two desks, a phone, a file cabinet, a typewriter, some chairs. The office of the battalion commander, a lieutenant colonel, was in the same Quonset. "I run a tight outfit, chaplain," he had said to Gershon the day before. "I like my officers to be aware of that. If you're entitled to your own jeep according to our T.O., you'll get one, of course. By all means, find yourself an assistant. You're not interested in military tactics, by any chance? I didn't think so. Good luck, chaplain, and welcome to engineers."

That morning he sat at his desk and made some phone calls, then walked over to the motor pool and the carpentry shop. He stood around awhile, chatting with the men. The street talk and gestures of all his early years flowed smoothly from him as he stood amidst men from Detroit, Chicago, Boston. They talked baseball and weather and neighborhoods. Reluctantly they returned to the reality of the day. "We can have it ready for you tomorrow morning, chaplain. Oiled, greased, ready to go. A what? Well, sure. We'll wire it to the front bumper guard. Sure. It'll hold. Anytime, chaplain."

He interviewed three men that afternoon, all regular attendants at his services, and chose one of them—a tall gangly clerk from the military police company; quiet, efficient; a Jewish boy from Boston —as his assistant. Then he typed and sent through channels a request to have Jewish services transferred from the medical battalion chapel to the chapel in the nearby infantry regiment. He had lunch at the officers mess. He ate scrambled eggs and listened to the talk about construction projects. The entire division was in transition to permanent housing, sewage, roads, power. Some of the talk was technical. He sat at the same table with John Meron and listened quietly. He returned to his office and prepared his monthly report. He stated that he had been reassigned and offered no explanations. He did not know what to say. At fifteen minutes to five he cleared his desk, locked the drawers, and walked up the winding path to his room.

A few minutes later, Meron came in.

"Tired," he murmured. "Long day."

He lay down on his bed and put his hand over his eyes.

Gershon turned off the phonograph.

"You can play it, chaplain," Meron said, his hand over his eyes. "No problem."

Later, at the bar, Skippy asked, "What's the movie tonight, Stuart?"

The orderly gave him the name of the movie.

Skippy, whose full name was Edward Skipworth, raised his beer glass in a sweeping gesture. "Another epic of the West, gentlemen. How long is the first reel?"

"It's a three-beer reel, sir."

"Thank you, Stuart."

The battalion commander, standing at the bar with a martini in his hand, asked Gershon, "How was your day, chaplain?"

"Fine, sir."

"We want you to feel yourself part of us, chaplain."

"Thank you, sir."

"We're bringing civilization to this place, chaplain. Roads, sewage, power plants. Did you see the story in *Stars and Stripes*?"

"Which story was that, sir?"

"'Civilization Fights Boredom. Morale at an All-Time High.' You didn't see it?"

"No, sir. I missed that one."

"Fine story. They didn't mention us, though. There's a meeting of our officers tomorrow at eighteen hundred you might want to attend."

"I have to go to Seoul tomorrow, sir. I'll have about a thousand men at Ascom City for the Jewish High Holidays. There are some details I have to take care of."

"Why doesn't the man in Seoul worry about it?" The battalion commander sipped from his martini glass and gazed narrowly at Gershon.

"There isn't any man in Seoul, sir. I'm the only Jewish chaplain in Korea."

"Are you really? I wasn't aware of that. You cover a large territory. You're the only Jewish chaplain in Korea, and you've just been made Special Troops chaplain?"

"Yes, sir."

Some of the officers were standing around listening to the conversation. The major who was the battalion adjutant said, "My God, the infinite wisdom of the army."

"We're having a field exercise in the middle of next week, chaplain," said the battalion commander. "I think you ought to join us for that. What do you think, Paul?"

"Very important," said the adjutant. "Definitely."

"I have to be in Ascom City for most of next week, sir," Gershon said. "The High Holidays are next week."

"Is that right? Well, I hope we see you around from time to time, chaplain," the battalion commander said. "Can I buy you a drink?"

"Thank you, sir. Yes. Scotch on the rocks."

"You heard the chaplain, Stuart."

"Yes, sir," said the orderly from behind the bar.

Gershon returned to his quarters after dinner and found Meron writing a letter. The lieutenant was bent over the paper and barely noticed Gershon's presence. Gershon began a letter to his aunt and uncle. The Jamesway was silent save for the scratchings of pens on paper. Somewhere nearby an armed forces radio announcer was giving the news. Meron put down his pen, read the letter, folded its many pages, inserted it in an envelope, sealed it, addressed it, and left it face-up on his desk. He yawned and stretched and looked at Gershon, who had long completed his letter and was trying to get into a passage of Kabbalah, without success.

"You want to see the movie, chaplain?"

"I don't think so."

"Neither do I. The wholesale slaughter of Indians doesn't appeal to me. Are you married, chaplain?"

"No."

"I'm engaged. I like writing to my fiancée. We promised we'd write every day, and I haven't missed a day yet. Not a day. I've made it a habit."

"You have to really want a habit like that."

"You better believe I want it."

"I wish a girl I know wanted it."

"Not enough mail, chaplain?"

"Not from her. She writes articles for philosophy journals and lectures for her classes. She doesn't seem to like writing letters. Listen, I want to ask you something. If I needed to have something built for religious purposes, can I give the request to the colonel?"

"What do you want built, chaplain?"

"It's called a succah. It's a kind of booth or hut with wooden sides and an open roof covered with leaves and branches."

"You'll have to include the specs with the request."

"I can do that."

"It shouldn't be a problem, chaplain. The colonel is pretty good as long as he knows you're giving him a full day's work. He wants his bird before he goes home. His wife's father is a three-star general in the Pentagon. The colonel really wants that bird. He keeps us in a sweat, but he knows what he's doing all the time. He's sharp. We're not going to see much of you here, are we? Why did they give you Special Troops? That's four thousand men, plus all the Jewish personnel in Korea. You're either very good or somebody doesn't like you." He thought for a moment and grinned. "Or both."

"I wish I knew," Gershon said. "I don't."

The next morning he flew to Seoul and was informed by the Eighth Army chaplain that for some reason the Jewish chaplain they were expecting daily would not arrive until some time in October. The second chaplain would come soon after. "I wish I knew what to tell you," he said. "I don't know what's going on and I can't get any answers. Can I help you in any way with your holiday arrangements?"

"Everything's all set up."

"The people at Ascom like the way you do things, chaplain."

"I'm not doing anything special."

"Do you need a lift back to the airfield?"

"Yes, sir."

"Use my jeep and driver."

"Thank you."

"Happy new year, chaplain."

"Thank you, sir."

He flew back in a rainstorm and landed in rain and fog. He called battalion from the airstrip, and a jeep and driver were dispatched to bring him back. He climbed the hill to his quarters, feeling very tired. The rain had become an annoying drizzle. He entered his room and saw John Meron sitting in a chair and looking at his bookcase.

The second lieutenant rose awkwardly, his boyish features flushing.

"Sorry," he murmured. "Admiring your books, chaplain. Sorry."

"Don't be silly, John. Read whatever you want. How was your day?"

"Nothing special. I really like your books, chaplain. I didn't touch any of them, you understand. I wouldn't do that. Are these Hebrew? Aramaic? They look old. I really admire your books. I have a friend who goes in for books. He's a Jesuit priest. A great guy. Boy, does he buy books."

"Borrow whatever you want, John. Anytime. Just keep the line straight. You know, keep the books lined up straight. I have a friend who used to enjoy pushing them in. I think I'll take a shower and head down to the club. I can use a drink. Did you ever fly in an L-19 through a rainstorm? I thought I would become the reason for a memorial service."

He went back down the path and along the division road to the shower. He had some drinks in the club and sat around talking with the officers. After dinner he sat through the first reel of a movie musical. In the darkness of the club he heard Skippy's voice. "How long is this second reel going to be, Stuart my boy?"

"It's a three-beer reel, sir."

"Thank you, Stuart my boy."

"I think we're going to have to take out the bridge across your beer supply, lieutenant," came the voice of the battalion commander in the darkness.

"That would constitute an abridgment of my rights, sir."

There was laughter from the officers in the room.

The movie came back on, a garish color spectacle of skin and nonsense.

Some time after the movie Gershon returned to his quarters. The night was cool. He found Meron asleep. He read for a while and went to bed. He slept and woke and sensed again, with a shiver of fear, a presence near his books. He saw no one. He fell asleep.

The next night he waited until Meron had completed his "nightly," as he called it. When the letter lay sealed and addressed on his roommate's desk, Gershon asked quietly if he might impose upon him for a favor. He needed careful diagrams of the succah, with a list of the lumber and the man-hours required to accomplish the work. He could draw the hut, but he was not sure he would be able to translate the drawings into lumber and men.

"Let's see the drawing, chaplain."

Meron watched Gershon sketch the hut on a sheet of airmail paper.

"That's no problem," he said. "But I don't think they'll let you put brush on the roof. The brush here has bugs and things, and some people think it may cause hemorrhagic fever. And I don't think they'll let you take branches off live trees. Let me think about it. Can't you use anything else?"

"It has to be brush, or something like leaves."

"Use a camouflage net."

"What?"

"A camouflage net should do it, chaplain. It looks like brush and leaves. You'll have some sunlight coming through it."

The succah needed the leaves and branches of living wood, not the dead gnarled strings of a net.

That night, in the darkness of the Jamesway, Gershon had a dream-like vision. The man who appeared to him in this vision listened patiently to Gershon's words, then smiled in his disdainful way and said, There is no wood available, Loran? In all of Korea?

It's a big succah, professor.

The seminary also builds a big succah, Loran.

We can't use brush. There is a danger of disease from insects.

Disease?

Yes, professor.

And your only solution is to use a—how do you call it?—a camouflage net?

Yes.

Well—use it.

Thank you.

Loran.

Yes?

You are not taking care of yourself. You look thin. To injure your body is a far more serious violation of Halacha than to build a succah with camouflage nets. Do you feel all right?

I feel fine, professor.

Take care of yourself, Loran.

Professor. Wait. Please. I have—another problem.

Yes?

Professor Keter doesn't answer my letters.

No? Write him again. The fact that he does not answer your letters does not mean that he does not read them. Enjoy your succah, Loran. And he gave Gershon the traditional greeting in Hebrew for the Jewish new year.

For a long time his image remained in the dark silent air of the Jamesway—the roundish pink face, the blue eyes, the silver hair, the lips with the haughty disparaging smile—the image of Professor Nathan Malkuson. Then, slowly, it faded.

The days went by. As he rode around the division, driven by the tall silent soldier who was his new assistant, he saw the transformation that was taking place all through the valley. Old and worn tents and Jamesways were being replaced by new Quonsets; permanent buildings of stone and wood were being erected; the drab and gray heaviness of blotched outside walls was being repaired and painted. On the way north to the infantry regiment one day he saw rows of new Quonsets on the hill behind the medical battalion and the skeleton of the structure that would be the new chapel. In the engineering battalion the officers Quonset was under construction on the crest of the hill above the present line of Jamesways. The tents of the enlisted men gradually disappeared. One afternoon during that week, while digging out a large rectangle of earth for the cement floor of a Quonset, a bulldozer opened a vast common grave that contained more than thirty skeletons of boys whose age could not have been more than fifteen or sixteen. Gershon was in Seoul when it happened, and he learned of it in the officers club that night from Meron.

"What did they do?"

"They covered it over and moved the building somewhere else."

"Why were they killed?"

"Who knows?"

"Who killed them?"

"The communists."

In Seoul that afternoon he had seen a policeman beating a young boy, beating him on a street, with his club, beating him, the boy cowering, head bent, standing beneath the blows, men and women passing by, averting their eyes.

"I hate this place," he said to Meron.

"I don't know anyone who doesn't, chaplain."

"How was your day, chaplain?" the battalion commander asked.

"Fine, sir."

"We don't see you, chaplain. You seem to be everywhere except with us. The G-4 has approved your little construction project."

"Sir?"

"That—what was it?—that succah." He pronounced it "sookky."

"Oh. Yes, sir. Thank you."

"What good are you to us if you're never here, chaplain?"

Early the next morning Gershon gave a character guidance lecture to the reconnaissance company, then flew down to Ascom City. He talked with officers and sergeants about quarters for the Jewish personnel coming in to attend services for the High Holidays; he talked with mess sergeants about food. On the way back he watched through the flimsy window of the aircraft as the sun went down in a spectacular display of colors, deep red and yellow and orange and violet playing across the sky. It seemed a strange and discordant sight: broken light splashing pastel loveliness across the blood and suffering of the broken land.

He returned to Ascom City a few days later. Nearly one thousand men came into the base from all over the country. There were two days of services. He rode back to the battalion in a typhoon. His assistant drove the jeep skilfully. They went along flooded roads and over bridges beneath which streams had turned into torrents. The wind tore at the canvas top and sides and at the plastic windows. He returned exhausted to his quarters and found a letter from his aunt. His uncle was not too well. She wished him a happy and healthy new year. They should all be together again soon and in health. He should be careful. Did he need anything? His uncle sent his love.

Two days later there was a half-page story in *Stars and Stripes* about the High Holiday services. His picture was in the paper, as well as his jeep with the blue and white wooden tablets wired to the front bumper. Prominently mentioned after his name in the caption beneath his picture was the engineer battalion.

He returned to Ascom City in the second week of September to conduct the service for the Day of Atonement. He fasted all that day, and all that day he stood on his feet, leading the service in the thronged chapel. He felt oddly light-headed at the end of the day and ate little. He slept in Ascom City that night, and in a dream he was in the dormitory elevator with Professor Malkuson and the elevator jammed between floors and he stood there calmly discussing some passages of Talmud with the professor until the elevator started up again. The next morning he returned to the battalion.

That afternoon a squad of men from one of the battalion companies was brought over to the area near division headquarters. There on a knoll on the edge of the division parade ground, which fronted the offices of the commanding general and the division chaplain, Gershon chose an area of ground. He watched as the men measured it, marked it with cords, began cutting the wood. The next day there was a story in *Stars and Stripes* about the Yom Kippur service. Once again there was his jeep and the name of the battalion.

"You're making us famous," Meron told him that evening.

Gershon did not respond.

"Are you all right, chaplain? You look awful."

"I think I'm still recovering from the fast."

"I've got some really good cookies my fiancée sent me."

"Thanks, no. John, I could use a drink. Will you join me?"

"No thanks, chaplain. I've got my nightly to work on."

The succah was completed the next day. Gershon watched as the men pulled the camouflage nets over the top of the succah. They used two nets. A cool and speckled dimness settled upon the interior of the succah. Outside, the parade ground baked in the early afternoon sun. Gershon thanked the men and shook their hands. He thanked the sergeant and patted his shoulder. The men left.

Gershon stood alone outside the succah. He could smell its fresh-cut wood. He circled it slowly. It seemed larger than he had thought it would be when he had outlined its dimensions on the piece of paper for Meron. Clean, clean. New wood everywhere, two-by-fours, plywood, the interior bare, the earth uncovered. He would have chairs brought in and tables for an altar and wine and cakes for Kiddush. The power cord strung from the nearby Quonset would give them light. He came through the door and stood inside the sudden shadows that lay upon the bare earthen floor. The air was cool. He held to himself in a silent and motionless embrace the tranquility of this hut that he had caused to be built—this memory of a wilderness wandering and of booths dwelt in during ancient harvests.

Men came from all over the division to attend the services of the Festival of Booths. He preached about the temporary and the permanent in life, about the need to build again and again despite all the minor and major destructions visited upon us by man and God. And he would come to the succah in the early evenings and sit in its shadows and listen to the soft winds moving through the camouflage nets.

One morning he came to the succah and there was the G-4, dark eyes, dark hair, short of stature, saturnine.

"Nice, chaplain," he said. "Very nice."

"Thank you for approving it, sir."

"You seem to enjoy having engineers do your building for you, chaplain. What next?"

"I can't think of anything, sir."

"Praise the Lord. Good luck, chaplain."

"Thank you, sir."

He came into the succah one evening that week and sat in a chair in front of the table he had set up as an altar. On the table lay the palm frond and citron he had been sent airmail from the Jewish Welfare Board in the States. These were the living symbols of the festival, its green and golden life. Two bulbs burned brightly below the canopy of camouflage nets. It was a cool evening. Always you invited guests into your succah; that was an ancient tradition. And always there were invisible guests there as well—*ushpizin,* they were called—the patriarchs Abraham, Isaac, and Jacob. You shared the loveliness of the hut, the sweet sadness of its intimate, bare, and temporary beauty. There was a knock on the door.

"Yes," Gershon heard himself say, for he knew who waited outside.

The door opened. Nathan Malkuson entered and was followed immediately by Jakob Keter.

Gershon stood. They exchanged the greetings of the festival.

How did you manage such a thing in this barbaric land? asked Nathan Malkuson.

I thought of it. A gentile drew up the plans. The engineers built it.

They sat in chairs before the altar.

An unusual roof, said Malkuson, looking up. What do you say, Keter? Is it not an unusual roof?

Unusual, said Jakob Keter. It conceals and reveals simultaneously. It hides the sun and lets in the sun simultaneously. Unusual. Yes. How are you, Mr. Loran?

All right, I guess, professor.

I do read your letters, Mr. Loran.

This is not exactly a proper succah, Loran, said Professor Malkuson. A synagogue and a succah at one and the same time. Interesting. And unusual. But all things considered—

Do you read, Mr. Loran? Do you study?

Yes. I'm trying.

Do not stop studying, Mr. Loran. In a place where there are no people, you be a person.

It is a big succah, Loran. You had in mind the seminary succah when you drew up the plans? The camouflage effect is intriguing. I think we will study a little, and then leave. What do you say, Keter?

A little Talmud cannot hurt.

Not nearly as much as a little Kabbalah.

What shall we study, Malkuson?

Gershon sat very still and in his vision studied Torah with his two teachers, his *ushpizin*, his guests in the silent interior of his succah on this cool Korean night.

The next day he saw with amazement the full-page spread on the succah in *Stars and Stripes*, the story of its construction by the battalion and a brief account of the festival. There were many photographs. He had not thought they would turn it into so big a story. "Fine story, chaplain," said the battalion commander. "Let me buy you a drink. Getting some nice calls about that story. Very pretty succah."

After dinner that evening Gershon walked down the path from the officers mess, crossed the compound, went past the guardpost and along the division road to the parade ground. He stood for a moment on the knoll near the door to the succah. The sky was paling into dusk from its brilliant stream of sunset colors. He saw over a distant hill a single star. He gazed at its flickering brightness. Another star appeared, not far from the first: pinpoints of bluish light bearing down upon him from—his own world? another galaxy? living stars? the lights of stars long dead? He came into the darkening interior of the succah and sat in a chair before the altar. The camouflage nets were dark now overhead. Night came as he sat and with it the canopy of starry sky. Through the nets he could see many stars. How alone he felt on this speck of cosmic dust that was his home. Still, there were questions to be asked, and he waited. He sensed after a while a puff of wind in the darkness, a growing invisibility around him. A descent had been made into his succah. Yes. Ask Him. Ask Him now. He was here, in all His power. Ask. Listen. Please. Why do You make them suffer so, these people, this land? Jews suffer because many think them to be the reconnaissance troops for the world, and such troops take the highest casualties. But to suffer merely because you are in the path of empires! How meaningless such suffering! Explain it. Please.

There was no answer.

Gershon remained silent. One does not act rudely toward a guest. They sat together in the darkness until the air grew cold. Gershon shivered and rose and left the succah and returned to his battalion.

Four days later he watched with sadness as the succah was dismantled. The plywood and two-by-fours were piled into a truck. The camouflage nets were folded. The men went away. Gershon stood alone on the empty earth, which still bore the marks of the two-by-fours that had framed the succah. It was the first week of October. The air was cold. An L-19 buzzed lazily overhead. He felt a wearying melancholy settle upon him. Nothing now until Chanukah. Into the fall and winter now. A lengthy tunnel of darkness now. He stood there a long time on the scuffed and trodden earth of the vanished succah. Then he walked back slowly to the battalion.

The new chaplain arrived ten days later, an efficient, friendly career soldier, a major, who acclimated himself cheerfully to the

Seoul chapel. Gershon liked him but could not take his cheerfulness for too long without in some strange way feeling himself made melancholy by it. This chaplain took responsibility for the Jewish personnel of Seoul, Inchon, Ascom, Pusan, and I Corps at Uijongbu. Gershon tended to the line divisions.

The days grew short. Sharp coldness invaded the nights. He faced the winter with a determined sense of calm, whose source he could not understand but which he found distinctly pleasurable.

The officers Quonsets were finally completed in the middle of October. One day a sergeant appeared in Gershon's office, the same sergeant who had assigned him to the Jamesway about seven weeks before. That night Gershon talked with his roommate. When it came time for the officers to leave the Jamesways, Gershon chose to room with John Meron. He packed his belongings and moved to the Quonset on the crest of the hill.

Two weeks later the second of the new Jewish chaplains arrived in Korea.

He announced his arrival to Gershon in a curious way. Gershon had no idea who he might be. He had asked about those who had originally been slated to come and when they had not appeared had simply lost interest. He had recognized none of the names given him.

The weeks before the arrival of the new chaplain were of a calmness he had not thought it possible to achieve in this land. He rode by jeep and plane throughout the line divisions. His jeep was known; men hailed him as he drove along the roads. The air was cool and autumnal, graced with clear light and with sunsets that emptied him of words. All through the land now he saw the faint beginnings of rebirth from the carnage of war: the start of permanent dwellings in villages, clean new shops in the nearby Korean market, paved roads. The engineers were busy, busy. He saw little of the officers save when he ate with the battalion. When he was in his office it seemed an endless line of men trooped in to see him. They came from all the Special Troop outfits of the division. He felt himself chaplain of all the valley. His assistant typed with swift and silent efficiency, cared for the files, drove him about. On occasion when Gershon heard him speak in the accents of his native New England, memories were evoked in him of seminary years that seemed so distant now it was as if they had never been.

He received a letter from Karen, her first in more than a month. Her father had been ill—a mild coronary just before the High Holidays. The family had been plunged into a turmoil of dread. He was well now, almost fully recovered. Two of her papers had been accepted for publication. She enjoyed the clippings he sent. But why did he need to travel around so much? And he looked so thin. She missed him. She loved him. She would try to write more often. Did he know that Jakob Keter was spending the semester at the University of Pennsylvania? Did he want her to send him some cookies and things? Her parents sent their very best. He shouldn't worry about her father. He was really all right now. And Gershon dreamed of her that night, held her to him, felt upon his fingers the moist warmth of her flesh, dreamed until there came over him the moment of exquisite release.

Officers came and went in the battalion. There were parties for those leaving—sayonara parties, they were called—boisterous affairs that Gershon would attend for a while, then slip away from to return to his quarters—invariably to find John at his desk writing his letter. He would read and listen to music and wake in the morning and go to his office or leave for a trip to a distant unit. They knew him now at the airstrip. And he knew the pilots of the division air company. He knew the MP and recon company sergeants, the ordnance and quartermaster sergeants, officers and noncoms up and down the valley, in the distant regiment, in the other line division.

It was in those final days of October that the medical battalion moved to the hill. He watched the completion of the new chapel as he rode by day after day along the main supply route. It rose on the hill like a white light, the steeple, without a cross, shining against the clear blue autumn sky. The old compound was now the division replacement depot. Chaplains interviewed and evaluated all enlisted men who came down with venereal disease. He saw many every week who had it. Often they caught it at that replacement depot on their first night in the division. He would drive past the compound and see himself walking across it in the bitter snows of the past winter, bent forward against the wind. He saw the fear in his eyes, felt the pounding in his heart. How strange that he had not heard that loud beating of his heart for such a long time now. He sensed that he had conquered something inside himself. He did not know what it was, but he was certain it lay vanquished, and the thought filled him with exultation each time he drove by the old medical battalion compound. The chapel was gone. The hospital was gone. All was gone to the hill. He did not once ride up to that hill. He felt no need for that. His was now the world of the river valley.

There were maneuvers in that valley and its nearby hills, the thud of heavy guns, infantry charges. Jets wheeled overhead. Tanks roamed the valley and churned the earth. American and Korean troops moved up and down the main supply route in trucks and jeeps. He slept two nights in the field with the battalion. The day they returned he flew to the regiment in the north. Then he flew to the division near Panmunjom. Then he drove to the artillery unit in the hills. Leaves had turned and were beginning to fall. The land was bathed in soft browns and reds and yellows and seemed to have become comforting to his eyes. The fields were still green, flowers sparkled on the hills. He saw farmers working the terraced earth, children on the roads on their way to school, old men in flowing white garments and tall stovepipe hats watching him stoically as he rode by. Once he saw on the road an old man wearing a tall dark skullcap, and he was reminded of his uncle. He came close to sensing a dignity and strength in the suffering people of the land. Yes, there was disease, there was filth. There were pimps and whores and thieves. Armies, the most peripheral of guests, always brought out the peripheral from among their hosts.

Early in the last week of October came the first night of frost. Water that John had left outside in their five-gallon can froze solid as iron. He rode to Seoul that day for an administrative conference of Eighth Army chaplains and in the late afternoon visited the Jewish chapel. The chaplain cheerfully showed him around. A new section had been added on to it. The building now had, in addition to the chapel, a lounge, offices, a refrigerator, a freezer, a stove. "I asked and they gave," said the chaplain. "Good people, fine people.

Can I treat you to a kosher dinner, Gershon?" They ate together in the lounge, served by a Korean woman. A Korean university student interested in Judaism ate with them. The talk rambled. The student talked reluctantly of his childhood in a village near Pusan, the loss of his two brothers in the war. What was the next holiday of the Jewish people? he wanted to know, speaking softly and not looking directly at either of them. What did it mean, Chanukah? How was it celebrated? They talked of the American presence in Korea. The Americans should leave, the student said quietly. Then the South Korean army would invade the north, Gershon said. Yes, said the student. The north would be defeated and the Chinese would enter the war, said Gershon. Yes, said the student, and the Americans would return and they would all then be able to complete the conquest of the north and reunite their sacred land. The conversation turned back to Chanukah.

On the way out of the chapel Gershon asked about the incoming Jewish chaplain. He was due in a few days, said the other. No, it wasn't the one they had expected, it was someone else, he didn't have the name and couldn't understand the cause of all the confusion. Did Gershon want to take some chicken back with him to the battalion?

That week parkas were issued to division personnel. On a day toward the end of that month Gershon drove to Seoul and recorded six broadcasts for the armed forces radio station. He returned to the battalion late in the afternoon and came into his room. He was alone. The new rectangular oil furnace burned silently. Over the radio he had bought a few days before at the PX came news of a threat of war in the Middle East. He washed and changed into a fresh uniform. He sensed something wrong about the room. He did not know what it was. They had arranged the room in the Quonset precisely as they had the Jamesway. He looked slowly around and shrugged and put on his battalion scarf. He wondered what the movie would be that night. He stood at the door a moment, gazed around the room, then opened the door and stepped out. It was nearly dark. The air was cold. He closed the door and started down the path toward the officers club. Then he stopped. His eyes now saw vividly what they had looked at but had not seen before. A slow

wheeling of the world occurred then for him, a shuddering movement through all things near and far. He turned and ran back up
the path and threw open the door and stood there in the doorway,
staring at the bookcase near his desk. Some of the books on the
shelves had been pushed in.

From his office in the deserted headquarters Quonset he called
Seoul. Then he called the medical battalion of the division near
Panmunjom. A few minutes before noon the next day his jeep pulled
off the road and into the compound of the distant medical battalion.
The jeep came to a stop in front of the headquarters Quonset. Stand-
ing outside waiting for him was Arthur Leiden.

7

On the telephone the day before he had said, "Arthur, is it you? Is it really you?"

"Hello? I can hardly hear you. Hello?" The voice came through as if muffled by water. "Who is this?"

"It's Gershon. Can you hear me now?"

"Barely. Dear Gershon. Hello."

"I can't believe this. What are you doing here?"

"I drove by to surprise you. You got my message?"

"I saw the books. Yes. I thought you were in the navy."

"The navy is a long story, dear Gershon. I was sufficiently suave but insufficiently secure for the navy. Hello? Can you hear me? This is a terrible telephone, Gershon. Is this the best they can do in this place for telephones?"

"Arthur?"

"Yes?"

"Will you be in your battalion tomorrow around noon?"

"I wasn't planning on going anywhere tomorrow."

"I'll see you then."

"Hello? Gershon?"

"Yes?"

"Are you going to Japan anytime soon?"

"I have a religious retreat in a few weeks. Why do—?"

"I've got to get to Japan."

"You just got to Korea, Arthur."

"I know where I am, Gershon. Is getting to Japan a problem? What do I have to do?"

"We'll talk when I see you tomorrow."

"What?"

"I'll see you tomorrow, Arthur. We'll talk about Japan tomorrow."

"How can we run an army with this telephone system?"

"Goodbye, Arthur. It is you, isn't it? Arthur?"

"It's me, dear Gershon. Yes."

He climbed out of the jeep. They stood a moment in the sunlight looking at each other. Incredibly, Arthur's face was deeply tanned. He wore a combat outfit and a field jacket and cap. His name was on a patch over the right breast pocket. He looked slightly stooped, and he squinted in the bright noonday sun.

They shook hands. Gershon said, "Hello, Arthur. You're not a vision, are you?"

"You would know that better than I, dear Gershon. Am I beautifully unexpected?"

"That's an apt way to put it. Yes."

"This whole place looks to me like a vision. You've lost weight, Gershon."

"About thirty-five pounds."

"Are you all right?"

"I've never felt better in my life. Do you have an assistant and an office yet? Are they giving you a jeep?"

"I only just got here. I'm not even sure I know what day of the week today is. My spacetime has suffered curvature and fluctuation. The mass of this mess is too much for me. A joke from Uncle Albert. Never mind. Are you hungry? I woke up too late for breakfast. Let's get something to eat. How do you keep kosher in this place? You'll have to teach me everything."

Gershon turned to his assistant, who sat looking at them from behind the wheel of the jeep. "Howard, get some lunch. Meet me back here in an hour. This is Chaplain Arthur Leiden. Howard Morten. Also from around Boston."

"Really?" said Arthur with only mild interest. "Where?"

"Chestnut Hill, sir."

"Newton Centre," said Arthur. "Neighbors."

"I'm pleased to meet you, sir. Are you related to Charles Leiden, sir?"

"Yes. I'm related to Charles Leiden. I like your jeep, Gershon. I like those tablets. There was a piece on you and your jeep in an issue of *Stars and Stripes* in Camp Drake. I saw it the night I laid over in Japan. What night was that? I forget. They even had a story on you in the local paper in Albuquerque."

"Where? What were you doing in Albuquerque?"

"I was serving your uncle and mine, dear Gershon. That's right. Our God was not kind to His humble servant. I seem to gravitate toward certain dark holes on the planet, and sometimes with nearly the speed of light. It wasn't enough that I grew up near there while they made the fucking bomb—if you'll pardon the expression; I had to be stationed there too. What do you call that? Irony? God's gambit with His frail servant?"

Two enlisted men went by. Gershon and Arthur returned their salutes. Three two-and-a-half-ton trucks passed along the road, sending up clouds of dust. An ambulance went past the battalion guard-post and turned onto the road. Two elderly Korean men walked slowly by on the road, the A-frames on their backs laden with brush. The autumnal noon air carried odors of sour cabbage and sewage.

"Am I supposed to get used to this?" Arthur asked. "Is that the idea?"

"I don't know what the idea is, Arthur. This place has just been through a war."

"Another moment of glory in the history of the species. Come on, Gershon. Let's eat."

They started across the compound, a narrow, flat stretch of terrain at the rim of a small valley. On the crest of the hill beyond the battalion were gun emplacements and observation posts that faced a river and a bridge and more gun emplacements and observation posts and a long length of naked gullies and rock-strewn flatland and then the gun emplacements and observation posts of the communist army.

"Have you seen this place?" Arthur asked. "Have you been around here?"

"I've been conducting services here once a week for months."

"They've put me at the end of the world." He was silent a moment as they passed a noncom. "That idiot MacArthur wanted to use the bomb on them. How do we ever manage to survive our generals?"

"Arthur, I think—"

"I'm quoting my mother, dear Gershon. I will be discreet. Trust me. Mouth closed. A general is a deity. I know. What do I do about kashrut up here, Gershon? I haven't eaten traif since I left Harvard."

"Didn't he tell you anything in Seoul?"

"My God, Gershon, he's such a smiling clod. He put my teeth on edge. I spent twenty minutes with him and fled."

"We'll talk to the mess sergeant. What did you eat in New Mexico?"

"I lived off the generosity of our brethren in Albuquerque and Los Alamos. You would be surprised at how many members of our tribe are involved in the protection of our land through weapons development. You would be surprised at the weapons. Enough said. The enemy is everywhere, right? Especially the F.B.I. and the C.I.D. and all the other letters of the alphabet. God, I'm hungry. What day is today? I'm not kidding. I've really lost track of time."

They sat in the officers mess over scrambled eggs and coffee.

"The navy danced me round and round," Arthur said. "They were sure, they weren't sure. I was cleared, I wasn't cleared. They approved, they disapproved. My father started making phone calls. Then my mother started making phone calls. My mother makes extraordinary phone calls. Nothing. No one could buck the security people, and they were in no hurry. Finally the seminary released me."

"How do you mean, released you?"

"From my chaplaincy obligation."

Gershon stared at him.

"What is the poor bastard doing here, you are asking. Right? I volunteered for the army instead. That's right. The thought of being the only one in our class to escape the chaplaincy because of some stupid bureaucratic idiocy was too much for me, dear Gershon. How face the accusing light in all your eyes for a lifetime? Right? I thought of the air force and chose the army. Less fussy, the army.

Less hysterical. My father was disappointed. Very long naval tradition in the family. Listen. When we're done, will you show me how you work your files and schedule your services? How do you keep day-to-day records? Do you have anything to do with non-Jews, or is it only Jews who come to you? God, I'm tired all of a sudden. This time change has really knocked me out."

Some of the battalion officers had been stopping by to greet Gershon. The adjutant, a tall, red-haired major, said, "There's going to be a war out there, chaplain."

"I hope not," Gershon said.

"We may all see Jerusalem if there's a war out there," the adjutant said, walking off.

"What's he talking about?" Arthur asked.

"Don't you know what's going on?"

"I don't know anything. Listen. How many times have you been to Japan?"

"Twice."

"That's all? Twice?"

"This isn't a picnic, Arthur. This is a combat zone."

"Did you see Kyoto?"

"Yes."

"Did you like it?"

"Sure. It's a beautiful city. I think we—"

"I have to see Kyoto, Gershon."

"It's worth seeing."

"No. I mean I *have* to see it."

"Arthur, it's a long ride back to my battalion, and I don't want to navigate those mountain passes at night. You wanted to know something about files and things."

"Okay, dear Gershon. Okay. But first I must, I absolutely must, go to the john. Will you join me?"

Some minutes later, as they walked back across the compound, Arthur said, "Do you hear from Karen?"

"Yes. Not often, but I hear."

"I've lost all touch with them."

"Her father had a mild heart attack. He's recovered."

"Are you still studying Kabbalah?"

"Yes."

"With Keter?"

"Informally, you might say."

"He's in Philadelphia for the semester. He went there in the summer from Jerusalem for some kind of specialized surgery and decided to be near his doctors for a while, so U of P invited him to teach."

"I didn't know about the surgery. Is he all right?"

"Keter is indestructible. He has an inexhaustible supply of incantations and all kinds of private agreements with the forces of light and darkness. Gershon, when can I go to Japan?"

"You'll be due for an R and R in early March, I think."

"March? I don't want to wait until March."

"Arthur—"

"For God's sake, Gershon, you don't think I volunteered to come here so I can sit on my—"

"Volunteered? You volunteered?"

"I didn't even know it was open until less than a month ago. Someone else was going. I made some phone calls. It was a mess. I didn't do all that just to sit here."

Gershon stopped. They were approaching the headquarters building. His assistant stood near the jeep, talking with a group of enlisted men. Gershon saw them all stare at Arthur for a moment, then look away.

"I think there's a religious retreat scheduled for January," he said. "What's in Japan, Arthur? What's going on?"

"January? I can wait until January. Yes. January is fine."

"Let me show you how to handle the files and the reports."

They worked together inside a small, windowless office.

"You're going to miss that Albuquerque sunlight after a while," Gershon said.

"You think so, dear Gershon? I've got news for you. I don't think I'm going to miss it at all."

"You ought to interview some kids and get yourself an assistant. And a jeep. You'll be covering your entire division. You'll probably need to do a lot of flying too. You've got units all up and down these hills."

"Maybe I'll get my name in the papers too."

"It's good to see you, Arthur. Really. It got very lonely here at times."

"What do we do for Chanukah? Anything special?"

"No. I'll have evening services and I'll light the candles. I'm not planning anything special."

"There's no way I can get to Japan before January?"

"Arthur—"

"Okay, okay. I'll call you later in the week. I hate those phones. How do we ever win wars with those phones?"

Later, on the road through the mountains, his assistant said, "Sir, Chaplain Leiden's father once talked to our high school at an assembly. That's how I remembered him. He's a physicist, isn't he?"

"Yes."

"Didn't he have something to do with the atomic bomb?"

"Yes."

"That's why I remembered him. Some of the other guys also remembered his name. Charles Leiden. That bomb probably saved my brother's life. He was all set to go in with the invasion of Japan."

"What did he talk about at the assembly?"

"I don't remember. Something about the future. I don't remember."

A wind blew through the mountains. The spines of the hills were bare and stony. Small valleys lay below the towering ridges. There was little traffic on this road. He could see villages and oxen and terraced hillsides and scrub brush and browning grass. The jeep bounced on the rough road, and he held himself relaxed in the hard seat, not fighting it, feeling the ruts and stones through the jeep floorboard, through his boots, into his legs and spine. He was glad he would not have to traverse these hills as often now as he had before. This was Arthur's territory now. How strange Arthur seemed, off balance somehow, the cool poise all on the surface. He thought a moment longer about Arthur, then forgot him. The sun had slid behind the hills. The road was in deep shadow. They drove in tense silence until they came down out of the hills. A hazy dusk covered his valley.

He washed and shaved and put on a fresh uniform. Wearied by

the jeep ride over the hills and disturbed by the nervous disorienta-
tion he had sensed in Arthur Leiden, he wanted silence in the room
and did not turn on the radio or phonograph. He remembered
clearly and with regret the inadvertent remark made long ago to
the F.B.I. agent about the cards Arthur had written. Could that
have hurt Arthur's entry into the navy? Why had he said that? To
this day he did not know. He had done so many things he could not
really understand, as if in obedience to some dark law of human
gravity which moved him pitilessly this way and that and lay beyond comprehension. Arthur Leiden in Korea in the next division.
They would share the line divisions as they had once shared a room.
How strange the machinations of the Author of light.

In the officers club, the battalion commander stood at the bar with
a martini in one hand and a copy of *Stars and Stripes* in the other.
The level of noise in the club seemed unusually high. The colonel
looked up from the newspaper. Gershon slid onto a bar stool and
ordered a Scotch on the rocks.

"Here he is," the colonel said. "Look what's going on, chaplain.
Your guys are starting the third world war."

Gershon looked at the newspaper. The Israelis had invaded the
Sinai Peninsula and the Gaza Strip.

"We're going to become a camel division," he heard someone say
behind him.

Two days later the division was put on yellow alert and went out
to the field. Gershon lived with his battalion, slept in a tent, rode up
and down the division to be with his Special Troops. In the Middle
East there were paratroop drops, tank battles, the storming of fortifi-
cations. The Israelis conquered the Sinai and the Gaza Strip. Gershon
was in the field five days and lost all contact with Arthur Leiden.

At the officers briefing the day before the battalion was to leave
for the field, the colonel had said, among other things, "And keep
your hands on your wallets. The slicky boys will be out there like
locusts. Are there any questions?"

Gershon did not know why he raised his hand. From somewhere
a dimly remembered conversation surfaced. Two noncoms in the

waiting room at Kimpo? Or was it Tachikawa? No, it was on board the C-124 during his last flight from Japan, after the R and R and the days in Kyoto and Tokyo. "Sir," he heard his voice in the crowded room. Could they detect the faint quiver? "Maybe we can offer something to the Turks and get them to stand perimeter guard for us."

There was a murmur of voices, a subdued stir of surprise. Every head in the room turned to look at him.

"What do you have in mind, chaplain?" the colonel asked in a faraway tone.

"I don't know, sir. Maybe they could use some ditch-digging equipment for a while. Some such thing." Why had he said that? Strange how calm he felt, his heart did not race, the faint tremor was gone out of his voice.

The colonel looked at him from across the room. "Let me think about it, chaplain. Any more questions, gentlemen?"

For the five nights they slept in the field, Turkish troops patrolled their perimeter. The Turks usually shot the thieves they spotted; or—so went the rumor—they castrated them or, in the winter, staked them out naked in the snow and left them to freeze to death. On the last night it rained. Gershon, dressed and half-asleep, heard the sound of nearby rifle fire. He did not leave his sleeping bag but lay very still listening to the rain on his tent. No one talked about it in the morning, and he said nothing.

They returned to the compound in the cold November rain. In the club that evening, officers thumped him on the back. Not a single theft had occurred.

"I think I'm going to take a Turk home with me," the adjutant said. "Give me a secure feeling."

"Have a drink, chaplain," the colonel said. "Stuart, a Scotch on the rocks for the chaplain."

"Yes, sir."

"The medics got themselves creamed," said Skippy.

"No," someone said. "Really?"

"All the slicky boys the Turks kept away from us descended on the poor medics."

There was laughter.

"Your guys don't have to worry about slicky boys, right, chaplain?" the colonel said. "A four-day war. That's a great little army your guys have out there. Great tactics. A classic. Anytime you have another idea, chaplain, let me know."

"Right," said the adjutant. "Right."

After the movie Gershon started back to his quarters in the rain. He went carefully up the path. Guards patrolled the wire fence perimeter. They wore ponchos and moved slowly. He found John Meron inside writing his nightly letter.

John looked up. "How was the movie, chappy?"

"Not bad. I like Sinatra." It was late. He began to get out of his clothes. "This bed will be a pleasure tonight."

"Weren't those Turks something? The last time we went out, the colonel had his wallet slickied right from under his pillow while he slept."

"I didn't know that."

"They even slickied one of my fiancée's letters. With these guys for allies, who needs enemies? Bless the Turks."

Gershon yawned. "Have they ever hit the compound?"

"Not since I've been here. I'd like to see them try it."

"Boy, am I sleepy."

"What's that? A good luck charm? I always meant to ask what that was."

"Yes. An old man in my synagogue gave it to me."

"Like a cross? No. A Saint Christopher."

"Something like that. God, this bed feels good."

"Chappy?"

"Yes, John."

"Were you planning to go to Japan soon on R and R?"

"I'm not due for R and R until about January."

"Do you think we might go together? I don't like going alone, and I don't go where the others go."

"That's a good idea, John. Let's think about it seriously."

"Actually I haven't been to Japan yet. Not yet."

"Where did you go on your last R and R?"

"I haven't taken an R and R yet, chappy."

Gershon raised his head from the pillow.

"I didn't want to go alone. I was a little afraid of the temptations."

"Well, we've got to get you to Japan, John. We'll work it out."

"The new chaplain. I heard his father is Charles Leiden."

Gershon looked at Meron. "Where did you hear that?"

"I don't remember who told me."

"Yes, he is."

"Wow. Charles Leiden. Does the chaplain know any physics?"

"He studied physics at Harvard."

"Then he got the call?"

"Something like that, John. Boy, I can't keep my eyes open. I'm sorry. I couldn't sleep out in the field."

"I started out in physics and then switched to engineering. I couldn't keep up with the brainwork. Did his family—did his family know Albert Einstein?"

"Yes. He used to call him Uncle Albert."

"Really? My God! Uncle Albert."

"Good night, John."

"Good night, chappy. I'll turn the light off soon. I'm almost done with this nightly."

"The light doesn't bother me, John. I'm used to the light."

"Uncle Albert. My God."

The next morning in his office Gershon said to Howard Morten, "It isn't necessary for you to tell the whole world who Chaplain Leiden's father is."

The assistant's face reddened.

"I thought you were the quiet type, Howard."

"I'm proud of who he is, sir."

"Let him tell it. All right?"

"Yes, sir."

"I never would have taken you for a talker, Howard. What do I have this morning? A character guidance lecture at recon?"

"Yes, sir. His father saved my brother's life, sir. I love my brother. You know how many times my mother and father and I have thanked Einstein and Szilard and Oppenheimer and Fermi and Teller and Leiden and all those who worked on that bomb? My

father had a special prayer of thanks he made up for them the first
Yom Kippur after the war. I was a kid. I watched him cry in the
synagogue. I remember it, sir. I remember it like it was this past
Yom Kippur. He cried like a baby, my father, as he thanked all
those scientists for making the bomb and ending the war. He even
made up a prayer thanking President Truman. You want to hear
how those prayers went?"

"No."

"I remember them. I memorized them."

"Howard."

"Yes, sir?"

"Get the jeep."

"Yes, sir."

"And stop talking about Chaplain Leiden's family."

"Yes, sir."

During the period of the field alert, France and England had invaded Egypt. Paratroops had been dropped outside Port Said. Naval
ships shelled the city. Commandos stormed ashore. The city sur-
rendered. Tanks headed for Suez City. Eisenhower, in the midst
of his campaign for reelection, was enraged by the war. The Russians, who had just invaded and subdued Hungary, now threatened
military intervention in the Middle East. In the field Gershon had
sensed all about him the dread of oncoming atomic war. British
troops were twenty-five miles away from the southern end of the
Suez Canal when London decided to accept the United Nations
cease-fire demand. But no troops would be withdrawn. This was
November 6. The battalion had returned from the field, but all
knew they might be alerted again at any time. In the officers club
there was subdued talk of the next war. Skippy named it Atomic
War One.

"How long do you think it would last, colonel?" he asked.

"About three beers, lieutenant."

"That short?"

"Maybe four."

"Atomic War One. A four-beer war. I wish the Middle East would go away. Stuart. Oh, Stuart. Here you are. Save me four beers for the war."

The first indication of the strange trouble came after the service on the Friday evening in the second week of November, three days after the cease-fire. Gershon's previous assistant, Gabriel Rosen, once again a hospital orderly, came over to him during the social hour and said, "Some of the guys who couldn't come down tonight asked me to tell you this, chaplain. I heard it from others too. We got a big problem."

Gershon's distaste for Gabriel Rosen had not diminished with time or distance. Others stood around listening.

"The Jews are being blamed for starting a world war, chaplain. There's a lot of bad feeling around."

"Has anyone else heard this?" Gershon asked.

Others had heard it.

Two days later Howard Morten said in the jeep on the way to the infantry regiment in the hills, "There's talk in the battalion and in recon, sir. I heard it myself. Bad talk. The Jewish men don't know how to answer. They don't know why the Israelis started the war."

"Do you know why, Howard?"

"I'm not sure, sir. I don't know anything about politics."

"Is it anti-Semitic talk?"

"Yes, sir. Everyone is afraid of an atomic war."

They rode on awhile in silence.

"Sir, do you want me to go over the mountains or across the river?"

"When did it rain last?"

"The day we got back from the field."

"Take the river."

The next morning Gershon called Arthur.

"How are you, Arthur? How goes it in the mountains?"

"It's terrible," he heard Arthur say in a muffled voice.

"What's the matter? Can't you hear me?"

"I hear you fine. This place is very strange. Everyone is walking around like it's the end of the world. Have you been out to the field?"

"Yes. We were alerted again this past Saturday morning. We packed up and were ready to go, but the alert was canceled."

"Everyone here thinks there's going to be an atomic war. I keep getting funny looks. A lot of people are avoiding me. Your assistant has a big mouth, do you know that?"

"Are you set up all right? Do you have an assistant and a jeep?"

"I'm set up. I found an assistant. A very quiet type. I don't like nosy people."

"I remember."

"Can you hear me?"

"Yes."

"I don't want to talk too loud. You can hear me? My assistant tells me there's a lot of anti-Semitic talk going on around the division. Because of the Israelis and the war. Do you have anything like that where you are?"

"Yes."

"I'm not going to worry about it. I just wanted you to know. I'm not used to having almost no one talking to me, dear Gershon. I'd like to hit your assistant in the mouth. Listen, is there any chance I might get to Japan before January?"

"No. Arthur, can you meet me in Seoul tomorrow? In the Jewish chapel. Around noon."

"Tomorrow? What for?"

"I want the three of us to talk about this anti-Jewish feeling."

"What's there to talk about, Gershon?"

"Arthur, unless you have a very important previous appointment or you hear from me to the contrary by four-thirty today, let's meet in Seoul tomorrow."

"All right, dear Gershon. Tomorrow. It will be worth it for the kosher lunch."

Gershon called the chaplain in Seoul. Yes, there had been some vague talk, the chaplain said cheerfully. Nothing to be concerned about. Tomorrow at noon? A meeting? Why not? Happy to host the two of you. What was wrong with the new man? A strange fellow. Moody. Tomorrow. Fine, fine.

Meron said to him in their quarters that night, "My fiancée writes that everyone back home is scared, chappy."

"Everyone is scared everywhere, John."

"I wonder how that new chaplain feels."

"That bomb ended the Pacific war, John."

"That bomb may end everything, chaplain."

"Would you want the Israelis to let themselves be bled to death by all those raids?"

"I don't know. But it may be the end of the whole world, chaplain. The whole world."

It rained that night, and in the morning the main supply route oozed with mud. Clouds covered the tops of the hills. Roadside streams had risen in the rain. Vehicles splashed mud onto his jeep. He rode in the rain and mud to Seoul. The streets were wet and crowded with traffic. He rode warily through Seoul now, always remembering the cart and the runaway horse. Near the train terminal were the hordes of scrofulous beggar children. The city looked dismal in the cold rain. He felt chilled and sensed a sudden oncoming vision. He closed his eyes and immediately saw a hill and two graves and a towering sand-colored stone wall. Sunlight shone on the wall from a blue sky. There were bare, rolling hills and a hot yellow wilderness. He opened his eyes. The wipers arced monotonously across the windshield. Was that snow? Yes. A wet snow was falling. It fell briefly, slanting and splattering against the jeep. He closed his eyes again but saw only reddish darkness. The snow was gone by the time they turned into the Seoul compound. He stepped from the enclosed jeep and felt a cold wind on his face.

The chapel was warm. He was greeted cheerfully by the chaplain, whose name was Solomon Geiger. Gershon sat in the lounge drinking hot coffee. He heard a jeep stop outside. Arthur came in.

"Hello," Chaplain Geiger said. "Both young warriors have now arrived. Can I get you a cup of coffee? We can have lunch if you want. I have a fresh salami. Or I can heat up some chicken."

They sat in the lounge, eating and talking. Arthur said little. His flaxen hair was cut short and seemed stark beneath his small dark skullcap. He was restless. He looked ungainly in his boots and uniform.

"It's nothing to be concerned about, I assure you," Chaplain Geiger was saying with a smile. He was a middle-aged, balding man with a paternalistic air. A permanent aura of cheery optimism had been stamped upon him like Lincoln on the penny. "It will pass. I've seen it before. Ignore it."

"The men are telling me they can't ignore it," Gershon said.

"Don't make so much of it. What do you say, Chaplain Leiden?"

"I'm new here," Arthur said. "Right now I'm listening."

"I think," Gershon said, "that each of us should have a service in a different place each night of Chanukah and use the occasion to talk about the reasons for the war."

Chaplain Geiger said, "Now, now, I don't know if that's wise, Gershon. Is it wise, do you think? The President disapproves of the war. The Secretary of State disapproves of the war. Are you going to justify it?"

"Listen, there's a lot of bad talk out there. Our men should be told how to respond to it. What do you think, Arthur?"

"Whatever you say, Gershon. You know more about this than I do."

They talked at length about the schedule of services and what they would say.

"I will cover Seoul and Pusan and Inchon and I Corps," said Chaplain Geiger. "I haven't your sense of urgency, Gershon. I don't enjoy running around this place. I'm not even sure I want to go to Japan. Maybe once. Maybe. Stay put and be safe. Would you like another coffee? Be careful what you say about the war. A soldier does not criticize his Commander in Chief. Be careful."

Some time later they stood in the doorway of the chapel. Chaplain Geiger shook their hands effusively. "A safe trip. Isn't this weather terrible? Tell your boys to drive with care. Isn't your father the atomic physicist? Yes, I thought I knew the name. Come back soon. Yes, yes. I will send the schedule of Chanukah services to Eighth Army. Yes."

Gershon walked with Arthur to where their assistants waited with their jeeps.

"Are you all right, Arthur? You aren't sick, are you?"

"I feel terrible, but I'm not sick. How can you stand him? He's so cheerful."

"I don't have to stand him, Arthur. I only have to work with him."

"It will take me a week to recover from this meeting. I have a need to retch."

"He isn't that bad, Arthur."

"No one has a right to be that cheerful, dear Gershon. Not in this world."

"Is there anything you need up in division that I can help you with?"

"Yes. Get me to Japan."

"What is this with you and Japan? What have you got there?"

Arthur gazed at him for a moment. They stood in the rain outside the chapel.

"I want to see it," he heard Arthur say as if from very far away. "I'm tired of the sand and the burned earth. I need to see it."

Gershon stared at him.

"Arthur."

Arthur Leiden blinked rapidly. "Yes," he murmured. "Yes. What can you know about it, for Christ's sake?" He shook his head and looked at Gershon. "Do you think we might be able to go to Japan together?"

"I don't see how, Arthur."

There was a brief silence. The rain fell upon them hard.

"Will we be meeting here often?" Arthur asked.

"I don't know. It's a good idea to keep in touch."

"I'll see you."

"Take care of yourself, Arthur."

Gershon watched as Arthur's jeep pulled away.

"Aren't you coming, sir?" he heard Howard Morten call. "It's pouring."

They rode back to the battalion in the rain.

It rained the next day too. He rode along the winding mountain passes to the artillery battalion and saw a Jewish soldier who had been caught in a village with a Korean girl. The soldier was nineteen years old and from Detroit. He sat wretchedly on a chair and talked to Gershon.

"They hate me, chaplain. They're going to throw everything at me."

"Couldn't you wait until you got to Japan? These villages are diseased."

"My sergeant is an anti-Semite, chaplain. He hates Jews. He's going to throw the whole thing at me."

"Sure," Gershon said.

"I'm telling you, chaplain. It's true."

"Everyone is an anti-Semite. Right?"

"My God, what am I going to tell my family back home?"

"I'll see what I can do," Gershon said.

"It's the third time the MP's caught him, chaplain," the sergeant said. "I sweet-talked them out of it before. I can't do it no more."

Gershon rode back to the battalion in the rain. On the way he stopped at the regimental library on the nearby infantry compound. He found the Henry Smyth book on the development of the atomic bomb by the American government, and took it out. He had read it quickly two years back. He wanted to read it again. In one of the regimental Quonsets he talked to a young Jewish soldier from Omaha.

"What did you think you were doing?"

"I don't know."

"That was a direct order. How could you disobey a direct order?"

"I don't know why I did it, chaplain." He was short and pale-skinned, with dark hair and a caged look. "I hate this place."

"You don't hate it enough. You were confined to the compound because you caught yourself a good case of venereal disease. Why did you leave the compound?"

"They're after me because I'm Jewish. The captain hates Jews."

"Really? What do you think your family will tell you when they find out about this? Do they also hate Jews?"

The boy stared miserably at the floor. "They're going to put me in Leavenworth, chaplain. Oh my God, my God."

"I'll see what I can do," Gershon said.

Late that afternoon the rain stopped. The air grew suddenly icy cold. The muddied earth and puddles of rain began to freeze. The earth cracked and snapped beneath vehicles and boots. Gershon came out of his room and started wearily down the hill toward the officers club.

The door to the officers club swung open. The division chaplain stepped out and let the door close behind him. He saw Gershon on the path and came quickly toward him.

"They told me you were here," he said. What he had to tell Gershon was not pleasant, he said. He had not wanted to tell it to him over the phone, he said.

Gershon stood there staring at him. A jeep went by on the road, breaking the frozen surface of the earth.

He called Arthur and the Jewish chaplain in Seoul. He packed a bag. Very early the next morning Howard Morten drove him to the division airstrip. An L-20 Beaver took him from the airstrip to Kimpo. His emergency orders—carried through the chain of command by clerks whom he knew by their first names and cut for him at an odd hour of the night—got him immediately on a C-119 flight to Tachikawa. He sat silent and numb in that boxcar of an aircraft, the roar of the twin engines deafening. In Tachikawa he waited two hours and was put on board a Military Air Transport Service DC-6. Somewhere beyond Wake Island he gained a day. He landed in Hawaii in humid daylight and in San Francisco in chill darkness. He flew through the night to New York. A cab took him through the starkly familiar streets of the neighborhood. He rode in a dreamlike trance. It was early morning. The broken streets were littered with filth. He saw the burned and boarded houses. The odors of mildew and decay filled the hallway of his house. He let himself into the silent apartment. He put his bag down in the living room. The apartment was cold. The living room seemed a closet. His cousin stared at him from the photographs on the end table. He thought he could hear the distant barking of a dog.

In the small kitchen he sat awhile at the table over a cup of coffee and a buttered roll. The walls badly needed painting. He went into his room. The bed, the dresser, the bookcase, the desk, the chair. Pale morning light filtered through the edges of the window shade. The room was very cold. There were cracks in the paint on the wall near his bed. He could not remember those cracks. He had not seen his aunt and uncle in ten months. An aura of submissive despair clung to the apartment like a foul scent.

Some minutes later he let himself silently out of the apartment and went down to the basement. He went past moist and grimy walls to the furnace. It lay huge and black, its bowel a bed of white ashes and faintly glowing coals. He shoveled into its mouth fresh coal and stepped back from the flames. He leaned a moment on the handle of the shovel and gazed at the fire. Then he went back to the apartment, washed his hands and face, lay down on his narrow bed, and fell asleep.

His aunt woke him. She held the robe tightly about her. He had called her from San Francisco. He rose from the bed and held her and felt the quivering of her fragile form. She wept, dried her tears with the sleeve of her robe. How pale he looked, she murmured in her whispery voice. How thin. No, he was well, could not remember when he had ever felt better physically. When could they go to the hospital? He sat with her at the kitchen table and watched her eat a breakfast of cooked cereal and coffee. Her hands trembled. She had aged a decade in a year. Outside, the street was coming slowly to life: cars, schoolchildren, a man's voice raised in a shout.

They took the subway and walked along a wide boulevard in cold gray air to the hospital. There in a room with five others lay his uncle amid tubes and tanks and hovering orderlies. He felt the sudden surging beat of his heart and looked away, unable to endure this vision of torment. Then he looked back, and in that moment his uncle opened his eyes and gazed at him. The face chalk-white, the goatee wispy and white, the skin wrinkled and papery, the eyes pale and filmy in bluish pools—he had seen that face everywhere during the past months; they were faces that had gazed so long at emptiness that even despair was a comfort. His uncle raised a hand and Gershon took it, felt its dry bony warmth, its feeble clutching. The hand fell back; the eyes closed.

In the corridor the resident said they would know in a day or two, it was touch and go, he was in very serious shape, lungs filled with fluid, heart erratic, very serious. He seemed surprised at Gershon's detailed probings into medical procedures and peered for clues at the insignia on his uniform. His aunt stood at his side in shriveled dread. They returned home in the afternoon. Their Shabbat dinner that evening was eaten in silence. He lay in his room and listened to the radiator dying.

In the synagogue the next morning a prayer was said for his uncle's recovery. The old man who had taught him Aramaic came over to him after the service. Gershon had the amulet, yes? He wore it, yes? He himself did not believe in such nonsense. But how could it hurt? Was he still studying Kabbalah? Had he found anything in it that could make sense of this insane world? A pity about his uncle. A pity. God would help. Yes. He shuffled away, speaking to himself through his stained beard.

He saw his uncle again the next morning and afternoon, then took the subway to Manhattan. He walked down a cold and windy side street toward the Hudson River. Karen met him in the hall, and he held her in a long silence, and they went up the stairway together to her apartment. She had let her hair grow long. She wore a light-gray sweater and a tweed skirt and no makeup. Her face was flushed. She was an untidy housekeeper, and the apartment was strewn with her books and papers. She had prepared dinner. They ate at a small table. Her father was fine, back at work; her mother was fine. Yes, she felt good having her own apartment, away from her parents. Yes, her work was exciting, exhausting, challenging; she was writing a book; she had been offered an assistant professorship at the University of Chicago, an extraordinary opportunity; but she was not sure she wanted to take it; what was Gershon planning to do? He was planning to survive, he said. No, afterward, she said. He didn't know, he said. Did she know that Arthur Leiden was in Korea? No, she had lost track of Arthur, had heard he was in the navy. She had glanced away for a moment at the mention of Arthur's name. They sat together near a window that looked out on the dark night sky. He drew the shade. I missed you, he said. I missed you. She was warm and silent in his arms.

He spent the next morning and afternoon with his uncle and then rode the subway again to Manhattan. His uncle had developed a very high fever, the resident told him the following morning. Gershon held the old man's burning hand. But the fever broke during the night, and when Gershon entered the room the next morning he found his uncle weak but clear-eyed. Now it seemed he might recover, and the nurses would not let Gershon or his aunt visit too long. They went back home. Gershon made some phone calls. He lay on his bed but could not sleep. He walked up the staircase to the roof. A winter wind blew a gale around the stairwell. The roof was deserted. He stood near the parapet and gazed out at the neighborhood. An aircraft droned by overhead, concealed by the clouds. He went back downstairs and took the subway to Karen's. They walked together in the cold night along Riverside Drive. A fog lay upon the river. He felt all about him a pervasive unsubstantiality; he was inside a vision that he was experiencing in his quarters in Korea. John sat nearby writing his nightly letter. That was the real world; this was a strange theatrics, a conjuring by those fearful of a focused gaze. Later in her apartment he held her and felt upon his lips the hardened nipples of her breasts. Turn off the lamp, she murmured. No, he said. No. She moved against him, moved. You've changed, she said into his ear. I knew you would change. Oh, she said. Oh God.

The next day they let him stay with his uncle all morning and most of the afternoon. In the evening he took Karen to a movie, then visited for a while with her family. How is our Richard Leiden scholar? her father asked. How is it on the other side of the world? Later, in her apartment, Karen said, Yes, he was at Harvard and I was at Radcliffe. But he began to go a little crazy. And I didn't want to marry into that family. They're strange people. They frightened me. I didn't want my father-in-law to be one of those who had helped make the bomb. I didn't want that for the rest of my life. Won't I see you again before you leave? Yes. Saturday night. Yes. Oh you've changed. Do you know how much you've changed?

His uncle said to him the next morning, trembling, feeble, Thought it was a dream. They let you come? Saw you and felt strength. Terrible there, Gershon? He stayed with him most of the day and kissed him when he left and felt on his lips the tears on the warm bearded face. He said to his aunt that night during the Shabbat dinner, How can you stay here? How? She said, glancing about, whispering, Here we belong. Here. Your father built this house. Your father. Yes. Now our house. What else is there?

He lay awake much of that night in his small room. He heard sirens. Somewhere in the neighborhood a house burned. He saw it the next morning on the way to the synagogue—an apartment house much like theirs. Windows broken and charred; hillocks of wet and blackened debris on the sidewalk.

He took the subway to Manhattan that night. This is more difficult than last February, she said. No, she said. I don't understand anything about Arthur. I don't want to talk about Arthur. Yes, she said. Oh yes, Gershon, you can do that again. Yes. Please don't change too much, she said. Please, Gershon. And she cried openly when he left.

Very early the next morning he rose and dressed and prayed. He stood with his aunt in the doorway to the apartment. She sobbed and clung to him. What else do I have? What else? Oh take good care of yourself, Gershon. Go with God. Come back in health. He went out of the apartment house. How do you live almost a lifetime with two people, and love them, and really not know them? What sort of energy or accident brings together loving and knowing? A wind blew along the street as he walked through its dismal silence.

He took a cab to Pennsylvania Station and boarded a train to Philadelphia. It was a cold cloudy day. The train moved slowly through the barren rot of the New Jersey marshland. He saw tall, pale-brown swamp grass, shanties, sheds, slums, the green slime of industrial waste, the spectral flames of refinery chimneys—a squalor more vile than anything he had yet seen in Korea. In Philadelphia a cab took him quickly through deserted Sunday morning streets to a cluster of stone buildings. He walked up a stone staircase into a marble hall and down a corridor to a door. He knocked and the door opened. In the doorway stood the tall, trim figure of Jakob Keter, dark suit, white shirt, bow tie. They shook hands. He looked thin, pale. His handshake was firm. Well, Mr. Loran, welcome. The train was not late. Have you had breakfast? Would you like a coffee? Leave your bag here. There is a little place on Walnut Street. We will have coffee and talk. You have changed, Mr. Loran. Yes. Excuse me. Rabbi Loran. Yes. You have changed.

They walked along a quiet street to a cafeteria. The air was cold, raw. They sat at a back table. Bright fluorescents glowed on the ceiling. The place was nearly empty but very warm. The heat misted the windows. They talked quietly together. No, he had not heard that Arthur Leiden was in Korea, Jakob Keter said. Was he well? And how was the winner of the first Richard Leiden Award? Was the army experience worthwhile? Was he able to study? A letter was on the way to him, mailed a week ago: Rabbi Loran's last re-search paper had been accepted by a noted scholarly journal. Yes.

He, Jakob Keter, had taken it upon himself to submit it. Rabbi Loran was surprised, yes? It was a splendid paper. Gershon stared. What research paper? For a moment he could not even recall its contents. The fluorescents hummed loudly overhead. No naked light bulbs here hanging from bare black cords. Vaguely he heard someone say, How do you know all this about the morale of the men, chaplain? He looked down at his coffee cup. Why had that suddenly returned to him, that meeting about the hill? He had not written that paper to have it published. It was not good enough for publication. Why had Keter submitted it? Why had it been accepted? No. He remembered it clearly. It was a damn good paper. Yes. He was happy it would be published. But many would read it, many. What would they say?

Jakob Keter was still talking to him, had not ceased talking, the normally expressionless face curiously relaxed, lively, the eyes sharp and bright. Rabbi Loran was reading Luria? Interesting. The writings of Moses Jonah of Safed could be of great help in clarifying his teachings. There are many manuscripts. They require evaluation. He had published extensively on this subject. As a curiosity, a bit of gossip, did Rabbi Loran know that Luria was in the pepper and grain business? From that to the doctrine of light and sparks and the withdrawal of the light that was God to make room for creation and the terrible mistake at the very beginning when even God lost control and the light spilled. A strange poetry of light. Yes. Did Rabbi Loran know that Luria often took long walks with his disciples—yes, in Safed—and would show them the lost graves of great people whose locations had appeared to him in visions? Yes. So, he was reading Luria, the mystic of broken worlds. Interesting. Many scholarly problems were connected with the reading of Luria. Many.

They walked back to the university. Yes, he would be returning to Jerusalem in January. He longed for Jerusalem. This had been a bad time to be away, the Sinai war, the dread of atomic holocaust. Had the American army in Korea been alerted for war? The fedayeen raids had been a long nightmare. Terror day and night. How long should a country endure such raids? How long had America endured the raids of the Mexicans in the time of the First World War? But the thought of a rain of atomic bombs putting an end to the light of civilization. . . . He fell silent. Yes, the operation had been serious but not spectacular. It had required special hands, and the hands were in Philadelphia. He looked closely at Gershon. Why do I feel you have changed, Mr. Loran? Rabbi Loran. You are thinner, yes, but it is more than that. It was very kind of you to come to Philadelphia. Your uncle will recover, yes? Goodbye, Gershon. Take care of yourself.

He waited a long time on the corner before he spotted a cruising cab. It was a little before noon. The cab took him to the airport. He had time for a sandwich and a cup of coffee. He caught a flight to Boston. They flew through dense clouds and turbulent air. It was cold in Boston. The wind tore at him when he came through the doors of the terminal. The cab driver said, "How do you want to go, lieutenant?" He said, "The shortest way."

It was a long ride. They went through the city for a while, then along the river. There were no boats on the river. The water ran dull gray. They rode along narrow New England streets with tall, bare trees and old homes. They came out after a while into the wide center of a town and went up a side street and suddenly through the trees was the silver sheen of a lake. They turned into a driveway and stopped before the wide stone steps of an enormous Tudor home. He paid the cab, and it started away. It was not yet out the driveway when the large oaken front door opened. Arthur's mother stood in the doorway.

"It was good of you to come," she said. She wore a light-gray woolen dress and no makeup. Her words of greeting were spoken with no trace of a smile. "Did you have a pleasant flight? I detest flying. They wouldn't permit Charles to fly during the war. It was considered unsafe. Do come in. Did you tell us over the telephone that you could stay for dinner? I forget. Charles is in the library and asked us to join him."

She took him through a spacious, high-ceilinged center hall. A wide carpeted staircase with an intricately carved wooden banister led to the second floor. There were paintings on the walls and, on a small triangular corner table, framed photographs of Arthur on a horse and of a uniformed man who resembled Arthur. His dead brother? Charles Leiden sat in an easy chair in the library, gazing into the fireplace. He wore an old gray sweater and dark baggy trousers. He held a drink in his hand and looked up as Gershon entered. His gray eyes narrowed, then suddenly widened. A look of enormous astonishment came over his gaunt features, a sudden light of uncontainable joy. Abruptly Gershon heard the cold voice of Arthur's mother.

"Charles."

The man looked at her. "Elizabeth?" he murmured.

"You remember Gershon Loran."

He looked at Gershon and blinked and passed a hand over his eyes. The light faded from his face. He rose wearily and shook Gershon's hand. A curious tingling sensation coursed through Gershon's arm. This hand had helped create the weapon that Oppenheimer had called death light. "Good of you to come. Appreciate it. Do sit down. Drink? Certainly. Mary?"

A maid had materialized from somewhere. She went away and returned silently with Gershon's drink. They sat in the library and listened to the fire roar up the chimney. It was a large room, carpeted, paneled, and lined on two of its walls with bookcases. Beyond its windows were rhododendron and oaks and a long sloping lawn and a line of birches and the lake. The sky over the lake was dull-gray with clouds and dwindling afternoon light. There were a few other homes along the lake, elegant, mansionlike, with lawns and trees and trimmed shrubbery. He saw docks but no boats. All were no doubt gone inside for the winter soon to come.

"How is Arthur?" Charles Leiden said, gazing at the fireplace. "Tell me about Arthur. Is he well? He doesn't write, you know. Now and then he sends along a cryptic card. Were you alerted for atomic war?"

"Yes."

"My little gift to the world."

"Charles," his wife said.

He gazed in silence at the burning logs. Gershon sipped from his glass, the ice tinkling softly.

"I understand that Arthur is stationed with a medical battalion," Charles Leiden said.

"Yes."

"And you?"

"Combat engineers."

"Indeed?" He looked at Gershon. "How very interesting. Richard was with engineers. Our son. How curious." He looked back at the fire. "Has Arthur been to Japan yet?"

"No."

"He will certainly want to go to Japan."

"Charles, I think—" Arthur's mother began.

"He will want to see the handiwork of his parents. Tell me, Gershon—I may call you Gershon? I feel somehow that you are sufficiently close to us—tell me, is it very bad in Korea?"

"It's bad. They're beginning to rebuild it."

"The war was savage?"

"From what I can see, yes. I wasn't there during the war."

"You can tell from the aftermath?"

"Yes."

"One can always tell from the aftermath."

"We are all descended from Epimetheus, Charles," his wife said. "All."

"Not all, Elizabeth. Szilard knew. Others knew."

"Leo wrote the letter, Charles. Leo. The father of it all. Albert merely signed it. Must we go over it all again?"

"No. Gershon. May I ask a favor? Please put another log on the fire. Yes. Thank you so much. About Arthur. What was I saying? He will certainly want to see Kyoto. Wouldn't you say Arthur would be especially keen on seeing Kyoto? Elizabeth?"

Arthur's mother stared at her husband. Her lovely face was pale. "Yes," she said. "And Hiroshima."

There was a long silence.

"It would be rather splendid if Gershon and Arthur could see Japan together. Don't you think so, Elizabeth?" There was a pause. "Don't you?"

As if from a long distance away came her faint, assenting reply. "Yes. I think so, Charles."

"Gershon, can we send anything to Arthur to ease things for him?" Charles Leiden asked. "He tells us virtually nothing in his cards."

"Food would be helpful. Canned fruit, salamis."

"Perhaps we should send him bagels and lox," said Arthur's mother.

"Elizabeth, for heaven's sake."

"He should not be there, Charles."

"But he is there."

"It is one thing to fight for good and quite another to fight for empire. The American empire is detestable. Why is our son involved in it? Why is he there? It is against everything that he was taught. I cannot countenance his being there. But we will, of course, send him whatever he needs. Had he not chosen to enter the army, he would never have been sent there."

"I think I could stand another drink," Charles Leiden said. "Gershon? How about you?"

Elizabeth Leiden, who had not been drinking, took their glasses and went from the room.

Gershon sat in an easy chair and felt the warmth of the fire on his face. He saw the fire playing across the bony features of Arthur's father. Charles Leiden turned to him with a melancholy look.

"Arthur asked for the Korean assignment, didn't he?"

"Yes."

"So I was informed by—a friend. You were alone there for quite a while."

"Yes."

"His mother is unaware of this. She is very angry at certain people over the fact that Arthur is now there. She would be angrier if she knew it was his own doing. Do you understand?"

"Yes."

"He did it to get to Japan, didn't he?"

"Yes."

"How foolish and impetuous. We would gladly have given him a trip to Japan after his separation from the service. Why does he need Korea in order to get to Japan? Foolish. He tends to behave at times in an impetuous manner. I—fear for him."

He looked back at the fire. The last light of the day lay upon the windows of the library. In the silence that followed, Gershon glanced briefly at the bookcases and saw that many of the titles dealt with oriental art. The light from the fireplace played upon the warm, dark wood of the walls and bookcases.

Elizabeth Leiden returned with their drinks. "Dinner will be ready soon. I did tell you, didn't I, that our home is entirely kosher? Yes. That was Arthur's doing. The kosher Leidens."

"My wife believes in it not one whit, but is scrupulous in its observance," said Charles Leiden, sipping from his glass. "A curious state of affairs, don't you think? We are kosher, Fermi probably attends synagogue, Albert believed in Spinoza's God and helped raise money for Israel, Teller may end up teaching in a Jewish parochial school one day, Szilard has the soul of a Jewish prophet. And we tinker with light and atomic bombs, with the energy of the universe. Do you wonder that the world doesn't know what to make of its Jews? No one is on more familiar terms with the heart of the insanity in the universe than is the Jew, and no one is more frenetic and untidy in the search for an answer. We are always in a desperate rush. We offer apocalypses in a pushcart, messiahs in tobacco-stained caftans. How did I get on to this? Yes. Kosher dishes hardly constitute a solution to the problems of our species. But it is Arthur's wish. And so—" He drank from his glass.

"Charles, I'm going to see to dinner."

"By all means, Elizabeth."

"Gershon, your flight leaves at ten?"

"Yes."

"I'll have a cab come for you here."

"Thank you."

"We will be ready for dinner in a quarter of an hour."

She went out.

"What do you eat in Korea if you keep kosher?" Charles Leiden asked. "Or are there dispensations that rabbis are permitted to invoke?" He gazed at the fire. "I think we might enjoy another log, Gershon. Yes. Thank you. How do you keep warm in Korea? Do you burn oil? In Los Alamos we burned wood." He sipped from his glass and stared into the flames that leaped from the fresh log. "In many ways those were our finest years. Almost everything since then has been a darkness. We traversed frontiers every day. We were Olympians to ourselves. Titans. Prometheuses of physics. We were searching for a bomb to kill the Germans before the Germans killed us. Simple, yes? Good and evil. They used to post the daily casualty lists from the war fronts on our bulletin boards. We were happy slave laborers to our own dream. Invent the bomb, punish the Germans, save American boys, end the war. A benevolent apocalypse. Arthur senses nothing of that. He—"

Somewhere in the house the telephone rang twice, then was silent. The windows of the library were dark with the night. Charles Leiden leaned over and turned on a lamp. Soft yellow light filled the room.

"Not for a moment do I regret the work that we did on that bomb," Charles Leiden said. "And not for a moment am I without remorse over our having used it on the Japanese. I thought once—when I was young—that there might be other ways my name would be remembered. Yes, other ways. . . ."

He stared into the flames and was silent.

Gershon excused himself quietly and went from the room. In the small washroom near the stairway he urinated and washed his hands and face. A faint murmurous voice came from somewhere in the house—perhaps carried by the hot-air vents. The words were indiscernible. The voice died. A moment later the phone rang again and the voice returned. He was about to leave the room when the voice was raised to a volume sufficiently loud to make it audible. It was Arthur's mother. Gershon heard her say, "John, please tell that besotted son of a bitch that Charles is ill. We are unable to come down on Tuesday. Perhaps Thursday. Yes. Thank you. I don't wish to hear any more about this. Goodbye, John." Gershon stood very still in the washroom. A moment later he stepped out and returned to the library. Charles Leiden sat gazing into the fire. "Were we better off when we thought it to be phlogiston?" he murmured. "No." He was silent a moment. "I wonder."

Dinner was served with unostentatious elegance. The dietary laws in this house were no deterrent to culinary adventuring. Wine was served. Gershon noticed that Arthur's mother was not offered the wine by either the maid or her husband. Had Gershon been to Kyoto? Arthur's mother asked. Yes, he had been to Kyoto. What did he think of the city? A beautiful city, he said. He hoped to return to it on his next trip to Japan. He had not thought such beauty could exist anywhere, he said. Would Gershon like some more of the duck? Arthur's mother asked.

Later they stood near the heavy, dark-wood front door while the cab waited in the driveway, its motor running. "Have a safe trip, Gershon," Charles Leiden said. "Yes," Elizabeth Leiden said. "And give our love to Arthur." "Tell him to write," Charles Leiden said. "A Harvard education should certainly have equipped him with the facility to write more than an occasional postcard." They shook hands. Really good of Gershon to have come, Charles Leiden said. He hoped he had not burdened him too much with all his talk. One tended to garrulity when one's stock of years and memories attained to a certain level. "Goodbye, Gershon. Take care of yourself." "Yes," Arthur's mother said. "Do take special care."

"You might," Charles Leiden said, "you might, if you can, try to keep an eye on Arthur. He tends at times toward the erratic."

"Charles," Elizabeth Leiden said.

"Goodbye, Gershon."

He rode a long time through dark cold streets. Off on the left was the river, lights glinting on its surface. He sat back in the darkness of the cab and closed his eyes. Patches of the past week came to him in an uncontrollable rush. Where was he going? Back? Back to that world? He heard the raucous honking of a car horn. The cab driver cursed softly. Back. Yes. Back. What airline? He felt a long moment of panic, an inability to locate himself in space and time. The driver wanted to know what airline. He began to reach into his pocket, then remembered. He sat back and stared out the window at the indistinct shapes of the city.

He flew all night. Shortly before noon the next day he boarded a Military Air Transport Service DC-6 at Travis Air Force Base. They refueled in Hawaii. Between Hawaii and Wake Island they lost a day and he lost all sense of time. He landed in Japan in the early evening and in Korea the next day before noon. That night, at the service in the infantry regiment near the engineer battalion, he lit the first candle of Chanukah.

. . .

In the early evening of the day he returned to the battalion, John Meron had greeted him with unrestrained delight. "Hey, welcome back, chappy. You look beat. Can I get you anything? Yeah, we were out two days in the field this week. Did your uncle pull through? Hey, really, thanks for calling my fiancée. I appreciate that."

The battalion commander said to him in the officers club, "You just get back, chaplain? Did you see that article in the infantry magazine on the tactics your boys used in the Sinai? A friend of mine brought it over with him. Good to see you. Have a drink. Stuart, a Scotch on the rocks for the chaplain here."

Arthur said over the phone, "You talked to my parents? You *saw* my parents? You flew to Boston? What for? Never mind. You'll tell me when I see you. I can't talk over these phones. It's insane up here. They make us turn off our oil stoves at midnight. They're afraid of fires. What good is an oil stove if you can't use it? Maybe they'll let us burn wood. I didn't think of that. Are you all right?"

"I'm very tired."

"How's your uncle?"

"He's better."

"Listen, I don't enjoy making a nuisance of myself, dear Gershon. But is there any chance, any chance at all, that I might get to Japan sooner than January?"

"Yes."

"What?"

"Yes."

The phone line was silent.

"Gershon," Arthur said.

"There's a chance," Gershon said. "I'll see what I can do."

He called Seoul the next day. No, Solomon Geiger said, he certainly wouldn't mind it if Gershon waived his invitation to the religious retreat in Japan and enabled Arthur Leiden to go in his place. He himself had no desire to go to Japan. He preferred to stay put. He was glad to hear Gershon's uncle had recovered. "Happy Chanukah," he said cheerfully over the phone. "Be wise in what you say about the war."

Gershon wrote a letter to the Jewish chaplain in Japan. All during Chanukah he traveled through the division. There was no snow, but the air was sharply cold, and you could not breathe it mouth open for too long without a strange tightness starting somewhere in your back and chest. He rode the mountain passes and the dry riverbeds, conducted services, lit the Chanukah candles, talked about the war, answered questions. There was another story about him in *Stars and Stripes*—"The Circuit-Riding Chaplain"—and a large picture of him in front of his jeep. The battalion was mentioned in the first paragraph of the story, together with Solomon Geiger and Arthur Leiden. "Hey, who's your press agent, chappy?" Meron asked delightedly.

Through the office of the Jewish chaplain in Japan, Arthur received orders to attend the Jewish religious retreat at Oiso. He flew to Japan in the middle of December, the day before an eighteen-inch snowstorm fell on the line divisions. By chance his aircraft was the C-124 Globemaster named the *Thin Man*. He was in Japan six days. He called Gershon when he returned.

"I want to thank you, dear friend."

"You had a good time?"

"It's a beautiful country. The phones work. The toilets flush. A visit to the john is an epiphany."

"Did you get to Kyoto?"

The phone was quiet.

"Arthur, did you get to Kyoto?"

"Yes. Briefly."

"Did you see what you wanted to see?"

"Yes."

"What was it?"

"Kyoto."

"What?"

"Kyoto. Just Kyoto. Listen, Gershon. Are you going on R and R soon?"

"Yes. In January."

"I'm due for some leave. You think I might tag along?"

"You just got back, Arthur."

"I'd like to spend some real time in Kyoto. I'd like to—I want to see Hiroshima."

"Let me think about it, Arthur."

"There's a canal at the foot of Higashiyama. It runs from Lake

Biwako. I've never seen anything so beautiful. There are cherry trees on both sides. You can walk along it and see the temples behind white walls. There were leaves still falling. You can see old gravestones. It's quiet, quiet."

"Where is this?"

"In Kyoto."

"I thought you were only in Kyoto briefly."

"I know Kyoto, dear Gershon. What do you think of my idea?"

"It's a fine idea, Arthur. But it won't be easy to get permission for both of us to be out of Korea at the same time."

"Nishida used to walk along that canal. You can hear the flow of the water. It's a city of streams and ponds. You'll love the gardens and the stone lanterns and the white walls and black roofs of the houses. There's a five-story pagoda—"

"Who was Nishida, Arthur?"

"A philosopher. He wrote lovely meditations. The temples are exquisite, dear Gershon."

"I've seen some of the temples. You don't have to convince me that Kyoto is beautiful."

"It's beautiful, Gershon. It's beautiful to me in a way you'll never know. God, it's beautiful. I love it and I want to see it again and again, and I want you to see it with me."

"Sure, Arthur."

"I know it well, dear Gershon. We'll have a splendid time in Kyoto."

"I can't promise you anything definitely. I'll try to work it out."

"Then we'll go to Hiroshima."

"All right."

"I have to get to Hiroshima, you see."

"Yes."

"I have to, dear Gershon. Hello? Can you hear me?"

"Yes."

"God, I hate these telephones. I hate these piss tubes and outhouses and—"

"Arthur."

"Listen. Do you know that this country is a virtual dictatorship?"

"For God's sake, Arthur."

"We have strange friends. The great American empire. *Pax Americana*. When will you know about January, Gershon?"

"In a few days. You do have leave coming to you."

"Yes."

"You're sure."

"Gershon—"

"All right. I'll see what I can do."

He hung up the phone.

A thick and silent snow was falling upon the hills and the valley. He walked in the snow to the officers mess. A passage from the Zohar came to him as he ascended the path. "Rabbi Yitzhak said: At the time God created the world and desired to reveal the depth of His being from out of the hidden, the light came from the darkness and they were joined together. Because of this, out of darkness came the light and out of the hidden came the revealed and out of the good came evil and out of mercy came severe judgment, and everything is intertwined with everything else . . . the good inclination and the evil inclination, the right and the left." He walked slowly to the officers mess and ate a lunch of scrambled eggs and sat at a window a long time looking out at the white light of the snow.

Three days before Christmas the British and French withdrew the last of their troops from Port Said. The Israelis remained in the Sinai Peninsula and the Gaza Strip, but the threat of war was gone.

In the last days of December the weather turned bitter cold. Day after day the sun shone from clear blue skies through air that was still and brittle with frost. He rode up and down the bare and frozen land—services for the distant artillery and infantry units, a stockade visit to Seoul, a hospital visit to Ascom City, lectures to recon and ordnance, the weekly meeting in Seoul with Arthur Leiden and Solomon Geiger. The valley froze. He saw children skating on the iron surfaces of the paddies and men carrying brush on A-frames from the hills. One's breath vaporized in the air; horses steamed; plumes of gasoline exhaust rose from vehicles. The land seemed spectral. He remembered the last winter—where was he now, Roger Tat?—and wondered why he did not feel the bite of the cold now as he had then. He was grateful to the benevolent biology that had attuned him to the temperature of the land.

There was a New Year's party in the battalion officers club. He joined the singing and drinking. They sang folk songs and pop tunes. Skippy played the piano and drank beer; he drank nine bottles of beer that night, then later walked a straight line back to the officers Quonset in the dark, stood a long time at a piss tube, and went to bed in his uniform. The battalion commander had, two days earlier, received his colonel's eagle; the party was in part a celebration of his promotion. He threw an arm across Gershon's shoulders and thrust his handsome features close to Gershon's face and bragged loudly about "his chaplain" and "the great little army the chaplain's guys had" and would Stuart give the chaplain another Scotch on the rocks. It was a happy party.

Arthur requested and received ten days of leave. But on one of his trips to Seoul he stopped at a café on a side street, a hangout for university students, and had coffee and some pastry. He came down with an intestinal infection. For a while the doctors thought it might be hepatitis, but the tests proved negative. Gershon flew to Japan with John Meron.

8

They flew in a C-124 Globemaster. About one hundred and fifty enlisted men and officers were on board. They left at four-thirty on a Sunday afternoon and landed in Tachikawa shortly before eight. They took a bus to Camp Drake and a cab to the Imperial Hotel in Tokyo. They washed and had a light supper. They walked the neon wonderland of the city's night. John Meron seemed stunned. They passed tiny shops and brightly lit theaters. In a teahouse on a quiet street they drank coffee and ate pastry. The interior of the teahouse had three levels and was in the shape of a circle. The tables were arranged around a large railed circular shaft. An open elevator moved slowly up and down the shaft. There were musicians on the elevator. They played Viennese music. You heard them even when you could not see them. Gershon sat there watching the elevator move slowly up and down. The tables and chairs were white. The décor was rose and white. The music was soft, dreamy. He had been to this place before. John yawned. They took a cab back to the hotel and went to sleep.

The weather was cold but kind. They spent the next three days in Tokyo. In a small Japanese restaurant, after the first day of sight-seeing, they sat on tatami before a low table and were served dinner by kimono-clad waitresses who padded in and out of the paper-walled room. Gershon wore a gray suit and a dark tie; John wore a blue suit and a blue bow tie. Paper lanterns hung from the ceiling. The table top was lacquered and reflected the soft lights of the room and the white of the dishes. They ate slowly in a cloud of gentle pleasures: scents and odors and food and drink and the soft rustle and padding of the girls, dark kimonos, white kimonos, lovely faces, and the short rapid openings and closings of the sliding door. Afterward they went to a Japanese musical, then walked through the blaze and tumult of the city's lights. They had coffee and pastry in the circular teahouse with the orchestra that went slowly up and down on the elevator.

In their hotel room John said, "I thought we destroyed Tokyo, chappy."

"We bombed it and burned it."

"It's incredible."

"Are you going to sleep, John?"

"I want to write my letter. I missed last night."

"I'm going down for a newspaper."

In the vast lobby he bought a copy of the English-language Japanese newspaper and walked slowly back toward the elevator. His ears caught bits of a conversation that startled him. He stopped and peered around discreetly. Two men sat in an easy chair near a large potted plant, talking and gesticulating.

"—an impossible situation," he heard one of them say.

"From one week to the next," said the other.

"The fluctuations are terrible. It is driving Lichtman crazy."

"Will you lend him the money?"

"Under such circumstances? With the Hong Kong dollar as unstable as a drunken Cossack? Do I look crazy to you?"

They were middle-aged, well dressed. They were speaking in Yiddish.

"I'll go over this weekend and have a look," the first one said.

"You won't change my mind. Unstable currency is like an unstable child. God protect us from both."

He took the elevator to the room. He got out of his clothes and washed and lay in the bed. He felt warmed and surfeited by the day. A brief vision of Arthur drifted before his eyes—Arthur in their seminary room asking him to explain a passage from the Zohar for the next day's class with Jakob Keter.

"What will we do tomorrow, chappy?" John asked. He was addressing the envelope.

"We'll see the parks and the imperial palace and the zoo. There's plenty to do, John."

"I don't want to leave the city."

"We won't leave the city, John. We'll go to Nikko on Thursday and to Hakone on Sunday. Those are one-day trips."

"I enjoyed myself so much today I feel a little guilty."

"What do you mean?"

"That my fiancée isn't here."

"You won't do her any good by a long tour with misery, John. You'll come back worn out. What kind of joy will she get out of that?"

"I wish she was here."

"I wish a lot of things, John. I wish my friend Arthur was with us."

"I wish a Jesuit priest I know was with us. We grew up together." He was silent a moment. "I hear us sounding like little kids, chappy. I wish, I wish, I wish."

"I haven't sounded like a little kid in a long time, John. It's refreshing."

John put the envelope on the desk.

"Why does this place bring out the kid in us?" Gershon asked sleepily.

"I don't know, chappy. It does, I guess."

"Are you finished with that letter? Let's get some sleep."

"All finished."

"Maybe it reminds us of when we were kids during the war," Gershon said.

John was quiet.

"A thought," Gershon said. "A fleeting, sobering, final word from your chaplain. Our thought for the day. Good night, John."

Early Thursday morning, on their fourth day in Tokyo, they boarded a train and rode north out of the city for about an hour and a half. They got out at Nikko and walked along a street to a bridge. There were hills and tall green trees. It was a brisk cold sunny day.

"Toshogu?" Gershon said to an old man on the bridge.

"Hai. Toshogu."

"Arigato."

They crossed the river gorge and walked on awhile in a forest of ancient cedars. Everywhere were temples and shrines. They descended a broad outdoor staircase of ten stone steps and stared at a huge stone torii that stood twenty-seven feet high. Sunlight shone on the granite. They gazed at the carvings on the white and gold entrance gate, stared at the stone lions and iron lanterns, walked through long red-lacquered corridors, marveled at the carvings on brackets, columns, and friezes, at the paintings, ceiling decorations —dragons, phoenixes, pheasants, monkeys, cranes, ducks, apricots, pines, owls, chrysanthemums. On one ceiling a fairy played a harp, on another a huge dragon made a strange sound to a visitor's clapping hands. High on a wall a cat slept among peonies. A mirror in a dragon-decorated chamber was the sacred spirit of a deity. Gershon saw himself in it and looked away. They wandered in and out of hushed rooms that had been shaped with the beauty of a special grace. They walked in silence. John's boyish face was awed. Gershon felt deep inside himself a strange and inarticulate stirring, the feeling he had in the summer in Kyoto—a tentative stepping upon forbidden thresholds.

They walked back to Nikko and had lunch in a teahouse. At the station they took an electric tramcar the six miles to Umageshi and a cable car across a river. The tram was crowded. They rode a bus along a paved climbing mountain road—sudden turns, vast green hills, deep gorges. An aerial ropeway brought them to a lookout point and they stood in the flood of early afternoon winter sunlight and gazed at a distant expanse of blue lake and hills and sky. They returned to Umageshi and took another bus that ran along a dry riverbed. Gershon kept looking out the window at the riverbed. They crossed a bridge and started up a narrow winding road with waterfalls on both sides. After a while the bus stopped. On the left of the road an elevator took them down to the foot of the gorge. They came out onto a parapet and looked up, and there, about three hundred and fifty feet over their heads, they saw Kegon Falls, a boiling rush of water that burst across the top of a granite cliff and fell to the shadowy boulder-strewn gorge, where it cascaded between huge wet rocks and rolled churning out of sight into the depths of the mountain. Huge patches of bluish ice coated the face of the cliff and the boulders. The water hurled lacy spray into the air, and Gershon thought he could feel mist brushed against his face by the currents of air blowing through the gorge. He felt his lips moving of themselves; he was saying something without having thought to say anything; and when he became aware of his lips working he could not remember the words they had formed.

They stood there a long time. They had coffee and pastry in a hotel on the shore of Lake Chuzenji. They sat with three Japanese men and one woman around a stove in a dining room of glass walls that looked out on the lake and the ring of hills beyond.

"Kekko," Gershon said to them, waving a hand at the lake.

They looked at him and smiled and nodded. They all sat around the wood-burning stove looking out the windows at the hills and the lake.

John was tired when they returned to Tokyo that evening. They had dinner in the hotel. John went up to the room to write his letter. Gershon took a cab to a club on a small side street. He sat alone for a while at a table and drank Scotch. The place was noisy and smoky. A five-piece band played American dance music. A girl came off the dance floor and went over to him.

"Chap-san," she said. She was very beautiful, with long dark hair and very dark eyes. She wore a tight dark-green dress and a red flower on a dark ribbon around her neck.

"Hello," he said. "How are you, Toshie?"

"I have someone now," she said. "Please wait for me, chap-san."

"I'll wait."

He waited about an hour. Another girl came over while he sat there. He shook his head and she went away. He sat staring into his glass. The day pulsed slowly within him—the trams and buses, the temples and shrines, the faces of people, schoolchildren in blue and white uniforms, tall trees, the cold of the mountain air, the explosive rush of the falls.

"I am free now," someone said, and he looked up and she stood there smiling. They danced a long time, and he held her softness to him. Then they sat at the table, and she drank the colored water that was supposed to be wine and he had another Scotch. They talked softly. Yes, his friend had been in to see her. "He is very sad, your friend. Why so sad? Two chap-sans, and one so sad. But very nice to look at. Very handsome." They danced and talked, and he took her in a cab to where she lived with her mother, and then rode back to the hotel.

John was asleep. The envelope lay face up on the desk. Gershon washed and got into bed. He lay awake a long time. What had he said in that gorge in the presence of that shimmering rush of power? He could not remember. The falling water had broken the sunlight, had set it in vibrating motion across the long surface of the spill—lights playing, breaking, flowing, crashing upon the rocks below. He could not remember. He was sleepy.

"How did you know about all that, chappy?" John had asked on the train back.

"About what?"

"About exactly where to go. The temples and the falls, and the lake. What buses to take. How did you know all that?"

"I read a lot, John."

He wondered why he could not remember. He fell asleep.

They wandered through Tokyo the next day, bought some shirts on the Ginza, had lunch in a little restaurant. Gershon sat at the window and watched the crowds go by. Once they had been the enemy. They had killed his cousin. Arthur's father had—he could not grasp it.

"Aren't you eating?" John asked.

He looked down at his plate. "I was thinking. Yesterday's enemy, today's friend. There are better ways to conquer the world than by making it bleed."

"Your thought for the day, chappy?"

"Right. Here's another thought. One for yesterday. I missed yesterday. I was taught when I grew up that the Jewish religion made a fundamental difference to the world. You know what I mean. Well, more than half the world is on this side of the planet. They don't even know what Judaism is, and they're perfectly and marvelously content without it. This is a rich culture, probably no more violent and cruel than our own. Do you think Christianity has made a big dent here?"

"I don't know, chappy."

"Anyway, that's my thought for yesterday. Sobering. At least to this one Jew. I'm done eating, John."

Later they walked beneath the arched roof of the Asakusa outdoor market. The street was crowded with shoppers. The shops were small and neat. In the indoor shrine at the end of the street, people crowded before an altar on which stood an image. Candles burned in tall black metal candelabra. Women stood with their hands together, praying. Children prayed softly. Before the altar was a railing. An old man stood at the railing. He wore a hat and a brown coat. He had a long white beard, a flowing beard that lay upon his chest and seemed possessed of a life of its own, like a waterfall. It caught the soft lights of the candles and glints of the sunlight that came through the door of the shrine. In his hands he held a prayer book. His body swayed slowly back and forth, back and forth, as he prayed. His eyes opened and closed behind rimless spectacles that flashed and flared with the lights of the candles and the sun. Gershon looked at him. Had he seen him somewhere before? He could not remember.

"Do you think our God is listening to him, John?"

"I don't know, chappy. I never thought of it."

"Neither did I until now. If He's not listening, why not? If He is listening, then—well, what are *we* all about, John? That's my thought for tomorrow. I think we ought to go back to the hotel."

The day was Friday. Gershon's Shabbat began with dusk. He remained by himself in the room; John went out for a walk. He sat in an easy chair, reading a work by Chaim Vital on the kabbalistic thought of Isaac Luria. He put it aside after a while and took up the second of the two books he had brought with him, a volume of the Zohar. He began to read the commentary to the Torah portion of that Shabbat, the section that tells of the Revelation at Sinai.

He read, "When a man spreads out his hands and lifts them up in prayer and supplication, he may be said to glorify the Holy One in various ways. He symbolically unites the ten *sefirot,* thereby unifying the whole and duly blessing the Holy Name." He read this and thought of the Japanese he had seen praying in the shrine.

He read, "It is true that the Holy One is glorified for the sake of Israel alone; but while Israel is the foundation of the sacred light from which comes forth light for the whole world, yet when heathen nations come to accept the glory of the Holy One and to worship

Him, then the foundation of the light is strengthened . . . and then the Holy One reigns above and below. That is exactly what happened when Jethro, the high priest of paganism, was converted to the worship of the true God of Israel: the whole world . . . gave up their idols, realizing their impotence." He read this and thought of the beauty he had seen in Nikko.

And he read, "It is written: And all the people saw the thunderings. Surely it ought to be *heard* the thunderings? We have, however, been taught that the voices were delineated, carved out, as it were, upon the . . . darkness, so that they could be apprehended as something visible . . . and because they saw that sight they were irradiated with a supernal light. . . ." He read this and thought of the waterfall roar he had heard the day before. Sound and sight had yielded a single vivid representation of power and beauty; it had lifted him from himself; he remembered that now. And he remembered the words he had spoken, the blessing. "Praised be Thou, O Lord our God, King of the universe, who has fashioned the works of creation." He was being taught the loveliness of God's world by a pagan land.

And he read, "At that hour all the mysteries of the Torah, all the hidden things of heaven and earth, were unfolded before them. . . . And when all the fleshly impurity was removed from the Israelites their bodies became . . . lucent as stars and their souls were as resplendent as the firmament, to receive the light. Such was the state of the Israelites as—"

There was someone in the room. He had heard nothing, but he knew there was someone with him in the room, and he looked up.

Jakob Keter and Nathan Malkuson stood near the closed door.

Ah, we did not wish to disturb you, Jakob Keter murmured. He wore his dark suit and red bow tie and was hatless.

Shabbat shalom, Loran, Nathan Malkuson said. We were watching you. You read the Zohar as a commentary on the Torah portion? Rashi, Ibn Ezra, the Midrash—all are inadequate?

I remembered some passages I wanted to look at again, Gershon said quietly, hesitantly.

Yes? Jakob Keter said without expression. I can imagine the passages.

May we sit down? asked Malkuson.

Please.

They sat on the sofa.

A comfortable room, said Jakob Keter. These are people who love plants and flowers, yes? The passages you read require thought.

This is a beautiful world, Loran. Beware of its allure. The Mishnah is clear on the matter of paganism.

Malkuson, Jakob Keter said. The Mishnah is old. We need a new Mishnah. If not on many things, then certainly on the matter of paganism. Our Christian friends can learn from this as well.

You are tampering with the core of things, Keter. The very heart.

That is the only area worth tampering with, Malkuson. Everything else is the periphery. He was silent a moment, gazing around the hotel room. I liked the last visit better, Mr. Loran. Yes. In the succah it was nicer. Especially with the camouflage nets. Do you not think so, Malkuson?

It was not exactly a succah, said Nathan Malkuson with a measure of his usual disdain. But it was certainly nicer in a way than this elegance.

They work hard. It is often a dangerous labor. They are entitled to occasional elegance. Still, the succah, Mr. Loran—Rabbi Loran—the succah built by your engineers was of a special beauty. Yes.

Are you going? asked Gershon. They had risen from the sofa.

Unless there is some other matter, said Malkuson.

Yes, Gershon said. About Arthur.

They looked at him.

What should I do? I feel—

You feel? said Jakob Keter.

Trouble. Doom.

Perhaps— said Jakob Keter.

Yes?

Perhaps you should try to make visible the sounds he hears.

What?

Yes. What do you think, Malkuson?

I agree. On this matter we are in agreement.

I don't—

You will think about it, Mr. Loran. Yes?

Gershon was quiet.

We should go now, Mr. Loran. This is sufficient. Yes?

Yes.

Read the Midrash, Malkuson said. Read Ibn Ezra. If you must have Kabbalah with the Torah, read Ramban.

The Zohar will not hurt him, Malkuson. Not this one.

Read Rashbam. Read Seforno.

Shabbat shalom, Mr. Loran. Rabbi Loran.

Shabbat shalom, Loran.

Shabbat shalom, Gershon said.

They were gone.

He sat alone in the hotel room. John came in a few minutes later. He had enjoyed the walk. What a great city. He loved the lights. He was grateful the chaplain had come with him.

They went by train south to Odawara on Sunday and took an electric tramcar to Miyanoshita. The tram went up tall hills. Gershon sat near a window and watched its climb. The hills were green with cedars and spruce. They had lunch at the Fujiya Hotel and took a boat across Lake Hakone.

"I can't get over how you always know what to do, chappy," John said, looking out the window at the lake. "This is beautiful, beautiful."

The day was blue, cloudless. A bluish luminescence covered the surface of the water. It was a small boat, and Gershon felt the heavy vibration of its engine and its path through the water. He gazed out the window at the spread of the lake. Then they rounded a bend and the concealing treeline fell away and, abruptly, there was Mount Fuji, enormous, snow-covered from base to top, alive in the light of the sun, its conical vastness so awesome he felt it as a presence against his eyes. And he spoke again, with full awareness now, the blessing he had uttered at the waterfall.

"Fuji-san," he heard a Japanese woman say softly to her child.

"Look at it, chappy," John murmured.

"Yes," Gershon said. "Yes." And he pressed his warm forehead against the boat window. The rhythm of the engines traveled along the cold glass to his forehead. He felt it in his eyes, the thrumming of the boat. Sun and sky played out a vast world of light upon the mountain, turning patches of its snow here and there bluish-purple and soft green and mauve and pink and stark clear white. He felt himself overwhelmed and closed his eyes. The vision of the mountain lingered.

Some of the Japanese on the small boat were taking pictures. He heard the clicks of the cameras and imagined he saw the mountain imprinting itself upon their film. He opened his eyes. There it was again, in its snow-filled enormity. He abandoned himself to it, to this sacred mountain of Japan, this god.

That night he left John in their hotel room writing his letter and took a cab to the club. She came over immediately to his booth. He ordered Scotch. She drank the colored water.

"Chap-san have a good day?" she asked softly.

"A very good day."

They danced in the dim light to the music of the band. She smelled clean. She came to his shoulders in height. He could see the straight lines of her dark hair and the curve of her eyes. She smiled shyly beneath his gaze. He was with her until the club closed. In the cab home he said, "Can you do it?"

"Chap-san meet mama-san."

"Now?"

"Tomorrow, chap-san."

"You understand?" he said. "Two rooms. Everywhere. You understand?"

"I understand, chap-san."

She had a soft musical voice. In the darkness of the cab her voice seemed a warm reddish light. I'm tired, he thought. It's the mountain and the Scotch. I'm really tired.

John was asleep when he returned.

The next afternoon John went off on his own, and Gershon took a cab to the club. She was waiting for him outside. They rode together to where she lived with her mother, a narrow street, an alleyway, crowded with tiny wooden houses. There were children everywhere and the curious faces of old women. He followed her through a narrow hallway. At a door he removed his shoes. She led him into a small room. They sat on the tatami. The room was bare save for some low pieces of furniture whose function he could not make out.

She went from the room. He sat alone, listening to the muffled voices of children. A door slid open. An old woman entered the room silently and sat on the floor. The girl, her daughter, sat beside her. The woman wore a gray-colored kimono. She was very old and seemed tired. She spoke softly to her daughter. They spoke together, nodding from time to time at Gershon. He would remember afterward that in the course of the talk a bit of furniture suddenly became a table, and cups and saucers appeared and tea and fire, and he breathed the aroma of the tea and held in his hand a steaming cup from which he sipped slowly. They sat in silence, drinking the tea. The sounds had disappeared. The room had expanded. The old woman nodded, her face without expression.

Gershon said, "Your mother understands?"

She said, "My mother is happy."

"I mean it," he said. "Two rooms."

"Yes, chap-san."

"Where will we go?"

"I will think, chap-san. Kobe, yes. Inland Sea, Takamatsu, Miyajima. Beautiful places."

"Hiroshima," he said.

The two women looked at him. The old lady spoke briefly to her daughter.

"Hiroshima not kekko," the girl said.

"Hiroshima," he said.

"Hai," she said. "Hiroshima, chap-san."

The old woman spoke to her again and she replied. The old woman looked down at the floor and was silent.

He took a cab back to the hotel.

John returned some minutes later, laden with packages. "Got to send these to my fiancée, chappy. You can outfit a whole house from here at less than half what it would cost you back home. I love this place."

"Let's get something to eat, John. I'm starved."

"I've got to do some more shopping tomorrow, chappy. Will you mind?"

"No, John. I'm all right on my own. No problem."

The next morning Gershon took the train to Odawara and the

tram to Miyanoshita and the boat across Lake Hakone. There was the mountain. He felt drawn to its majestic light-filled rise, its splendrous whiteness. The old man who stood next to him leaning on a cane murmured, "Ah, Fuji-san," and then spoke softly toward the mountain in Japanese.

Gershon returned to Tokyo in the early evening. He had dinner alone in the hotel and spent an hour over coffee and pastry in the tearoom, listening to the music and watching the small orchestra move slowly up and down on the elevator. He took a cab to the club and was there until it closed.

The next day he and John flew to Korea, and that evening they were back in their room in the battalion.

He lay in his bed and listened to the night. Siberian winds beat against the walls. He had felt the cold on his exposed flesh as he had stood earlier at the tube. In the darkness the stove burned quietly. He heard John's deep breathing. An intense vision appeared inside his closed eyes: the white, lyrical grandeur of Mount Fuji. He felt a slowly rising sensation, as if he were becoming weightless, and then an abrupt lurching fall as the vision faded. He was back in Korea. Yes. He settled slowly in the bed and slept.

In his office the next morning he put the ringing phone to his ear and heard Arthur's voice, thin and metallic. "Hello? Gershon?"

"Yes, Arthur."

"How are you?"

"Fine."

"Is it snowing where you are?"

"Yes."

"It's awful up here. We're entombed. How was your R and R?"

"Excellent. How do you feel, Arthur?"

"Terrible. You should have waited for me, Gershon. Why didn't you wait?"

"You should have stayed out of that café, Arthur. You know better than to eat the food here. Don't you listen to orientation sessions?"

"I couldn't go in there and not eat anything. I couldn't just sit there, dear Gershon. A few more times and I'll be used to the food."

"What do you mean, a few more times? Have you been back there?"

"Listen. Do you know that this country is really a dictatorship? Do you know that?"

"Are you getting involved with these students? For God's sake, Arthur. There were riots here last spring."

"We owe them something, Gershon. Did you set up our trip?"

"I'm working on it. I've got us an interpreter. Arthur, don't get involved with the activists here. You're an officer in the American army."

"I know what I am, dear Gershon." The tinny connection could not conceal the sudden flare of anger in the voice. "I'm an offspring of killers, that's what I am. You think I left physics and entered the rabbinate just so I could sit on my rear end? We owe them. Hello? Can you hear me?"

"Yes."

"I said we owe them."

"I heard what you said, Arthur."

"Are you going to be in Seoul next week?"

"Yes."

"That was a good idea you had, dear Gershon. The weekly meetings in Seoul." There was a brief pause. "I wish you had waited."

"I couldn't wait. My roommate couldn't wait."

"Goodbye, Gershon."

He sat at his desk. Outside the window, snow fell thickly through the gray air. It snowed all day.

A Quonset burned down that night in a distant infantry unit. He heard of it the next day at lunch, along with the rumored report that two nights back the Turks had caught a slicky boy on their compound stealing cameras and had staked him out naked in the Siberian winds.

The battalion commander said jovially, "Chappy, remember that great idea you had about the Turks?"

Yes, Gershon remembered.

"The medics remember it too," said Skippy. "I'll bet a beer they remember it."

That night Gershon's assistant woke and saw a shadow next to his bed. He drew in breath. The shadow moved. An icy metallic object was pressed between Howard Morten's eyes. He heard a whisper and felt his flesh crawl. "This forty-five gun, soldier boy. You shout, I shoot." He closed his eyes in terror and listened to the silence in the Quonset.

"I was never so scared in my life," he said to Gershon in the morning.

"What did they take?"

"My footlocker. Camera, slides, letters. Everything."

John said that night, "It's going on everywhere, chappy. They hit the tank company last night. Did you hear about it?"

Yes, Gershon had heard.

"We try to build up this place, and they tear us down for it. How about that, chappy? Does it make any sense? I'm sleeping with this under my pillow."

Gershon stared at the dark glinting metal of the .45 automatic.

"Anyone comes through our door at night, I shoot him first and ask questions later."

His voice was empty of posturing. Gershon watched his expert handling of the weapon and knew he would use it. John sat writing, the weapon in its belt and holster on the desk near the letter.

Gershon rode the jeep into Seoul early the next week and found Arthur in the chapel. His flaxen hair was uncombed, and he looked haggard. They shook hands.

"You're losing weight, Arthur."

"It's this parasite I picked up. You look good, dear Gershon. Doesn't he look good, Sol? Asia agrees with our Gershon."

"You liked Japan?" Solomon Geiger said. "Arthur tells me you liked Japan."

"There's a lot there to like."

"That's why I'm staying put here. Who needs the temptation? What did I want to ask you? Yes. Do you know a boy named Gabriel Rosen? He tells me he was your assistant in the medics."

"Yes."

"He's been to services here a few times. A sincere boy. I'm bringing him here as my assistant."

Gershon looked at the round pink face of Solomon Geiger.

"A fine boy. Devout. Well, what is on our agenda for today?"

They sat in Solomon Geiger's office, discussing service schedules, a Jewish boy who was in the Seoul stockade for disobeying an order, and preparations for the observance of Purim and Passover. Arthur sat drinking tea and glancing repeatedly at his watch. He crossed and uncrossed his long legs. Gershon saw the darkness in his blue eyes. You live with someone for two years and you hardly know him. Arthur had not wanted himself known. Privacy; reticence; carefully demarcated boundaries—those had marked his relationship with Arthur Leiden. He had no reason to believe that would change now. Arthur drank four cups of hot tea in the time they sat there; he contributed little to the discussion.

Later they stood outside the chapel near their jeeps in the cold afternoon air.

"Why don't you come along?" Arthur said.

Gershon said nothing.

"It's only a crowded room with a bunch of kids smoking and drinking coffee. Most of them know English."

"Is this the sort of thing you did at Harvard?"

"I did a lot of things at Harvard. Most were stupid. Will you come?"

"No."

"All right, dear Gershon. All right."

"Be careful, Arthur. Politicians get shot here."

"Politicians get shot everywhere. It's a mark of our enlightened species. God, it's cold. I can't remember winds like this in Boston. Are you having a problem with thieves in your area? It's bad where we are."

"How did you get started with those students?"

"The Korean kid who hangs around the chapel began to talk to me about Chanukah. He said you told him it was a liberation war. I told him about Purim and oppressed minorities and about Passover and freedom from slavery. It isn't just a lot of dead words and ideas to me. He was really impressed, dear Gershon. He thought Judaism was just another Western bourgeois religion. I showed him how wrong he was." Gershon looked at the half-mocking smile on Arthur's wind-reddened face. "You could tell him about Shabbatai Zvi and revolutionary messianism, right? About the power of Kabbalah and dreams. We have a thing or two left to teach, don't we?" Arthur gazed up at the pale light of the afternoon sky, squinting.

"My head doesn't stop hurting. That parasite colonized me to a remarkable extent. We do have something left, don't we? I wasn't wrong to leave physics. We're not all a bunch of money-hungry merchants or black-frocked reactionaries or blood-congealed scholars. Are we? We're not all theoretical physicists who helped the country make bombs to drop on the wrong enemy." He looked intently at Gershon. "What do you think, dear friend?"

Gershon stared at Arthur as if he had never seen him before.

"My father in his infinite wisdom incinerated them," Arthur said softly through clenched teeth. "I owe them something."

"That was a war, Arthur."

"Don't tell me what it was. I know what it was. I was there. I saw the fucking death light when it went off. Pardon my feral vocabulary. You never saw a light like that in your life. It was white and eery, and everything it shone on was sharp and clear and frozen-looking. I saw it through the window of the little house we lived in. You know what it was, dear Gershon? It was the whole species going down the piss tubes, is what it was."

"Arthur—"

"I'll see you around, Gershon. I put in again for that leave. There won't be any problem. Sometimes I think people are glad not to have me around. Very different from the seminary years. Here I seem to remind people of their worst nightmares. I'll see you, dear Gershon. I must go to the john."

He walked off quickly toward the rear of the chapel.

It was dark when Howard Morten turned the jeep from the main supply route onto the division road. To the right of the road Gershon saw the tank company perimeter lit with burning drums of waste oil. Dark smoke curled toward the night sky. The fires burned with lurid red and yellow flames. Guards patrolled near the burning drums. Their orders now were to shoot night intruders. The division seemed spectral, tense with anticipation of attack.

"I thought they were supposed to be our friends," Howard Morten said in a frightened and dismal voice.

"Make sure that weapon of yours is working next time," Gershon said. "I don't want to hear you've brought along a weapon you're not sure you can use."

"Yes, sir. I'm really sorry about that."

He turned the jeep into the battalion compound. Gershon sat back in the seat. Strange how comforted he felt by the knowledge that he was back in the battalion. Wash and shave and change clothes. Relax in the club. Comforting. Yes. He wondered if Arthur was driving through the mountain passes now in the dark.

He woke abruptly in the night to the sounds of nearby rifle fire. He reached for his flashlight and turned it on and saw John awake in his bed, upright, the .45 held in both hands and pointed at the door.

"Turn off the light, chappy, and get your head back on the pillow."

He lay in the darkness and felt all around him the presence of sudden death.

The rifle fire ceased.

He heard a faint stirring and a click. "Go to sleep, chappy," John said quietly after a while. "Let's both go to sleep."

Gershon lay awake a long time, listening to the darkness.

In the morning on his way down the path to the officers mess he saw the colonel standing outside the Jamesway that served as his private quarters. The colonel stood without a cap or a coat and looked at the cut in the thick canvas wall of the Jamesway along one of the ribs. Snow had fallen during the night on top of the frozen snows of the past weeks. Footsteps were visible in the snow, small footsteps that led from the Jamesway to the nearby perimeter fence. The fence had been cut along a post. The cut section could be folded inward or outward and then back onto the post and the cut would remain indiscernible to the passing guard.

"My tape recorder," the colonel said. "I bought it last week. He reached in and took it." His breath vaporized in the air as he spoke. "How about that, chappy? We should have had the Turks on our perimeter again. He knew just where it was."

The colonel stood there staring in amazement at the Jamesway wall and the perimeter fence.

That afternoon Gershon walked over to the Quonset near the road that housed battalion supply and signed for a bayonet and a sheath. In the room that night John looked at the bayonet, then looked at Gershon. He said nothing. Gershon slept with the sheathed bayonet under his pillow.

He dreamed that night of his cousin. He had not dreamed of him in years. Outside their apartment house stood a scrawny sycamore. In the weeks of the long summer after his parents had died, his cousin had taught him how to throw a penknife. The trunk of the sycamore was their target. How to hold it, how to aim it, position of fingers and wrist, forward motion of arm, the bark chipping each time, for Gershon could not get the hang of it; he threw with a rush, with anger, with poor control. Think you're the point, Gersh, his cousin kept saying. You're the point. Hold it this way. Yeah. Right. Now think they're the tree, that's right, the ones that killed them are the tree, look right at the tree, throw, easy, easy, try it again. Again. You got it. That's it. You see? Now try it again. The knife quivered in the bark, and the sunlight came through the network of branches and leaves and spangled the shiny blade. Now let me show you some tricks with it, his cousin said. Some neat tricks. Come on, Gersh. Come on. Don't be afraid.

He woke from the dream and did not know where he was. When he remembered, he reached beneath the pillow and felt the sheathed bayonet. The dream had been strangely comforting. He could still feel the touch of his cousin's hand upon his shoulders and arm. He fell back into sleep.

A warehouse over at quartermaster near the airstrip was broken into and looted that night. Along the recon company perimeter a guard shot and killed an enlisted man who was too drunk to respond to the halt calls. The next night Gershon woke again to the noise of nearby rifle fire and saw through the darkness John awake in his bed with the .45 in his hands, eyes fixed upon the door. Two nights later a Quonset burned down in the artillery compound in the hills, and the next day in the division newsletter was the order to shut down all oil stoves each night by midnight.

At the bar that night one of the officers said, "A toast to the army's infinite wisdom."

"I'll drink to that," Skippy said. "Stuart, I will need a beer."

"Eyes that do not see, ears that do not hear, stoves that do not burn," Gershon intoned.

The colonel smiled patiently.

"I sense rebellion in the ranks," Skippy said. "Do I hear the murmurous tones of mutiny against the wisdom of command?"

"How was your meeting, chappy?" the colonel asked.

"Bleak, sir. The percentage is high."

"Our men must keep warm," Skippy said. "If not here, then elsewhere."

"It'll go higher now, sir," Gershon said.

"VD doesn't kill you," the colonel said. "Fires do. Everything is a trade-off. Another martini, Stuart."

Gershon was awakened that night by soft footsteps outside the door. His heart surged in his head and throat as he reached for the bayonet and slipped off the sheath. Dimly he saw John sitting with the .45 in his hands. Gershon fumbled for the flashlight and as the door opened pressed the switch and saw clearly in the beam of light two enlisted men in parkas and with rifles. They stood frozen, blinking into the light.

"Orders to check all stoves, sir. See if they're off." They ran a flashlight over the stove. "Good night, sir."

John lay back on his bed. Gershon snapped off the light, sheathed the bayonet, and put it under his pillow. His hands were trembling.

"Don't know who's coming in the door anymore." He heard John's murmur of bewilderment. "Don't know if I can shoot or not. Nothing works here, chappy. Everything is against everything else. What're we doing here?"

Gershon lay awake a long time in the piercing cold air. He rose with his flashlight and went to the stove and turned the flow control lever. He threw a match into the pool of oil and set the lever at low. He went back to bed. John was silent. The air in the room slowly warmed. Gershon fell asleep.

He rode to Seoul the next day in air brutal with cold. Gabriel Rosen met him at the door to the chapel.

"You saved my life," he whispered. "It was Gehennom up there."

"What do you mean?"

"Chaplain Geiger said you gave me a good recommendation. They hated me up there. I was the only religious Jew. They—"

Gershon moved away from his sallow face and whining voice.

"Hello," Solomon Geiger called from his office. "Gershon? Come in. What do you think of this weather? It's Siberia."

Arthur was in the office on a chair near the desk. He looked pale and tired. They shook hands.

"How do you feel?" Gershon asked.

"Terrible. Every other day I disintegrate into a quivering bundle of cloacal needs."

"Try kimchi with the coffee. Your needs will become continuous."

"I had no idea you were so cutting a wit, dear Gershon."

"I had no idea you were so involved a politician, dear Arthur. Sol, would it be all right with you if Arthur went with me to Hong Kong and then to Japan? It's only a matter of another five or six days."

"I will have no objection to that, Gershon."

Arthur looked at Gershon and said nothing.

"Do we have an agenda for today?" Solomon Geiger asked. "I don't like meetings without agendas. Gabriel, bring Chaplain Leiden a cup of hot tea and then close the door. Did you check my jeep? Is it all right?"

After the meeting Arthur said, as he walked with Gershon to their jeeps, "I don't want to go to Hong Kong. What have you got me going to Hong Kong for?"

"I want to see Hong Kong, but I don't want to go alone. Also, I don't want to fly to Japan from Hong Kong and find out that your cloacal needs have kept you in Korea. Come on, Arthur. We may as well see as much of this place as we can. I'd go to Bangkok too, but there are riots off and on in Bangkok."

"Why do I have the feeling, dear Gershon, that you really don't want me too far away from you? Is that an inaccurate perception? Never mind. Let me think about Hong Kong. What's down there besides British imperialism? My God, it's cold! Why are we standing out here in this wind? Where did you get that idea for your jeep? I always meant to ask you that. The tablets, dear Gershon."

"They're a copy of the tablets I once had made for my medical battalion chapel. I went portable, so to speak."

"I didn't know you were with the medics."

"Oh, yes. I was their sacrifice, Arthur. Not now. Another time. Lead the way and I'll be right behind you."

In the jeep he told Howard Morten to follow Arthur's driver. They rode through a wide street that paralleled briefly the bleak frozen Han River and the vile shanties along its banks. The road curved and ran on awhile. Arthur's jeep stopped in a narrow street crowded with shops and ramshackle houses. He followed Arthur down a flight of stone steps into a large café dense with noise and cigarette smoke. There were tables and chairs and students in dark uniforms and dark caps. Arthur stood in the center of the din, looking around. Gershon felt the gaze of curious and hostile eyes. He followed Arthur to a table. Two students sat at the table. Gershon heard, vaguely, Korean names; he sat next to Arthur opposite the students. A waiter came over. Arthur ordered coffee and pastry. Gershon looked at the waiter and shook his head. The waiter went away. One of the students smiled politely at Gershon and abruptly began to talk. This was the student with whom Gershon had once spoken briefly in the chapel: dark uniform, dark cap, dark, intense eyes. He said, "I thank the chaplain very much for his kind explanations. Very good explanations. We explain Korea to chaplain one day. Explain history and culture and mountains and climate, most beautiful climate in entire world, no climate like climate of Korea, but all is sadness in Korea now because country is divided, and people are very poor and must steal and sell themselves to live, and government is very corrupt." Gershon's head hurt with the noise; his eyes burned with the smoke. The student kept on talking. Arthur sat very quietly, drinking coffee and eating pastry. His face looked flushed. The light in the café was dim. The student talked to Gershon a long time.

Later Gershon stood with Arthur outside the café in the piercing wind that blew along the narrow street.

"I don't think they trust me very much," Arthur said.

"Why do you say that?"

"He said more to you in an hour than he said to me in all the weeks I've been going here. They know who I am."

Gershon said nothing. He beat his gloved hands together against the cold.

"I feel I want to help them," Arthur said, "and I don't know what to do."

The wind was unable to drown out the torment in his voice.

"There's going to be blood in the streets here, Arthur. I don't want us to get caught in it."

Arthur gave him a long look. Then he nodded. He brushed gloved fingers across the strands of flaxen hair that stuck out beneath his fur cap and blew along his forehead.

"Will you be back here again, Gershon?"

"No."

"For some reason they like to talk to you. They think you're a serious man of God. Why would they think that, dear Gershon? It must be your face, your manner. Maybe they saw you written up in *Stars and Stripes*."

"Good night, Arthur. I've got to get back."

"Shouldn't we be helping these people?"

"I don't know. I'm not cut out to be a riot planner. I lost my parents to a riot. Stay away from their food, Arthur. They really won't kill you if you don't eat and drink their food. Are you all right?"

"I think I need to use their john."

"Good night, Arthur."

He left him there in the darkening street and rode back to the battalion.

Again guards came in the early morning to check the stove, and again Gershon lit it after they left. There were no guards the next night, and Gershon and John slept through until the morning. Two nights later the guards came again. There followed the strange shadow-filled ballet of flashlights, .45 automatic, guard check, closing door, and Gershon's lighting of the stove. Nothing was ever said between Gershon and John about the warmth that entered their quarters on the heels of the investigating guards.

The colonel called Gershon into his office.

"At ease, chappy. Have a seat. I meant to call you in earlier on this, but you're all over the place. I gave you top rating on your January efficiency report. Outstanding."

"Thank you, sir."

"I want to read my remarks."

The words were a military paean of praise. Gershon gazed at the handsome face, the dark close-cropped hair, the meticulous uniform.

He listened to the rapid reading, the flat tone. He remembered F.B.I. men with that same quality of voice. A long time ago. No, not so long ago.

The colonel finished reading and looked up. "Chaplain, we're proud to have you with us. When you get to Hong Kong you might want to look up an old friend of my wife's father. Anything I can help you with, just let me know."

Later Gershon sat in his office and stared out the window at the gray winter sky. He had no perception of having done outstanding work for the battalion; in fact, his sense of things was that he had done little for the battalion and that most of his work had been with other units. He had cared intensely about the medics and somehow had failed; he cared little about the engineers and somehow was succeeding. He understood none of it and after a while shrugged it away and returned to his work.

He called Arthur later that day.

"What have you decided?"

"I haven't decided anything yet."

"No Hong Kong no Japan, Arthur."

"You never struck me before as being this adept at the art of persuasion. Why do you want me to go to Hong Kong? Why don't we spend all our leave time in Japan?"

"There aren't many Chinese in Japan, Arthur."

"Are there Jews in Hong Kong?"

"I think so. But I'm not going to Hong Kong to meet Jews."

"You've turned strange out here, dear Gershon."

"So have you, Arthur."

There was a pause.

"Arthur?"

"I'll go."

"Fine."

"Then we'll go to Japan."

"Yes."

"Kyoto and Hiroshima."

"Yes. And other places."

"The girl will come along as interpreter?"

"Yes."

"Are you sure it's all right?"

"I have it all arranged."

"I don't really want to go to Hong Kong, dear Gershon."

"Arthur—"

"But I'll go anyway. I am persuaded."

"Good. How do you feel?"

"Terrible. I think I'll take your advice and stop drinking their coffee."

"Shabbat shalom, Arthur."

There was a pause. Then, "Is it Shabbat already? Yes. What do you do all day Shabbat over at your place?"

"I study Kabbalah."

There was another pause.

"Right. Kabbalah. Shabbat shalom, dear Gershon."

He saw Arthur in Seoul the following week.

"Everything is all set," Arthur said.

"I have a check list I made up of things to take along. I'll make a copy for you if you want."

"How efficient of you, dear Gershon."

"Don't forget to take your dog tags. And a raincoat."

"What about my galoshes? My vitamins? My pills?"

After the meeting they stood outside the chapel near their jeeps.

"Geiger's pious cheerfulness will lead me to sin," Arthur said. "That new assistant of his is a Gothic creation. They make a handsome couple."

"Are you going over there again now?" Gershon asked.

"Yes."

"I'll come along."

Arthur looked at him.

"To keep you from drinking the coffee. I don't want you messing up my trip to Hong Kong."

"Am I to keep away from their tea and pastry as well?"

"All kidding aside, Arthur, you can really get very sick from their food. If you miss out on the Hong Kong trip, you'll end up in Hiroshima alone."

"You've turned unbearably officious out here, dear Gershon. What am I to do about you?"

"Stay away from their food."

"And devious. You've turned cleverly devious. Like some nuclear physicists I know. You're becoming a pain in my rear end."

Gershon looked over at the jeeps. They were parked on the road near the chapel. The assistants sat behind the wheels, waiting.

"I'll eat whatever the hell I want," Arthur said. "Who appointed you my guardian? Did my parents say to watch over me, I'm erratic? Did they? They had people watching over me all through Harvard. They once even asked Karen to watch over me. I don't need you to go to Japan with. I'm quite capable of going to Japan by myself."

"All right," Gershon said softly. "I'll see you around, Arthur."

"Go to hell, Loran. I didn't come to Korea to have you wipe my nose. I want to see the city my father helped blow up. I want to see the city my mother—" He stopped. Gershon stood looking at him and saw a coldness that was not of the frigid winter afternoon. Arthur turned abruptly away and went to his jeep. Gershon watched the jeep drive off.

He heard nothing from Arthur all the rest of that week.

That Friday night he conducted the service at the nearby infantry regiment. Walking back along the poorly lit, ice-encrusted division road, he heard someone fall in step beside him. He looked, and it was Jakob Keter.

Shabbat shalom, professor.

Shabbat shalom, Mr. Loran.

A jeep went slowly past them in its own tunnel of light, its tire chains rattling.

You are a little frightened concerning your journey. Yes?

Yes.

Why have you chosen to go to Hong Kong?

I don't know.

A strange response. There is a chance I may not accompany you.

Gershon said nothing.

It is a descent that may not only be difficult but also menacing. Have you considered that, Mr. Loran?

Yes.

You will also go to Macao?

I'll try.

I may not accompany you.

I thought there was no place you would not go.

You are not omniscient, Mr. Loran. Still I might go.

Will Arthur go?

I also am not omniscient, Mr. Loran. Our Mr. Leiden is difficult. I do not understand him. And I do not indulge in fortune-telling or crystal-gazing. I am an academician, not a practitioner. Will there ever be sufficient light on this road? It is a menace to one's well-being. Your army cannot afford lights? Is there anything you need to discuss with me concerning the Zohar on this week's Torah reading?

They walked on awhile together, talking quietly.

Later he came into the room and found John at his desk, writing, the .45 in its holster next to the letter. He read and went to bed and woke in the night to the sound of rifle fire that seemed to be going off right next to his ear.

"Stay down," John said in a whisper.

There were shouts outside, the noise of boots on ice. John dressed hurriedly and went out. Gershon followed a moment later. The sky was clear, the air bitter cold. He saw a crowd of dim figures near the perimeter fence a few feet from the Quonset. Someone brushed by him quickly. It was the colonel. Gershon followed in the path opened through the crowd by the colonel and saw the figure on the ground near the fence, strangely bent and twisted, a hand looped over a strand of wire, legs moving awkwardly of themselves on the frozen earth, small cries emanating from the bloodied mouth. He saw the colonel being saluted by a lieutenant. Brief flurries of whispered words were exchanged. "We called the medics, sir," he heard from somewhere in the hushed crowd.

"I want a full report on my desk by o-eight-hundred."

"Yes, sir."

"I want the guard in my office at that time."

"Yes, sir."

The figure on the ground moaned softly and stirred, and Gershon felt a clutch of horror deep within himself. Then it let out a wail. It coughed and arched its back over the earth and lay still, moaning. There were dark stains on the iced earth.

A light came along the road. It bounced and flared with the frozen ruts and turned into the compound. Even in the darkness Gershon saw the markings of the ambulance; the deep red lines seemed to pick up the light of the stars. The figure screamed briefly as the stretcher-bearers moved him. Then it fell silent.

The crowd dispersed.

The colonel spotted Gershon. "We've got us a slicky boy, chappy, and I've got me a mountain of paper work." He looked along the path. "He was right outside your quarters, wasn't he? Lucky night for you. Sharp-eyed guard. He'll get a commendation for this. God, it's cold. Get inside, chappy. You look frozen."

In the room he could not stop shivering. He moved the oil flow lever and lit the stove. John sat silent at the edge of his bed. The .45 was strapped to his waist. His face was pale, drawn. The room had warmed considerably before Gershon realized he had inadvertently violated the commandment against making fire on Shabbat. It was nearly dawn before he was able to sleep.

He saw Arthur at the meeting in Seoul during the week. Afterward they came out of the chapel and stood in the winter sunlight. Gershon felt the sun strangely cold on his face.

"I'm not sure I want to go," he heard Arthur say.

He was quiet.

"I don't see the point to Hong Kong, dear Gershon. Really. Why do you insist on going?"

"I'd go to India if I could afford it and had the time. But I can't."

"India?"

"So I'm settling for the next worst thing. I need to see it. All right? I don't know why exactly. Most of the time I don't entirely understand what I do and why I do it. Is that so terrible? Frankly, I'm getting tired of your whining and your heroics. I don't give a shit whether you come with me or not. Do whatever you want."

He strode to his jeep and climbed in and rode away. He found John writing. After dinner he wrote to his aunt and uncle and to Jakob Keter and to Karen. He lay awake a long time in the darkness. He knew John was awake too. No guards came that night to check the stove.

. . .

Some days later in the evening he stood in a noisy customs room. All around him were Koreans. He thought he heard German and looked around and saw some Europeans. The room was crowded. He was jostled repeatedly. The sour odor of kimchi hung in the stove-warmed air. The Korean customs officer looked closely at his orders and went through his bags with the measured insolence of one who knew how completely he dominated this moment of another's life. Arthur appeared in the customs room after Gershon was already aboard the Korean National Airlines DC-4. He came onto the aircraft, slipped into his aisle seat, and did not look directly at Gershon.

The engines coughed in start-up sequence and settled into their pre-takeoff rhythms.

Gershon felt the weariness of all the Korean weeks come suddenly upon him and the swift dissolution of the tightness with which he had been warding off the other side.

"It was not quite necessary for you to be so offensive, dear friend," he heard Arthur say.

He mumbled a barely coherent reply and a moment later could not remember his words. He leaned back in the seat. The wing lights flashed outside his window. He saw the lights reflected on the dark snow along the runway. The aircraft trembled into takeoff. As if drugged, he tumbled into a deep sleep.

Arthur sat with his eyes wide open, staring at the dim overhead reading lights. He refused the drink offered him by the stewardess.

They flew southward through the night.

Part Three

9

He slept and woke and slept again and woke finally into the early morning to a window vision of tall hills. Next to him sat Arthur, awake, sullen. He felt in his ears the descent of the aircraft. His head hurt and his throat felt raw, and it occurred to him that he might be ill. Below lay a pale land of hills and plains and an expanse of slate-colored water. They flew between mountains so close it seemed their wings would brush the peaks. A city suddenly appeared beneath them on the wedge of coastal plain between the mountains and the sea. They landed heavily and after some minutes came to a stop. He saw the wing reflected in the rain puddles on the tarmac. In the distance hills and water faded off into blurring mist.

Arthur stood and reached for their jackets and coats. "I wish I knew what we're doing here."

"We're looking for Chinese kabbalists," Gershon said, and coughed.

"Are you all right?"

"Sore throat." Passengers were moving past them to the door. "Come on before they turn the plane around and go back."

"Wasn't there another airline we could have flown?"

"Not last night. The pilot was American."

"I didn't know that. I wish you had told me that."

"Were you worried, Arthur?"

"I was petrified. I hate flying."

"A physicist who hates flying?"

Arthur did not respond. He followed Gershon out of the aircraft. A cheerful British passport control officer stamped their orders, and a customs official made chalk marks on their bags and breezily waved them through. A cab took them along the wet, crowded morning streets. There was a faint fragrance of flowers in the cool air. A light rain was falling. They looked through the streaked windows at the rickshaws. The sight of the humans between the shafts shocked them both. Gershon, feeling achy and feverish, had a sudden vision of the horse galloping crazily up the street between the shafts of the cart and missing the jeep by the bare distance of the heat that rose from its glistening body. He smelled again the rush of warmth and sweat, felt again the jarring swerve of the jeep as Roger Tat turned the wheel. Where was he now, Roger Tat, the Bible-reading composer, the Mormon who had two or three times saved their lives? Strange how people drifted in and out of your life, and you never really got to know them. Even if you lived with them in the same room. Whom did he really know? No one. How could he ever know anyone when he barely knew himself?

The cab driver, a portly middle-aged Chinese, was saying something to them. Gershon looked away from the strange city in the window of the cab and saw the driver talking to their reflection in his rear-view mirror.

"First time Kowloon Hong Kong?"

"That's right," Arthur said.

"Stay long time?"

"Six days."

"Not long. Go shopping? Suits? Nice jewels?"

"Maybe. Are we going shopping, dear Gershon? This is your show."

"Maybe we'll go shopping."

"Are you all right?"

"Headache."

"Here nice places buy suits and jewels. Queen's Road, Hong Kong. Take ferry." He handed them two cards.

"Sure," Arthur said. "Thanks."

"You say go Peninsula Hotel?"

"Yes."

"Very nice hotel."

"Do you have any aspirin on you?" Gershon asked.

"I've a small pharmacy in my bag. Are you sick?"

"I don't know."

"If you're sick we'll certainly have a fine time here."

"I didn't come here to have a fine time. Are you going to Hiroshima to have a fine time?"

"That's very different," Arthur said, his voice suddenly low.

"I'm going to wander around and look."

"At what?"

"I don't know. At this half of God's world."

"Splendid. Listen. Tell me your big secret. Why did we really just now spend ten hours in a Korean airliner? Not to mention one hundred and forty-five dollars in air fare. What are we doing here? Are we sightseeing?"

"We're going shopping."

Arthur looked at him. "You said 'shopping,' dear friend."

"I really could use that aspirin," Gershon said, and gazed out the window.

They were on a wide boulevard that was a confused mass of pedestrians, rickshaws, double-decker trams, autos. Coolies weaved through the crowds with loaded bamboo shoulder slings. White-sleeved patrolmen in traffic pagodas directed the maelstrom with marionette gestures instantaneously obeyed by all.

Gershon heard Arthur murmur, "What am I doing here, dear God? What?"

Gershon said, looking out the window at the Chinese and English signs on the shops, "There were riots here last October."

Arthur said, "There is a noticeable edge of hostility to your humor these days."

"Aspirin will cure it. Have you been paying attention to the Chinese girls in their cheongsams?"

"In their what?"

"The tight slit skirts."

"How do you know what they're called?"

"There's a fine regimental library next door to my engineers."

"Gershon the student, forever the student. Karen would look nice in one of those."

"As a matter of fact, she would. But the Chinese girls look especially nice."

"Did we come here to look at Chinese girls?"

"Aren't they part of God's world?"

"I don't know. Theology is your department. Is Korea part of God's world?"

"Definitely. Except for my old medical battalion. The chapel was too nice. I'm sorry. I'm not making sense. I may be a little feverish. Here we are."

The cab had stopped at the hotel. The door was opened. Porters came for their luggage. The rain had turned into a drizzle.

"Have nice time Hong Kong," the driver said. "Queen's Road, nice shopping. Nice clothes, nice jewels. Goodbye." He dove into the traffic stream.

The room faced the harbor. From their windows they could see Salisbury Road and the Kowloon Canton railway tracks and the Star Ferry pier. Across the narrow oceanic lagoon was the island of Hong Kong—the brief flatland of dense urban growth and the sudden rise of Victoria Peak, its crown obscured by low clouds. The lagoon was crowded with junks, sampans, ferries. They crisscrossed one another's wake like skating water bugs. An American aircraft carrier rode at anchor, huge, massive, awesome with dormant power. Freighters were tied up in the harbor. A convoy of cargo junks entered the lagoon. Gershon saw on their flags the yellow star of Communist China.

He leaned the side of his head against the cool glass of the window. They had unpacked. He had swallowed two aspirins. His head still ached. He stood near the window, very still, praying the morning service and gazing out at the Chinese world below.

He had journeyed the farthest distance he could from his own world. Why? He did not know. He wanted to look, that was all. Arthur could not understand that. They had entered the city that lay on the overlapping rims of two warring cultures, each seen as barbarous by the other. This was a between-world. He wanted to look at it. He looked out at the harbor. There was something strange about the harbor. He remembered the walks along the Hudson River—alone, with Karen, with Jakob Keter. There was something missing here. He was done with the service and began to remove his tefillin.

"Not like the view from our room in the seminary," Arthur said from the other window.

"I liked the seminary view."

"Did you see that aircraft carrier?"

"Yes."

They stood there a moment gazing at the carrier. Gershon glanced at Arthur and saw him close his eyes. His handsome face was pale; his flaxen hair was in disarray beneath the dark leather thong of the tefillin box he wore on his head. He looked back out at the water. Something was wrong, and he did not know what it was. How lightly the boats moved back and forth between mainland and island. He felt chilled and light-headed, but the pain was nearly gone now from his head. He knew he should eat, though he was not hungry. Gazing out the window, he thought for some reason of Professor Malkuson's study in the room above his in the seminary. He remembered the test in the elevator. All these memories simply because he was standing next to Arthur and looking out a window. How the streets teemed with people. A city without enough food or water or space and with too many fires, typhoons, and visitations of plague. What else? What had he read in those books he had borrowed from the infantry regiment's library? The large region of farmlands beyond Kowloon—the area called the New Territories —might have to be returned to mainland China in 1997 when the lease on it was due to run out. A precarious existence, thin, tenuous —so the books had characterized the city. He wished to wander through this menaced and thriving world, this strange simultaneity of darkness and light. The books had lured him. As had Skippy. "Spent a week there, chappy. Fantastic place. Got a name you can call if you ever go. Nice people. They'll show you around. Take you to places you'll never see on your own. You ought to go, chappy. You might never get another chance." Yes. That was probably why he had come. But what was wrong about the harbor?

He heard Arthur removing his tefillin. The clouds had begun to thin. Pale sunlight struggled through onto the grayish water. He heard Arthur say, "That's curious."

"What?"

"Have you noticed any sea gulls anywhere?"

Gershon looked out the window. Of course. The ships, the harbor, the lagoon— He had a sudden vision of the gulls circling the tug-boats on the Hudson. The old Italian man selling ices on Riverside Drive. "Thanka you, thanka you."

"No birds," he heard Arthur say, and he looked at him and saw him standing at the window with his eyes tightly shut. His head was cocked to one side, and he seemed to be listening to something. "No birds," Arthur said again. He had released the finger thong of his hand phylactery; now the thong began to unroll of itself along his arm. Gershon saw it spilling slowly out of his sleeve and spiraling onto the carpeted floor.

"Isn't it too early for birds?" Gershon asked. "It's February." And he answered his own question, "Not here. Not this far south."

Arthur opened his eyes. He stared out the window and a look of surprise came over his features, as if he had expected to find himself somewhere else. He looked at Gershon. "Hello," he said, and smiled weakly. He noticed the dangling thong and raised it quickly from the floor. "Sorry," he murmured. "Lost myself there a moment. Memories and all that." He was silent, gazing out the window. Then he looked at Gershon. "We ought to get something to eat."

"I want to make a couple of phone calls."

"How's your head?"

"Much better. Are you all right, Arthur?"

"No. But it's not anything you can help. Whom are you calling?"

"A friend of my CO's. And a girl."

"A girl? Chinese?"

"Persian."

"Jewish?"

"Muslim."

"Muslim? Did you say Muslim, dear Gershon?"

"Yes."

"My God," Arthur said. "You have changed out here, haven't you?"

"Would you take along your antibiotics when we go out? In case I need them."

"Where are we going? Shopping?"

"Looking," Gershon said. "All I want to do is look."

"You expect to need antibiotics just from looking?"

"I had better make those phone calls."

"About the birds," Arthur said. "After the bomb went off, there were sections around Los Alamos where it rained dead birds. I saw more than a dozen birds fall into our yard. They made faint thudding sounds. I was looking out the window and saw them fall. It was pure chance that I saw them. Pure chance, dear Gershon. I remember what they looked like. They smelled charred. Their eyes were burned out. You know, sometimes I think I don't mind it too much that we will probably kill ourselves. We're a terrible species. But we're going to kill all the birds too. Anyway, my mother buried them. My father—my father wasn't home at the time. Sorry to trouble you with my bizarre memories. Go ahead with your phone calls. Excuse me."

Gershon watched him turn away from the window, place his tefillin bag carefully on the bureau, and cross quickly to the bathroom. He turned and looked out the window at the pale sunlight on the tumultuous harbor.

Later that morning they crossed to Hong Kong in a ferry crowded with noisy Chinese. Along wide and narrow streets filled with the clamor of shops and crowds and the odors of outdoor cooking, they walked and looked and listened and said little to one another. They wore their coats in the cool air and carried their cameras, and most of the Chinese they filmed smiled at them and others seemed embarrassed. One woman, eating rice with chopsticks out of a white lacquered bowl behind tall baskets of potatoes in an outdoor vegetable market, saw their aimed cameras and shouted at them and turned her back. Tall concrete tenement houses lined many of the streets and climbed the foothills of the encroaching mountains. Laundry hung from the windows. A huge billboard festooned with oriental letters and faces announced a theatrical offering. Nearby was a Coca-Cola sign, and down the street at a service station the flying red horse of Mobilgas hung suspended in the air against a background of light-gray three-story houses with enclosed porches and flat roofs. Tall, thin-trunked palm trees grew from the sidewalks. A child in a gleaming red baseball cap laughed shyly at

Gershon as he snapped his picture. Another gazed at him wide-eyed from a bowl of rice. Camera visions frozen on film. Was his mind like that, freezing visions onto a film of memory? How did it work, memory? No one really knew. The Japanese he had seen photograph Mount Fuji—what did they do with the pictures? Were they worshiped as icons? He did not know. He knew nothing about this world where he had lived now for a year. He knew its periphery, the faces it yielded to photographers. He was a soldier, and soldiers were the most peripheral of a culture's exports. Arthur had begun to penetrate beyond the periphery by attending those student meetings. What did that mean to him—an act of atonement for his father, whose bomb had obliterated periphery and core in two oriental cities? Gershon did not know. Why was he suddenly thinking all this on a clangorous Hong Kong street? He did not know. His head was hurting again, and he felt cold.

On Queen's Road they turned into a white stone Victorian-style building and went up a flight of stairs. They waited in a spacious room furnished in the antique elegance of the Victorian world. You expected that a picture of the great queen would adorn one of the papered walls. Instead there were color photographs of Hong Kong and Kowloon: the harbor, the view from Victoria Peak, the Aberdeen floating restaurants, the farmlands in the New Territories, an old farmer guiding a wooden plow through a rice field behind a water buffalo, a vast, white, exquisite home on a hill with what seemed to be a gilded angled roof and a lettered sign that read Ankars on the foot of the curving path that led from the road to the house. They sat in silence in this Victorian room, and Gershon thought, Yesterday at this time I was in a jeep on the way from battalion to Seoul in a snowstorm. The jeep skidded into a shallow ditch. MP's pushed us out. Glad to help, chaplain. No sweat, sir. Yesterday. Yes.

Somewhere in the room an inner door opened soundlessly, and a woman stepped through it and came toward them, hand extended. "How do you do? So sorry to keep you waiting. Mr. Loran, Mr. Leiden." She shook their hands warmly. "I am Patricia." She looked to be in her late twenties. She wore a dark-blue dress with a small white artificial flower near the right shoulder. She had short dark hair and dark eyes and brown skin and was possessed of the charm and vivacity often taken on as compensatory characteristics by the ungifted and the plain. "So kind of you to bring greetings from Lieutenant Skipworth. So very kind. Do sit down." She spoke in hushed tones. "Will you be long in Hong Kong? We must think what to do. You must come have dinner with us one night. Shall I take you to see a street shelter? Yes. Tomorrow morning perhaps. We take them off the streets, you know, and provide them with a place to sleep. We are a city of refugees. You must come and meet my father. Do come. I am so glad to meet friends of Mr. Skipworth. Is he well?"

They followed her out of the room and along a silent corridor through an oak door. They were in a carpeted oak-paneled room. Behind an enormous dark-wood desk sat a large, brown-skinned man in a dark business suit and vest. He wore thick-lensed glasses and had small lively eyes and graying hair. He rose and shook their hands energetically.

"My good fellows, how nice to meet you. Friends of one of my daughter's friends, I hear. Dashed good of you to stop by. Fine chap, that Skipworth. Has it up here, you know." He tapped his head and winked an eye. "Quite an extraordinary chess player. Are you staying long? We must have you over for dinner. Patricia will make the arrangements. I've an appointment in a few moments. Leiden. Leiden. You aren't by any remote chance, sir, related to the physicist Leiden? By Jove, sir, are you now? Well, we are honored, sir. Do you hear that, Patricia? Well, how fortuitous indeed. We shall have you over, and we shall talk. Good day, gentlemen. So very good to have met you."

They went down the stairs and out into the noisy street.

"What does he do?" Arthur asked.

"He's a lawyer. A solicitor."

"Will we see them again?"

"Sure. Why not? They'd be hurt if we didn't."

"It's your show, dear Gershon."

"Are you upset?"

"No."

"You're a lousy liar, Arthur. Did you bring the antibiotics?"

"Yes."

"I think I'm running a fever. I feel chilled."

"I brought the aspirin too."

"Maybe you should have studied medicine."

"I thought about that. But my brother wanted to study medicine. The one who was killed in the war. I walk in enough shadows as it is."

"No one in your family was ever a rabbi?"

"In my family? Hardly, dear Gershon. Hardly."

They had lunch in a small restaurant on Queen's Road and then spent the afternoon wandering through streets and shops and alleys. They went past the post office and the fire brigade building. The sun was warm. Gershon had taken two aspirins, and the chill he had felt earlier had now subsided. They walked on and, after an abrupt turn that seemed not to be on Gershon's map, found themselves in a section of horrid squalor—shacks and rotting tenements and the odor of raw sewage and stony faces staring at them from broken doorways and windows. They were lost for an interminable half hour in a festering labyrinth of alleys vile with gutter filth and putrid water. Through this winding and maggoty warren they wandered with mounting apprehension and horror—had they stumbled into a leper world?—until they turned a corner and saw a rush of traffic and plunged into a wide street that led them eventually to Connaught Road and the ferry.

There was a telephone message for them at the Peninsula Hotel when they returned. An invitation to dinner at eight that night. They were to take a cab to the Ankars on Victoria Peak. The message was signed Pat.

"I'm tired," Gershon said. "My fever is back up."

"I'll call her and tell her we can't make it."

"No."

They rode the elevator to their room.

That night they took the ferry across the lagoon and gazed in awe through the windows of the throbbing boat at the splendor of light that bathed the darkened island.

"He never knew what he was doing when he discovered neon," Arthur murmured to the windows. To Gershon's query he shrugged and said nothing.

The cab took them on a dizzying climb along a winding mountain road and deposited them before the white edifice they had seen in the photograph earlier that day. Chinese servants brought them inside. There were Pat and her father. She looked lovely in a tight red cheongsam, and he looked lordly in a dark-blue brocaded dinner jacket and white silk cravat. "Ah, good evening, dear chaps. Good evening. So very glad you could come. We will make a splendid evening." They walked on carpeted floors through elegant and richly furnished rooms. In a flowering garden they saw far below them the lights of Hong Kong and Kowloon. Gershon sensed the girl come alongside him. Arthur and her father were talking together softly some distance away.

"How did you enjoy your day in Hong Kong, Mr. Loran?" the girl asked.

He had taken two aspirins before leaving the hotel. He felt well. They talked awhile about Hong Kong. The garden was dimly lighted. He sensed her body warmth and smelled the scent of her perfume and felt the discomfort of the rush of blood within him.

"How long have you lived in Hong Kong?"

"We came soon after the war. It was quite unstable in Persia. We were fearful of the Russians."

"Is there a city more unstable than Hong Kong?"

She smiled at him in the dimness. "Perhaps not. Perhaps it is a creative instability. I like it here. I did not like it very much back home. There were riots, and my mother was killed, and we fled. Look at them. They are talking quite intently. My father has a high regard for your friend's father. Are your parents alive?"

"No."

"I'm so sorry."

"They were killed during the riots in Palestine in the late thirties."

He gazed out at the lights on the island and sensed her looking at him.

"We are Muslims," she said softly. "We are not Arabs."

"I understand," he said.

"Did you live in Palestine?"

"No. I've never been to Palestine. My parents went there to buy land. My father had the idea that he would build apartment houses for the poor. He was not a very good builder, but he wanted to learn. I'm told he had great plans to build up Jerusalem. Anyway, they shot him and my mother while they were out in some café one night, and that was the end of that."

He was quiet then, gazing out at the lights and sensing the sadness in her silence. Arthur and her father came over to them from the other side of the garden. "We have a most illustrious guest with us tonight, Patricia. He is on intimate terms with many of the great of the world. It is a privilege to have both you gentlemen in my home. Shall we begin dinner? A most extraordinary fish has been prepared for us by my cook. Will you have wine? I myself do not drink spirits, but I do not object to having it served in my home. Come, Patricia. Are you all right, my dear? Shall we go inside?"

They sat in a sumptuous room and were served by silent servants who seemed able to perceive each of their wishes as it journeyed from mind to mouth. Tall tapers burned in silver candelabra on the table. They talked of Hong Kong and Communist China and the British who ruled the crown colony and the Chinese refugees who continued to steal across the borders. The girl ate slowly, delicately, and from time to time glanced at Gershon. Arthur said very little.

"And where do you gentlemen go from here?" Mr. Ankari asked at one point during the meal.

"Kyoto and Hiroshima," Gershon replied.

"Hiroshima," the man said and gave Arthur a swift involuntary glance that he obviously wished he could immediately call back. He had committed some sort of impropriety; he seemed embarrassed. "And Kyoto," he said quickly. "A most magnificent city. I have been to Kyoto. You are in for an experience, my dear chaps. More coffee? Wine?"

Arthur sat very still, staring down into his cup. The dancing lights of the tapers played upon his frozen features. Gershon looked at him and felt for the first time in their lives together the heavy pull of compassion. He looked away. No. He would have none of that. Too many deprivations. Too many abandonments. Too many. It was the wine and the fever, that was all. He glanced across the room at the tall wide window that faced out toward the garden—and restrained a cry. There in the window, peering in, was the long face of Jakob Keter. He closed his eyes quickly and turned his head.

When he looked again the face was gone. He heard Arthur saying something about the poverty in Hong Kong and the possibility of rage and riots. Patricia's father said, "Oh, indeed, we have our share of troubles. But we do our best. We do more than survive. We have charities. We have the brothers Kadoorie, your co-religionists, who are giving thousands in charity every year to help our farmers. No room here in government for the soft-minded. We will deal with the troubles as they come. No reason today to be overly concerned with tomorrow. We are not without a sense of charity, you understand. But we are a profit-motivated people, have always been, will always be. Dashed fortunate it is too, else there would be no city here today. I say, are you all right, Mr. Loran?"

Gershon had again seen the face of Jakob Keter in the window that looked out on the garden. It was the fever, all right. His head throbbed.

They returned to the garden after dinner and sat on white metal chairs looking out at the city. Patricia had brought Gershon two aspirins, and he felt better now.

"Perhaps you will let me show you one of our street shelters tomorrow morning," she said.

"Of course," Gershon said. Arthur was quiet.

"We do fine things here for our poor," she said.

"Almost entirely on a voluntary basis, you understand," said her father. He leaned over and spoke quietly to Arthur. Gershon could not hear what they were saying.

Patricia said softly, "It is quite fine here, you know. But it is lonely at times. Were you raised in America?"

"Yes. In New York. In a section more like where we got lost this afternoon than where we are now."

"Were you very poor? Forgive me. That was bad form. I do apologize."

"That's all right. Yes, we were very poor. We're still very poor. I'll only have the money I save from the army. That's not Chinese poor. But it's poor."

"What will you do after the army?"

"I don't know."

She looked at him.

"I don't," he said.

She was quiet. He sat with her silently in the dark and flowered night.

Later they clustered outside the double-door entrance to the house. The engine of the cab throbbed softly in the driveway. "A most memorable evening," Patricia's father was saying. "You see? I said we would make a splendid evening. It was my honor to have such gentlemen in my home. Good night. Good night. All my very good wishes."

Patricia's handshake lingered warmly upon Gershon's hand. "Good night," she murmured. "How good to have spoken with you."

"Good night," he heard himself say. "Thank you."

"You will need to take a *wallah-wallah*," her father said. "One of the small boats. The driver will show you where they are. The big ferries do not run at this hour. Give the boatman no more than fifty cents. Good night, my dear fellows. Good night."

They drove down the mountain in the darkness. Arthur sat very still. At the pier they hired a cross-harbor motor launch for the five-minute ride across the lagoon. The boat pitched and rolled in the dark, choppy water. The hotel lobby was nearly deserted. In the elevator Gershon looked at Arthur and saw his face drained of color, the pale-blue eyes wide and unblinking. What was he seeing? What was he hearing? And Gershon felt again the drawing pull of compassion. And this time he let it linger. The elevator door opened. They went to their room.

Late that night Gershon woke with a fever and lay still in his bed. He thought he had heard a sound in his sleep that had raised him into wakefulness. The room was silent save for Arthur's heavy breathing. Gershon's throat hurt, but he chose to return to sleep rather than leave the bed for aspirins. At a moment of light drifting he heard through the darkness of the room the voice of Arthur. "Not Abraham, no," said the voice clearly. And, "Jonah, Jonah." Then it was silent.

Gershon lay very still, enveloped by the thunderous pounding of his heart. He had no notion how long he lay there, unmoving, before he was able to fall asleep.

In the morning they crossed to Hong Kong and stood with Patricia in a Quonset-like building that had been divided into small cubicles crowded with bunks—planks of wood braced with vertical two-by-fours. Emaciated Chinese lay in the bunks and gazed at them vacantly. A young Chinese with a camera materialized from somewhere and spoke in Chinese. Two men climbed out of their bunks and stood beside Gershon and Arthur. They were thin and pale-skinned, and the bones were prominent on their gaunt faces. Bulbs flashed. The photographer spoke again. The two Chinese nodded and turned stiff smiles upon the waiting camera. Again, the sudden lights.

Outside on the crowded street Patricia said, "I do hope that wasn't too much of a bother for you. We show the pictures to people. They see that foreign visitors come to view our work. It helps us to raise funds. We bring the Chinese in off the streets. Many thousands sleep in our streets. It's all so very sad and sometimes hopeless. We had two other such shelters. One recently burned down. That was most unfortunate. We're raising funds to rebuild it. It would be so nice to erect additional shelters but I'm afraid our efforts to secure sites have thus far been fruitless."

"You have many fires here," Gershon said, making it more a statement than a question.

"Indeed. Terrible fires. Are you all right, Mr. Leiden? You're so quiet this morning. Shall we go?"

She drove them to the pier. A green and white ferry sat solidly in the water. Arthur went aboard.

"Shall I see you again?" she asked Gershon.

"I'll call you," he said.

"My father was so pleased you were able to come last night. It was a most pleasant night."

"Yes."

"My father detected some discomfort in Mr. Leiden and wishes to apologize for his enthusiasms and indiscretions. Have you the schedule for Macao?"

"Yes."

"Goodbye, then."

Gershon boarded the ferry and saw Arthur near a window and moved alongside him.

"Her father apologizes if he made you uncomfortable last night."

Arthur stood at the window staring out at the water and said nothing. After a moment he asked, "Where will we be next week at this time?"

"Kyoto, I think. Yes. Kyoto."

"I wasn't sure."

The crowded ferry moved slowly away from the pier and started toward Kowloon.

"No sea gulls," Gershon heard Arthur say. "Curious."

"I asked Pat about that. They never throw anything away. There's nothing here for gulls to eat."

"What do restaurants do with the partly eaten food?"

"They sell it. I think there's a market here in used food."

Arthur was silent. The ferry slipped into its Kowloon pier. They walked up the wide street to the hotel.

"I'm not very hungry," Arthur said. He sounded as sullen now as he had on the flight from Korea.

"We'd better eat something," Gershon said. "And we'll have to get a few things for Shabbat. We'll make Shabbat in the room. All right?"

They had lunch in the hotel and shopped briefly and then hired a cab to take them around Kowloon and the New Territories. The sky was gray with clouds, the air was autumnal. They saw with their tourist eyes beaches and eroded hillsides and old fortresses with people packed into tiny rooms. They passed brown cattle and water buffalo and small farms and terraced rice fields. They stood on a hillside and looked across a river at the border communes of Communist China. Later, on the way back, they passed a wild rhesus monkey on the side of the road, one of its arms extended in appeal, and it occurred to Gershon that this was the first instance of begging he had seen since their arrival. Insufficient food, insufficient water, insufficient shelter, and no beggars. Surely there were beggars somewhere. Later, along a section of Kowloon waterfront, they wandered among people whose homes were the boats moored to the docks, and they saw some of the stupefying and tumultuous boat life of the water people of that land. A vast array of sampans and junks and launches; a dense jungle growth of masts. On a small street their cab halted to let a Chinese funeral procession go by. Through the open windows of the cab Gershon and Arthur heard the ragged tune of the marching band. The musicians were playing "Bye Bye Blackbird."

"Let's go back," Arthur said.

"All right. Just another turn off this road."

They went past a low hillside of shanties made of scrap lumber, tin, tar paper, and sacking. The squalid dwellings clung precariously to the sloping earth. An old man was adding straw matting to a tilted roof.

"Did you bring the aspirin?"

"Yes. Is your fever up again?"

"I think so."

"I'm glad it's Shabbat soon. I'm a bit tired of all this touring."

"What do you think you're going to be doing in Japan?"

"I don't know exactly. But it won't only be touring. Haven't we done sufficient looking for today? I'm really becoming weary of it."

"I like the way they keep building. It's a mess, and it looks hopeless, and they all keep building and trying. Even the crooks here keep trying. Especially the crooks."

"What do you know about the crooks?"

"I read a lot. This is a strange city."

"Gershon the scholar. We haven't done any real shopping yet. Do we still have time today to let you do some heavy shopping?"

"Wrong, dear Arthur. We've done a lot of shopping."

Their driver, a strangely taciturn Chinese of indeterminate age, abruptly came alive. "Gentlemen want nice place tonight? Girls? Very clean. Yes?"

"No," Gershon said.

They returned to the hotel to prepare for Shabbat.

That evening Arthur listened soberly as Gershon chanted the Kiddush over a paper cup of red wine. The bottle, purchased in a nearby shop, stood between them on the trim desk they had converted into a dinner table. Gershon said the blessing for bread over the rolls they had bought in a bakery not far from the hotel. They ate slowly a dinner of canned fishes and vegetables. They sang together a few Shabbat melodies. There settled upon them the languor and somnolence of the evening. Sirens sounded in the distance, distracting Gershon for a moment. Arthur seemed to have heard nothing. He poured himself another cup of wine and said quietly, "You know, my family doesn't observe Shabbat. They don't observe anything. Except kashrut. I made them do that. They thought I needed an analyst when I told them I had applied to the seminary. They still think I ruined a great career."

"Would you have been a good physicist?"

"I think so. Yes. My father thought that I might be the one who would unify the wave and particle theories of light. That would have made me another Albert Einstein. God, he put together everything—matter, energy, space, time. Someone now needs to put together quantum theory and relativity. Uncle Albert once told me he thought I might do it. I used to make strange jumps in my thinking. But I thought we were going to destroy everything with all that knowledge. In my second year at Harvard I began to hate it. All I could see were dead bodies over the surface of the whole planet. And birds with burned-out eyes. I started to study privately with a local rabbi. Twice a week and a lot of homework. He said I did six years of work during the two and a half years I studied with him —whatever that meant and however he measured it. Have some more wine, dear Gershon. This is good wine. Anyway, he suggested the seminary. Do we have enough fish for tomorrow? Have we eaten all the fish?"

They had not eaten all the fish. There was plenty of fish.

Arthur sipped from his wine cup. His face was flushed. He went on speaking softly in his Boston tones. "My parents were angry when I told them about the seminary. Especially my mother. We don't fight loudly. It's all done in subdued fashion, with carefully chosen words. 'Really, my dear Arthur, I ask you to reconsider. What in heaven's name has possessed you?' And, 'What's the point to your entering so benighted a calling, dear boy? This is, after all, the twentieth century.' There was a good deal of that, a lot of talk about this being the twentieth century, and it went on for quite a while. I think my mother saw me as some sort of vindication of my father's name. They would send me into physics to prove their faith in the country no matter what the country might be doing to my father for his ideas about bombs. He had begun to have second thoughts by then and was in trouble with all kinds of committees in Washington. I don't know the half of what went on. I didn't want to affect physics. I wanted to affect people. What good is physics in the hands of a species that is still partly reptilian? We'll kill ourselves with all that physics. I left to go to the seminary. And there we met, dear Gershon. I must say, this wine is really good. We should have bought another bottle."

"We can ask to have a bottle sent up. I just won't sign for it."

"Sent up? God, we're in Hong Kong, aren't we? In Hong Kong. I·had this queer sensation for a while that we were in our room in the seminary."

"We never talked this way in the seminary."

"No. That's right. We had to come all the way to Hong Kong. What does your kabbalistic mind make of that?"

"I'm not sure, Arthur."

"Neither am I."

They looked then at each other and after a long moment they looked away in faint embarrassment.

"How's your uncle these days?" Arthur asked.

"As well as can be expected, I guess."

"Do you hear from Karen?"

"Yes. She thinks she'll take that job with the University of Chicago."

"It was her father who taught me."

"I assumed as much."

"What will you be doing after the army?"

"I don't know."

"The award wasn't of much help to you, was it?"

"It may have been. I learned a lot of Kabbalah. I got to know Keter very well."

"He's a strange bird. I never liked him."

"You never liked Kabbalah."

"Magic. Numerology. Emanations. Ascents. I don't have the mind for Kabbalah. I used to watch you with amazement. The way you ate up those weird books."

"Weird? Maybe. Those books are really records of the religious imagination, Arthur. When I was a kid I once went up to the roof of our apartment house in Brooklyn and looked up at the stars. I remember I raised my hands in supplication—a little like the gesture of the monkey we saw today on the road. I felt something touch me. Oh yes, something touched me. I've been waiting to feel that touch again. Is that childish of me? This is, after all, the twentieth century. But sometimes when I read those texts I'm on the roof of that building again. I don't know why I feel that way. They say things in those books that no one dares to say anywhere else. I feel comfortable with those acceptable heresies. God originally as sacred emptiness; ascents to God that are filled with danger, as if you were going through an angelic minefield; creation as a vast error; the world broken and dense with evil; everything a bewildering puzzle; and the sexuality in some of the passages. I like the sexuality. I especially like the ambiguities. Wow, Arthur, listen to me go. I'm saying more to you tonight than I did during all our seminary years. That is really good wine. Where was I? Yes. Ambiguities. You can't pin most of it down the way you can a passage of Talmud. I can live with ambiguity, I think, better than I can with certainty. Doubt is all that's left to us, Arthur. Doubt and desperate deeds. Excuse the bad alliteration. Is there no wine left, my good man, my friend, my lapsed physicist? Shall we conjure up Elisha to do a number for us as he did for the Shunammite woman? What say you, dear Arthur? Perhaps Keter will come to our aid. I am able to conjure up Keter from time to time. I have visions, you see. Oh yes. Yes. Visions. What?"

"I said I talk to Uncle Albert sometimes."

"Really?"

"Yes."

"I'll be damned. I thought I had the corner on visions in our class."

"We still talk physics. Sometimes we talk religion. He was not at all observant. I—loved him." His voice cracked. He cleared his throat. "I think he was the only human being in the world I truly loved. I think he knew that. I think that was the reason he agreed to speak at the graduation. He was pretty sick. That was how we got Truman. We asked Uncle Albert to ask him. I think that was how we did it. Not really sure. Poor sick Uncle Albert coming all the way from Princeton. Beg pardon, beg pardon, dear Gershon. Am becoming maudlin. Dislike sentimentality. We should finish our meal. No more wine anyway."

"And then I think we should go for a walk and clear our heads."

"Splendid idea, dear Gershon."

They chanted the Grace After Meals and cleared off the desk and went from the hotel into the cool night. They walked for a long time through the lighted and crowded Kowloon streets. Late that night they returned to the hotel and prepared for bed.

Gershon said as he lay in the darkness, his head very clear now, "I remember pretty much all that I told you, Arthur, and there is nothing of it I regret."

Arthur said quietly, "The same here, the same here. No regret."

"Shabbat shalom, Arthur."

"Shabbat shalom, dear Gershon."

Gershon woke early and dressed and prayed the Shabbat service. He prayed in silence, facing the window and the sea and the green rise of Victoria Peak from the city at its base. The air was clean and golden with sunlight, the water greenish-blue. He closed his eyes and saw the silent words of the prayers. A passage from the Zohar commentary to that day's Torah reading surfaced easily into light. "A man should be careful not to let others overhear his prayer. . . . Prayer becomes absorbed in the upper world, and the speech of the upper world should remain inaudible." A curious passage. "When the silent prayer soars aloft . . . to the third heaven. . . ." He was losing the thread of his own prayers.

Behind him Arthur stirred and woke. Gershon returned to the prayer book.

Arthur dressed and prayed, and Gershon sat in one of the soft chairs reading the Zohar. Arthur chanted softly. He was tone deaf. There was an awkwardness about the way he pronounced some of the more difficult words. Gershon struggled to keep himself inside the book. He read, "At the turn of the four seasons of the year a sound arises in the four quarters of the world through which the sinister side is stirred up, interposing between one sound and another, and at the same time obscuring the light that streams from on high. . . . That interposing sound is the sound or noise of war, the noise of the evil forces. . . ." Now he was gone deep inside the text, its rivers of imagery and mixture of metaphors. He read of the evil power that impaired the light of the moon and darkened the light of all Israel; the fish that swallowed Jonah and was actually the belly of the underworld, the grave. He read that the world was created by means of the Torah and is sustained by the Torah, and he asked himself, Even the oriental world? He read and paused awhile over this passage: "A wise man knows for himself as much as is required, but the man of discernment apprehends the whole, knowing both his own point of view and that of others. . . . He apprehends the lower world and the upper world, his own being and the being of others." He read of the star that appears in the evening of every sixth day and turns into a fiery mass and extends itself around a thousand thousand mountains and draws out of itself a vast explosion of colors into which the star plunges, concentrating itself more and more until it approaches the concealed point that is the source of all light. He read an intriguing passage about the power of incense: "Prayer repairs damage which has been done, but incense does more—it strengthens, it binds together, it is the greatest light-bringer. . . ." Arthur was talking to him.

He looked up.

"You were lost in there, dear Gershon. As usual."

He blinked and felt the text slide out and away.

"Anything interesting?"

"What?"

"Anything interesting?"

"Yes."

"How do you feel?"

"I'm all right. The throat feels better."

"What was interesting?"

"A lot. You said something in your sleep about Jonah the other night. I think it was the other night. There's something here about Jonah."

"Really? What did I say?"

"I don't remember. I think I was feverish."

"What does the Zohar say about Jonah?"

"It's a long passage, Arthur."

"You don't remember what I said about Jonah?"

"You've often talked in your sleep, Arthur. I've never paid much attention to it."

"One way or another, people talk," Arthur said. "Most people. I was thinking about Jonah the other day. He was a foolish man who inadvertently saved a city. Even Abraham couldn't save a city. But silly Jonah did. I think we ought to make Kiddush and eat."

"All right, Arthur."

At one point during their meal Arthur said, "You keep drifting in and out, dear Gershon. Where are you now?"

"Here."

"Where were you a moment ago?"

"With Keter on Riverside Drive. Near the memorial to the dead firemen." He had seen him clearly—dark suit, red bow tie, bald head. There had been gulls over the river.

"You have an extraordinary memory. I would never have remembered that monument. What did he look like in your imagination, our Professor Keter?"

"He was his usual humorless self."

"I'll bet."

"He told me to be careful during our trip to Japan."

Arthur put down the bread he had raised to his mouth. "What do you mean?"

"I have no idea."

"What are you talking about, Gershon?"

"I have no idea, Arthur."

"You have a strange sense of humor."

"I have about as much of a sense of humor as has Keter. It was a vision, Arthur. Let's finish up and go out for a walk."

"I don't understand. You mean you actually saw Keter just now?"

"I think so."

"Dear Gershon—"

"You see Albert Einstein."

"That's the imagination working."

"Right. All right."

Arthur looked at him.

"I'm not a religious fanatic, Arthur. I will not leap at you with my bare hands."

"What are you, Gershon?"

"Scared."

"A scared twentieth-century Jew with visions."

"Something like that."

"I lived in the same room for two years with a guy who thinks he has real visions?"

"Poor Arthur."

"Talk about not talking. Have some more fish. Are we out of fish? I want to hear about your visions."

"I'm not sure I want to talk about that, Arthur. This is, after all, the twentieth century."

"I would never have known if you hadn't told me. Excuse me."

Arthur left to go to the bathroom. Gershon sat alone, staring out the window at the sunlight on the harbor.

In the afternoon they walked along shop-lined streets and were caught up in the pedestrian tumult of Kowloon. They did not talk about visions. At dusk they returned to their room.

Shortly after eleven-thirty that night they boarded a long solid double-decker ship, a steamer named S.S. *Takshing.* Their cabin was small and clean, with two narrow bunk beds, two chairs, a chest of drawers, and an armoire. There were yellow globe lights on a wall and a motionless caged fan on the ceiling. The air smelled vaguely of disinfectant.

A few minutes before midnight Gershon and Arthur came out on the upper deck. The ship did not seem crowded. They felt the throb of the engine through the deck floor. Precisely at midnight the steamer shed its tie lines and moved away from the shore. Gershon watched the water widen between himself and the pier and, sharply, fleetingly, saw himself standing on a Hudson River quay, watching his parents depart for Palestine. Don't break any more windows, Gershon. Watch out where you throw the baseball. He stood at the deck railing and gazed up at the sky. It was a cool night. The sky was clear and canopied with stars. He could almost feel its cold touch.

"I hope they have a good navigator on this boat," Arthur said. "I don't want to end up in a Communist Chinese prison."

"Maybe we'll end up in the belly of a whale."

"My name isn't Jonah, dear Gershon. I never saved a city."

"Look at the stars, Arthur. He really understood them, didn't he? Your Uncle Albert, I mean. He could really navigate the whole cosmos inside his head."

"I think so."

"That was some navigator."

"Yes," Arthur said.

"I'm a lousy navigator. I never know where to make my turns. It's all guesswork and instrument flying and a lot of fear."

Arthur said nothing.

Gershon turned to him. "Mystics are often full of fear. The one doesn't necessarily cancel out the other."

Still Arthur said nothing.

They stood on the deck and gazed at the dark world of sky and water all around them. There were tiny lights in the darkness from other ships and the distant shore, dots of light like stars borrowed from the sky. The steamer sailed slowly and ponderously toward Macao.

They woke in the early morning to the sound of shouts. They dressed and prayed and came out on deck. Below them the wharves were thronged with women working the tie lines of ships.

A light rain was falling. The harbor was crowded with junks. All around was a watery delta world—a peninsula, low granite hills, offshore islands, slow-moving vessels. The small city lay before them like an old watercolor paled by too much sun. Low buildings in the Spanish-Portuguese style. Yellow, pink, beige, lime—a pastel world. They came down off the steamer. A Portuguese police officer stamped their leave papers. They took a cab through wet waterfront streets to a hotel.

Later that morning they joined a group of tourists and were driven about the city in a small bus. Municipal library, cathedral, observatory, outer harbor. Gray bleak sky. Macao famous for its firecrackers, incense sticks, Chinese wines, dog races, gambling casinos.

There were no rivers in Macao. "Can the American gentlemen in the back hear me?" The guide was a middle-aged woman who wore a light-blue raincoat and a red kerchief. She was short and round and nervously eager to please. Gershon dozed intermittently as they rode along wide and lovely boulevards lined with tropical plants and trees. He woke and saw a distant net tied to poles off the shore and, as they went by, saw the net sink suddenly into the sea. Chinese pedaled by on trishaws. The bus passed low rectangular wooden buildings with corrugated metal roofs. Women sat inside behind baskets and stalls of vegetables. Some of them carried infants in papoose fashion on their backs.

The guide droned on about the history of Macao. Arthur sat quietly, looking out the window at the beige-colored houses, the arched windows, the colonnaded streets, the Chinese lettering on the signs. Tall, leafy trees grew behind the closed beige walls of some government buildings. They stopped in a garden and descended into a haven of landscaped pink and yellow flowers and embowering trees and red benches and narrow walks. There were birds, and Gershon closed his eyes a long moment and listened.

The rain had ended. They got back on the bus and rode awhile and stopped. The guide was saying something about beggars. Gershon saw women selling lettuce and onions. Some had infants on their backs. Inside a crowded open-air temple, women placed sticks of smoldering incense in boxes of sand before a fire that burned in a large octagonal-shaped stone urn. Smoke poured upward and drifted out through the open roof. Women stood before the fire, hands clasped in gestures of supplication. A woman threw into the flames a bit of paper on which she had written something a moment before. Gershon watched her swaying gestures and out of the corner of his eye saw that Arthur was watching too. She swayed back and forth, her clasped hands moving up and down, face to thigh, face to thigh. The child on her back accompanied placidly her swaying motions. The aroma of incense was sweet, strong. An old man sat on a low chair against a far wall, playing a reed instrument. The music filled the noisy air of the temple with what seemed to Gershon a strain of sweet melancholy. How the women prayed, how they prayed. And the children on their backs—infant accents to their mothers' incense-accompanied prayers. He wanted to ask the guide about the temples and the prayers and the gods to whom the women were praying, and he came outside and stood on the top step of the stone stairway that led down to the street and saw a crowd of beggars near some of the tourists in his group. He looked around and could not see Arthur. Then he saw him with the other tourists, taking photographs of the beggars, his flaxen hair startlingly clear amid the dark hair and tattered rags of the beggars. One of the beggars was a heavily built man, slightly stooped. The lower half of his face was covered with a rag. He had black eyes and wore a wide-brimmed hat and a long cape. In one hand he carried a stick and in the other a metal cup. He pushed through the other beggars toward Arthur and banged on the cup with his stick. Gershon, standing at the head of the stone stairway, could sense through the crowd and the distance Arthur's annoyance at the sudden din made by the stick on the metal cup. Arthur backed away. The beggar followed, beating against the cup. Gershon started down the stairs. He had gone down two steps when he saw Arthur stop. He could feel his flash of anger. He saw Arthur lower his camera and reach into a pocket and hand some coins to one of the beggars standing alongside the man in the cape. Then Arthur began to turn. There was a shout, a clanging beat of wood against metal. Abruptly the entire crowd of beggars surged forward around Arthur, beating the cups. The women in the vegetable stalls at the foot of the stairway turned to look at the noise. He saw the frozen looks on their faces and looked at the throng and could not see Arthur. Then he saw him, surrounded, the cups and sticks of the beggars raised toward his face. A high keening wail, a fused clamor of anger, now accompanied the pounding of sticks upon metal. Some of the beggars were beating their sticks against the stone pavement. Gershon saw the tour guide trying futilely to edge her way through the crowd. He came down off the stairway toward the crowd and pushed between two ragged screaming crones, pushed firmly, steadily, as he had through the crowds at the fires in his neighborhood, a slow shove here, an opening there, feeling the roughness of the vile rags they wore—were any of them lepers?—fusing with the jostling bodies and sliding between them slowly so they would not notice his motions and begin to eddy around him—and there was Arthur, looking frightened, staring around for a way out, and Gershon had his hands firmly on Arthur's shoulders and was pushing heavily now through the crowd. Someone stumbled and fell. There was an angry roar. They were out and half running, and the guide was there near the bus, and they were on board. "Not to give to them, not to give to them," the guide said in a high, frightened tone. She seemed to have gone to pieces. "You did not listen to me." The other tourists scrambled into the bus. The driver started the bus along the street. Behind them the beggar throng turned away, silent, sullen, waving the sticks.

"Are you all right?" Gershon asked.

"No," Arthur said. He was clearly shaken. "Who said that charity redeems you from death?"

"They didn't touch you, did they?"

"I thought they would use my head for their sticks."

"Did they touch you?"

"No."

They rode on. Arthur sat back in the seat. He closed his eyes.

The guide came over to them later as the group stood outside the bus on a street filled with shops. Was the gentleman all right? She was so very sorry. Macao beggars notorious with tourists. Did the two American gentlemen wish to go shopping or were they interested in seeing something else of Macao, something more intriguing than shopping? Yes? Fine. They could walk down three streets and turn left into a small street and go to this number and give the porter inside this piece of paper. Yes. It would not be long, and they would all be waiting for them here when they returned. She was so sorry about the incident with the beggars, so sorry. This would be of interest to the Americans, oh yes.

They went along the street and turned and walked slowly through an alleyway that led downward and abruptly widened and became a cobbled street. Old houses lined the sides of the street. They saw no one. They went through a green door that fronted an old beige-colored two-story house. Inside, an old man with an incredibly wrinkled face and palsied hands glanced at the piece of paper in Gershon's hand and pulled on a rope. A bell sounded in some far region of the building. The room they waited in was dimly lighted and scented with—perfume? incense? A door opened soundlessly and a woman appeared—gowned, perfumed, stately; a Chinese woman of middle age. "I greet the Americans," she murmured. "Please to follow. Please." A dim corridor. A carpeted stairway. A curtained room. Carpeting, mirrors, a dresser, a chair, a wide bed. The woman spoke murmurously, with quiet pride. A baby. An infant. Oh yes. Surely to die. Surely. Or all family would die. No food, you see. So loved by father. Sold to here. Oh yes. And raised. And now happy and fifteen years old and working here. Life saved. Yes. Sleeping now. Americans wish to meet? No? Perhaps wish to see upstairs? Interesting upstairs. A corridor. A stairway. A small room. A wide bed. Two thin, robed, middle-aged women. Robes shed. Breasts saggy, ribs protruding. The scent of cheap perfume thick in the room. A phallic instrument appears. Each takes a turn playing the role of the male as they writhe on the bed, heaving, grunting, faking the end with small gasping cries. "Americans wish yes?" they say eagerly afterward. "Yes? Two dollars? Yes? Two, two, yes?"

"No," Gershon said.

They came out into the cool air and made their way back through the alley and along the street to the group. The tour guide looked at them and smiled and turned away.

"Are we planning to do any more shopping, dear Gershon?" Arthur asked.

Gershon said, "Not today."

They remained in Macao overnight and walked leisurely through the city the next morning. They went to the frontier and stood around awhile staring past the guards at the land across the border. They walked beside the sea and through congested streets and tropical gardens. They encountered no beggars, no pimps. In a café beside a small exquisite garden they ate lunch and watched junks slide smoothly across the golden sheen of the sea. Somewhere behind the pastel façade that enveloped them, somewhere very close by, was the dark world, the other side. They did not want to think of it now. They sat together quietly in the café near the garden and the sea, and they ate and rested.

A little before three o'clock that afternoon they boarded the steamer to Hong Kong. They were back in their hotel that night.

All the next morning they wandered with Patricia through the bizarre statuary of the Tiger Balm Garden.

"That was a millionaire with a strange imagination," Arthur said in front of the statue of a horned, black-skinned man in chains.

"They depict Chinese folk tales and Buddhist stories," Patricia said. "Quite loved by the people."

"What am I to make of you?" Arthur asked, speaking to a duck-billed sailor in a white uniform who was drinking from what looked to be a bottle of whiskey.

"Maybe he was on board a ship with Jonah," Gershon said.

"Maybe he just met a kabbalist talking to someone in a vision," Arthur said.

Gershon laughed. Patricia stood between them, puzzled.

"Shall we see more?" she asked.

They did not think they wanted to see more.

Later that afternoon they crossed in a taxi sampan to one of the floating restaurants in Aberdeen. Patricia wore a white, tight, high-necked dress, and they wore suits and ties. They chose their own fish, live from tanks set in the sea, and then sat upstairs in a glass-walled room, waiting to be served and looking out at the sunlight on the water and the endless bustle of the boats. They sipped their drinks. Arthur was unusually quiet, and Gershon sensed his thoughts. Japan tomorrow. Japan. They ate slowly, with a leisure both had rarely known and amid the dreamlike elegance of a European world long gone.

They returned to shore in a boat rowed by a young woman with an infant on her back. She pulled on the oars, back and forth, back and forth, long deep pulls, and the infant went low over the stern, its head snapping back and coming forward, until Gershon was certain the child would fall into the water. He saw Arthur staring at the mother and her child.

The boat slid slowly alongside the pier. A boy came up to them from the crowd of Chinese on the pier, his thin hand outstretched in the gesture of a beggar. The woman climbed out of the boat and brushed him gently aside, then went back into the boat.

Standing on the pier, Gershon looked into the little boat and saw the woman tickling the hands and naked feet of the child; he saw the child throw back its head and laugh with delight.

"I do hope you had a pleasant time," he heard Patricia say quietly. She stood beside him. Arthur was a few steps away, looking at another young woman with a child on her back.

"Yes," he said. "We're very grateful."

"It's I who am grateful." She hesitated a moment. "Would you care to come up? I've a friend I can ask to join us."

He looked at her. She smiled.

He didn't think so, he said. It was late. The trip tomorrow. No, he didn't think so. But he was very grateful, he said.

She understood, she said.

They drove her home. They shook hands. "You will give my very best wishes to Lieutenant Skipworth," she said. "Do have a fine time in Japan. It was most pleasant being with you both. Are you certain you won't come in? Daddy is away for a time tonight."

Gershon thanked her. No. The trip. Packing. He felt Arthur looking at him.

They took the cab down the mountain to the pier and a ferry across the harbor to Kowloon.

The next morning, a few minutes before ten o'clock, they boarded a Japan Air Lines DC-6.

"You're sure there was no other flight to Japan?" Arthur asked, staring out the window at the engines. "Is the pilot an American?"

"I don't know. Do you want me to find out?"

"No."

"It's a good airline, Arthur."

The engines came on one after the other, roaring.

"Did you get all your shopping done?" Arthur asked.

"I got more done than I thought I would. It was only six days."

"Why didn't we go in with Pat last night?"

Gershon did not reply.

"I asked—"

"I was afraid it would get complicated."

"We're not saints, dear Gershon."

"No. We're certainly not saints."

The plane took off soon after ten o'clock. They flew through the day, refueled briefly in Okinawa, and landed in Tokyo late that night. A cab brought them to the Imperial Hotel.

A distant siren, riding on the early hour, broke his fragile sleep. Its wail grew faint, yet lingered strangely, an echo of his morning fears.

This was the hour he had learned to dread, the hour of questions. No time of day or night seemed so filled with the weight of darkness as this hour before the twilight of morning. It had begun in early childhood with the murder of his parents—the sudden snapping awake to some inner or outer disturbance—and had plagued him intermittently through the years; a malevolent background to the death of his cousin, the loss of friends, neighborhood fires, a street killing. Why had it chosen this Tokyo night for its appearance, this pre-dawn ghostly messenger with its relentless questions, coming to him through a black tunnel from the other side?

He lay very still in his hotel bed. It would make no difference if he rose and went to the bathroom and returned to the bed. It would still be in the room; this was its appointed hour. Only a light would drive it away; but he did not want to wake Arthur, who had gone to sleep exhausted by the full day of flying and in a dark and brooding mood—clearly fearing and anticipating their journey through Japan. "I'm glad you made me come with you, dear Gershon," he had said, lying in bed with his arms over his eyes. "I think I would have gone to that student café and made myself ill again. I want to go and I don't want to go. It's—awkward. You're a wise and good man, Gershon Loran. Wake me when you get up in the morning or when the Messiah comes—whichever happens first. Good night, dear friend."

He did not feel wise or especially good. He felt himself fearful and uncertain about most things, and never more so than at this hour when there hovered about him what he had come to call the four-o'clock-in-the-morning questions.

Listen, listen, came the seductive whisper from the darkness. I journey from the other side with a burden of chill truths. Why are you so afraid? Is it possible that illusion is more welcome to you than truth? Listen. Listen. When in all the history of your species have you ever produced so vast and panoplied a parade of great minds across so large a portion of your planet in so short a time as you did in the first decades of this century? Your generation and the one yet to come are the children and grandchildren of these giants. What have they left you? They were your greatest gifts to yourselves; they were of a special grace. How you trusted them. What heritage have they given you to hold in your hands? Can you answer me?

He lay silent, waiting. The air seemed cold.

Gershon, listen to me. Are you listening? They cast vast shadows, your century's giants. From whom do all of you flee—Karen to Chicago, you to the rim of the world, Arthur to Hiroshima? Would not the shadows be a comforting darkness if they yielded warmth and light? What do they yield, Gershon? In truth, what do they yield? What fungus horrors have grown in the soil of those shadows? The truth, Gershon. Tell yourself the truth.

The soft insistent voice carried within itself the coldness of a tomb, the emptiness of an infinite space. Gershon cringed. His heart beat thickly, drumming in his ears. He lay silent, listening.

Yes. Listen. Your parents. Yes. Why did they leave you to go to Palestine in spite of the menace of riot and death? To build on the sacred soil, to build in the sunlight on the sand and the hills? Were they not molded in your eyes of heroic clay? Recall how much pride was mixed with the fear you felt as you watched their ship slide away. They were builders, yes; two small people, your mother and father, but of a grandeur that far surpassed whatever you now see in your combat engineers. And why were they killed? They were warned; they should not have gone to that café. An errant act of defiance? This is our land, and we will sit in its cafés. Can you hear their words? Listen to the hidden point of truth deep within you. Their defiant building broke your life. Is there no rage in you, Gershon? No rage? And no envy, no sense of awe? How far will all of your generation flee to escape the shadows cast by the parents of your century?

Far, he thought. Far. There were those whose parents succeeded.

But I am not one of those. Have the first generations of this century's parents succeeded? What went wrong? Yes. Far. How he dreaded these cold and burning truths! Rage and envy and awe. Yes. He lay silent, cringing.

And your teachers, Gershon, your Keter and Malkuson. You turn your head away. Why? Do my truths hurt? Listen. Your Keter and Malkuson—are they not also among the giants of your century? Are they not to your century's Talmud and Kabbalah what Einstein was to its physics? What greater gifts of scholarship could Jews have given to themselves? Recall the feelings of your years in their classes. Yes. It lingers still. The play of light from awesome minds upon dusty ancient texts. How the light gave life to the words! Do you remember? Yes. Yes. They swallowed you with their minds. How does one contend with such giants? Would you have found comfort in their shadows? The scholar of Talmud has the hauteur of an ancient king, and the scholar of Kabbalah has the secularism of a logical positivist. Disrespectful? I deal in truths, Gershon. Matters of respect I leave to moralizers. I am from the other side. Why do you shield your eyes behind your hands? Is my darkness too keen, too bright? Listen. You lie in your bed in your Tokyo hotel on the eve of your journey through Japan. Where are you going? And why? Why your flight into the army? Why your journey to Hong Kong and Macao? Do you flee from the shadows of the giants of your century, the great ones whose lights blind the eye and whose faults numb the heart? They fill you with hurt, with anger, with awe, do they not, these giants? They make ashes of great ideas, do they not? Do you flee to pagan worlds remote from the civilization of your teachers—to test their teachings? To escape their visions, their echoes, and the shadows that lie between what they are and what they teach? How far will you flee? Or are you done? Did your journey end in the fused light and darkness of the Macao brothel? I ask cruel questions of truth, Gershon. Truth. I come from the other side.

How cold it was now in the room, how dark. The dimmest of lights seemed to have been drained from the air. Was this the realm of the other side? Yet there were truths in those words. How could truths emanate from such darkness? His heart thudded wildly. He lay silent, wondering.

The silken voice went on. And Karen. Consider Karen. Are not her parents thought to be among the great of the clergy of your century? Power, power, they cast long shadows of clerical power. Does she flee them, your Karen? Why do you avert your eyes? I believed you to be no longer fearful of the direct stare into truth. You seemed to have learned so quickly in Korea—away from the power and ashes of the great. Yes, how swiftly you changed. Do not avert your eyes. Am I cruel? Are you too raw, too lacking in defense? You do not listen to me at any other time. You are running or reading. I detest the activities in which you so fussily engage yourself as a barrier against my questions. I am not without feeling, though I dwell in the kingdom of the other side. Are you listening? Your Karen flees to philosophy to avoid the tawdriness of clerical politics, and she flees to Chicago to avoid the seaminess of clerical power. Yes. How silent you are. Is it that you are surprised at the energies and insights possessed by the realm of darkness?

And Arthur. What of Arthur? Can you sense his broken world? It was the winds of his darkness that I rode into this room tonight. He was a child of the most golden of the promises of your species— the promises emanating from the unlocking of the universe by his adopted uncle, his family, their associates, their friends. They held in their hands the light of creation—and returned to the world the light of death. Walk in *that* shadow, Gershon. Taste and see *that* shadow. You will begin to understand Arthur, who flees from world to world—physics to revolution to the rabbinate to the Far East to Korean activists to—where? what? Does he search to locate himself in a corner of the world untainted by the shattered promises? Now he flees to Hiroshima—to find what? He is among the most bloodied of your generation. He has the most to forget, and can forget nothing.

Gershon spoke up and said to the darkness, He has a friend.

Yes, said the messenger. There is some refuge in relationships. Yes. I am not one to say that all is lost. But listen to me, Gershon. You are the bereaved children and grandchildren of a broken century. There are no more dreams. There is nothing to wait for. Nothing. Consider my truths with care.

Gershon was quiet. There was a faint stirring in the darkness. And a sigh.

I leave now. It is almost light. Your illusions will soon return. Ponder my questions. I do not make the journey from the other side merely to torment you. We can make a cautious alliance, you and I. You have a mystic sense, and an eagerness to break old barriers and confront the new. Old ascents bore you. Am I not right, Gershon? In truth, we are all you have left if you wish to attempt new answers. Leave the dust to the pious and the old, to the professional peddlers of illusions. Shall we not deal in truths? Ah, I feel the light below the rim of your world. What contempt you will have for me soon! Now you still have in you the respect of fear. But soon— Consider. There is some merit in darkness. There are times when light is a menacing distraction. You need the fires of the other side, dear Gershon, if you are to move beyond the pale of the old and the dry and the illusions that are truly dust. There is already so much of me in your Kabbalah. Are we not by now well acquainted? Consider me. Yes. Consider me with care as you journey through your broken century.

The room fell silent. The palest of lights appeared in the rims of the draped windows. He closed his eyes. After a while his heart grew still. He slept.

Arthur woke him. He had pulled back the drapes. The room was filled with the morning sun.

"You were talking to yourself in your sleep, dear Gershon."

"I was?"

"You must have been dreaming."

"Yes."

"What day is today? Oh, yes. We're in Tokyo. Right."

Gershon felt as if he had not slept. He rose wearily and went to the window. The questions, so clear in the darkness, now seemed blurred. What was the meaning of that proffered alliance? An alliance with what? Evil? No. Something more alluring than evil. What? He shook his head in confusion. The city looked brown and drab, a dusty hive of impassive pushing crowds—so different from the blaze of its neon nights. There was a small garden on the street below. He stood at the window looking down at the city and the garden. Tiny trees and shrubs and flowerless plants; a winter garden, waiting. An airplane droned by overhead; the windows rattled noisily, were still. Arthur came out of the bathroom.

The day was cloudy and cold. They spent much of the morning in an office of the Japan Travel Bureau and came away with their itinerary, plane tickets, and hotel reservations. A wind blew through the streets. Traffic was thick, noisy, a dark and churning river. Dense crowds of people moved by. Many wore white face masks against winter germs.

"You're certain you know what you're doing?" Arthur asked on the crowded street.

"We can't travel alone. You know how easy it is to get lost in this country? The cities don't even have street signs. And we're going very far south into rural areas."

"You explained it to her?"

"Yes."

"Is there a bathroom anywhere around here? I need a bathroom."

They went to the club that night and sat at a table with Toshie. She wore a tight black dress with dark-green flowers. Dark eyes, small nose, a graceful curve of lips; she looked lovely and fragile. Why was she here? To keep from starving? He thought of the Macao brothel and pushed the thought away. The club was crowded and noisy. Arthur had gone to the dance floor with another of the girls.

"Your friend very sad again tonight, chap-san," Gershon heard Toshie say. "Why so sad?"

Gershon did not respond.

"Very handsome, very sad," she murmured. "Chap-sans will go to Hiroshima?"

"Yes."

"I am worry about Hiroshima. Bad memories for me, Hiroshima. Brother dead, aunt, uncle, many."

"The war was a long time ago, Toshie."

"Not so long, chap-san. Memories like yesterday."

He was quiet. She seemed sad, troubled. He said quietly, "Toshie, it will be all right. You understand the arrangements?"

"Ah, yes, chap-san."

"Two rooms."

"Ah, yes. Yes."

"We'll be back Sunday and we'll meet you Monday. Then we'll all fly to Osaka, take the steamer to Takamatsu, then a train, a boat, and a train to Hiroshima. Okay?"

"Hai, chap-san. Okay."

"Have you ever been out of Tokyo, Toshie?"

"No, chap-san."

"It will be a fine trip. I forgot to ask about your mother."

"Thank you, my mother is well, chap-san." She was silent a moment. Then she said softly, "You are a good man, chap-san. Another drink? No? Dance? Chap-san now look as sad as Arthur-san. Trip will be very nice. But you not be too good to me. Yes? I like to dance with you, chap-san."

He and Arthur remained in the club until a little after midnight.

"She's a beauty," Arthur said. "Those eyes. You had to see her mother about this?"

"Yes."

"I'm a little jumpy, dear Gershon. I'm not sure I know what I'm doing."

"You're running."

"What?"

"Nothing. Let's find a cab and get back. I'm tired."

They returned to the hotel and went to sleep.

There were no more four-o'clock questions. Very early the next day they took a train to Kyoto and began their final journey together.

10

◢◢◢ Arthur was in love with the city of Kyoto. It was a love he made no effort to conceal, a passion for the city's temples and gardens, its trees and stones, its wide business streets and narrow residential alleyways, its hills and rivers and streams and ponds, and especially its people. It was an inarticulate passion that found expression in the way he would look around, draw in breath, widen his eyes, let his face relax in a smile, shed his polished and often caustic New England manner and walk the streets like a beggar with hat in hand, eager for any morsel that might be offered him. This passion was a surprise to Gershon Loran, who was not to understand its source until many months later.

They stayed during that weekend at the Miyako Hotel amid an Eden of landscaped gardens. They walked to shrines and palaces and temples. They crossed a river, they went past shops, they saw a wood-block exhibit, silks, porcelains, ivory and wood carvings. The streets were clean and washed with sunlight; there were many winter-leaved trees. The sand courtyards of the temples were swept clean and combed. They walked for hours on Shabbat, and walked again that night and Sunday morning. It was only on the train on the way back to Tokyo that Gershon thought with surprise how silent Arthur had been throughout that time, save for the one hour on Shabbat when they had studied together some passages of Kabbalah.

He seemed to want to embrace all the city. He stood in the sunlight of temple courtyards, and he stooped and caressed with his palm the frozen seas of white-gold sand. A woman of an incredible old age—brown, wizened features, sunken eyes, black kimono,

carved wooden cane—gazed at him with expressionless eyes from
the steps of a temple as he ran his hand slowly over sand in the
courtyard, over the stone lantern near a bent tree, the intricate carv-
ing on a pillar; watched him until he turned and caught her eye
and inclined his head to her in a barely perceptible nod, and she
closed and opened her eyes in acknowledgment of some shared
secret message that had passed between them. He touched the
parapets of bridges, the pebbles of narrow garden lanes, the shadows
of passing clouds on the stained white walls of simple dwellings. A
child stared at him from the window of a passing tram, and he
waved and embraced himself with his arms, and the child laughed.
He stopped to gaze at a chrysanthemum in the entrance to a shop—
where did chrysanthemums grow in the winter?—and gazed at one
again in the windshield of a cruising cab. He seemed intoxicated
by the city; even the overhead power lines formed patterns of fascina-
tion for him. He stopped for a long moment at a service station and
stared in silence at the flying horse of the Mobilgas sign, as if asking
himself where he had seen that before on this journey. Sudden doors
in garden walls, stone urns beneath leafy winter trees, a man in
knickers sweeping the pebbles before the red columns of a vast
temple complex, a wide long pebbled road leading to a huge red
torii set against hills and the blue sky, the gentle serpentine curve
of a dwarf tree along the edge of a silent pond, a bank of trees reflected in the still surface of a dark-green pool, a pagoda covered
with gold leaf, a lone cyclist along curving lines of tram tracks, a
lotus-shaped fountain in a temple courtyard of sand, the mirror
surface of a pond that returned to him his pale face and blond hair,
light and shade and the lacy shadows of tiny trees, women in
kimonos and Western garb, old men in puttees and worn army
caps, a distant smokestack beyond a misty line of trees and dark
roofs, a tram rounding a corner, crowds of pedestrians crossing a
street, huge billboards, a gushing fountain in a busy square, the
gentle arc of a wooden bridge in a temple garden of rock and
sand—all these Arthur Leiden touched with wordless and luminous
passion. Gershon had never seen him so transformed, so possessed
of open radiance, so easily moved by all around him, so hungry, so
eager. The city was a woman, and he embraced it with all the tender
and gentle adoration one brings to a first love.

On Shabbat morning, as they prayed together in their hotel room, Gershon listened to the melody in Arthur's words. The flattened sounds of his tone-deaf voice, the rhythmic rise and fall, had begun to form a lyric music all their own, a haunting bridge of sound between his silence and the city. He heard him chant and sing some of the kabbalistic prayers that are in the liturgy of the Shabbat morning service. "The Lord is master over all His works," he sang. "He is blessed and acclaimed by all living things. . . . Good are the luminaries our Lord has made, with wisdom, knowledge, and skill were they fashioned. . . . They are filled with splendor, their brightness sparkles, their light is lovely through the universe. . . ." Some time later Gershon heard him chant, "For our sins we were exiled from our land," and looked up from his own prayer book with surprise. That was a wrong prayer, and Gershon knew that Arthur was certainly aware of its inappropriateness to Shabbat. Arthur had chosen to chant it, and was chanting with an intensity of feeling that brought a tightness to Gershon's heart. He said nothing to Arthur about his prayers that Shabbat morning; he would not break the strange bond that had been established between him and the city.

Late in the afternoon they returned from a long walk through temples and shrines, and Arthur said, as they entered their room, "Let's study some Kabbalah, dear Gershon. Anything pertinent to our being here. Is there anything?"

Yes, there was something—passages in the Zohar to that day's Torah reading. They sat in their room before a glass wall that looked out on a hill of green winter trees and late afternoon sunlight. Gershon read, "The guarding of the universe is from above downward, that is, from the upper world which was formed by the expansion of Thought. We thus understand the meaning of the passage, 'Unless the Lord guards the city, the watchman watches in vain.' The watchman here refers to the watchman of Israel— Metatron, the head of the angelic host. Protection depends not on him but on the higher world."

"It doesn't do too good a job sometimes," Arthur said.

"What doesn't?"

"The upper world. Protecting cities. Go ahead, dear Gershon. Read."

"Mr. Loran, read," Jakob Keter used to say in class. "Read." He thought he could hear his voice. He saw him in their seminary classroom, behind the desk, standing, dark suit, white shirt, red bow tie. The sun came through the windows. Pigeons strutted on the high ledge of the dormitory building.

He read, "The Torah was given in the midst of flaming fire, itself being written in white fire upon black fire, the letters floating high in the air. . . . And the Torah emerged from the inner Voice, called Great Voice. . . ." Gershon paused, trying to remember something once told him by Jakob Keter. He could not. He went on. "The world is divided among forty-five varieties of light, seven of which are assigned to the seven abysses. . . ." They agreed that the passage was obscure and difficult. Gershon turned some pages. He read, "The nearer a thing comes to the realm of the hidden and undisclosed, the less is it made mention of. . . . On the same principle, the Divine Name Sublime, the essence of the hidden and unrevealed, is never uttered. . . . Thus it is throughout the Torah, which contains two sides: a disclosed and an undisclosed. And these two aspects are found in all things, both in this world and in the upper world."

He paused and looked at Arthur.

"I like that," Arthur murmured. "That's very good."

Gershon said quietly, "What aren't you telling me, Arthur?"

Arthur looked through the glass wall at the green rise of the hill.

"All right," Gershon said. "We'll go on."

He read, "Rabbi Simeon explained the verse: 'Then they said to him: Tell us, we pray, inasmuch as you are the cause of this evil that is upon us, what is your occupation? . . .' There is much to think about, he said, in this text. The men put their question to Jonah with profound wisdom. They wished to find out whether he was of the seed of Joseph. . . . They said, in effect, 'If you are of the seed of Joseph, pray that the sea may cease of its raging. . . . If you are of the seed of Jacob . . . then pray to the Master that He may send His angel to save us. . . .' They further asked, 'What is your occupation? . . . Where do you come from?' . . . that is, Who were your forefathers? . . . And 'What is your country?' . . . Is it a country that deserves punishment? Thus all the questions put by them had a good reason."

Gershon stopped reading. There was a long silence.

Arthur looked at him. "You picked some good texts, dear Gershon."

"I'm trying to help."

"Do your kabbalistic powers enable you to read minds?"

"I have no kabbalistic powers."

"Then don't tell me what you do have. You picked some fine passages. It's getting dark."

"Do you want to study some more?"

"No."

"What do you want to do?"

"I want to sit here very quietly and watch the hill get dark. Then let's go out and have dinner and go to a geisha house and listen to some Japanese music. Then we'll just walk. All right, dear Gershon?"

"Sure."

"You picked good passages, Gershon. Studying Kabbalah with you is like walking under an artillery barrage. Find something good for next week when we're in Hiroshima. All right? Look at the way that hill is changing color. My God. . . ."

They ate dinner in the hotel and took a cab to a geisha house, where they sat with Japanese on straw mats and were served green tea by white-faced geishas and listened to two geishas play soft and mournful music on stringed instruments. Muted sounds, the silken movements of kimonos, Arthur's half-open eyes, the strange calm in his face, and the love, the clear and palpable love that shone from him like a morning sun—all these Gershon saw and felt and heard that night. Later they walked through the quiet streets of the city, past lantern-lit tiny houses, along streams, through wooded parks, across a black and running river, past temples darker than the night. A thin crescent of new moon hung in the sky like a lantern of silver light. They caught a cab back to the hotel and went to bed.

Gershon woke abruptly in the night, his heart pounding. There was someone in the room. Arthur was asleep. The room was very dark.

I come with my burden of truths, Gershon heard from the darkness. Why are you still afraid?

Go away, Gershon said.

I am sent. I cannot go. Gershon, will you listen?

No alliances. Go away.

Gershon. I quote your own Zohar to you. "What is profane has no share in the side of holiness but belongs entirely to the other side, to that of impurity. Thereon is based the separation which we have to make between the holy and the profane. Yet, for all that and despite their separateness, the holy contains a particle of the left side." You know the passage? Yes. You are concerned about your friend? I understand. I am not without feeling. Perhaps I will go now after all. Have a safe journey, Gershon. When you study your Zohar in Hiroshima do not avoid its truths.

The silken voice was silent. Slowly his heart grew calm. He fell asleep.

In the morning they took a cab to the train station.

"I don't want to leave this place," Arthur said.

Gershon said nothing.

"You were talking in your sleep again, dear Gershon."

"I don't remember anything."

"I'd like to come back here again."

"Not on this trip."

Arthur looked out the window of the cab at the sun on the violet hills. "God, I'd like to be able to get back here again soon. I'd like to try and live awhile with a family. We didn't really meet any of the people. Maybe I could spend some time in a monastery."

"We could skip Hiroshima."

"No, we can't," Arthur said, staring out the window. "We can't skip Hiroshima, dear Gershon."

They stayed at the Imperial Hotel that night. The next morning they rode by cab to the club. The small street seemed drab without its night blaze of concealing neon light. Toshie stood on the street in front of the club with a small valise. She climbed in and sat in the front seat next to the driver. He looked at her and said nothing. They rode to the airport, weaving through the heavy traffic. A pale sun shone on the brown and gray streets. They passed sections of the city that lay gutted and charred; they passed the broken ruin of what had once been a cemetery.

"Fires in the war," Toshie said softly. "Bombs. Very terrible fires."

Arthur shifted in his seat.

The driver, a thin Japanese in his early twenties, said nothing to them all during the long ride.

They took off for Osaka in a Japan Air Lines DC-6. It was a two-hour flight. Arthur went repeatedly to the toilet. Gershon asked him at one point, "Can I do anything to help?"

"No."

"Are you all right?"

"Not too good." His face was chalk-white.

"Arthur-san sick?" Toshie asked.

"A little," Arthur said. "Stomach."

"I buy Arthur-san medicine in Osaka." She seemed concerned.

Arthur thanked her. He had brought along his own medicine, he said. He always traveled with medicine.

They sat together in the rear of the aircraft. None of the passengers looked at them.

In Osaka they took a cab to the Tenpozen Pier. They had lunch in a café. The owner knew no English. Toshie spoke in Japanese. Outside, beyond a tangle of wharves and warehouses and cargo ships, lay the long dark surface of the sea. Arthur drank tea and would not eat. He sat staring out at the water.

Later that afternoon they stood at the railing of a white steamer and watched themselves move away from the shore. Sea gulls wheeled overhead. There were loud cheers from the crowd on the pier. Long colored streamers stretched from the people on the pier to the passengers, tightening as the distance widened, then falling slowly into the water. Some of the passengers looked to be honeymoon couples. A low, white, blinding sun shone on the water; sea and sky were stark white. They passed a white lighthouse and a fishing boat. The passengers milled about on the wide deck. Some began to move off to their cabins. The shoreline grew hazy. The steamer headed into the open sea. A salt wind blew against their faces. They stood near the rail, staring in silence at the darkening sea. None of the passengers stood near them. Distant hills faded slowly. The air grew cold.

"Seto Naikai," Gershon heard Toshie murmur and was about to ask what the words meant when he heard Arthur excuse himself and walk stiffly away in the direction of a nearby toilet. What could they have eaten that had made him ill? Perhaps it was the green tea served Saturday night by the geishas in Kyoto? Perhaps it had nothing to do with food? Perhaps—? Toshie was talking to him quietly. He did not understand what she was saying. A young couple walked by. Toshie looked out at the water. He listened and stared at her and did not respond.

"I am sorry, chap-san," she said, looking troubled.

He was quiet.

"Two, three days, chap-san," she said.

He stared at the dark sea, felt the muted vibrations of the ship.

Arthur came back along the deck.

"How do you feel?" Gershon asked.

"Very bad."

"Your medicine not help you, Arthur-san?"

"No."

"What did you eat, Arthur?"

"I'll be all right. Let's forget it. I think I want to lie down. Do you want to go inside?"

The steamer was scheduled to dock at Takamatsu at eleven that night. Gershon had taken one cabin with two bunks. Arthur lay with his hands over his eyes. Gershon, sitting in a chair near a porthole, looked at him and saw he was asleep.

"Your friend is very sad, chap-san," Toshie said. She was sitting on the second bunk, her legs folded beneath her. She looked small and lovely. "Why are we go to Hiroshima? For your friend?"

"Yes."

"Why, chap-san?"

"I don't know."

"Ah," she murmured, and looked curiously at Arthur. "So."

Arthur slept until shortly before they arrived in Takamatsu. They hailed a cab and rode to the Kawaroku Inn. The two girls who received them knew no English. Toshie spoke to them in Japanese. There was some confusion about the rooms. The girls looked at Toshie, then looked at Arthur and Gershon. It was finally straightened out. They went to their separate rooms. The room to which Gershon and Arthur were brought had tatami on the floor and sliding walls. There were no beds. On a low lacquered table stood a vase with a simple and astonishing arrangement of yellow-white flowers and bare black branches. One of the girls brought Arthur a lacquered bowl and a pitcher. She bowed.

"Toshie," she said, and poured a yellowish liquid into the bowl.

"What's this?" Arthur asked.

The girl pointed to her stomach and said again, "Toshie."

"Toshie wants you to drink it," Gershon said.

"What is it?"

"It's probably for whatever it is that's been keeping you so busy lately."

"Should I drink it?"

"I would drink it. If the Korean crumpets didn't kill you, this won't."

"Home remedies."

"Maybe it's chicken soup."

"My mother doesn't know about chicken soup." He drank it down slowly. "It's not chicken soup. I've been slain. I want a simple ceremony and a modest burial. No big stone."

"You have it."

The girl bowed and went from the room.

After a few minutes Arthur said, "I think I feel better. This is a beautiful room. Was it your idea to stay at a Japanese inn?"

"Yes."

"Do we visit the girl before we go to sleep?"

"I don't feel like visiting."

"She seemed a bit forlorn as she went into her room. Did you notice? Good night, dear Gershon. You know, I think this stuff really works. What do we do tomorrow?"

"We'll tour around. There's an island and some parks we might want to see."

Arthur said, "You're sure we don't visit? A social visit."

"I'm delighted by your quick recovery," Gershon said. "Good night."

Gershon slept soundly that night on the floor on a mat and hard pillow and beneath a heavy quilt covered with dragons and flowers and bamboo lanterns. He woke in the morning to the whisper of a sliding wall. Two girls were in the room with bowls and pitchers of water. They bowed. Arthur stirred and woke and sat up. He looked around in surprise. His hair was wild, and he brushed it from his eyes. He saw Gershon and blinked and shook his head.

"I didn't know where I was for a minute." He looked at the girls. They bowed to him.

"How do you feel, Arthur?"

"I'm all right. Do they stay here while we get dressed?"

"Not if we don't want them to."

"That stuff really worked. Toshie's chicken soup."

"I'm glad."

"Look at the sun," Arthur said. "It's glorious. Did you see that we have a garden out back all to ourselves? This is a fine room, dear Gershon. Must thank our Toshie for the chicken soup. God, that's a beautiful garden. Look at it."

The garden—a miniature landscape of stones and moss and low shrubs and a dwarf tree—lay in the pink light of the morning sun. The twisted tree stood brushed with gold. The garden seemed as soft and yielding as flesh, and Gershon felt himself ambushed and mesmerized by it.

The beauty of that tiny garden flowed beyond the boundaries of the inn and embraced all that they saw and did that day. They took a ferry to Megishima Island and wandered from the pier through groves and along climbing paths to a hill which looked out on the sea. A wind blew. Toshie wore a beige coat and a white flowered kerchief over her head. The long ends of her jet-black hair brushed across her face. Gershon stared at the sea. The water was greenish-gray. The sun shone through a thin screen of ashen clouds. Gershon took Toshie's arm as they went back down the hill. There were many young Japanese on the island. Some looked to be high school or university students; others were newlyweds. Many had cameras. They scampered about among the rocks and trees, laughing and taking pictures. Arthur stopped to aim his camera at one of the girls, and she laughed and hid her mouth behind her hand.

"Arthur-san better," Toshie said to Gershon. "He will take medicine again tonight and tomorrow he will feel fine."

"What did you give him?"

"Mama-san make for me. Very healthy medicine."

He felt the warmth of her hand in his.

"I fine tonight, Gershon-san," she said, averting her eyes. "I finish."

He said nothing.

Arthur came over to them. "Happy kids," he said, nodding toward the scampering youngsters. He looked at Gershon and Toshie and grinned. "Look, ma, no bathroom. I thank you, dear Toshie."

Gershon saw the pink color that rose to her cheeks.

"Come on," he said. "Let's catch that ferry back."

Later that day they rode a bus to Ritsurin Park. They rode through narrow streets fronted by small houses with earthen walls. Everything looked clean, neat, doll-like. They were not dolls, Gershon reminded himself. They had waged global war, carved an empire, caused millions to suffer and die. They had killed his cousin. Why was he so enchanted by this land? How they fused together nature and man! All one flow of world. No separations. Or was that merely the facile view of an outsider? No, he had read a lot about Japan. That was a good library, that library in the infantry regiment. Not many used it. Strange. He had not thought of Korea for days. They were passing by wooden houses with latticework windows and doors. On the side of the road near an entrance to an alley was a small shrine. He pointed to it.

"Jizo," Toshie said. "Protects little children. Jizo in many places, chap-san."

"We saw that shrine in Kyoto," Arthur said. He was sitting across the aisle from Gershon. "Remember? In those narrow streets."

The passengers in the bus sat quietly, not looking at them.

"Give Jizo flowers to help children," Toshie said, looking out the window. "We had Jizo in Tokyo near our house. Jizo did not help in fire bombs. Children die. Fire was like ocean. Ashes and smoke like big storm. Air was on fire. All Jizos get burned. Very bad, chap-san." She looked at Gershon. "War very terrible. I am happy there is no more war. But very strange. People kinder during war. People nicer. Help each other more. Now not so. Very strange."

Arthur looked away. They rode on in silence.

At the park Gershon helped her out of the bus. She leaned lightly on his arm. They walked through landscaped gardens and along winding ponds. The park seemed nearly deserted. There was a zoo and they fed young deer, and Gershon felt the leathery nibbling of their lips on the palm of his hand. Arthur took many pictures. Toshie, suddenly surrounded by jostling deer, was frightened, and Gershon pushed his way through and brought her out. She laughed and covered her mouth, then put her hand on his arm. Gershon noticed Arthur looking at her. They walked through an art gallery and an apricot grove. The air was still. They stopped at a teahouse for something to eat, and Toshie ordered for them in Japanese. Arthur ate slowly, looking out the tall windows at the forest of pine trees and the long finger of dark-green pond near the edge of the teahouse.

"Kekko," Gershon said.

"Hai, Gershon-san."

"I wish everything would stop now, dear Gershon. I wish I could take a picture of this and have it become the real world. I wish we weren't going anywhere tomorrow or in fifteen minutes or whenever."

I wish, I wish, I wish. Where else had Gershon heard or said this? He could not remember. He saw Toshie looking at Arthur.

"We can stay over if you want," Gershon said.

"No, we can't," Arthur said.

On their way out of the park they became lost in a green maze of gardens and ponds. An old woman came by, and Toshie spoke to her briefly. Gershon saw the old woman's sidelong glance at him and Arthur. It was dark when they got back to the inn.

They ate a dinner of fish at the inn and walked awhile through the town and then spent some time together with Toshie in her room. Arthur described his encounter with the beggars of Macao. "He pulled me right out, our Gershon. Just as he pulled you out, dear Toshie. Gershon our savior. I have it on film. A record for all generations. Did I film you saving me in Macao, dear Gershon?"

"I can't remember."

"Plunges right in. Through beggars and deer. Splendid friend. Are you sure I can't have any of this?"

"Very bad for you now, Arthur-san."

"Drink a little for me, dear Gershon."

"I am."

A while later they said good night. She stood at the door, her eyes lowered. A deep-pink color lay on her high cheeks. They walked through hushed corridors to their room. A moment later a girl entered with a bowl and a pitcher.

"Toshie," she murmured, bowing.

Arthur drank it down. She bowed and left.

Gershon was getting out of his clothes.

"I wonder how many bar girls get a chance to see this much of their country," Arthur said.

"I don't know. Not many."

"You're doing her a spectacular favor."

Gershon said nothing.

"She's going to want to repay you, dear Gershon. I read somewhere that they feel burdened by favors."

"I know all about it, Arthur. We worked it out."

"I'm sure you did," Arthur said. "What time do we get up in the morning?"

"About eight. We take a train to Matsuyama, a boat to Ujina, and another train to Hiroshima. We should be in Hiroshima about ten tomorrow night."

"You're sure you worked it all out?"

"I'm sure, I'm sure."

"Maybe we ought to have spent more time with her tonight. Maybe we ought to go back—"

"Arthur."

"Yes?"

"Good night."

"Good night, dear Gershon." A moment later he said, "She ought to bottle that Japanese chicken soup or whatever it is. An incredible remedy for jumpy Jewish stomachs." Then he said, "Look at the moonlight on the garden. Can you see it?"

There was no answer. He listened to Gershon's deep breathing. All that saki. He lay on the floor beneath the heavy quilts, staring at the bluish sheen of moonlight on the garden. A train, a boat, a train. Hiroshima. It was a while before he could fall asleep.

· · ·

In the morning they rode south and west by train through dense clusters of hamlets, farms, and brief cities. They rode in third class, and their car was crowded with families. Arthur sat awhile with Toshie, and Gershon struck up a conversation with the man in the seat next to him, a middle-aged Japanese in a baggy suit and a rumpled fedora. The man appeared transfixed by the countryside that flashed by beyond the window. Gershon offered him a cigarette. The man looked momentarily startled. Then he nodded, little rapid movements of the head, and smiled. Ah, so, yes, thank you. American. Thank you. He spoke English well. He owned a ceramics factory in Tokushima. American should visit Tokushima. Almost rebuilt. Yes. Almost all city destroyed in war. Yes. Bad war. American come to stay with his family. Yes. He handed Gershon a card. Happy to have stay. He opened his briefcase and pulled out three small clay figures—a horse, a Buddha, and what looked to be a Shinto god. American take, yes? A gift. Thank you for cigarette. Thank you. The man smiled and nodded happily as Gershon packed the figurines carefully into the smaller of his two bags. Then the man turned to look back out the window, and it was as if Gershon were no longer there.

At Matsuyama they took a cab to the Takahama Pier. Gershon helped Toshie out of the cab and heard her say quietly, "Please do not be so good to me." Arthur was paying the driver. The smell of the sea was very strong. They boarded the boat.

A cold wind blew across the water. The boat moved slowly away from the pier and then settled into the labor of the sea crossing. They slid by tiny islands. The hull of a fishing boat flared blindingly in the slowly setting ball of the sun. Banks of fiercely colored clouds covered the distant hills. The water grew deep purple. Waves broke against the bow. They stood at a window and watched the night come onto the sea. Gershon felt Toshie next to him, against him. Arthur stared across the water, his face pale, expressionless. Light and color drained slowly from the sea and the sky. They stood at the window and looked out at the darkness. Winking dots of light formed vague outlines of hills and shores. The boat pitched and bucked in the wind. Gershon thought he would be sick. He felt Toshie's hand on his arm. They docked at Ujina a few minutes before nine o'clock and took a train and a cab. Gershon helped Toshie into the cab. "Please, chap-san," he heard her say softly. "I do by myself. Please."

A light rain was falling. They rode through night streets. Arthur was very silent. He sat next to the driver. Gershon could feel his silence. They pulled up at their hotel.

It was a new and huge American-style hotel. The lobby was large, brassy. Their rooms were small, sterile. Arthur and Gershon took Toshie to her room and then went one door down to their room. The corridor was a long, narrow, carpeted tunnel of silence. In their room Gershon looked out the window and saw the rain and the black night and the scattered lights of the city. Behind him Arthur was sitting on one of the beds and staring down at the floor. He said something but Gershon could not hear the words.

"What?"

Arthur looked up. "Why are we here? I don't know why we're here."

Gershon looked at him.

"I can't think what I had in mind. Why did we come?"

"It was your idea, Arthur."

"I know. But why did we come?"

"To look around. To go shopping."

Arthur was silent a moment. Then he said abruptly, "You know, we never had any idea what he was doing. All the years on that mesa. The kids in school, no one knew what their fathers were doing. What am I doing? Why are we here?"

"I think we ought to wash up and get something to eat before they close the dining room."

"That light was so bright a blind girl saw it. Did I ever tell you that?"

"I think so. Arthur—"

"He came home afterward and washed up and went to sleep. He looked excited. My mother didn't know what was going on. All she knew was that she had buried a lot of charred birds in our yard. Am I sounding maudlin?"

"Yes, frankly."

"Then I shall stop immediately, dear Gershon. I shall not spoil our heretofore pleasant trip. Are you hungry? Let us scoop up our Toshie and have some dinner. God, what a vacuous room this is. It reeks of empty souls. It must have been built by engineers and physicists. Are you going to visit Toshie later? You realize that you have a problem."

"If there's a problem, it's mine. Please stay out of it, Arthur."

"By all means, dear Gershon. Absolutely. Why do you suppose it's raining tonight? Is that a kabbalistic omen of some kind?"

"The Japanese think that rain is a blessing."

"Really? I didn't know that."

"The Israelis do too. Most people do."

"You're a treasure house of folklore, dear Gershon."

"Let's eat dinner, Arthur."

Toshie responded immediately to Gershon's knock. She looked very tired and kept her gaze averted. They took the elevator down to the lobby and crossed over to the dining room. Arthur stopped for a moment to buy a packet of picture postcards. The brown, green, and red packet had printed on it in black the words "Peace City of Hiroshima."

They ordered dinner but ate little. A dry and brittle air had settled upon them, a sobering sense of unease. Toshie picked at her food, looking small and sad. There were very few people in the dining room. From somewhere outside came the sounds of American music. Arthur sat looking through the postcards as he chewed slowly and half-heartedly on a morsel of fish. Gershon sensed all around them, and in the darkness of the city, the black portal to the other side. Here a chasm had been opened to the empty future of the race. His mouth felt sand-dry. No matter how much he drank, he could not ease the sensation of dryness that thickened his tongue and throat. And yet—and yet he felt too a strange eagerness of expectation, a heightened sensuality that had located itself in his abdomen, a keen desire for the look into the nakedness of things. What was it really like out there in this first city to feel the light and fire of the atomic age? Here he sat, in its very midst. He would know soon enough. All the darkness and light of the species were here in this city. Toshie was saying something to him. He bent his head toward her.

"I am very sorry, chap-san. I cannot eat. Very, very tired."

"I'll take you upstairs."

"I'm done," Arthur said.

"Don't forget your cards," Gershon said.

At the door to Toshie's room, Arthur said, "Are you feeling all right?"

"No, chap-san. But will go to sleep now."

"Good night, Toshie."

"Good night, dear Toshie."

"Good night, chap-sans."

She went into her room.

The two of them looked at each other.

"We talked about it at least a half-dozen times, Arthur. She agreed."

"The head agrees, the heart cannot. An old story, dear Gershon. I'm tired myself. Let's go to sleep. Isn't this an awful room?"

Arthur was in the bathroom. Gershon sat at the small desk, reading the picture postcards. Beneath the picture of an atomic cloud he read, "Think of it that this Single Cloud killed or injured some 140,000 citizens and damaged 92% of the city!" Beneath the picture of a view of the city from the skeletal remains of the Industrial Exhibition Hall he read, "A single A-bomb turned the vast land of 3,628 Acres into Atomic Desert." Beneath a picture of a river and a park he read, "The devastated city with seven rivers is now under Rehabilitation." Beneath a picture of banks and offices he read, "Of those who witnessed the terrible scene of the atomic disaster, who could have expected Hiroshima thus far revived?" A picture entitled "Radiant Ray" showed a gray stone stairway. Above the picture he read, "Stone Step (Bank). The flash left the shadow of a man who was seated there at the moment. In this neighbourhood everything was exposed to a heat above 5,000° 280 m. from the explosion center."

Gershon looked carefully at this last picture. A section of the stone was clearly darker than that all around it. The picture filled him with a dread so overwhelming and unexpected that he felt himself beginning to tremble. Death light on a picture postcard. He left the cards on the desk and went over to his bed and lay down.

Arthur came out of the bathroom.

"All yours, dear Gershon."

"I was looking at your postcards, Arthur."

"Yes? I'm contemplating sending one to the Boston area."

"I don't think they need that, Arthur."

"You don't? What do you know about it?"

"Not very much."

"You don't know a damn thing about it."

"All right. I'm sorry. I don't want to butt into your family affairs. Listen. I think I made a mistake."

Arthur looked at him.

"I was absolutely sure I had it worked out. I wanted her to have a good time. A free fun time. No payments. It's all screwed up. I think she's miserable. What do I do?"

"You'll think of something, dear Gershon."

"You're not amusing me, Arthur."

"I don't very much feel like amusing anybody right now. I don't even know *what* I feel. She'll survive. She'll think you're another strange American." He sat on his bed. "I took a sleeping pill," he said. "I was afraid I wouldn't be able to drop off." He lay down and stared up at the ceiling. "We're here and it's all out there. Isn't it? I feel it. The city that little Arthur's daddy helped blow up. We were heroes, all the kids in our high school, when everyone finally found out what our fathers had been doing. That lousy little special school they set up for us in Los Alamos. Boston was a joy after that school. Everyone was proud. All the mothers were proud. God, listen to me. It must be the pill. It's a nice feeling. Nice. Floating. Yes. All very proud until started to hear words like mass murder and crime of Hiroshima and horror and other things like that. Unpleasant. Lost many friends. Funny looks. Some girls don't let you touch them. Begin to feel leprous. Listen, very grateful you came with me here. Deeply grateful. Good friend Gershon. Was afraid to come here alone. Don't know what might do. Funny feeling being here. Can't take hold of it. Grateful, dear friend. Don't worry about Toshie. Nice girl. She'll forget. Forgive, forget, right, God, oh God, oh God—" He dropped suddenly into sleep, as if he had been clubbed.

Gershon sat up in the bed and looked at him. Arthur's mouth was open. He was breathing softly. The pale, slack face—Gershon remembered the tan he had once sported—looked vulnerable, boyish. His father one of the giants of the century. Shadows on a broken generation. Gershon washed up and climbed into his bed. He slept and woke in the early morning and waited. The dark room was silent. No messenger. No silken voice. No questions. Strange. He fell back asleep and woke some hours later to a morning brilliant with sunlight. Arthur stood at the window, staring out at the city. He was fully dressed and was wearing his phylacteries and praying the morning service.

Gershon padded over to the window in his bare feet and looked out. He faced a nondescript sprawl of a city—low red- and black-tiled houses, a river, then more houses leading to the foothills of a range of green and purple hills. There were bridges over the river. The city looked drab and dusty. Off to the left was a wide, parklike area, with walks and broad stretches of brushed sand-colored earth and a scatter of young trees and white posts. Near the edge of the park stood a curious cement structure that looked like a saddle. Gershon recognized it from its pictures. He stared at it, dimly aware of Arthur's atonal chanting. He dressed and washed and prayed. They picked up Toshie—she seemed wan and distraught. They had breakfast in the hotel and went out into the city.

It was a warm day, the air clean and radiant with sunlight. They walked in silence along a riverbank. The water, reflecting the cloudless sky, was deep blue. Busy streets. Traffic. People. Work. Normalcy. Crossing to the park, they were nearly run down by a hurtling cab. Arthur pulled Toshie back to the curb. She was shaken and spoke loudly in Japanese to the disappearing cab.

Inside the broad, bare park, they wandered slowly along naked paths. Few people were about. The warm air and bright sunlight seemed a mocking dissonance to the darkness Gershon sensed in Arthur as they approached the saddlelike monument to the victims of the bomb. They stared through its cavelike opening to the nearby ruin of the exhibition hall, the only building in the center of the blast that had survived—a shell of a building, charred brownish stones, blasted windows, skeletal ribs of a dome. Beyond it flowed a wide slowly curving river, very blue. The banks of the river were the color of sand. The entire city seemed built on sand-colored earth.

Standing in front of the monument, Arthur said quietly, "Isn't there anything we ought to say?"

Gershon said, "What do you mean?"

"We killed all these people. Shouldn't we do or say something? Anything?"

Gershon saw Toshie looking at Arthur, puzzled.

They walked away from the monument. Gershon saw Arthur blinking in the sunlight. He brushed hair out of his eyes.

"Arthur-san feeling okay?" Toshie asked.

"No," Arthur said. He had brought his camera but had not taken any pictures.

They spent the rest of the morning wandering about the area of the blast. They looked at the Peace Tower, visited the museum, stared at atomic-melted slates and bricks and at pictures of the desert that had been made of the city by the explosion.

"Some turn deserts into cities, others turn cities into deserts," Arthur said. They were standing outside again in the sunlight. "Depends upon your line of work. Right, dear Gershon?"

"We firebombed Tokyo, Arthur. No one feels guilty over that."

"Why do people keep saying that? They know damn well it isn't the same. All those brains to produce a bomb. Think of it. The best brains we had. I wish Jews hadn't been involved. Somehow there's something wrong in that. I can't put my finger on it. I feel it tearing at my head. I'd rather we were blamed for stopping it than dropping it. An inadvertent rhyme. Sorry."

"It was supposed to have been used against Germany."

"Yes," he said. He looked across the expanse of sand-colored earth at the monument. "I know all about it. I've heard all the arguments. I lived all the arguments. I used to hear them at night before going to sleep. All my parents' friends, all those scientists, all those great minds, arguing. I'm telling you how I feel, Gershon. How I *feel*. I know about all the thinking. God, isn't there something we can say? You know, I think I hate this city. I think I really hate it. It cries out too much. Look at it. Bare and raw. I can smell the death. Look at that monument. It's vulvar, and it reminds you of the real possibility of an end to our species. You want a neater contradicion than that? What does your kabbalistic soul tell you about this city, dear Gershon? You know what my soul tells me about this city? It tells me that my father helped kill nearly one hundred thousand people. I'm sorry. I'm talking too much and too loudly. Really sorry, dear Gershon, dear Toshie." He turned away from their stares and looked into the open face of the monument. A dark cool cave. Shadows.

They ate lunch in a café, then toured the city. There was little to see. Pale-brown boulevards with center islands of low trees and patchy grass; gray and beige buildings; rivers; distant hills. Toshie walked with them, silent, withdrawn. At one point Gershon took her arm to help her up a steep curb. He heard her say, "Do not be so good to me. You Jesus Christ?" Arthur heard her too.

They returned to the hotel, burdened by a dark and weighty fatigue. They sat in a noisy bar over drinks. They had dinner. They walked awhile. Little was said. They went to their rooms. Arthur took a sleeping pill. "Does the trick, dear Gershon. Drop off like a rock. Have one?" Gershon refused. "I can't imagine that there's nothing to say," Arthur murmured from his bed. "Nothing?" He fell asleep.

In the early morning they rode a train and a ferry to the island of Miyajima. There they wandered for a few hours among the shrines. Delicately arched wooden bridges, a mirror pond, stone lanterns, the special grace of dwarf trees, a five-storied pagoda, dense greenery, shrines built on platforms in the water. Set in the sea amid its own deep and shimmering shadows and looking like a towering portal to the water and mountains beyond, was the great red torii of the Itsukushima shrine. In the brochure Gershon had brought along, he read that "the inhabitants did not dare to chop down the trees for long years, as they believed that God dwelled inside the evergreen trees." He read that "the Goddess of Itsukushima is worshipped as a Guardian of marines" and that today the shrine "is chiefly used for Shintoism." He read, "Its population, which counts about five thousand, are not allowed to have their cemetery on the island." He paused over that and read it again. In the official guidebook to Japan, he read, "The main shrine consists of three parts: the holy of holies, where the goddesses dwell; the inner part which only the priests enter; and the outer part for public worship. Along the corridor in front of the shrine are exhibited the utensils and sacred vessels used in Shinto worship. . . ."

Toshie had brightened as they had walked along the seafront shrines. Gershon had seen her pause against the red railing and look out at the water and speak something into the air, her eyes closed, her hands raised in a brief gesture of supplication. Now she stood near a black stone figure of an animal-like god and was talking with Arthur, whose troubled silence had not been eased by their journey to this sacred island. They returned to their hotel in Hiroshima in plenty of time for Shabbat.

Gershon had arranged for them to eat in the hotel dining room without paying or signing. The manager understood. Jewish? Ah, yes. So. Of course. Yes. Cold fish? Yes. Yes. They would pay when they departed. Certainly. Thank you so much. Yes.

They ate dinner. Toshie, looking drained, nearly fell asleep at the table. When they were done, she excused herself and went to her room. "I so very tired, chap-sans. Please. Good night."

They walked to the monument. It looked eery in the darkness. "Isn't there anything we can do?" Arthur asked. "God, we're all so helpless."

Gershon listened. His voice in the dark night conjured up images of frightened and supplicant children.

Arthur said, "Do I sound unnecessarily maudlin to you, dear Gershon?"

"No."

"It's a weight, a sore. It doesn't lighten, it doesn't heal."

Gershon was quiet. After a moment he heard Arthur say, "Ah, what difference does it make what we do or say? We're such dumb brutes, all of us. Let's go to sleep."

They walked back in silence to the hotel. In the room Gershon said, "You can get hooked on those pills, Arthur." Arthur said, "Yes? Where did you hear that? In your medical battalion? They let me drop off. You ought to try one. It might cut down on your nocturnal mumbling. Can I interest you?"

"No."

"Good night, dear Gershon."

When Gershon woke in the morning Arthur was not in his bed.
Nor was he in the bathroom. After some moments he went over to
the window and looked out. He dressed quickly and left the hotel
and walked along the river to the park and the monument. The
sun was harsh, bright. Arthur stood in front of the monument. His
skullcap formed a black circle over his hair. He held in his hands
a prayer book. Gershon moved alongside him.. Arthur gave no
indication that he was aware of Gershon's presence.

He was reading softly, but clearly, from the Book of Psalms.
His voice, agitated, stumbled over some of the Hebrew words,
stopped, went on, stumbled again. He read, "My God, my God, why
have You abandoned me; why so far from delivering me and from
my anguished roaring?" He read, "The benighted man thinks,
'God does not care.' Man's wrongdoing is corrupt and loathsome;
no one does good. The Lord looks down from heaven on mankind
to find a man of understanding, a man mindful of God." He paused
for a moment, his lips working soundlessly. He seemed deeply
agitated. He read, "O God, You have rejected us, You have made a
breach in us; You have been angry; restore us! You have made the
land quake; You have torn it open. Mend its fissures, for it is col-
lapsing." He read, his voice breaking, "O God, endow the king with
Your judgments, the king's son with Your righteousness; that he
judge Your people rightly; Your lowly ones justly." He paused and
looked up and his eyes fell upon the dark interior of the monument.
He glanced away and looked down at the prayer book. He read,
"O God, heathens have entered Your domain, defiled Your holy
temple, and turned Jerusalem into ruins." He stopped. His voice
broke. He took a number of rapid, gulping breaths. He went on.
"They have left Your servants' corpses as food for the fowl of heaven,
and the flesh of Your faithful for the wild beasts. Their blood was
shed like water—" he stopped again, cleared his throat, "like
water around Jerusalem, with none to bury them." He read, slowly,
his voice now barely audible, "O you who dwell in the shelter of the
Most High and abide in the protection of Shaddai—I say of the
Lord, my refuge and stronghold, my God in whom I trust, that He
will save you from the fowler's trap, from the destructive plague.
He will cover you with His pinions; you will find refuge under His

wings; His fidelity is an encircling shield. You need not fear the
terror by night or the arrow that flies by day, the plague that stalks
in the darkness or the scourge that ravages at noon." He stopped.
He put an arm across his eyes. There was a long silence. From the
distance, as if floating across the park, came the muted traffic sounds
of the city. Some Japanese had come up to the monument and looked
curiously at Arthur. They sensed something; a quick glance, a brief
impassive stare, and they drifted quietly away.

He stood there now and began to recite the words to the Kaddish.
Gershon listened to the awesome words of the prayer for mourners
—the public sanctification of the name of God; the affirmation of
meaning in the very presence of the most unassimilable of darknesses
—and a coldness of terror brushed against the back of his neck. His
heart began a wild beating. Arthur was reciting the words in English, reading from the prayer book in his hands.

"Magnified and sanctified be the name of God throughout the
world which He hath created according to His will. May He establish His kingdom during the days of your life and during the life
of all the house of Israel, speedily, yea, soon; and say ye, Amen."

"Amen," someone answered, and Gershon looked up with surprise
and realized that he, Gershon, had answered, and he continued the
required response, "May His great name be blessed for ever and
ever." Without a listener's response the Kaddish was meaningless;
the response was the soul of the Kaddish, its living center.

Shadows, came the whisper from the dimness inside the monument. They left you shadows. Join me, Gershon. This is such a
weariness. To build, to build? Why?

"Exalted and honored be the name of the Holy One," Arthur said.
"Blessed be He, whose glory transcends, yea, is beyond all praises,
hymns, and blessings that man can render unto Him; and say ye,
Amen."

You belong with me, came the whisper from inside the monument. With me, Gershon. From the time of your parents' death.
From the time of your cousin's death.

"Amen," Gershon said.

A middle-aged Japanese couple had stopped near the monument.
They looked at Arthur and Gershon and did not move away.

What a dryness of the heart and soul there is in all this, came the silken whisper. Nothing, nothing.

"May there be abundant peace from heaven, and life for us and for all Israel; and say ye, Amen."

We will hear one another again, Gershon, came the whisper. It is in the nature of things. Yes.

"Amen," Gershon said.

"May He who establisheth peace in the heavens, grant peace unto us and unto all Israel; and say ye, Amen."

"Amen," Gershon said.

"Amen," came a faint echo, and Gershon looked around and saw the Japanese couple turn and walk slowly away.

Arthur closed the prayer book and stood silently before the monument. He looked at Gershon and looked away. His eyes, dark, tormented, seemed ringed with fatigue, as if he had not slept the night before. He turned and walked slowly away from the monument. Gershon walked beside him. They went along the river, then crossed the wide street to the hotel. Gershon felt Arthur's hand touch his arm, rest upon it a moment, the fingers exerting a brief and gentle pressure. Nothing was said. They went into the hotel.

Toshie looked ill. She had slept late and had gone to their room and knocked on the door. Thinking they were in the dining room eating breakfast, she went downstairs. She looked for them in the dining room, then in the lobby. She wandered about with a mounting dread of having been abandoned. Alone. In Hiroshima. The city of fire and death. She considered asking at the desk if the Americans had checked out. But she was ashamed. She would wait in the lobby. And that was where they found her—in the lobby, on a chair, looking small and frightened.

Gershon regarded her with a feeling of dismay. "I'm sorry. I didn't think we'd be away so long. I'm really sorry."

"I think you go away and leave me."

"No."

"I was very afraid."

They had hurt her. Arthur looked at her and looked away.

During lunch she said, "We leave tomorrow, Gershon-san?"

"Very early."

"I am very tired."

She excused herself.

They watched her go, a small, dark-haired girl. They said nothing.

That afternoon they sat in their room, and Gershon read aloud and translated passages from the Zohar on the day's Torah reading.

He read, "We have compared the former with the latter generations, and found that the former were conversant with a higher wisdom by which they knew how to combine the letters that were given to Moses on Mount Sinai, and even the sinners of Israel knew a deep wisdom contained in the letters and the difference between higher and lower letters, and how to do things with them in this world."

Arthur said, "They knew how to blow up the world, that's what they knew. They did all the right mathematics and dropped it down the block."

Gershon read, "In the exposition of the verse, 'Hear, O Israel, the Lord our God, the Lord is one,' we have learned that 'one' signifies the Community of Israel who clings to the Holy One, blessed be He, since, as Rabbi Simeon said, the union of male and female is called 'one,' the Holy One, blessed be He, being called 'one' only in the place where the Female also is, since the male without the female is called half the body, and half is not one. When, however, the two halves are united, they become one body and are called one. At the present day the Holy One, blessed be He, is not called 'one.' The inner reason is that the Community of Israel is in exile, and the Holy One, blessed be He, has ascended aloft and the union has been broken so that the Holy Name is not complete and is therefore not called 'one.' "

Arthur said, after a silence, "That's a very audacious statement, Gershon. I like that. A strong imagination made that statement. If God isn't one, is He two? Very daring, that."

Gershon read, " 'Until the day be cool and the shadows flee away.' This refers to the secret known to the Companions, that when a man's time comes to leave this world, his shadow deserts him. Rabbi Eleazar says that man has two shadows, one larger and one smaller, and when they are together, then he is truly himself."

Arthur said nothing.

Gershon went on. He read, "If there are any righteous, then they suffer first for the sins of the age, and if not, then those children for whose sake the world is preserved suffer first, and God takes them from the world although there is no sin in them."

"I don't understand that," Arthur said.

"Neither do I."

"You're supposed to be the Kabbalah expert, dear Gershon."

"I understand the words. I don't always understand the mind that spoke them. Shall I go on?"

"One more. I'm getting tired."

Gershon read, "Rabbi Yosi then discoursed on the verse: 'A voice is heard in Ramah, lamentation and weeping, Rachel weeping for her children because they are not.' We have learned that on the day when the Sanctuary on earth was laid waste and Israel went into captivity with millstones on their necks and their hands bound behind them, the Community of Israel was banished from the house of her Husband to follow them; and when She came down She said: 'I will go in front and weep for my home and my children and my Husband.' When She came down and saw her home devastated and the blood of saints spilled in its midst and the holy shrine and temple burnt, She lifted up her voice, and higher and lower angels trembled, and the voice ascended to the place where the King dwelt, and the King was minded to turn the world into chaos again. Thereupon many armies and hosts went down to meet her, but She would not accept consolation. Hence it is written, 'A voice is heard in Ramah, Rachel weeping for her children because they are not'; or, as we should rather translate, '*He* is not,' referring to the Holy King who had gone aloft and was not in her midst."

Gershon stopped. There was a long and uncomfortable silence. Arthur shifted in his chair. "You know how to pick them, dear Gershon."

"Thank you. Another one?"

"No. I want to get some sleep. The damn pill didn't work last night. I like your Kabbalah. God, I'm tired. Listen. Thanks for being out there with me. Thanks for—answering." He lay on the bed and closed his eyes. "It was bad out there alone. Bad. I had to say or do something. I couldn't think of anything else. Probably would have offended some of our seminary professors. Sorry. Couldn't think—" He was asleep.

After a moment Gershon went over to the window. He sat in a chair and looked out at the monument. There were many people around it now in the park. Hazy sunlight covered the city. He sat there a long time, looking out at the monument. Light drained slowly from the sky. Behind him he heard a subdued whisper. Not one. Not one. See? And gone. In your own precious Kabbalah. We are more allied than you acknowledge, Gershon.

He said nothing. Darkness settled slowly upon the city.

That night, after Shabbat, the three of them ate dinner together in a quiet restaurant away from the hotel, and then walked awhile. And very late that night Gershon woke and saw that Arthur was not in the room. He lay awake a long time, his heart beating wildly. He slept and woke when Arthur returned. He lay very still and said nothing. From the darkness of the room came the sounds of soft and sibilant laughter.

Early the next morning they took a train to Osaka. They arrived in the afternoon. A cab brought them to the airport. They took a plane to Tokyo. The air was dense with rain and turbulence. Arthur sat white-faced; Toshie was repeatedly ill. They landed in rain. A cab brought them through narrow streets to the small house where she lived. Arthur said goodbye to her in the cab. Gershon stood with her in the doorway. A lantern shone dimly upon her lovely face. She looked exhausted.

He slipped an envelope into the pocket of her coat.

"I'll try to see you again on my way home. If I can."

"Hai, chap-san. You are getting wet in the rain."

He looked at the cab and saw Arthur staring at them through the closed and rain-streaked window. The engine was loud in the alley stillness of the neighborhood.

"Goodbye, Toshie."

"Goodbye, chap-san. Sayonara. He very sad and kind, your Arthur-san. Hai. Last night he come into my room. Very sad. He say to me his father is very big scientist who helped make bomb to drop on Hiroshima. He ask forgive. He say to me his mama-san help to save Kyoto. I not understand. He cry like little baby. I hold him and am mama-san to him. Hai. Please, chap-san, do not tell him I tell you. Take care your Arthur-san. Yes? Have safe trip to Korea, my chap-san. Have safe trip to America."

He held her to him. "I wish you a long and happy life, Toshie." And he kissed her.

"Ah, chap-san. You will write to me one day. Yes?"

"Yes."

"Sayonara, chap-san."

She went through the doorway and was gone.

He stood there a moment in the rain. Then he got back into the cab.

"What were you two talking about for so long?" Arthur asked.

"We were saying goodbye."

"That's all?"

"Yes. Should we have been talking about anything else?"

Arthur said nothing. His face was barely discernible in the darkness of the cab.

"Take us to Camp Drake," Gershon told the driver.

"Very long ride," the driver said. "Very late."

"I know how long and late it is," Gershon said.

The next day a C-124 brought them back to Korea, and the Japan journey of Gershon Loran and Arthur Leiden came to an end.

He took the train from Seoul. It moved with tortuous slowness, stopping frequently, lurching forward, stopping again. At one point it rode backward some distance, then stopped and went on ahead, slowly. He sat at the window and stared through the streaked glass and the iron grate. Freshly fallen snow covered the hills and fields. He saw jeeps and trucks moving slowly along the main supply route. The car was crowded with soldiers. They passed a cluster of huts in a nearby valley, and he saw a scrawny dog loping through the snow, its breath steaming. He closed his eyes and leaned back against the hard seat.

At the station he got a lift in an MP jeep. "Hey, good to see you, chappy. Yeah, isn't that the truth? Worst weather. There's half a foot of ice under this snow. Yeah, you better believe it. Sure, take you right to the guardpost."

Mounds of snow lined the sides of the division road. There were trenches in the snow all along the battalion compound. A narrow path through waist-high snow led up to his Quonset.

He came inside. The room was empty. Everything was as he had left it—desk, bed, books, phonograph, records. A sheet of writing paper and an envelope lay on John Meron's desk, waiting for his nightly writing. He put down his bags and took off his cap and overcoat. Then he sat on his bed and stared down at the floor. After a while he got to his feet and began to unpack.

John came in some time later.

"Hey, chappy. Great to see you. How was it?"

"It was excellent, John."

"You look good. Did you do all the traveling you wanted? You were lucky to be away. These last two weeks were one long snow-storm. It's really great to see you again, chappy. We got some new men in. Do you realize we have only three months to go? Three months!"

Yes, he realized that.

At the bar in the officers club that evening, Skippy said, "Aren't they nice people? I thought you'd like them, chappy. Pat wrote and said she enjoyed being with you and your friend. Nice people."

The colonel shook his hand, patted his shoulder, and bought him a drink.

Later he lay in his bed in the dark and listened to the wind on the walls of the Quonset. It blew down from the north in stiff, icy gusts. Images of temples and gardens filled his vision. The sun over the sea. Toshie's hurt face. Arthur's broken voice. The monument. Train rides, plane rides, boat rides, a child in a brothel, raging beggars. It was a long time before he was able to sleep.

In his office the next morning he sat behind a mound of correspondence on his desk. There were letters from his aunt and uncle. They were well, eager for his return. Only a few more months, his aunt wrote. They were praying for his health and safety. There was a letter from Karen. She was on the verge of accepting the University of Chicago offer. Did Gershon know what his plans were for the coming year? She loved him. Would he please write soon.

Letters from distraught parents who had not heard from their sons; letters from angry wives who had heard rumors about their husbands; a letter from a minister asking the chaplain about a soldier named Martin Shawn, who was with engineers and who had been counseled by him before entering the army—had that soldier yet found Jesus? Memos. Reports. Counseling appointments. The schedule of his character guidance lectures for the remainder of the month. Copies of the division daily bulletin issued during his absence. Howard Morten sat silently as Gershon quickly sorted the mail. Normally taciturn, he had greeted Gershon's return effusively; the bare office, the mail, the phone calls had nearly overwhelmed him. It was clear sailing now to the end; he had a little over three months left before he went home. He watched Gershon's swift sorting of the mail, then sat down at his typewriter with his next few days of work.

Gershon penned a quick reply to Karen. He did not know what he was going to do next year. The phone rang.

It was Arthur, his voice thin, distant.

"Hello. Gershon? Is that you?"

"No. It's your Macao guide."

"What? Hello!"

"It's me, it's me. How are you, Arthur?"

"I can barely hear you. Can you talk louder?"

"Can you hear me now?"

"Yes. We're buried in snow up here. It's terrible. Are we really back?"

"I'm afraid so."

"I can't believe we're back. Listen. Are we still going to have those weekly meetings in Seoul?"

"Definitely. Especially with Pesach coming up. There's a lot of planning we have to do, Arthur."

"Okay. I'm not arguing with you, dear Gershon. I just wanted to know."

"Do you intend going back to your Korean students?"

"I don't know. I intend going back to Japan as soon as I can."

"You just came from Japan, Arthur."

"I want to see Kyoto again, dear Gershon."

"You'll be due for an R and R in about four months."

"I don't want to wait four months."

"You want me to utter a kabbalistic incantation that will get you there sooner?"

"I'll take all the help I can get."

"What's in Kyoto, Arthur?"

"Kyoto."

"What?"

"An incantation or two can't hurt, dear Gershon."

"Goodbye, Arthur. I'll see you next week in Seoul."

The next afternoon Gershon went over to the nearby regimental library and found two books on Kyoto. He took them out. He returned to the regimental area that night to conduct the Purim service. A small group of worshipers listened to him read from a scroll the story of the deliverance of a Jewish community from an ancient Persian persecution. Later that night he sat in his room, listening to Bach and reading one of the books on Kyoto. John sat at his desk, writing.

In Seoul the next week Arthur walked into the Jewish chapel and heard Solomon Geiger say, "Today or tomorrow. He wants an answer."

"Go," Gershon said. "How can you possibly not go?"

"Go where?" Arthur asked from the doorway.

"Ah, the other wanderer is here," Solomon Geiger said. "Your friend here wants to turn me also into a wanderer."

"There's a retreat in Oiso. Solomon has been invited but isn't sure he wants to go."

"I'll go," Arthur said.

"You just returned," Solomon Geiger said. "I'm going. Gershon has persuaded me. I pride myself, you understand, that I have managed in the chaplaincy to avoid—trouble. I had a chance once before to go to Japan. Now I'll go. What shall we talk about today? Is there an agenda?"

After the meeting Gershon and Arthur stood outside the chapel near their jeeps. The sky was heavy with snow.

"Are you going back now?" Gershon asked.

"Yes."

"I'll call you during the week. Tell your assistant to be careful on those mountain passes."

"He's a good kid, dear Gershon. He's careful. You be careful. You don't have much time left here."

Gershon stood in the freezing wind and watched Arthur drive off. He rode over to the post library and spent some time leafing through books on Japan. It was snowing when he returned to the battalion.

It snowed all the next day. Trucks with plows went up and down the division roads. Toward evening the snow stopped and a wind blew its powdery surface in wild swirling waves across the valley. The sun was out in the morning, blinding. At night the wind returned and froze the surface of the snow. Gershon sat in his office working on reports, on his mail, on the transportation schedule for the Passover services. He tried calling Arthur but the lines were down. A helicopter flew by overhead in the direction of the medical battalion on the hill. In the early evening he trudged through the snow to the club and sat at the bar over a drink and a cigarette. Later that night he sat in his chair, reading about Japan.

He saw Arthur again the following week in Seoul.

"Are we getting all the snows of the planet here, dear Gershon? How is one to survive?"

"It's a bad winter, Arthur. The Koreans I talk to tell me they can't ever remember this kind of a winter."

"The phones are terrible. Are you having trouble?"

"All the time."

"What do they do if there's a war?"

"Don't say it," Solomon Geiger said. "Don't even think it." He knocked on the top of his wooden desk. "Pooh pooh! Can we get started, Gershon? What's the agenda?"

On the path outside the chapel after the meeting, Gershon said to Arthur, "Are you all right? You look tired."

"I don't sleep very much. The damn pills don't work."

"Why don't you have one of your doctors look you over?"

"Maybe."

"Is your stomach any better?"

"Sometimes it is, sometimes it isn't."

"You're in great shape, Arthur."

"I haven't been in great shape in a long time, dear Gershon. The face and the hair are my greatest asset, my Anglo-Saxon mask. Listen. How do I get to Japan without waiting four months? Will you figure out some way for me? What am I going to do here after you've gone?"

"I'll leave you with some incantations."

"Yes," Arthur said. "Right."

"You'll be fine, Arthur. Just take care of yourself."

"I'm trying, dear friend. I really am. But it's turning out to be just one more thing I'm failing at."

They stood there for a moment, looking at one another in the bitter-cold wind.

"Take care, Gershon."

"You take care, Arthur."

They shook hands. Arthur drove away. Gershon spent some time at the post library, then returned to the battalion.

He spoke to Arthur again twice that week regarding preparations for the Passover service at Ascom City. It was a complicated task, involving shipment of Passover foods, new dishes and utensils, preparing an army kitchen so that it would be kosher for Passover, and transportation and housing for a thousand men. No, he said wearily to Arthur. There was no possible way of getting him to Japan now. He spoke once on the phone to Solomon Geiger about ways of preventing the theft of silverware, about discipline among the Jewish troops during the two-day stay at Ascom City. He wrote letters, interviewed enlisted men who had come down with non-specific urethritis, gave two character guidance lectures, and that Sunday flew up to the regiment in the hills for a morning service. The L-19 jerked in the winds like a kite. The mountains were white, the jagged peaks menacing. He flew back that afternoon in a snow squall.

He was in his quarters with John Meron in the early evening when someone tapped on the door. John said, "Come," and the door opened and the division chaplain stood there and closed the door behind him. Overcoat and cap. Glasses. A schoolteacher. He brought into the warm room the chill scent of wind and snow.

Gershon stared at him and put down the book on Japan he had been reading. He felt a lurching sensation, a rush of shadowy air, and the sudden thick surging of his heart. Something had happened to his uncle.

The division chaplain cleared his throat. He was the bearer of ill tidings, he said. He hadn't wanted to call. It was very bad. He had just been notified from headquarters in Seoul. It hadn't been on the radio yet.

Gershon saw John staring at the division chaplain from his desk. He had been writing his letter.

A C-124 had crashed about half an hour ago on takeoff. Yes, at Kimpo. Yes, it was full. No, there was no definite word on casualties. But the man who had called him from Seoul had said that there were some dead.

Gershon, listening, wondered why the division chaplain had come in person. Was he going around to all the unit chaplains and telling them their men might have been in a plane crash? Abruptly he stiffened, remembering. He said, "Was Chaplain Geiger on that plane?"

He was sorry, the division chaplain said. Deeply sorry. It appeared that Chaplain Leiden had been on the plane and was not yet accounted for. There was much confusion. He might be fine. Still—

"You mean Solomon Geiger," Gershon heard someone say, and then realized he had said it. He had not recognized his own voice.

No, he had just spoken on the phone with Solomon Geiger, the division chaplain said. It was Arthur Leiden. The young man whose father was the physicist. He was so very sorry. There would be no broadcast of names until the families were notified. But he had wanted Chaplain Loran to know. He had to go now. There would be no end of work to do. If he could be of any assistance, any assistance at all. He cleared his throat. He was gone.

John Meron said, "God, chappy—"

"There's got to have been some kind of mistake," Gershon said. He was putting on his parka. John leaned forward and snapped on the radio. A Japanese song. Gershon was outside, half-running through the narrow trench in the snow that led from his quarters and around the officers mess and the club and down to the headquarters Quonset. Alone in his office, still wearing his parka and fur cap, he called Seoul. A thin, quavering voice responded.

"Seoul Jewish chapel. Private Gabriel Rosen speaking."

The voice conjured up in Gershon the picture of the boy's thin face, dark hair, shifting eyes.

"Gabriel. What's happening?"

"Chaplain Loran, sir?"

"Yes."

"Chaplain Geiger just went out. You know about it? It's awful, sir. They say there are lots of casualties. They say—"

"Was Chaplain Leiden on that plane?"

"Yes, sir. He was. He went instead of Chaplain Geiger."

"Ask Chaplain Geiger to call me when he returns."

"Yes, sir."

"Will he be back soon?"

"I don't know, sir. He went out to the airport."

"Goodbye, Gabriel."

"God, I don't know what to tell you, sir. They say that—"

"Remember to ask him to call."

"Yes, sir."

He hung up the phone. He sat there at his desk. A dull and heavy tightness had come into his chest. He found he had stopped breathing, and he stood and took deep gulping breaths. His hands were freezing. He had on his parka and his cap, and still his hands were freezing. It was cold in the office with the oil stove out. He sat down at the desk. The top was bare, all his papers locked away in drawers. Arthur. It was absurd. No. Why wasn't Geiger calling? He sat there, waiting. It was a mistake. Arthur could not have been on that plane. He had spoken to Arthur on Thursday. He had said nothing about going to Japan. Absurd. He stared at the phone in the canvas pack on the wall near the desk. After a few minutes he called the Seoul chapel again. There was no answer. Damn that stupid Gabriel Rosen. He sensed to his surprise how enraged he felt that it had been Gabriel Rosen who had confirmed Arthur's presence on the plane. Someone else should have told him. Why? He did not know. He sat there at his desk, waiting, and feeling the rage against Gabriel Rosen. After a while he called again. No answer. He left the office and went back up the snow-packed path to his quarters.

Inside the heated room John said, "It just came over the radio, chappy. Seven dead so far."

Seven out of—what? Ninety? One hundred? Soft music floated from the radio.

"Skippy was just here," John said. "We had some of our boys on that plane. Was your friend on it?"

"I think so, John."

"God, chappy—"

"He was on it, John. The stupid bastard was on that plane. He had no right to be on that plane. We just got back. What right did he have to do that?"

John stared at him.

"He was going to spend the rest of his life atoning for his father's mistake. That's stupid, John."

The music ceased abruptly. An announcer came on with news of the crash. Engine exploded about one minute after takeoff. Prop tore loose and cut through fuselage and elevator controls. Crash landing on ice in Han River. Ninety-two passengers. Eleven dead so far. Will interrupt regular programs with further news as soon as it is received. Now resume with the music of Glenn Miller.

Gershon went back down to his office and once again called the Seoul chapel. There was no answer. He walked back to his Quonset in the bitter wind. It was dark. He ate supper quickly in the officers mess. The talk was subdued; by now all knew. The colonel put his hand on Gershon's shoulder and murmured, "Really sorry, chaplain." After supper Gershon again called Seoul. Again, no answer. Damn that stupid Gabriel Rosen! Why wasn't he near the phone? He returned to his quarters. John was writing his nightly letter. The radio now reported fourteen dead. Later Gershon lay in his bed and listened to John's soft breathing. Deep shadows filled the dark room, darker than any darkness he had ever known before.

He came into his office the next morning and was removing his parka when the phone rang. It was Solomon Geiger.

Yes, Arthur had been on the plane. Could Gershon come down to Seoul?

"Today?"

"Yes."

"What's the matter?"

They would talk about it in Seoul. When could he expect Gershon?

"Two hours."

Solomon Geiger hung up.

Gershon stared at the phone, and a long shudder moved through him.

The main supply route was heavy with traffic and treacherous with frozen snow. The ride took nearly three hours. He sat in Solomon Geiger's office. Solomon Geiger had gone through the night without sleep. At the airport. Terrible. A horror. Yes. His round face was ashen, his hands trembled. They could not find Arthur's body, he said. It was somewhere below the ice in the Han River. They were looking for it. One other body was missing.

Gershon sat back in the chair. He heard the blood surging in his ears. After a moment he heard himself ask, "Why was he on that plane?"

Because Arthur's phone calls had been endless, his pleading relentless. Because Solomon Geiger had decided to change his mind. Too much trouble. Too cold. Too much snow. He didn't know why he had changed his mind. The Japan chaplain had counted on Geiger. He needed someone for that retreat. Could Geiger find a replacement. If he could, they would get the orders cut in Japan. Geiger had called Arthur. The orders had come through at the last minute. Arthur had taken an L-19 to the military airstrip near Seoul and had barely made it to the plane. No one thinks there will be such an accident. He was doing Arthur a favor. He himself had never really wanted to go to Japan. If Gershon had not talked him into it—

Gershon sat very still, no longer listening. A strange and muffling heaviness had settled upon him. He moved slowly beneath that heaviness—first to the bathroom, then to the chapel, where he stood a moment staring at the Ark, then back to Solomon Geiger's office. They sat together awhile, reworking Arthur's schedule of services, dividing between themselves the assignments he had undertaken for Passover. Gershon said he would handle the services for both line divisions; he heard himself say that, but it seemed to him—how strange!—that he was actually watching and listening to someone else. One Gershon was watching and listening to another Gershon.

He heard Solomon Geiger say, "We will have to write a letter to his parents."

He heard himself say, "Do they know?"

He heard Solomon Geiger say, "I was told they would be notified. Probably by now they know."

He heard himself say, "He was stupid. Why did he have to do that? What right did he have? He was no hero."

He heard Solomon Geiger say, "What do you mean?"

He heard himself say, "Why does He break the world this way? What are we to do?"

He heard Solomon Geiger say softly, "Gershon, Gershon."

He heard himself say, "What if they don't find his body?"

Solomon Geiger did not respond.

Gershon drove back to the battalion.

It took four days to find Arthur's body. They were helped—that mysterious "they" that Solomon Geiger kept referring to each time Gershon called him; Gershon never asked about their identity—they were helped by the sudden thaw that set in with the coming of April. A vast portal had opened somewhere, and warm air surged through. The snow ran off the hills; the roads turned to oozing mud; the valleys reappeared; the ice melted in the Han River. They found Arthur's body. Then they found the second body, that of an eighteen-year-old enlisted man. Both had been in the tail section of the plane near the toilets, the section that had sheared off on impact. All the dead had been in that section.

During those four days Gershon worked at his desk, drove along the muddied roads to his various units, flew to Arthur's division to conduct a service, and wrote letters to the parents of the two enlisted men in his battalion who had been killed in the crash. He did not write to Karen. He was waiting to hear about Arthur's body. He kept reading about the crash in *Stars and Stripes* and hearing about it on the radio. It was being very widely reported. He worked and read and listened and felt himself a passive observer. Often he heard Arthur's voice, the lilt, the New England accent; and often he saw Arthur—quite clearly saw him—driving off in his jeep, walking the streets of Hong Kong, gazing at a Kyoto garden, looking at Toshie, staring at the Hiroshima monument, asking him to explain a passage of Kabbalah, Keter would kill him the next day, he was not prepared. Dear Gershon, he kept hearing him say. Dear Gershon.

The nights were difficult. He could not sleep. He thought he might go over to the medical battalion and ask for sleeping pills, but he did not really want to yield to that. Also he had no wish to seek out that battalion; he had not once been on that hill since his transfer. And so he lay awake in the darkness of those nights, listening to Arthur, watching Arthur—how sharp the images were! Surely he was alive! He could hear him! Touch him!—and sensing in the darkness all the malignant stirrings of all his past abandonments. Yet there were no whispered questions. The seductive voice did not appear. But he knew it would come. Always in the past it had come. It would come, it would come, and he did not know how this time he would be able to withstand it.

And then Solomon Geiger called to say that they had found Arthur's body.

"What do we do?" Gershon asked after a silence.

"Nothing. They will fly it home to his family for burial. Do you know the family?"

"Yes."

"Apparently they have considerable political influence. The crash will be very seriously investigated. The seating arrangements on those planes have already been altered. They will no longer fly with soldiers in the upper deck. It is a very unfortunate business. Will you write to his parents or shall I?"

"I'll write."

"Will we continue our weekly meetings?"

"Yes."

"I cannot begin to tell you how sorry I am, Gershon. My heart is very heavy. If I had not yielded to the temptation to go—" He broke off. There was a brief silence. Then he said, "The army is planning a memorial parade for all the dead in the crash. They have asked one of us to speak. Do you wish to?"

"All right."

"I'll see you next week, Gershon. Take care of yourself." He hung up.

Gershon wrote three letters that afternoon—to Arthur's parents, to Karen, and to Toshie. He worked on his March monthly report; it was four days overdue. Later he walked back to his quarters

through the mud of the compound. Climbing the hill, he felt someone behind him and he turned. He saw no one. The compound
was quiet. Jeeps, trucks, bulldozers, ditch-diggers stood parked in
neat rows near the maintenance sheds. It was a warm afternoon; all
the dark cruelty of the winter was gone. He walked back to his
quarters in a darkness that emanated from a realm altogether without wind and weather.

At his desk that night, while John sat writing to his fiancée,
Gershon wrote to Jakob Keter and told him of Arthur's death. He
folded the letter and put it into an envelope. He addressed the
envelope, sealed it, and sat there a long time, staring at it. He went
to bed early, but it was hours before he was able to sleep.

He found the next morning, when he put on his phylacteries,
that he was unable to pray. He was alone in the room. It was a
warm morning, and there was no fire in the oil stove. He stood
near his bookcase, and the words would not come. He knew the
words, but he could not get them past his throat. This surprised
him, for he felt no sense of anger and even thought that his grief
had diminished somewhat. He had a sudden vision of Arthur praying in their hotel room in Kowloon, the phylactery strap spiraling
down off his arm and onto the carpeted floor. He removed his
phylacteries and went out of the room into the warm morning.

At the infantry regiment chapel that night he conducted the
service and spoke briefly about Arthur. The chapel was crowded.
He went very quickly through the service and later walked back to
the battalion alone through the cool, star-filled night. That Monday
during the meeting with Solomon Geiger in Seoul, he was all business, cool, detached. He tried to avoid mention of Arthur, and he
acknowledged without comment the date for the memorial parade.
Solomon Geiger looked at him curiously.

"You are losing weight, Gershon."

"I'm fine."

"No one is fine in all this, Gershon. You have to take care of
yourself. You have less than two months left here."

"I think we ought to go on with this food list. We'll never be
ready if we don't cover every item on this agenda today."

Solomon Geiger nodded heavily, his eyes sad.

The days were now permanently warm, the air blue and clear. Slowly a cover of green spread across the hills and the valleys. Farmers began working the fields. Ball games sprouted on the compounds. The mud had dried. The dirt roads were firm. Some of the main roads were being paved. Gershon worked; he rode, he flew, he interviewed, he lectured, he conducted services. He spoke briefly one day at the large military parade in Seoul that honored the dead of the crash. "Splendid, chaplain, splendid," men with birds and stars on their uniforms said to him afterward. "You were extraordinary, Gershon," Solomon Geiger said. "Yes?" he said. He had spoken from scant notes and could remember nothing of what he had said.

A letter arrived from Toshie. "Dear Chap-san, It was so very good to hear from you and to know that you were safe and well. I was worry about you when I heard that big airplane accident had happened. I'm very sorry that you lost your very good friend by the accident. I cry when I read this in your letter to me. He was very good person, and I will always remember Arthur-san. Your best friend, Toshie."

A letter arrived from Karen. "Darling Gershon, I was stunned, as were my parents, by the news. We learned of it two days before we received your letter; one of the newspapers here carried a final list of all the casualties. I was so terrified of seeing your name that I never thought I might see Arthur's. There it was, and I couldn't believe it. His poor parents. My father was talking this morning about a memorial of some kind in Arthur's name. My parents send you their very warmest good wishes. Take care of yourself. I have told Chicago yes. Are you really uncertain about next year? What shall we do? All my love, Karen."

A letter arrived from Arthur's mother. "Dear Gershon, Thank you for your comforting letter. It was good to hear from Arthur's friend. He wrote to us of your trip to Hong Kong, Macao, and Japan. He wrote of you with warmth and deep appreciation. We can find no consolation in the absurdity of his death. Time may dull the pain; nothing will make up for the loss. Is there a chance you might stop off in Boston on your way back home after your release from the service? Both Charles and I would very much appreciate seeing you once again. Please accept this expression of gratitude for your kindness. Yours sincerely, Elizabeth Leiden."

The days passed, one sliding slowly into another, longer and warmer now, the fields and hills deep green, dust rising now on the roads, heat now in the afternoons. He worked, he rode, he flew. He could not pray. He would put on his phylacteries; but he could not pray. Instead he would read aloud passages from the Zohar. Once he was reading loudly with his back to the door, and he turned, and there was John, looking surprised and shamefaced; a murmured apology came from John as he turned and left, closing the door softly behind him. Gershon continued reading.

Passover came. Nearly a thousand men were transported to Ascom City by truck and train. The supervision of food preparations, the Seder services, the morning and evening services, discipline, cleanliness, study sessions—he was drained nearly to exhaustion and he sat around his office for some days after the festival, staring down at his desk, writing letters and reports, daydreaming, seeing himself in Hong Kong, Macao, Japan. All the arduously mended pieces of his fragile world lay in shards everywhere around him, and he did not know what to do.

In May the hills turned brown from the burning sun, and one day he looked up, and there were the fires again, leaping along the slopes, and he asked around, and no one knew why the Koreans burned their hills. One of the fires abruptly changed course and took a path directly toward the battalion. Gray ash fell on the compound; smoke clouded the air. Orders were issued to evacuate the area, and the battalion moved out to the field. He lived a day and a night in a tent in a small valley, and Turks guarded their perimeter, and no one was disturbed. The fire was fought back, and in their quarters afterward John said he was glad they got to the fire before the fire got to them, the division ammunition dump was directly behind them on the hill, and Gershon looked at him, and John nodded and said nothing more.

The heat and dust of May became relentless. He rode around in his face mask and felt the yellow dust all through him and even after long showers in the stalls down the road from the battalion. He saw little of Solomon Geiger now. He gazed for long moments at a time at the calendar on the wall near his desk. He could not grasp it. Day after inexorable day.

One afternoon at the start of the second week in May he packed his books into his footlocker. The Talmud tractate he had brought with him he packed too. He kept out only a volume of the Zohar and a kabbalistic work by Chaim Vital. Two enlisted men came and took the footlocker away.

Skippy went home—with an enormous hangover from his sayonara party. Two other officers went home.

It seemed to Gershon as he traveled around that everywhere now the roads were being paved, the tents were disappearing. He had lived through a between-time with the army in Korea. Now it was coming to an end. And he discovered, to his astonishment, that he was vaguely regretful. He had learned so much, suffered so much, and survived. He was only sorry that his time here was nearly over; he was not sorry enough to want to extend it.

He found as the days went by that he missed Arthur very badly. The anger and numbness had slowly turned into an ache, a poignancy, a heavy and persistent sense of the melancholy capriciousness of all existence. He was still unable to pray. He read often—and aloud when he was alone—from the Zohar and from the book by Chaim Vital.

On a hot sunny May afternoon his replacement arrived—a seminary graduate from Columbus, Ohio, young, tall, clear-eyed, and self-assured. He brought regards from Professor Malkuson. Gershon spent some days showing him around. He had been assigned to the medical battalion on the hill.

John Meron went home. "God, it was good being with you, chappy. You really made all those months bearable. I'm really sorry about your friend. You must really have been hurting because I heard you sometimes talking in your sleep. Here's my address. Maybe you'll want to write me one day. You're a good guy." And he was gone. His bed remained empty.

The colonel went home. The adjutant went home. There were new faces everywhere.

He heard nothing from Jakob Keter.

At the end of the second week of May he went through the battalion and the division with his installation clearance certificate.

The check list for his clearance contained these items, among others: troop information and education officer, unit and regimental supply, enlisted or officers mess, quarters assignment, post exchange cards, courts and boards, classified documents, efficiency reports, field military 201 file and allied records, military pay record, post motor pool (he turned in his jeep; the Star-of-David insignia was lost somewhere; he never found out what happened to it), postal officer, health jacket, dental jacket, special projects officer. In the area on the sheet of paper marked "library," a librarian placed the large round stamp of the special services library above his signature.

He went to the medical battalion on the hill for chest X-rays. All were negative. He saw no one he knew. He wandered about the hill in the hot sunlight of that May afternoon and recognized nothing. The white buildings of the hospital, the new Quonsets for the enlisted men, the officers quarters, the stone and wood and glass building that was the officers mess, the paths with white-painted stone borders—everything neat, clean, orderly. On the crest of the hill stood the chapel—large, white, and dazzling in the sunlight, its steeple tall, majestic. It contained no crosses.

He stood on the hill near the chapel and looked down into the valley behind the battalion. The village was gone. In its place lay an ugly sprawl of a town, shacks, sheds, huts, farmhouses, shops, and, no doubt, brothels. Dogs slept in the shade of the dusty houses. He recognized nothing of the old village, nothing. After a while he turned away and got into his jeep, and rode back to his battalion.

The Saturday night before he left there was a sayonara party for him in the officers club. Someone had drawn a cartoon on a large sheet of oak tag. It showed Gershon, and one of the officers who was leaving with him, in a rowboat with a mast. The officer was rowing. The boat was surrounded by sharks. Gershon sat on the top of the mast, a pelican on his head, a spyglass in his eye. "Going home!" read the cartoon. "Congratulations!" It was a loud and noisy party. Gershon drank a great deal. They sang many songs. He was drunk when it was over, and someone helped him to his bed. He lay in a stupor and listened to the darkness. And finally, in the early morning, there it was, the silken voice. How you protect yourself against me, it whispered. But now is it not time to talk?

He fell into a drunken sleep.

The next day he rode to the office of the division chaplain. He thanked him for his kindnesses, for the difficult messages he had had to carry to him. "Good luck to you, chaplain," said the division chaplain. "God bless you." They shook hands.

He called Solomon Geiger. "Good luck," he heard Solomon Geiger say. "You'll call my wife, yes? Have a safe trip. I wish you health and a long life."

Three days later, in the early morning, he loaded his bags into a jeep. The officer with whom he had shared the sayonara party was in the jeep with him. Howard Morten stood there, silent. He was going home in ten days. They shook hands. The jeep took Gershon out of the battalion, out of the division, out of the valley, through Seoul, and into Ascom City.

Two days later a C-124 Globemaster brought him to Japan. All during the flight he sat staring out at the engines, waiting. In Camp Drake they were all restricted to the base; their flight could be called at any time. He did not see Toshie. Three days later a DC-6 took him away from Japan.

They refueled at Wake Island. Over the Pacific he gained a day. Near Hawaii one of the engines went bad. They waited six hours in Hawaii for the engine to be repaired. He sat in the passenger lounge, foggy with the fatigue of travel and altered time, and watched them working on the engine.

They landed in San Francisco in the morning of the next day. He made some phone calls. His aunt wept into the phone. His uncle was barely audible. Karen sounded subdued. "Yes," Elizabeth Leiden said. "Please. It is so very good of you to have called."

For a day and a half he waited on lines, signing his name again and again. And then he was out, it was over, he was free.

He stood on a sidewalk, tasting his freedom. He felt hollow. He hailed a cab. That night he flew to Boston.

He landed in the sunlight of a pale New England dawn. Inside the terminal he made a quick phone call. Outside on the street there were no cabs, and he had to wait awhile before one pulled up. The city was still asleep. He rode through the quiet streets, feeling light-headed with lack of sleep, looking at the grass and trees along the river, the sheen of the sun on the surface of the water, the stately buildings of the universities, the clean blue of the morning sky. He remembered the old houses. The trees were full now. There was the lake, barely visible through the trees. The cab brought him to the driveway of the Tudor. Banks of azaleas lined the front of the house. He paid the driver and watched him leave. He saw the cab as a jeep pulling away from the Seoul chapel after one of their meetings, Arthur inside. He rang the bell on the ornate oaken front door, and it seemed to him that he waited a long time before it was opened.

Elizabeth Leiden stood in the doorway. "I'm so sorry to have kept you waiting. I was on the phone with my daughter. Do forgive me. Please come in, Gershon. It was so very good of you to come."

He entered the house, and there were the high-ceilinged center hall, the wide staircase with its carved dark-wood banister, the paintings on the walls—and, on the small triangular table, the framed photographs of Arthur and his brother. Arthur on a horse. Arthur smiling. Gershon looked away.

Elizabeth Leiden was talking to him. He had not heard her. He turned.

"—down soon. He has not been well. Have you had breakfast, Gershon? Oh, that's dreadful food. You will have breakfast with us." She wore a pale-blue summer dress. There were tiny lines around her eyes. Her face had no makeup on and looked pale and drawn. "Are you out of the army now? Entirely? Do come with me into the kitchen. What would you like for breakfast? Arthur used to like—" She stopped. "Forgive me. Come along, Gershon."

He followed her from the center hall through a long corridor and into a spacious kitchen. Sunlight streamed through the windows and fell across a table and chairs, the glistening stove and sink, the closets. Motes whirled slowly in the slanting beams. Beyond the rear windows lay the lawn, green now, and the oaks, and then the line of white birch and the lake. The water shimmered through the trees, lights of silver and gold. There were small boats in the docks that fronted the elegant homes on the lake. Gershon stared through the trees at the boats. He turned away.

"Shall I scramble some eggs?" Elizabeth Leiden was saying. "Lately I have gone back to cooking. I am now quite good at it. Was Arthur eating well? I'm sorry. A pointless question. We do miss him. Well. Eggs it shall be. Charles? There you are. Look who is here."

Gershon had heard the steps along the narrow hallway. Now Charles Leiden stood in the sunlit kitchen, blinking in the light. "How good of you to come, dear fellow. I do appreciate it. Did you have a pleasant flight? Fine. May I sit down? A bit weary these days."

They shook hands and sat at the table. Elizabeth Leiden busied herself at the stove. Charles Leiden, in a light-brown sweater and dark baggy trousers, looked haggard. His features were gaunt, high bony cheeks and sunken gray eyes, and his hands trembled faintly. He looked at Gershon. "Well," he said. "Tell me about yourself. Are you done with the service? What will you do now?"

Gershon said he didn't know.

"I remember that for the longest time I also wondered what I would do. I am not entirely certain to this day why I chose physics. I thought I might uncover the secrets of the universe. I thought—" He stopped and shook his head. "Please forgive me. I do tend to go on sometimes. Ah, breakfast is served. Elizabeth has returned to cooking now and then, and a splendid return it is."

They ate quickly and with awkward small talk. Afterward Gershon stood alone in the library. Charles Leiden had excused himself and was somewhere upstairs; Elizabeth Leiden was cleaning up in the kitchen and had refused Gershon's offer of help. "Another time. Now you are our guest, and a weary one at that. Do wait in the library. I shall be done quickly."

He stood before a wall of books, scanning the titles. This was clearly part of Elizabeth Leiden's library, for there were many volumes on oriental art. He noticed a set of three thickly bound volumes with no titles on their spines, and he reached up and took one down. It was a collection of scholarly papers written by Elizabeth Leiden, all of them on the religious art of ancient and medieval Japan. A second volume contained three of her monographs. The third volume was made up of essays and a monograph—all on

Kyoto. He had turned to the closing pages of the monograph and was reading the summary when he heard her footsteps in the hallway. He did not put the volume back on the shelf. He was standing there with the volume in his hands when she entered the library.

She regarded him without expression. He closed the volume and replaced it on the shelf. Charles Leiden came down the stairs and entered the library. He walked slowly and was somewhat stooped. He had an envelope in his hands.

"Why don't we sit down? Please. Elizabeth? Gershon? You might be interested in this, Gershon. It is a letter from Arthur, one that he wrote when he returned from the trip the two of you took. It was the only letter he wrote to us. He favored postcards."

Gershon watched him remove the pages from the envelope. Elizabeth Leiden sat very still in an easy chair, her hands clasped in her lap. She seemed pale.

"There is much in it that is quite personal and I shall not read that to you. His relationship to us was, at times, something of a— problem. But he tells us here what the trip meant to him." Charles Leiden put on dark, shell-rimmed glasses and read from the letter. "He writes, 'I did not want to travel to Hong Kong and Macao, but it turned into an extraordinary trip. All the world, it seems, is a grayish sea of ambiguity, and we must learn to navigate in it or be drowned. That may not be much of a learning to you both; but it has been brought home to me here. And each of us treasures the places where he was taught best regarding the nature of things— some in a slum, others in Los Alamos, still others on Asiatic streets. Gershon is rather remarkable. He studies texts as a commentary and a balance to what he sees. What shall I do for my balance? I shall see. Perhaps I have found something already. I am powerfully drawn to Kyoto. It has, as you can well imagine, a special significance for me. At any rate, my stay there with Gershon was inexpressibly beautiful. I thank you for that city. Perhaps I shall live there for a while when I am done with the army. We shall see. I do apologize for the card I sent you from Hiroshima. It was quite tasteless of me. There was a moment of anger that had somehow to be assuaged, and the card was written and mailed before I had much time to think. I do want to thank you for thrusting Gershon upon me—or thrusting me upon Gershon—a gesture I at first deeply resented but which proved in time to be possessed of a special wisdom. I wish there had been more moments among the three of us when I might have perceived that wisdom. Perhaps in the future. Now I must conclude, for I am off to Seoul for another of those weekly meetings of Jewish chaplains established by Gershon. I look forward rather keenly to seeing him again. He is quite changed— hardly the shy and reserved fellow he was in our seminary years. He appears to have shed a chrysalis of some sort. I do not know how I shall manage here when he leaves. Do write me soon about yourselves. Your—'" and here Charles Leiden's voice, which had been firm through the reading, suddenly broke, and he cleared his throat, "'your son, Arthur.'"

There was a long silence. Elizabeth Leiden looked down at her folded hands. Her face was expressionless. But a slight tremor played briefly along the lower rim of her lips.

Charles Leiden said softly, "I was searching earlier for the card Arthur sent us from Hiroshima, but I appear to have misplaced it. There was on it, as I recall, a photograph of a stone stairway with a shadow that remained on the stone after the blast. The message Arthur wrote on the card was somewhat cryptic but hardly indecipherable. He wrote, 'Shadows on stones and shadows on lives.' That was all. And he signed his name. The irony in all of this, you understand, Gershon, is that you never visited the city of the real moral tragedy. Hiroshima is an arguable stain, but Nagasaki was without doubt an act of utter cruelty. Why not have dropped it on an island after the point was made in Hiroshima? Nagasaki turned my stomach. We were in the hands of the witless. At any rate, I thought you would want to know about this letter from Arthur. I am sorry if I stirred up too many painful memories."

"Charles," Elizabeth Leiden said quietly.

He lapsed into silence.

Gershon said after a moment, "Mrs. Leiden, what did you have to do with Kyoto?"

She seemed startled. She said after a pause, "Not very much, Gershon. It was to be the target of the first bomb. In roundabout fashion I succeeded in getting the target changed."

The soldier son of a close friend of Henry Stimson's, the then

Secretary of War, had dined with him one night and praised the qualities of Kyoto. The soldier had once studied with Elizabeth Leiden. Stimson requested confidential memos from a small number of academicians on the advisability of Kyoto as an incendiary bomb target. All consulted with Elizabeth Leiden, and all urged against it. Stimson then removed Kyoto from the target list for the first atomic bomb. "It was quite inadvertent, you understand. I had no direct hand in the affair."

"You had more of a hand in it than you ever acknowledged, Elizabeth," Charles Leiden said. "You never wished to acknowledge it. You helped save Kyoto and helped destroy Hiroshima." He had folded the pages of Arthur's letter. Gershon watched the pages disappear into the envelope. "You managed to slip a word to Harry Truman one evening. Hardly indirect, Elizabeth. Inadvertent, yes. It was our part in all the inadvertence that Arthur found unendurable, Gershon. Quite by chance you destroy a city, and quite by chance you save a city. To me, the fact that Kyoto was chosen at all is a comment on the superficiality of the minds of some of our leaders. That and Nagasaki and the new bomb—it was enough. Perhaps I waited too long. Shall we go outside? It's a bit of a warm day, isn't it?"

They came out of the sun porch door. A flagstone path led through a lovely garden and onto the lawn. They walked on grass beneath the tall and leafy oaks. There was the lake, shining between the trees. They walked in silence through the white birch and gazed at the gold and silver surface of the water.

"We used to swim down there," Charles Leiden said. "Arthur was—" He stopped. He said after a moment, "You cannot imagine how much we miss him, Gershon. You cannot imagine how deeply we regret not having given him a better life."

"Charles," Elizabeth Leiden said. Her voice seemed to fade off into a whisper toward the end of the word. She turned away and stared through the trees at the lake.

They stood there in silence for a while in the sun and shade of the late morning. Then Gershon said he thought he had better leave, his aunt and uncle were eager to see him, and Elizabeth Leiden went off to call a cab.

"What a difference the years have made," Charles Leiden said.

"It is all a whimsical game, a nothing, really. And yet somehow I seem unable to reconcile myself to that. Otherwise why do I grieve that we now have no one to continue our name?"

They went slowly inside together.

A few minutes later they stood at the front door. Gershon shook their hands.

Elizabeth Leiden said, "It was so very good to see you, Gershon. Do come again. We still have a great deal to talk about."

"Yes, whenever you are in the area, dear fellow, do give us a call and come over. Any time. We should so very much like to see you again. Yes?"

"Yes," Gershon said.

He climbed into the cab and saw them watching him from the doorway. The cab brought him to the airport. He waited nearly two hours for a flight to New York. Another cab took him through the streets of his neighborhood. Burned houses and boarded windows. Little had changed. He came through the hallway of the apartment house. His aunt opened the door.

That was a night of tears and long silences and sighs. "Finally home," his aunt kept saying in her whispery voice. She was gray but clear-eyed. His uncle kept saying, "Enough away. Too long. But now what?"

He did not know.

He called Karen. She cried quietly over the phone.

He slept in his small room that night and listened to the sounds of the neighborhood—the cats, the quarrels, the cars, the voices of youngsters in the street. He slept and there it was; it had waited for him to return, and it came to him now in the darkness of the early morning and he lay caught beneath its terror, listening. The sun rose. The room grew still. He slept.

The next day he took the subway to Manhattan and walked the dusty city blocks to her apartment. He rang the bell and went up the stairs, and she ran down to meet him, and he held her on the stairway, and they nearly toppled downward. "Let me look at you, let me look at you. You've lost so much weight. Oh, I can't begin to tell you how good it is to see you. Come upstairs. Can I get you something to drink? It's so good to see you, Gershon."

They sat in her apartment over cold drinks. There were plants
on the windowsills. He stared at the plants and listened to her talk.
She had waited and waited to hear from him, she said. What else
could she have done? She was right to have done it, he said. "Con-
fronted by a certainty and an uncertainty, you decide for the certainty," he said, not certain that he really believed it.

"But what will we do?" she asked. Could he come to Chicago?

He didn't know.

Later they walked along Riverside Drive to the Fire Department
monument. There he stood a long time, and she stood beside him,
wondering about his silence. Sunlight bathed the stones with a
luminescence that hurt his eyes. And from the trees somewhere behind him he heard again the silken whisper.

They crossed the Drive and walked beneath the trees. Beyond the
parapet lay the river, wide, bright, tugs and barges moving upon it,
sea gulls wheeling about. She spoke of her students, a paper she had
published, the book she was writing. She was not pretty, but when
he held her to him or when she spoke of her work, the flush that
came over her face gave her a surprising comeliness. She talked of
Arthur, and her voice grew low and tremulous, and it was clear
she felt some of the pain of that family. A memorial scholarship in
Arthur's name was being established at the seminary, she said. Her
father was working on it.

"Do you have to go to Chicago?" he asked. "Isn't there anything here?"

Not now, no. In a year or two, perhaps. But she felt she wanted
to leave New York for a while, get away from—get to learn how to
live somewhere else. And Chicago was exciting, it was a great university, a great department, a rare opportunity, and a certainty.

"Yes," Gershon said. "Right. I understand."

"What will we do, Gershon?"

"I don't know," he said.

"Will you start trying out for pulpits?"

"No," he said. "I don't think I want to do that."

They walked over to her parents' apartment. Her father greeted
him effusively. "Good to see you, my boy. You've lost a lot of weight.
Was it a worthwhile experience? Except for the tragedy, of course.

There will probably be a memorial in his name. Have you any plans? We are going to our summer place soon. You are welcome to be our guest any time. Good to see you."

Karen's mother stood by, nodding and smiling. Karen stared at the floor and was silent. Gershon took the subway home.

He came into the seminary the following week and entered the dormitory building. The elevator took him slowly to the sixth floor. He knocked on a door and entered.

Professor Nathan Malkuson sat behind his desk in the book-filled study. "Loran," he murmured, and rose and extended his hand across the desk. "It is good to see you. I thank you for calling. Please, please, sit down."

Gershon took the wooden chair opposite the desk. Malkuson sat and looked at him. The blue eyes, the slightly florid features, the silvery hair, the small round dark skullcap, and the vague fixed smile on the thin moist lips.

"So," he said after a silence. "It appears we have a problem."

Gershon was quiet. He looked at Malkuson and did not avert his gaze. Through the open window came the distant sounds of an airplane and the cooing of the pigeons on the ledge.

"I understand," Malkuson said. "There was once a time in Paris, when—" He stopped. "It is of no importance. You are now of importance. I will tell you. Do what you are doing. Either it will return or it will not. Prayer is not the only commandment. The study of texts is also commanded. There are those who tell us that even the scientific study of sacred texts is a sacred act. So do what you are doing, Loran. Do you understand?"

Gershon nodded, gazing directly at the man behind the book-laden desk.

Malkuson sighed softly. "You were very close?"

"Yes."

"It is a great tragedy. The last of the sons." He looked down at the books. There was a long silence. Then he raised his eyes and directed his gaze at Gershon, and Gershon did not look away. "I will tell you, Loran. What is of importance is not that there may be nothing. We have always acknowledged that as a possibility. What is important is that if indeed there is nothing, then we should be prepared to make something out of the only thing we have left to us—ourselves. I do not know what else to tell you, Loran. No one is in possession of all wisdom. No one."

Gershon sat in silence, looking at Nathan Malkuson.

"What will you do?" Nathan Malkuson asked.

"I don't know."

"Did you study Gemara while you were in Korea?"

"Not much."

"Did you study Kabbalah?"

"Yes."

"Did you study with *éntheos,* Loran?"

"Yes," Gershon said. "Yes."

There was a pause. Professor Malkuson rose slowly and came around the desk. Gershon got to his feet.

"Let me know if I can be of help to you, Loran," Malkuson said. "Now or any time."

"Thank you."

They shook hands. Gershon took the elevator down and went out of the building and rode the subway home. He was one station away from his stop when, staring out the window at the rushing darkness of the subway tunnel, he was abruptly struck by a thought of singular horror. He felt coldness on the back of his neck. He went up the stairs of his station stop and out into the street. Early evening, warm and pale with fading sunlight. He walked quickly through the streets of the neighborhood. In the apartment he made a phone call to the Leidens in Boston. There was no answer. He called three more times that night. Still no answer. He went to bed.

The voice, coming in the early morning, mocked him from the darkness. No, it whispered. No.

Soon after he rose, he called the Leidens again. No answer.

He saw Karen that day. They walked together near the river. She was leaving early the next day with her family. She would return in a few weeks and pack her belongings for the move to Chicago. What would Gershon be doing?

He didn't know.

"I'll wait if you wait," she said.

"Is that fair to you?"

"Maybe not. But the alternative may be unforgivable. I love you," she said. "You crazy kabbalist."

They had dinner and went to the theater and, later, he held her and she moved against him, warm, her face against his, warm. She wept when they parted.

The next morning he called the Leidens again. Still no answer. When he called that night the phone was raised on the third ring and he heard, clearly, the voice of Elizabeth Leiden. Why, what a surprise, she said. They had just returned from a physics conference in Princeton. How good to hear from him. Was everything all right?

He asked her if anyone was saying Kaddish for Arthur.

There was a very long silence. No, she said. They believed in none of that, she said. Charles had said it for a few days and then had stopped, she said. Her voice had gone strangely flat and cold. Why was he asking? she said.

He merely wanted to know, he said. A friend asking about a friend. Would she please give his very best wishes to her husband, he said.

They hung up.

The days passed. Karen left the city with her family. Gershon walked the streets of the neighborhood or remained in his room, reading. Often he rode the subway to the Jewish Division of the Forty-second Street library, where a kindly balding gentleman in his forties, with a dark mustache and gentle eyes, placed before him volumes of Kabbalah. He read until his eyes teared. He took the subway home.

His books arrived from Korea. He removed them from the footlocker and put them into his bookcase. He went out and walked through the neighborhood. A near slum plagued with frequent violence; yet his aunt and uncle would not leave the building.

There was a fire in the neighborhood one night in July, and the sirens woke him. He lay in the sweltering heat and could not return to sleep. And then, strangely, he found himself on the roof of the apartment house, on its cracked and malodorous tar paper and amid its jutting pipes and valves and crooked rods, and he could not remember leaving his room and going through the narrow hall and up the rickety stairs and out the metal door of the staircase shaft. Overhead the sky seemed to have been washed in the blackest of ink. No stars, no pinkish glow of cloud cover. He could barely see his hands. He stood very still in the darkness, his eyes wide. Passages moved through him, and he felt the gentle pull of the words. He began the ascent, slowly, through the darkness of this sky to the darkness of the next and on to darknesses beyond all imagining. This was no surprise; all was now sealed to him. He had not wanted it in the past, when it had been easily accessible. Now. . . .

He returned slowly downward to the darkness of the roof.

He waited. There was someone on the roof with him, in a corner, near a jumble of pipes. He did not turn; instead he sat down slowly on the tar paper and placed his head between his knees. He felt the boniness of his legs against the sides of his face. There he sat a long time, waiting. Yes, there was someone on the roof with him. He sat very still, waiting.

Then he began a slow and determined descent into himself. This he did with the fiercest of concentration, moving with great care past fears and angers, past faces and shadows, deep and deeper still toward the silent, central, secret point of himself. And he sensed as he moved that someone had brushed by him on the roof and had entered him, and now they were together, and it was the whisper of the messenger from the other side, and it said, Good morning, Gershon. Yes, this darkness is morning. You take a strange journey. Have you no concern for me at all? And Gershon moved on toward the center, and the messenger said, Ah, Gershon. What can you find in here that you did not find out there? And Gershon moved on and still on and deeper and deeper still, and at the very deepest within himself he heard a voice, and the voice had a face, and it was the face of Arthur Leiden, and the voice was saying very softly, There must be something we can say or do, dear Gershon. There can't be nothing. And Gershon trembled and heard the silken voice of the messenger say, Ah, there was something. Yes, and what did it get you, dear Arthur? What? And Arthur said again, There must be something we can say or do. Something. And Gershon listened to them, to both of them within the center of himself, and then he heard distant words echoing from somewhere far beyond where he was now, words in Aramaic, and the words made the journey, and he listened, and the words were the words of the Kaddish, the sacred public affirmation of God, and he heard, "Magnified and sanctified be the name of God throughout the world which He hath created according to His will. May He establish His kingdom during the days of your life and during the life of all the house of Israel, speedily, yea, soon; and say ye, Amen."

How you play with words and people's feelings! came the faintly annoyed response. How you dangle your illusions before the eyes of the weak! How—

From somewhere came the voice of Arthur Leiden. "Amen," the voice said.

No, Gershon said. This is for you, Arthur, and others must answer. This is for you, for us, for all the broken ones of our generation and the ones to come, for all who live and will live in the shadows of the giants. To the in-between ones who cling with their fingernails to the shards left by the giants—so we can somehow mend the world or hold it together and then have it broken again in new acts of creation. You must not answer, Arthur. Others must answer.

And Gershon went on. "Exalted and honored be the name of the Holy One, blessed be He, whose glory transcends, yea, is beyond all praises, hymns, and blessings that man can render unto Him; and say ye, Amen."

He stopped and waited.

You are playing with me, came the sibilant voice. I am not a simpleton. I am from the other side.

"Amen," said Arthur Leiden quietly, faintly.

And Gershon said, Please, please, another must answer. And he continued, "May there be abundant peace from heaven, and life for us and for all Israel; and say ye, Amen."

He waited. There was no response. He waited. All his years and dreams he now brought to this waiting, and then he himself answered, "Amen."

And concluded, "May He who establisheth peace in the heavens, grant peace unto us and unto all Israel; and say ye, Amen."

And waited. And from the darkness came the halting and agitated response of the silken voice. "Amen."

There was a long, steep, dizzying ascent—and a silence. Somewhere in the neighborhood a dog barked. The air was stifling.

He got to his feet.

Ah, Gershon, how many more times will you need to be broken? I don't know.

You will go to him, and he will eat you alive. The giants eat the small ones. Some are infantile and cruel and are giants in only one or two things. He will break you.

No, he won't. Others stronger than him have tried.

Who?

You.

Silence.

You will hear from me again, Gershon.

I'm sure I will.

Why must one do or say something? Why?

I don't know, Gershon said.

He was suddenly alone on the roof. He went carefully downstairs and along the hall and into the apartment to his room. After a long time he fell asleep. He slept deeply and without dreams.

He spent his days reading and writing. He wrote a lengthy letter and three weeks later received a letter in return. He saw Karen the week she was in the city and the night before she left for Chicago. Yes, he would write. Of course he would write. They would wait. Another year or two. They would wait.

One day in August he packed his books into the same footlocker he had used in Korea. Men came and took it away. He waited. He went daily to his uncle's little synagogue to say Kaddish for Arthur Leiden. The old bearded man who had once taught him Aramaic and had given him the amulet to wear in Korea would answer "Amen" loudly. Gershon rarely prayed. He read texts instead.

On a day in the first week of September he packed two bags. His aunt and uncle saw him depart with pride and sadness, for they knew he had chosen to be with one of the giants. He embraced them. "You will write," his aunt said. "Yes," he said. "With God go," his uncle said. "Thank you," he said.

A cab took him to the airport. A Constellation carried him to Newfoundland and Shannon and Paris and Tel Aviv. An old rattling cab brought him along mountain roads to a sand-colored city on a hill. The air was hot and dry, the sun searing. He stood before a stone house on a narrow shaded street and rang a doorbell and waited. It seemed to him that he waited a long time, and he rang the bell again. He could hear it inside the house. The door opened and there stood the tall, trim form of Jakob Keter—clear gray eyes, sharp nose, clean-shaven unlined features. He wore an open-necked, short-sleeved shirt and light trousers and sandals over dark socks. "Well," he said. "You are here. Was it a difficult trip? I find all such trips arduous. Come, Gershon. Come inside. Let me help you with your bags."

The interior of the house was a cool stream.

Jakob Keter looked at him. "You will tell me everything later. Yes? Leave the bags here. Let me get you something to drink. First, we will go outside. You will sit and rest."

They came through the house and out into the garden.

"What shall I bring you, Gershon? Something cold? A coffee? I have splendid coffee which I brought with me from Switzerland. Coffee. Fine. I will be back very soon. Sit and rest. I know about such trips. Yes. They are quite arduous."

He went into the house, his sandals slapping lightly on the flag-stone walk of the garden.

The air was shaded by tall trees, through which streamed narrow pillars of light. Gershon heard nothing save the lazy flight of flies. The neighborhood seemed asleep. He closed his eyes. Mint-leaf plants scented the still air. A faint tinkle of dishes came to him through the partly open sliding door. Jakob Keter and the coffee. Soon. Yes. He did not think he had made a mistake. He would know soon enough. A bird sang briefly from somewhere in the branches overhead. Gershon Loran sat in the light and shade amid the yellow jasmine and purple bougainvillaea and the red and white roses of Jakob Keter's Jerusalem garden, waiting.

A NOTE ON THE TYPE

This book was set on the Linotype in Granjon, a type named
in compliment to Robert Granjon, but neither a copy of a classic
face nor an entirely original creation. George W. Jones based
his designs on the type used by Claude Garamond (1510–61)
in his beautiful French books. Granjon more closely resembles
Garamond's own type than do any of the various modern types
that bear his name.

Robert Granjon began his career as type cutter in 1523. The
boldest and most original designer of his time, he was one of
the first to practice the trade of type founder apart from that of
printer. Between 1557 and 1562 Granjon printed about twenty
books in types designed by himself, following, after the fashion,
the cursive handwriting of the time. These types, usually
known as *caractères de civilité,* he himself called *lettres fran-
çaises,* as especially appropriate to his own country.

The book was composed by American–Stratford Graphic Services, Inc., Brattleboro, Vermont. It was printed and bound by
American Book–Stratford Press, Saddle Brook, New Jersey.

Typography and binding design
by Dorothy Schmiderer

383
3